Plead More, Bodymore
Bodymore Book Two

Ian Kirkpatrick

STEAK HOUSE
BOOKS

First publication in the USA
Steak House edition published in 2022
Copyright © 2022 by Ian Kirkpatrick

Paperback ISBN: 978-1-7368870-5-9
ebook ISBN: 978-1-7368870-6-6
LCCN: 2022911730

Our books may be purchased in bulk for promotional, educational, or business use. Please contact your local bookseller to order.

Cover by Samuel Johnson
www.SpoopySamuel.com

Printed in the United States of America.

31   10   22   1

CONTENTS

ONE.

stic Jag's pacing from the small kitchen into the living room of my trailer. There's not much space, just enough for what little furniture my dad and I had: a crappy table holding my dad's stolen TV, his recliner, a TV tray, a folding chair against the wall, the cheap card table my dad and I pretended we ate at sometimes. Dad broke one of the chairs from the set a while back. I've got the scar on my left forearm where the plastic went in.

It's only been a few hours since I died, came back, shot my dad dead *twice*, and watched the reaper finally collect his soul for good. I don't know if it's hit me yet that he's not coming back. I'd call myself numb, but I'm hyped like I've been at a concert for the last three hours and I'm ready for more shoving and jumping and maybe a brawl in the parking lot where you can still hear the electric guitars and drums, but security's not gonna do a damn to stop anyone.

"I don't know what else to say, J." I shrug. "You said it yourself, I don't look normal and it's not drugs." Every time I catch my reflection, there's too much black around my eyes to be eyeliner and too much red to just be tired.

Then my hands are so pale that the blue and red veins running through them look too vibrant, like my skin's too thin.

Jag makes another lap across the kitchen, keeping his time in the living room short because it keeps him further away from Wayland, but there's not enough space. He runs into the empty chair at the table, then the table, then dad's chair, and he swears under his breath when his boot hits some broken glass left behind from a smashed bottle. With the next step, he kicks a plastic bottle of Barton's. He hisses a mixture of mostly, "Goddamn it, Joey," and "Shit" and "What the hell?" with a groan. Jag brings his cigarette to his lips, sucks hard, and exhales. "Your house always this bad?"

"When you kick the shit out of the furniture, yeah." I shrug. Look away. Maybe a little embarrassed that *this* is the first time Jag's really been in my house.

Jag's eyes catch on dad's gun sitting on the counter. He keeps looking at it like he thinks I'm gonna grab it or Way's gonna grab it and someone's gonna end up shot, but Wayland's still sitting in the folding chair on the other side of Dad's recliner. He's been tense since Jag's car pulled back up out front. His fingers curl so tightly around the seat that his knuckles are white. Every so often, he's muttering that he's fine, but it's pretty obvious he's not, so I've been trying to keep the storytelling short to get us out of here faster. Though, I don't even know where we'd go.

Not like this.

My foot's bouncing against the floor. I stand up. Jag stops pacing, points back to the chair, and says, "Sit."

With gritted teeth, I do.

I grab the box of cigarettes off the table and light another one. Jag takes a beer from the fridge. The house smells like my dad's ripe corpse, piss, and the pizza none of us have touched.

I breathe in the cigarette. Eyes stinging, I wipe them

with the back of my hand. "You saw my body, J." My foot's tapping again. The nicotine's doing nothing to calm my nerves while Jag's making me itch for another fight. I get stuck watching dad's recliner; he should've been sitting in it, he should've been telling me to get Wayland and Jag out. Somehow, the nasty red stains left behind by his splattered brain are darker. The stains of so many years of misery make the chair look like it's a bleeding, rotting corpse all its own. The spot that stands out the most is where his head was when he ate lead the first time. I take another hit from the cigarette, wiping at my eyes. A laugh bubbles out. I thought stains were supposed to fade with age, just like the bad stuff that happens to you, but they don't. Fifteen years isn't enough to make blood blend into brown carpets with every other mess?

Bullshit.

Jag leans against the wall by the table beside me. His beer bottle hisses. He sets the cap on the table, then the room's quiet. Jag's steps are heavier than mine. I wear sneakers, he's got on steel-toed boots, and they keep making me think it's my dad down the hall because he's supposed to be around. I mean, how long has it been since his ass hasn't been in the recliner or somewhere around it? I keep hitting my back into the flat, plastic cushion on my chair and I keep waiting to hear my dad yelling from down the hall, "You bitch," and "What's the noise?" and "What the hell's he doing in my house? I told you I never wanted to see that asshole's face again. I'm gonna lay him out if he doesn't leave right fuckin' now," and Jag'll say, "Let's do it old man," and he'll knock my dad out. Then when Jag's gone, Dad'll pay the favor back to me.

Irony is the only time dad met Jag was through the house window. Met's not an accurate word. He saw Jag drop me off a couple of times, yelled at him through the wall, then when I came in he said, "You're really planning to leave me, huh?" Any time he got that kind of insecure,

I'd say, "If I was gonna leave you, I would've done it by now, Dad," but it didn't matter. He never believed me and acted like he'd never heard it before. If he was dead all this time, maybe he actually never did remember.

Dead, drunk, something reset in him to replay his worst day, every day, and he couldn't escape it.

"Your regret will consume you," Charon's words echo in my head. "Everything you may not have liked about yourself, amplify it. Your regret will fuel you."

I'm leaning forward, checking down the hall toward my room and his. The bathroom door hangs open. I should be listening for his heavy steps getting off the chair or coming out of the shower after I finally forced him to wash after a week. None of the thudding is him; he's not here; he's not coming back and I still can't believe it.

"It was dark," Jag finally says.

"You took a picture, right?" I lean back.

"I'm not keeping a picture of a corpse on my phone," Jag says.

Wayland stands up with a jerk; his chair falls over.

Jag pushes off the wall, body tense. "Final warning, Cross. If you don't keep your ass in the chair, I'm gonna beat it until you can't make a different choice. Got it?"

Wayland's stiff. His fingers curl. I think he's actually going to jump Jag. I feel it. Then, his stare comes to me like he's remembering I'm still here. With trembling hands, he picks his chair up from the floor. He sits back down, never taking his eyes off Jag.

My teeth pull at my lip ring. I'm bouncing harder against the back of my seat too, but now with my head bobbing like there's music and I can't tell if what I'm hearing is from the neighbor's house or just in my head. "Give it a couple of days, J," I say. "Someone should call. Someone'll need to ID the body and I don't have anyone else left."

Jag turns back to me. He drags on the cigarette. "You

actually made me an emergency contact with someone?"

"Yeah?"

I twist away, turn to the table, pull at a piece of pizza even though I'm not hungry. Half of it is plain cheese. The side Jag got for me because he knows that's what I like, even if he thinks it's gross and laughs at me every time we order because *it's so plain.* "I can call Charon back if that'll make you feel better."

"Who?" Jag says.

"The dude in white who took my dad earlier?"

"Joey…" Jag presses his hand to his forehead, sighing. "You need to get out of this house. It's making you crazy."

"Are you fucking serious?" I stand up.

Jag straightens, directs me to sit down with his hand.

I ignore him. "You're telling me you didn't see him?"

"No." Jag crosses his arms. "I saw him, but you're stressed. He could've been a paramedic—"

"Literally what?" I sit down and pick up the bottle of lukewarm beer I've been nursing, though I don't drink it. My nail polish is chipped. My fingers are stained black and dried blood sits caked under my nails. A sip makes the cold move under my skin, from my hands to my toes. I'm hoping it'll cool off some of the nervous energy I've got telling me I need to get the hell out of this house and find the next person who deserves to meet my dad's gun. "Where was the ambulance, Jag? What about the raven? And who the hell ever cared about us Deadwood deadbeats anyway? The only kind of action we see around here is mics and badges trying to catch a promotion or their next paycheck." I'm looking at dad's chair again and the TV, turned off, and Jag not saying anything is making the house so quiet I don't recognize it as my house anymore. The TV should be blaring with sirens from *Cops* or game show ringers or obnoxious ads trying to sell my dad depression, death, or an erection on repeat. Sometimes, the ads got so daring, they tried to sell all three at the same time.

I bring a cigarette to my lips and lean back, bouncing. My head touches the wall behind me. My eyes close and I'm eight again, looking at his body in the chair with the phone pressed to my ear and the tears blurring my vision being the only things trying to take the image of a dead asshole away.

My head's throbbing and I feel it painfully teasing the tips of my fingers, adding to the trembling shakes I've had since I stepped back into this house.

Anger left behind by my dad makes the air thick. It ricochets off the tin panel walls pretending to be made out of wood with paint. It's not like I didn't feel it before; my dad's seething burned through his chair, left prints on everything he touched, and amplified every sound I made behind my closed bedroom door. Negativity fills my neighborhood like someone playing a stereo too loud. It's a constant block party where the neighbors are spectators to the private dances of the ruined lives that stain this city. Locals look the other way while tourists take pictures for macabre websites made famous by the tragic existences of others.

Funny how people only care ten years down the line when it's all over and there's nothing anyone can do to fix the destruction wrought.

Jag runs a hand through his hair. A sigh. He looks back out the window. I'd say he's checking on his car, but he's probably looking for badges. He turns back around, grabs the box of cigarettes off the table, and slides it into his pocket. The cigarette he already has hangs from his mouth. He plucks it out. "You pack a bag?" He glances at me, then the window. "I'm tired of being here."

"That's it, then?" I say.

"I'm tired of being here, Joey. It smells like someone died—"

"Because someone *did*, then his corpse rotted in a chair

for fifteen fucking years!"

"You've got to be kidding me." Jag tosses his cigarette into the tray on the table. "This is the biggest cope I've ever heard." He rubs his face. "Your friend's a killer, you're implicated, and reasonably, you lost your shit at someone who actually deserved it, but that's all that's going on here."

Wayland's out of his chair again. Fast. I've never seen him move so quickly. Eyes on Jag, he draws his fist back and throws a punch into Jag's face. It lands. Jag grabs Wayland by the arm and pulls him into the fist he's got up. The blow's powerful enough to knock Wayland back. Jag hits him again, pushing him off his feet. Wayland's on his knees, grabbing at Jag's legs with both hands. Jag hits Wayland in the head again, grabs his shoulders, and presses him into the ground. He turns Wayland over while he pulls one of Wayland's arm's behind his back. Wayland sneering, "Get off!" while Jag thrusts him harder into the ground every time he makes a noise.

"I warned you, Cross," Jag says. "Now back the fuck off." After securing one of Wayland's arms, Jag grabs the other. "Call the badges, Joey."

"I'm not a narc, J," I say.

"You'd let your *bestie* kill me? Is that where we're at?"

"You're being over-dramatic—"

"He's already killed a guy!"

"The circumstances were different." I grab my cigarette out of the ash tray and bring it to my lips. I don't get anything from it; I need to light it again for that, so I toss it back into the tray.

Wayland struggles. Jag pushes him into the ground harder and harder until he growls and swears and doesn't sound like Wayland anymore.

"Grab your shit, we're leaving," Jag says.

My entire body's tense and the house looks too dark suddenly. It's not the right time for this kind of shade, but it creates the temptation to hurt because this'll keep it hidden from everyone else. I blink a couple of times, hoping the room brightens. It doesn't. My anger spikes erratically until all I can think about is grabbing whatever's in arm's reach and throwing it and it's making me think too much of dad. Glass cracks, then a crash; my hand stings; Jag says, "Holy shit, Joey—" while Wayland's pushing against Jag saying, "Jo!"

Blood runs down my fingers. A small spot of red dots my thighs where some of the blood's dripped down the fresh cuts in my hand. My beer bottle's broken to pieces, some sit in my lap, some around my feet. There's a release of the overpowering emotion inside of me that comes out in something like a laugh and a sigh and I'm saying, "I'm fine, I'm fine," while getting up and using my body to hide my hand from Jag.

I grab the medical box from under the sink and put a couple of bandages over the cuts and say, "I'ma go grab my shit. That's what you wanted, right?" without turning around.

Jag says, "You want help?" and I say, "Not from you," with a snort and a laugh. I stop halfway to my room. The fingers on my unbandaged hand slide along the wall. I glance over my shoulder. "Wayland, wanna help?" I remain still, in place, eyes on Jag more than Wayland like I've got command and the stare will make him let Wayland go. Jag doesn't change position. Wayland pushes into Jag's grip, his knees trying to give him some kind of edge. Jag thrusts him against the floor again. "Jag. Let him go."

Jag keeps Wayland down while he locks eyes with me. He's got something to say, but he's not saying it.

I come back down the hall slowly, arms crossed, lips pursed. I shake my head trying to silence the calls for violence rattling inside it. "Jag, please. I'm trying to help him," I say.

"Yeah… That's a crime," Jag says.

"Give us a bit to figure this out... Please?"

Jag stands up fully before loosening his grip on Wayland.

"Thanks," I say. I put my hands out to help Wayland up. He takes them. I don't let go and walk backwards, tugging him with me. "We won't be long, 'kay?" Wayland and I are halfway down the hall when I'm letting go of one of his hands. Before we're at my room, I hear Jag swearing under his breath as he pops the cap off another beer. The pizza box opens, then closes. I close my bedroom door behind Wayland.

Take a breath.

Nothing about right now feels normal and I'm cussing at myself for what just happened, what I could've done differently, did I piss off Jag, and how the hell do I get him to understand things aren't as simple as he thinks they are? What if he changes his mind and he's not out there anymore once I've got a bag together? The only bag I have is the backpack I've had since first grade. I grab it from the back of my closet and toss it onto the bed. The silence is bugging me. I go to the small radio clock at my bedside and flip it on, letting the racket of rock fill my room. My hips swing as I move; I'm taking more steps than I need to, making them smaller and faster. I rip a pair of jeans off a hanger, grab another two from the floor, and put them all in the bag. My drawers have unfolded t-shirts and underwear. My hoodie's on the floor.

Wayland's still standing at the bedroom door, back against the wall, fingers now in his pockets, though he's watching everything I do.

I cross the room like I'm going for something, but I don't know what I'm looking for anymore, I just need to be moving. I get to the far side of the room, turn around, catch Wayland again, laugh. "You know you can come in, right?"

"Sorry—It's different this time." Wayland takes one

step in, but stops himself, then presses his back into the door again. The door clicks, hitting the frame, latch broken and loose from when dad beat it down like half a week ago.

"Dad's not here to get mad." I laugh.

Wayland shakes his head. "I don't care about your dad."

"Don't worry about J. He's been rough with you, but… he's not a bad guy, okay?"

"Right." Wayland exhales hard.

I turn around to look at him. His head's down; he's not wearing his glasses. I don't think I've seen him wearing them since he first went missing. His clothes are filthy. Smelly, blood-stained, and caked in dried mud. "We should get you something else to wear. My dad's clothes might be kinda weird on you, but at least it's better than *that*." I nod toward him.

"Okay," Wayland says.

I smile. He weakly smiles back. I go back to my bag, take the clothes out, and put them back in. I don't know what I'm doing but finding an excuse to move. I zip the bag closed. My fingers curl around the shoulder straps. My chest is tight, so I exhale. "You know… even with him gone, I still feel everything. Like… his hands are around my throat or my back's against the wall and he's slamming me into something again, but it's not even bad like it was. It's more like I'm craving the fight because I want to beat the shit out of him again. You know that feeling?" My eyes burn, go blurry, but stay dry. I wipe them and chuckle. It hurts.

"I don't like it, Jo."

I turn back to Wayland and he's looking at me.

"I want to go back; I want another chance to get it right."

"We got another chance, Way."

"That's not what it feels like."

I'm standing in front of Wayland. My hands are on both sides of his face. I'm looking into his eyes, stroking his jaw with my thumbs. Red, already swelling from where Jag hit him. Rabid energy goes through my skin where we touch, I'm not sure what it is, but something from him hits me like getting drunk on the hardest liquor I've had. "We'll figure it out, okay? Whatever we need to do to make it work, we'll do it."

Wayland leans forward. His stance turns him into a tower, making him feel more like Jag than Wayland as he cranes his neck. One of his hand's is on my hip, the other cups my jaw. I step back.

Wayland grabs my hand to stop me from pulling away. "What if we can't?" His grip tightens. His gaze grabs mine again; it's unlike the souls in Mortem. Though glossy, his face doesn't look empty. Everyone in the bar down there had checked out, but there's a feeling when looking at Wayland like he's too aware. Fear, anger, rage, passion, fire. Is that what I look like to him? "Jo... I've killed people," he whispers.

I breathe out hard. A flat laugh carries. It's kind of alarming how little I care about the death or the confession. "That guy at Leakin had it coming, Way—"

"It wasn't just that guy..."

"What?" I laugh the word.

"There were more," Wayland says, still soft, still looking worried.

"How many?"

"I don't know. Five, six maybe? Some of it's too blurry. Jo—I just know that when I came back, I found the guy that killed me. I had to and then there was the one that attacked you and then there were those people at Armistead who got in the way—"

"The couple?"

"Yeah." Wayland's almost panting. His anger's not like mine. A slow boil that's got him trembling as he tries to contain himself while mine leaks out constantly in movements I can't keep to myself. Swaying, bouncing, punching, shuffling, anything that keeps me going. "I saw you at the fort by yourself. I was coming to you, but then those people came out of nowhere and I couldn't stop blaming them for getting in the way. Something else *again* and they didn't want me to see you. They were working against me, Jo. But then after they were gone… I…" He looks down at his hands. They're discolored. Paler skin from death brings out the dirt and grime and blood trapped under his nails from every encounter he hasn't been able to scrub off. I don't know if there's a way to ever fully scrub off someone else. The dark circles under his eyes are darker than they should be, looking like he hasn't slept in years. "After I did that, I couldn't see you. I was messy again and I couldn't let you see me looking like that."

"It's kinda funny now how much I don't care…" I say.

"You did back then. I heard you when you asked if I put the body in my car."

"Did I?"

"Yeah."

I remember it; I remember walking around Armistead, calling for Wayland, hoping he was there so I could prove he did nothing wrong. With everything I know now, I should feel bad or scared or guilty or something, but there's a numbness inside like when I was at Lodgings in Mortem. Something's wrong with me, but I'm not even bothered enough by it to care. People are little more than annoying ideas and dead people are annoying ideas I don't have to think about anymore. I've made light of death for so long. There was never any hope to leave, so the best I could do was laugh. It had to be a joke when all I did at night was hope to stop existing so I wouldn't have to suffer anymore.

A week ago I opened the trunk of Wayland's car and

got sick at the sight of a body, but I don't think I'd do the same if it happened today.

"Don't worry about them, Way," I say. "Any of them. They all deserved what they got."

"Even the couple?" Wayland releases my hand.

"Virginians get what they get when they come to Maryland." I shrug. "Shouldn't've come to Bodymore if they didn't have a death wish. So… Don't worry about it, okay?" I wait until Wayland gives me a response, it's just a nod, but it's enough, then I'm back at the bed, unzipping the backpack again, forgetting what's inside. I count the clothing and close it again before tossing it over my shoulder. "I need you to be honest with me though, Way."

"What?" he says.

"Have you ever…" My chest tightens. It's hard to exhale. It's hard to talk. "If you ever think about hurting Jag, you need to tell me, okay?"

"Oh."

"I know what the impulses are like. I couldn't stop myself around my dad. So, if you've got a problem with J, tell me and we'll figure it out."

Wayland shakes his head rapidly. "I don't—" His voice cracks. "I don't have a problem with him."

"You'll tell me if something happens, right?"

"Yeah. Of course."

"Good." I'm reaching for my cigarettes only to realize I left them on the kitchen counter. I stuff my hands into my pockets instead. They rapidly tap against my thighs in the little space. I look around the room one more time. There's a hole in the wall beside the window from when I was sixteen and my dad tossed me against it then tried to punch me. I never fixed the hole; I never wanted to. It was supposed to be my excuse to get the hell out before he could do it again, but when I realized I couldn't leave, it became a reminder to lock the door and keep myself ready whenever he came down the hall, even if it only sounded like he was going for a piss.

A breath comes out like a laugh. I push my bangs back. I run my fingers gingerly along my forearms, tracing the scars left behind from falling, from dad, from things I did to myself. Even though I spent the last hour trying to prove to Jag I'm real and this is happening, part of me still feels like I'm dreaming, I'm not really there, and I'll wake up any minute now. I walk over to my nightstand and push the lamp off it.

"What'd you do that for?" Wayland says.

"To prove we're still here." I pat Wayland on the shoulder and smile. He smiles back, still small, but better than the last one. He steps away from the door and lets me open it. We leave the bedroom, but I pull Wayland by the arm into my dad's room next. I grab a pair of pants and the plainest sweater I can find in his closet. Neither look like they'd fit my dad right if he'd tried to put them on; probably why I don't really recognize them. I can't remember the last time he put on something other than sweats and a t-shirt. "I know it's not exactly your style and it kinda smells, but at least you'll get by without getting weird looks. We'll wait for you out there, yeah?"

Wayland looks at the clothing I'm holding. His hands tremble a little as he reaches for my arm. "Jo, I…" He takes a step closer. His hand touches my arm, but then drops to the top of the clothing. "Thanks."

"Any time, Way." I pat his arm again as I walk by. I turn on my heels to step back, watching Wayland. He watches me back until I go out the door, closing it behind me.

In the kitchen, Jag's eaten half a slice of pizza, but there's another empty bottle on the counter and another butt in the ashtray while he's smoking a new cigarette. The broken glass from my bottle isn't on the floor, table, or chair.

"You ready to go?" I close the pizza box and slide it

toward me.

"What's happening with your *boyfriend*?" Jag nods toward the hall.

"Stop being a jackass, J," I say.

"I'm only picking up what you're putting out," he says.

"I'm *sorry*," I don't mean to growl. I lick my lips, eyes turn to the kitchen window, face hot. There's not much in the window but the light makes an outline of my head like I'm a translucent ghoul with dark holes in the middle of my face. My foot's tapping, my heart won't stop throwing itself all around my chest and I don't remember feeling like this five minutes ago. "Sorry, J. No matter what it sounds like, I mean it. I'm just not—Feeling good right now."

Jag takes a deep breath. His voice comes out, then stops. Wayland comes down the hall. My dad's clothes don't fit right like I expected, but they're not bad. Baggy slacks held up by a belt bunch around his feet, the sweater also hangs around his stomach where there's too much fabric from accommodating the gut my dad got from drinking. His eyes flicker to where Wayland's still standing in the hall, stiff. "You got a ride, champ?" Jag says to Wayland.

"I figured we could drop him off on the way to your place," I say.

"Hell. No," Jag says. "He's tried to off me, like, three times already, Joey. You're insane if you think I'm getting back in the car with him."

"I thought we'd already established I'm probably insane." My eyes roll.

"And you want to drop him at *home*?" Jag grunts. "What if he kills his family?"

"I'm not talking about this with you, Jag." I grab my skateboard and I'm walking out the door now, going down the steps. I have to keep moving or I'm going to want to break something again. The desire keeps coming back strong. The voices, the images, the feeling of adrenaline like shooting up, and now Jag's bloody face is getting into my head, scaring the shit out of me. I look down at my hands, my own blood coloring the curves of my fingerprints. The voice in my head's says *do it again, do it again and break 'em open!*

I shake my head while I walk, almost stepping off the side of the wooden stairs. Instead, I trip the rest of the way down. Not far from the bottom of the steps, a big, black raven sits on the walkway halfway between the stairs and the driveway. Its glossy eyes lift, look at me, then past me. There's another one closer to the road between me and my neighbor's house. It's staring into my door too. "You should get going, Val. Don't wanna miss a meal, do you?" I say, walking toward the bird.

Its wings spread; it flies back, but only by a couple of feet to land in the neighbor's yard.

"You talking to birds now?" Jag says.

"They listen a lot more than you think." I stop when I reach Jag's car. The passenger door's unlocked. I toss my skateboard into the backseat. My bag goes next. Then, door closed, my ass presses into the window. I cross my arms. Check on the ravens. They're staring at Jag. I hold my breath, wait for a sound, a caw, a car, something that might make the ravens break attention, but nothing grabs them. They're tracking *him*. I walk back across the yard, take Jag's hand, and pull him forward, still checking on the ravens. I don't expect him to come with me so easily, but he does, glancing over his shoulder for a second to find Wayland in the trailer door. He turns, stepping sideways to keep an eye on him too.

"We're not that organized, J," I say.

"I'm not worried about you like that," Jag says.

I squeeze Jag's hands. "You ready to go, Way?" I say.

Jag shakes his head. "No." He takes his hands from mine.

I go back to the stairs; Wayland's still standing in my trailer's doorway, staring at something behind me. I follow him. It looks like he's watching Jag, the same way the birds are. Close, sharp, too focused. "Way?" I say.

Wayland shakes his head like he's snapping out of something. "I'm not going with you," he says.

"What?" I look back at Jag.

Jag shrugs, then he's opening the trunk to set the pizza down and climbing into the driver's seat of his Mustang. I wait until the car door closes, acting like it gives us some kind of privacy.

"What do you mean you're not coming? We're just dropping you off," I say. "What are you gonna do?"

"I'm going to figure it out," Wayland says.

"Figure what out?"

"How to get where I need to go." There's pain in his voice. It cracks a little, but he's stiff, like he's trying to hide it. He rubs the side of his head, closes his eyes, covers his face, and turns away.

"Where are you gonna go?"

"Home. Like you said. I haven't talked to my parents in a while and I should at least let them know what's going on."

"You sure?" My chest tightens.

"I just mean that I'm here. I shouldn't have let them worry so long."

"There're no instructions on this. They can't hold it against you."

"I should've done better, though."

Again, Wayland's not looking at me. I cross the yard, stop halfway. Look back at the Mustang. Jag's head's down, maybe looking at his phone, pretending he's not watching. I just hope he's not seeing what I see. Wayland's got a look that feels familiar, but foreign, a look like I saw in my dad and the Big Guy who killed me and every angry banger I've seen running around this city, thirsting for something they feel owed. It's not fair to say banger—It's not just them looking to rob everyone else of everything they can, looking for money and advancement and happiness. Sometimes, you'd think the miserable believe they can beat joy out of people—Like it's being hoarded in someone's pocket, and the only reason you're miserable is because someone stole it from you first. There's a finite amount of happiness in the world, right? So, maybe some gotta be miserable for others to not be.

"You sure you're gonna be okay?" I say.

Wayland takes the last step down, but he's still not looking at me. He breathes out hard through his teeth, his fingers curl, even without Jag near, his hands tremble. "Yeah. I have to be."

I close the space between us. My arms are around him and I pull him toward me. He doesn't wait to do the same. He's so much sturdier than I remember him being. "You're not alone in this, Wayland."

"Are you gonna stay with me?" Wayland says.

My front door goes out of focus. My nose is in Wayland's shoulder. He smells like my dad, my house, and sulfur. There's barely any sense of himself. My fingers curl in his shirt. "I can't. I have to talk to Jag."

"I know." Wayland let's go of me first.

I follow, putting a space between us. I grab out my phone and look over the screen like I'm expecting something to be there. "Text me," I say.

"I will," Wayland says.

"I'll always answer, okay?"

"Yeah." Wayland smiles, but it doesn't last.

My walk to Jag's car is slow, half backwards, watching Wayland while I open the passenger door. He doesn't move, even when I'm in the car, even when the door shuts, even when Jag reaches for the key hanging from the ignition.

"You good?" Jag says. His phone's sitting in the

cupholder with his box of cigarettes and his lighter.

I take a breath, using it to give me time to come up with an answer or at least enough enthusiasm to sound convincing when I say, "Yeah," but my voice still shakes. I glance in the side mirror. Wayland fills the frame while "Objects May Be Closer Than They Appear" lies to me at the bottom.

The Mustang roars. Wayland's getting smaller and I've become my mom, leaving someone I told myself I'd never leave at my shitty trailer, telling him to figure it out on his own. I push my fingers hard against my eyes, keep wiping, smudging the black so my eyeliner's probably everywhere, but at least that's all that's on my face. Jag glances sidelong and says, "Wipe your face. You look like trash," and I say, "Yeah? What's new about that?"

I've got my window rolled down; the air blowing in doesn't feel as cold as it should and the heater's only on mild, but it's burning my skin where it touches. The burn isn't uncomfortable though. Jag got the radio on and he's trying not to make conversation which works for me because I don't want to talk. I want to pretend everything's fine, he's satisfied, and since no one's asking any questions, there's nothing to explain. We pass by an abandoned office store; the wall outside says DON'T BE ALONE and brick townhouses just a street over say WANT, WANT, WANT, WANT in different colors, colliding off the wall onto the concrete and go from looking like paint to chalk to washing down the drain in the street. The smell of pizza makes its way out of the trunk, somehow overpowering the cigarette Jag lit. I hope there's beer back at his place.

My fingers tap my thigh until I'm in my pocket and getting out my phone and turning it over in my hands, trying not to message Wayland first, because he's driving or he's being picked up by his parents or he's walking somewhere and he needs to be alert because of what happened last time. But then I message him anyway.

JOEY   Everything's gonna be fine.

It's minutes before he sends anything back and even then, he only says, "OK."

I tap my phone to my thigh a couple more times.
New message.

JOEY   Trust me?

Minutes later, he says, "OK," again.

I crank the radio up, but it's not loud enough since Jag cranks it up after me. My foot's tapping to the music, and I drop my phone on the floor so I can't reach it as easily as before. My hand finds Jag's thigh because holding anything is better than holding onto that goddamn phone right now and it seems right. I close my eyes, trying to focus on anything but the seething anger and fear inside of me trying to get out.

Jag's saying my name before I realize we're at his apartment. I grab my bag and skateboard from the backseat, he's got the pizza and asks if I need help carrying anything. I say, "Nah. You've got your hands full already with me, yeah?" I smile; it's weak, but he smiles back.

The hall on his floor is quiet and it smells like someone's making spaghetti while someone else burnt popcorn sometime last week. The scent of popcorn sticks around, burnt or not. Dad hated it. "Melted butter smells like piss," he'd say, but if that was true, then he never would've smelled me making popcorn, right?

In Jag's apartment, he sets the pizza down in the kitchen, I set my skateboard against the wall by the door. My bag falls off my shoulders near that. I can't give a fuck about it. Jag's keys hit the counter with a jingle. The TV comes on, but the sound's low.

Everything feels heavy and jittery at the same time. Lit and worn out. Restless and exhausted, I don't want to move, but panic strikes when I'm standing still. It's nothing new, but all I want is to feel something to wear me down until I can't move or think or feel anymore.

I'm gaining on Jag until I'm running into him and he's stepping back, looking down at me. My hands go up his chest while I say, "Hey, J?"

"Hm?" He grabs my hips.

"Do you think it'd be weird if we fucked right now?" My hands are around his neck, drawing me to him.

"Why would it be weird?" Jag's still stepping back, guiding us to his room. He leans down, bringing his lips close to mine. His hands slide around my hips. He unhooks my belt and tugs the ends free.

I pull at his shirt. He grabs at mine and our clothing hits the floor. Jag turns us around so he can push me onto the bed and then he's on top of me. His lips are hot against my skin and I've never felt so hungry for his body before. Now, he's all I can think about.

The balance between his body and the bed keeps me from floating away, and the screaming in my head finds a quiet place to fuck off to so all I can focus on is feeling Jag. His smell, his voice muttering against my skin. The way I say his name feels different and I don't get why until we're done and his arm's hanging over me, holding me close, forming me to the contours of his body. At that moment, I'm not thinking about what time it is or how I'm gonna sneak into the house or will I wake my dad up, and what commercial break will be loud enough to cover me closing the door without drawing his attention. There's no rush to get out of here because there's no one at home I have to take care of.

I close my eyes to stop the tears from forming. I bring Jag's arm to my mouth so my lips can trail along his skin, to his wrist, then the back of his hand. The words I want to say scare the hell out of me. I never liked hearing them because they never felt real, like anything more than a saying that costs 15 cents to make, but $13.99 to pass on through a plastic, preprinted card that a million other people have given to someone else.

No one ever said you had to be real, just believable. Even the afterlife works like that.

Heat moves along my neck. A trail from Jag's lips and he says, "I'm glad you're here, Joey," and I'm thinking *me too*, but I can't say it; I'll look like an idiot when he changes his mind, so instead, I close my eyes, let my hand go limp, and pretend I fell asleep already so I don't have to say anything back.

TWO.

I'm alone when I wake up. Light bleeds through the thin blinds and reflects off the bright floor. The bed feels unfamiliar. Too good. Too warm. Too soft. The apartment's quiet. I grab a handful of blanket and take a deep breath. Jag's smell is all over the sheets. I roll onto my back and stare at the ceiling, letting what I can remember of the last day replay in my head again while I pretend it's all just a blurry dream. I don't believe in God, so I don't know who I'm talking to when I say, "Please tell me I didn't make a fucking mistake," and even as the words come out, I know they're stupid. My life's one giant mistake and I can't stop making bad decisions.

I shove the blanket back. I'm putting on underwear and grabbing one of Jag's worn-out shirts from the hamper because it's hanging off the side and takes the least effort to put on. It's yellow with old fashioned red lettering that reads AVERAGE JOE across the front. A couple of oil stains blotch it in black patterns. Never enough washing to get it out, but the laundry will fade the graphics before leftovers from the shop.

In the kitchen, a box of cigarettes sits on the counter

with a lighter. The pizza's been put in the nearly empty fridge. Orange juice, milk, cold coffee, a bag of three apples, condiments, lunch meat, bread.

I light a cigarette and put a slice of pizza in the microwave just long enough so that it's not stiff, but not long enough to make the cheese gooey again. While the timer counts down, I fill a glass with water and open one of the living room windows. The cool, fall air doesn't make much of a difference, but feels nice on my skin, like dipping into a pool of neutral water. I lean outside, elbows braced on the frame. My eyes close.

The microwave beeps.

I lean back in but stop. Val's down there. He's in one of the trees outside the parking garage, like he's waiting for someone to come out so he can take them away forever. My vision's still tinted red, but it doesn't seem as bad as it had been yesterday—like blood mixed with water instead of looking through a stream. I rub my eyes. Black spots take over, trying to make me go blind. The spots are gone when I try again. No birds on the cars. I lean out again for a better look. Nothing.

I snap the window shut, lock it, and open one on the other side of the apartment. I pace away from the window, go back to the other while I'm smoking, check again. No ravens. There aren't any ravens out there looking for me. I hear something. A caw. A laugh. A guttural snarl. I return to the open window. Lean out. Look.

Nothing.

I close and lock it.

I'm in Jag's room, opening the window, looking for anything out of place. My heart's pounding so hard I feel it in every part of my body. Cigarette pinched between my lips, I hunt for my cellphone. My jeans are on the floor by the bed. The pockets are empty. My phone sits on the nightstand, plugged into the charger I normally use, but I know I didn't do it. "Damn it, Jagger." Heat burns my eyes as tears blur my vision. I wipe them with the back of my hand, then my hand on the shirt I'm wearing.

The microwave beeps again, reminding me I've got pizza waiting. I put out my cigarette, go back to the kitchen, and grab a slice. My eyes catch on the printed schedule hanging off the fridge; Jag's working until six today. My heels tap while I eat. My hips press into the counter, my phone's in my hand. I have eight messages. The first three are from Jag saying, "Don't run off," and "We need to work some shit out when I get home," and "No sex next time."

I send, "Sure thing, J ;)" and delete the messages like I never got them.

The other five are from Wayland. Two from last night. The first's a three-second clip of some street I know too well to not recognize, even in the dark. I've lived in Deadwood for so long, I know the numbers on the light poles, which ones people like to use most for missing cats versus missing dogs or lowkey prostitution ads, and which poles don't work at all because someone just pulls everything down and leaves it in the gutter the second they see it.

I replay the video a couple of times, pausing it every second to look for why Wayland might've sent it. I turn the volume up and replay it again. He's breathing hard, running, stepping through brush or trees or something. It doesn't sound like anyone's chasing him. No swearing, gunfire, or squealing wheels, but that could've come before or after the video cuts off. I close my eyes and replay it again, just listening. There's a soft caw in the background and on another replay, there are distant rattling chains and a whistle. Something subtle, but I'm sure it's there.

The first two messages following the video were sent thirty minutes after it and just say "SORRY" twice. Then, two hours ago, Wayland sent two more messages.

WAYLAND	JO
	I NEED YOU
JOEY	Where are you?

I pace the small kitchen, reach for the cigarettes to light another one, but stop. I open the fridge. In the back corner's a six-pack with four cans left. I reach for one. My phone vibrates in my hand. I shut the fridge without grabbing anything. Wayland's text says, "MP" and I shoot back, "Coming."

My bag's sitting in one of the living room chairs. I grab a pair of jeans and my wallet. Once the box of cigarettes and the lighter from the counter are in my pocket, I've got my skateboard and I'm outside. There's a bus stop out front and the two or three minutes it takes for the bus to come feels like an hour. The ride isn't any better. I can't keep still, my foot's bouncing and when I try to stop it, the other one picks up. I probably look like I'm crazy or high or a little bit of both, so after three stops, I move to the back.

Doesn't help.

Irritation builds as someone's shitty music comes through the shitty speakers on the back of their phone; he's not even bothering with earbuds. The bus is just loud enough to destroy anything meaningful coming out of the phone, but not enough to drown it out totally, and what's left is tinnier than the music that should've been muffled. The combination feels like dragging a fork down the inside of my skull so all I can think about is grabbing the asshole three rows in front of me and bashing his head into the seat in front of him. At least unconscious, he wouldn't need his beats anymore, yeah? Be lucky if I don't toss the phone out the fucking window.

My growing anger makes the shaking worse. My feet roll from toe to heel and back. I run my hands along my skateboard's deck, then switch to spinning its wheels while it lays over my lap.

Not helping.

I grip the deck. I'm panting, smashing the skateboard over the guy's head with my fingers so tight, my bones hurt. "No," I say through a stiff jaw, eyes open. I'm still sitting, back bouncing against the bus seat, racket man with his racket phone still listening to his fucking racket *jams*.

I can't take it anymore and I pull the wire to get off the bus. I'm at the door before we're anywhere near the stop. He's on the higher floor, right in front of the door, bobbing his head, muttering something, but he's so uncoordinated or lazy or whatever that he's just making sounds no one else can hear. How is the phone still so loud?

The bus stops. I punch the sheet of plastic separating the upper-level seat from the door while I'm on my way out, saying, "My bad!" He's looking at me through the window when the bus pulls away, so I flip him off.

I skate the rest of the way to the park. It's not that far.

I'm at the east entrance on Franklin when I get my phone out to tell Wayland I'm here and ask where he's at. All he sends is, "BRIDGE."

I send back, "u ok?" and he doesn't answer.

Dumb question, I know.

I'm skating down the side of the road. The smell's strong. Must and mold and rot and sulfur. It's not usually so bad during the day, at least not when it's sunny like it is now. The place is worse when it rains, yeah, but the worst it usually gets is at night during a storm. Maybe someone's been busy sowing new secrets into the mud, but I pretend it's because I'm dead and that somehow makes the smell worse or maybe it's actually just me that smells. My sight's messed up from whatever the river did to me. I can't see better, it's just obscurity and a veil and sometimes it's graffiti showing up in a place it shouldn't be.

My wheels should be making sounds, but they're not.

I put my foot down, wipe my eyes, wait. A couple runs past me on the trail between the trees. A car goes by, radio coming through the windows. The rotting park smell lightens up, replaced with crisp fall air.

What the hell is wrong with this place?

A caw comes from somewhere in the trees. I can't tell how close. I look over the trees, but there are too many and the branches go from thin to thick and even the mild red in my eyes makes everything too dark like it's trying to hide the birds from me. I look over the park again, this time looking for a bit of white. Val might not stand out, but Charon would.

Yet, there are no chains and there's no white.

"Stop stalking me!" I let my board down. "I'll get to work when I'm done figuring some shit out, okay?" I hop back on my board and continue toward the bridge.

The short bridge is on the west side of Franklintown and near where Winans Way intersects. It's a wooden bridge with metal railings that goes over Dead Run, the creek, and connects the two sides of the walking path. Wayland's not standing at the entrance of the bridge. I walk across it to the other side, further from the road. The trees are brown, leaves thinning from winter. I don't know how there're still so many left on the branches to make the woods thick. I go down the short hill to the base of Dead Run. The closer I get, the more uneasy I am. My skin tingles all over with a soft reminder of the searing pain of regret.

Some of the mud along the shoreline is indented with fresh, sunken-in shoe tracks, but who or where they came from is unreadable. Probably left behind by the last asshat dumping a dog where he hopes it won't be found for a while. There's a foam cup from Kwik Mart floating in the water, the lid barely hanging on and the straw crooked. A bag of ranch Doritos sits further down the river, random strips of plastic, torn paper, receipts left behind, a soiled sock, but no lumpy garage bags from someone's midnight sins.

I'm back up at the bridge, walking across it again, looking around at the other end.

Wayland's not here.

A breeze passes by me, rustling trees. I open my eyes. It's just runner's already a couple feet down the path.

I lean my skateboard against the bridge, dig out a cigarette, and light it, jittery. Pace across the bridge again. "Wayland?" My voice comes back to me with a couple of rustling leaves, but nothing else. Two times in two weeks I've been out here calling his name. It being daytime isn't making a difference; this feels like the night he went missing. I jog back across the bridge. "Cross? You out there?"

I never realized how much I hated this goddamn forest. It's not just because it's a dumping ground, but because it eats everything too. There's a reason people come *here* to dump their trash or the life they're done with; there's a reason this place is called Murder Woods by the *dead;* there's a reason the Styx drops you here when you push through. The scars on my arm tingle every time I get closer to the bridge. It's unbelievable how I still remember every feeling from the night I picked up Wayland's car. My arm, my face, my desperation, the fucking end.

In the dark, you feel like you're tempting fate to do away with what no one's noticed is missing yet. The city lights on the horizon feel like another dimension; the world goes on without you, no one taking notice of the things you do in the cover of the trees and night and filth because the warm city lights will never touch the darkness. The golden leaves of the fall or green of the summer are a mirage, like the mist in the forest of the dead, they hide everything happening between the trees until you get lost in the darkness and can't find your way out without a guide.

But no one's coming for you here.

I pinch my cigarette between my lips and draw out my phone.

JOEY   Cross—
                  Where the fuck are you?

Another pass over the bridge. I don't want to be near the forest's edge. The trees shuffle, but there's no breeze. I look around. The birds should stand out against the gold. They don't. You can't see anything and in the yellow leaves, the red tint from death makes them look dipped in blood, or maybe the trees actually drink the blood from the bodies in the soil and that's giving the leaves color. I stop, stare, come closer to the trees until I'm off the path and standing underneath one of them. I pick up a fallen leaf from a pile under the tree. The surface is silky paper under my thumb. Dark veins, red, almost black, run through the leaf, coming from the stem and going to different edges while the rest of the leaf is illuminated and thin. When held up to light, it almost looks like skin.

The trees rattle again. I stop where I am, look up.

"If you're there, then say it!" I turn back around, eyeing the trees for birds like someone in the park's about to die.

It sure as Hell isn't gonna be me this time.

I cross back to the bridge. A dark blob stands out against the trees. I startle.

"Jo."

It's not a raven.

"Way." I run off the path to the forest's edge. He's standing in them, hiding behind branches and leaves and stumps, making no move to come out. "What the hell are you doing?" I laugh. I step into the grass that's thinning into mud; sticks crack under my feet. The closer I get, the more the light hits him and the branches move away. The shirt I gave him yesterday's discolored red and brown and black. Not dirt. At least… not all of it. "Cross… What happened to you?" I'm trying not to look at his hands because maybe it's looking too hard mixed with the paranoia and whatever dying did to my eyes that's making the mud look like blood.

In an instant, he lunges for me. He grabs hold of my arm. The cigarette falls out of my hand. He's pulling me into the trees, stepping backwards, pushing branches out of the way so they don't hit me when we walk by.

"Wayland—What's going on?" My legs stiffen to stop, but he doesn't falter, instead, he's pulling harder now.

"I messed up, Jo—"

"I told you last night, it's gonna be fine. What did you get on your clothes?"

"…Like I said—I… I messed up. I didn't know what to do."

We're getting so far into the trees there's no seeing the running trail anymore, but the sounds of Dead Run still echo. Branches wave, a soft whistle goes through the leaves. Wood turns to a plastic garbage bag, then another and another until I see four bags sitting on the ground between trees along with a crushed soda can and a log covered with initials and hearts and empty sentiments. The log's covered in something sloppy that had once been liquid but dried now. A box of opened garbage bags sits on the log next to discolored grass. A big knife sits beside that, crusted in mud and gore.

I wouldn't call the place a clearing. The log's a tree that became weak and fell over some time ago.

Wayland lets go of my arm; it drops to my side.

I look between the bags. "What—"

Don't ask questions. Questions get you killed. Mind your business. I'm not worried about Wayland hurting me, but the less I know, the better. The fewer answers I have, the more I can say I don't know if I'm asked and mean it. It's not a lie if I'm never told something directly.

"I just gave you those clothes yesterday, Cross. You look like you've been rolling around in the woods all night." I laugh in an attempt to breathe.

Wayland turns away from me, pacing between the trees. "I've been out here since last night, so… I guess you're not totally off," Wayland says.

"You told me you were gonna go home—"

"That was the plan, I just—I didn't make it. Something happened." He looks at the bags.

I can't stop myself from looking at them too. The smell of mud and blood and sulfur… it's stronger now than it was seconds ago. I turn away, digging into my back pocket for my cigarettes. I don't take one out, but turn the box over in my hands while my thumb taps my lighter's plunger too weakly to pretend it's gonna draw a flame. I watch the ground, trying to avoid looking at him without it being obvious I'm avoiding him. It's too late. The blood's staining down his legs, heavier on his thighs and the cuffs of his pants. The shirt's matted against his body. Dried blood chips all down his arms, starting heavier at his hands, discoloring his nails and fingertips, and going up to his elbows. I pull out a cigarette and put the box back into my pocket. Lighter and cigarette to the same hand. I push my bangs back, turn away. My feet crunch on dry leaves.

Wayland grabs my arm. "Please don't leave!"

I turn back to him. The black bags on the ground keep catching me every time I face him. "I'm not gonna leave, Way. I'm just… I'm thinking."

"They already came for the heart."

"Good to know, but not what I was thinking about."

"Okay." He releases my arm.

I'm still stepping back because I need to move. "After everything we've been through, you'd think I'd just…

abandon you over something like this?" A small laugh comes out. My throat burns in the back. Not vomit. Really, I should be feeling sick, guilty, scared, angry, something. I don't have to pretend there's not a body in the bags so I don't get sick. I keep thinking *they deserved it* without having to know about them and from there, I don't care enough to ask anything else. Wayland's always been the reasonable one between the two of us anyway and it's like he said a week ago, can't save a dead man walking; someone that doesn't matter is doomed to disappear. Everything else goes on, unchanged.

It happened to me.

I think I'm starting to get why the badges don't give a shit when people go missing. No one likes looking at the destruction around them. Acknowledging it means you have to worry about it coming for you.

Ignorance, even feigned, means you can get on with life without fear.

"How many?" I turn back to Wayland.

"One." Wayland carefully tries to pluck off the specks of dried blood on his arm. It gets caught under his nail. He brings his fingers to his mouth and uses his teeth to try and clean out his nails. His skin's so red with nail marks, stripped raw from how hard he's been tearing at himself.

"I meant bags."

"Just the four. I didn't want to put him all in one. It would've been heavier and looked weirder and—"

"I don't want a bunch of info, Cross. Thanks."

"Sorry—"

"Don't be sorry. Just practice. Like you don't wanna talk like this if a badge stops you. Get used to saying as little as possible, okay?"

"Okay."

"Badges hate benign shit." I snort. "They'll actually tell you to shut up if you share too much of it." I don't think I should be telling him to talk to the badges at all, he's too honest, but Wayland's life is so vanilla, I'm imagining Rocky sitting in an interrogation room with him while Wayland goes through his class schedule and the things he's learned over the last couple of years. I hate to say it, but even the few times I tried helping him with flashcards, I fell asleep.

I pace through the trees in the direction we came from, then back. "I'm trying to think... of how the hell to get you out of here and cleaned up without anyone noticing."

"I have a car," Wayland says.

"Where?"

"The west entrance. Not far from the bridge."

"How..." I put my hand up. "Never mind. Don't tell me where you got it. The less you say, the less I have to pretend I don't know." I go to one of the black bags. Picking it up, it's heavier than I expected it to be, and I struggle to lift it at first. The bag sags down with the feeling of wetness and a soft squish inside as it hits the ground again. A sharp stick pokes into the plastic side. I set it back down.

"What are you doing?" Wayland says.

"I think we should chuck these in different places. Not far, but like, at least not *together*. It'll make them look less connected and probably take longer to notice."

"You sure?"

I glance over the bag beside me again then back to Wayland. I pick the bag up again. "No, but my dad couldn't stop watching true crime shows. Pretty sure he was prepping for the day he finally offed me." I look into the trees with a short chuckle. "What you're supposed to do is spread the remains. It works for a while. Sometimes no one finds anything until you're already dead."

"Jo... I'm already—" A sheepish smile tugs onto Wayland's lips.

"Dead and *buried*." I smile back. Wayland's smile gets a little bigger, a little more relaxed, he almost looks normal.

I get back to work. I have to use two hands to carry just the one bag. Anything less and it'd drag on the ground, risk popping, risk spilling whatever it was hiding all over the grass and I don't want to find out if that'd make me vomit or laugh. Now that I'm holding it against me, I'm feeling the shape of someone's chest by their ribs, their shoulders, the stub from the neck, and disconnected spine.

The smell's so potent, it *feels* heavy.

Wayland picks up a bag with one hand, then a second with the other, reminding me that it doesn't matter what he looks like; he's still stronger than me. Even his arms aren't muscular in the same way Jag's are from working in the shop. He's trim, muscles firm, flexing from the weight of each bag that he's lifting with less effort than I need and it's like this that I'm reminded we're not in high school anymore. Wayland's a *man*.

He and I go deeper into the trees, moving fast. I tell Wayland to drop one of the bags into a couple of bushes. A little further, we drop another into a ravine. We go a little further still and I spin, letting the weight of the bag pick up momentum until I finally let it go. It smacks into a tree with a wet *thud*. I fall back into Wayland. His hands curl around my shoulder. My cigarette falls out of my mouth.

"Thanks." I stand back up on my own and pick up my cigarette.

"Any time." Wayland steps back. We're walking back to the log. I pick up the box of garbage bags. Wayland takes the knife and slides it into his jacket.

"You know you don't want to be found with the, uh, *tool*," I say.

"I guess I'm hoping I don't get found then?" He laughs, short and sharp.

"Yeah?"

A raven caws. I look to the trees. "Stop following us!"

"What?" Wayland turns around, fast, panicked.

"The birds." I point to a high branch in a tree like it'll out where the raven is. "I swear they've been following me around since you disappeared. I thought they'd stop after I died, but it feels like they're still everywhere."

"Do you think they're watching us?"

"I think someone's *being a lazy ass*!" My voice ricochets off the branches and reaches into the sky. Probably a mistake to yell. Probably better not to stick around here anymore. I'm going back through the trees toward the bridge.

"What about the last bag?" Wayland says, coming up behind me.

"Leave it. If someone finds the log, they're gonna look for shit anyway. Maybe if they think everything on the log's in one bag, they won't go looking for more."

"Okay." Wayland's close behind me. We stay off the main trail, but still have to get close enough that I can grab my skateboard from the bridge, assuming it's still there.

We keep off to the side of the road and a little in the trees while we get to the parking lot. I'm closer to the street and Wayland's on the other side of me, his hands in his pockets, his back arched, his eyes down. My elbow bumps his and I say, "What's wrong?"

"Nothing new. I'm just..." He sighs. "I'm glad you're here."

"Me too."

We're back at the parking lot and Wayland leads me to a silver Corolla, probably ten years old. Busted out taillight covered in red tape, bubbles in the rear glass, and it looks like it's never had an oil change, probably never had a car wash either. Wayland opens the driver's side and hits the lock. Inside, it smells like pot. There's a collection of burned CDs in the center console. I don't think I'm daring enough to put one in to see what's on it.

Wayland starts the car saying, "Where do you want to go?"

I'm working my phone out of my pocket. I look over the screen. A message from Jag says, "No." I don't know what he's referring to. I check the clock and put my phone back. "Jag's place… for a shower. You know how to get there?"

"No." Wayland's fingers curl around the steering wheel.

"Okay. I'll tell you."

I have Wayland put his clothes in a garbage bag the second we get into Jag's house. He's in the shower now and his clothing's in the washer. Just in case, I throw my clothes in the wash too. I'm going through Jag's closet, looking for a pair of pants he doesn't wear very often. The easiest way to tell is if there are no stains or tears, then you're probably good to go. There's a pair of slacks in the back that I don't think I've ever seen him wear. I'm at my drawer next, grabbing out another pair of black skinnies for me, a faded green tee with a UFO on it for Wayland, and a red band tee with a scribbled yellow monster on the front. Tentacles and eyes are all I see. I dress quickly, then take the other items into the bathroom.

The air's thick with steam. The mirror's too foggy to see anything but the vague shapes moving off reflections and rippled glass. I set the clothing down on the counter. The glass shower door slides open. Wayland's eyes catch mine. He looks down, he closes the door again, saying, "Jo!"

"Sorry. I brought you clothes." I'm turning away, grabbing the door, stepping back out of the bathroom as fast as I can. "You might need to roll up the legs, but that's it."

I close the door behind me. "Shit," I mutter. It comes out more like a laugh as I push my hair back and laugh again. "Sorry, Way!" I yell through the door. "I promise I didn't see anything!"

Wayland doesn't say anything back.

I shake my head, laughing again, then I'm in the kitchen, getting a beer out of the fridge, drinking it while I rinse Wayland's shoes off in the sink.

The bottle's empty when Wayland finally comes out of the bedroom. I'm not sure if it's because I was drinking fast or because he took forever getting dressed. His face's still red when he rounds the corner. His pant legs are rolled up a couple of times. He tried tucking his shirt in; it looks funny. "You should untuck that," I say, and he does.

The clock on the microwave says it's four-thirty.

I go back to the fridge and get two more bottles out, uncap them, and set them on the counter. "Tell me what happened." I push one of the bottles toward Wayland. The other comes to my lips.

"I thought you said you didn't want to know—"

"I want to know what happened to you *last night*, Way."

Wayland's eyes are moving around every part of the house like he's observing every detail about a pretty girl. They go to the fridge, sticking on everything from the random magnets to the receipts and coupons and Jag's schedule. Then he's looking over the counter, turning around, looking at the room, the blank walls, the couch, the chair with my bag in it, the bedroom, unmade bed, clothing in the hamper.

I smack the counter.

Wayland jumps, turning around instantly.

"You okay, Way?"

"I can't focus."

"You wanna go somewhere else?"

Wayland shakes his head, but says, "Yeah."

"We need to get rid of the car anyway. So we'll do that and then get something to drink." I grab the beers off the counter and put them back in the fridge. "Grab your keys unless you want me to drive."

THREE.

The red sign on top of the bar flickers the word BAITs; it stands for *Badass Idiot Train* and refers to a local indie band from a couple years back. Their first CD was titled *Moonchild*, their second *The Book of the Law*, and their third, *The Book of Lies*. A total of about thirty-two songs and nothing else was released because the band broke up. Something happened with the lead singer, I think. It's a shame; they were pretty popular locally, but just like everyone that goes missing around here, no one talks about them anymore. A couple years later, this bar popped up, run by the ex-drummer, Ralph Reagan and the lead singer, KC.

The place looks like a couple storage containers put together and painted, pretending to be a building. Small, rectangular windows line the topmost edge, barred like a jail cell, keeping the light out and the darkness in. Trees uproot the parking lot, sidewalk, and patchy grass that's mostly dirt and dead weeds anyway. The parking lot's uneven, broken, and unwelcoming. I've tripped on the cracks more than a couple of times when riding with a little too much confidence. Sometimes you're lucky if you can fit even five cars in the lot because people become jackasses when it comes to parking spaces. There's a spot for Wayland's car by a Jeep and an unmarked black sedan.

We're going for the door; sirens echo off the buildings a block over. Wayland stops moving, watching in the direction like he's waiting for the badges to turn down this way and nail him for the car. If we get inside soon enough, they shouldn't notice, right? Can't connect the car to us. It could belong to anyone inside. I take Wayland's hand. His brown eyes turn from the neighborhood to me.

"You okay?" I say.

"Yeah." He breathes out heavily.

"Good." I tug him toward the bar, stepping faster to pull him along. He doesn't resist. "Cause we're gonna have a good time. This is called problem-solving like an adult."

"How does this solve anything, Jo?" he says with a small laugh.

"Liquor takes your problems away, at least for a little while. Better than the solutions most people got—" My foot catches on uneven asphalt. I'm falling forward. An arm goes around me while the other holds my arm tighter, keeping me from hitting the ground. Wayland pulls me upright again, letting me go only when I say, "Thanks."

"Yeah." He clears his throat. His face has so much color to it now.

I pat his cheeks. His skin's warm to touch.

A caw like a laugh comes from above. A couple of clicks follow. It's too human. Then there's another caw, a second bird, then a third. Three ravens sit on the big tree by the bar's entrance. Only one of them's looking at me. Its attention shifts, going through me, checking on a noise behind me. A car passes; one of the birds jumps to the ground. Its beak digs into the dirt. I don't think it's actually pulling anything up. I follow where he'd been looking.

Three more ravens sit spread between the roof and a couple of trees by the bar. The biggest of them jumps down from the tree. He lands firmly. For a second, I'm sure I see a person, but there's still a bird when he's on the ground. Its eyes catch me, dark with a slight red ring around the outside, almost glowing in the sun. I count the birds one more time. Only six. No one's dying here, not yet at least.

I let go of Wayland's hand and slowly step closer. The raven flicks its wings but doesn't retreat. The ring around his eye is wet at the bottom, dampening his feathers.

A clear lid slides over his eye. He turns away, pecks the ground, looks at the bar.

"Something smell good around here, Val?" I say.

The bird caws softly, bends down, pecks at something in the weeds again. Looks like nothing.

"You know you can just talk to me if something's up, yeah?" I say.

"What?" Wayland says.

"It's gotta be Val in there, right?" I point to the bird. "Why else would he follow us around?"

"There are a lot of ravens around here."

"Never mind, then." I turn around, closing the space between Wayland and me. "I think I'm getting paranoid so... means I need a drink." I take him by the arm and pull him toward the door.

I'm tense; moving's not helping. I pull the door open too hard, it flies out of my hand even though it's heavy.

Wayland takes the door from me. I would've stopped him, but his hands are shaking, so I say, "Thanks," instead and walk in.

Wayland touches the small of my back when I pass. "Any time, Jo," he says, coming in behind me. The door shuts, heavy with a gust. The overhead lights are darker than I remember from the last time I was here, glowing amber like burning candles with a flicker now and then. It's not faulty electrical, it looks more like someone's trying to blow the lights out. Bodies like shadows paint stripes against the bright, neon labels illuminating the walls. There's enough light to see furniture and people, but details are hard to make out. Then, there are things I've never noticed before decorating the bar. A dream catcher, feathers, bones hanging from bones with string connecting parts to look like skeletons. One corner even has a homemade doll nailed to the wall made out of weeds or twigs or something.

I cross the bar without pause and climb onto the step at the counter. I smack my hands against the polished wood as a greeting. I don't see the bartenders anywhere. "Hey, Ralph, you here?"

The dim lights catch on smoke. Furniture's smooth in shape and muted in color, getting closer to gray. The guitar coming through the speakers sounds cleaner than anything I've heard in the last few days. A heavy beat, a voice saying life goes on if you just wake up, but don't mess with me or I'll burn you alive. It's speaking to my soul. My head rolls back. My lips are moving to a song I've never heard, but somehow, I know the words. Smooth, deep, boom, like the restlessness is from the other day isn't there anymore. My ass sways with the next beat, following after my head. My knuckles knock against the counter. A smile spreads on my lips.

Solace without a cigarette.

I almost feel normal.

"Bartender?" I say.

"Gimme a sec," a voice comes from the far end of the bar. Ralph stands rimming a glass with something. He pours a shaker into it. Blended into the background with the black tee, slim black jeans, messy black hair. He turns to me. Light catches on his pendant necklace. Shaped like a heart, it doesn't look cut, but rough-edged. The upper part of its white and misty. Red splotches pattern the edges of the bottom half while dark tendrils wrap around the insides like wire. Specks of red and gold reflect inside the white. A studded earring holds a black feather dangling from his right ear and eyeliner darkens his eyes in a way that's been out of fashion for a while now.

Ralph comes toward me, leaving behind some other guy with shoulder-length blond hair pulled into a loose ponytail, torn blue jeans, and a sleeveless shirt like the kind Jag likes to wear. This one's got band insignia on it. It's KC, the ex-lead singer from the same band Ralph was in, now his business partner.

I straighten up. "Why was I thinking... KC died all of the sudden?" I watch him, moving like nothing's wrong. Nothing shows on his face that he's dead like all the other ghosts around him. "He's been here since I've been coming here, but I'm just now thinking he died?"

"Yeah," Ralph says. "Because he died a while ago."

"Why am I just remembering it now?"

Ralph smiles. "Because things are a little different on the other side." He winks.

"You *know*?" I lean back.

Ralph's tongue brushes his lips. "What'll it be?"

Don't ask questions.

"Two shots of tequila, two cinnamon ciders," I say.

Ralph's eyes go from me to Wayland. Wayland's not sitting down; his arms cling tight to his sides. He's not shaking anymore, but he looks like someone who feels guilty and waiting to get caught for something. His breathing's rigid and he keeps scanning the room.

"You sure about that?" Ralph nods at Wayland then locks eyes with me.

"Party." I step back from the counter to grab Wayland and pull him toward the bar.

Ralph's already in motion, grabbing glasses from the counter, a bottle of Patron from the shelf behind him. Dark tattoos cover his arm; a big black circle is on the back of his hand, surrounded by what looks like half a thick halo. Tiny black circles dot each knuckle. Lines like a mixture of sigils and cursive almost look like shackles around his wrists, go up his arm, and disappear into his shirt sleeve. Silver rings decorate his fingers, some thicker than others, some plain, some with stones, the one on his left ring finger is silver with a large eye on it.

Ralph turns around, setting the shots down. "Patron," he says. He reaches under the counter. A fridge opens, he comes up with two ice-cold bottles. He uncaps them and pushes them toward us. "Cider."

I dig my wallet out of my pocket and give him my card. It's gone and back before Wayland and I have a chance to sit down.

"Keep the tab open?" Ralph says.

"Maybe," I say.

"Let me know." He turns away. He stops. "One thing."

"Yeah?" I say.

Ralph comes back to the counter, leaning in, arms folded. "In case you're unaware, things are a little different now that you're dead." My eyes meet his; I'm searching for the signs in his face. He's not alive knowing this shit, right? I didn't even know my own father was dead and I lived with his ghost for fifteen years. I'm looking for the death in his eyes; they're brown, a little dull, but still alive.

"What do you mean?" I say.

His eyes roll up, his head bounces slowly while he thinks. His tongue pokes the inside of his cheek. He smiles, though it's small. "Ghosts are sensitive creatures." His stare comes back to me. His smile lowers. "Keep yourself level; a fetish only helps so much. Pop off and you're not the only one that'll lose your shit."

"Ralph?" KC says, dipping behind the bar counter.

Ralph's rings tap against the counter as his fingers bounce. "Call if you need somethin'." One more tap, and he's gone.

"What do you think he means, Jo?" Wayland says.

I reach for the shots. "I don't know." I throw back the

shot and put the glass back down. I turn away from the bar for the first time and I get what Ralph's talking about. Maybe. Veiny, red eyes are playing a game at the pool table; a couple more red eyes sit in the corner of the room, drinking from glasses, smoking cigars, muttering to themselves. A pair of red eyes sit at the end of the bar. It's not just the red eyes that give them away, it's the black tendrils coming through their skin, wrapping around their necks and hands and arms, keeping them all tied to their pain. Some have sunken cheeks, some have overly bony arms, some look like their skin is too thin, almost transparent and ghoulish. I don't have the same tendrils going down my skin, but will it come with time? Is that rot and if it's inevitable for the dead... what happens when Jag sees me like that someday?

"You seeing this, Way?" I reach back for him without looking away from the patrons. My fingers find him after a couple of empty grabs.

His hand takes my arm. He nods, swallows, says, "Yeah."

They're all dead. Well, maybe not all of them, but enough of them that I don't understand how I never noticed. The crowd here was sometimes rowdy, but that's not uncommon for a bar, especially on this side of town when rowdy is the home setting for most. But so often I couldn't even recognize most of the people who were here, even being a regular. I figured that was just part of not paying attention, keeping my head low, trying to stay out of trouble. If I never remembered who they were because they were dead... What the hell is Ralph doing in this place or is this legitimately what the population of Bodymore looks like? Is the entire city a graveyard?

I grab my bottle off the counter. Wayland's shot's still there, untouched. I sigh. No pressure. Maybe if I drink more it'll get him to do the same. Throat dry, I'm drinking the cider fast, craving a cigarette halfway through. A chill goes down my arms; the song that comes on is too familiar and too honest. My lips follow along. I put the bottle on the counter and step back. My hands hang out, reaching for Wayland, finding his arm. I pull him from the bar as I take a couple of steps back. My legs are light, but still dragging. It's not the alcohol. It hasn't had the same effect since I came back, but I don't know what it is.

My eyes close and I'm just letting the music wrap around me and feeling the room, feeling the moment, letting it take me back. Smiling, swaying, I'm at the first high school party I got Wayland to go to.

Sophomore.

I was skipping school more and more. I think Wayland came this time because he really thought I'd never come back to school if he didn't. He never drank at the parties, but he dragged my sorry ass into his house so I didn't have to risk knocking shit over at home trying to sneak into my room. He'd turn the music on in there too cause silence makes me uncomfortable.

The air's suddenly tense. Wayland sucks in a breath, holds it. He's gripping my hip.

"Fuck," slips out of my lips and I'm not sure why.

Pool sticks touch the ground, laughter stops. My eyes open. Ralph's staring at me from behind the bar while he gestures something at KC. He nods, waving me over. When I don't respond to that, he waves again, harder. I pull away from Wayland. "What?" I say, going toward the bar. I bump into something. "Sorry—"

Someone grabs my arm. I'm yanked back. "You got a problem, bitch?" a voice says. Deep, angry, the only thing familiar about it is the rage. Instant, all-consuming, so over the top I'm feeling it in me. I'm nodding to the music, my skin's buzzing, and the music from the radio's getting muffled with the rush coming to my head.

My lips pull into a sneer. I laugh, turn around, ready to swing. "You wanna take that bet?" My hands are curled, and the voice is back, telling the guy to do it, *fucking do it and we'll see who lays who out*. The guy grabs me by the front of my shirt and uses it to toss me to the ground on the other side of him. My wrist snaps, but it's not any worse than any time I've fallen off my board. Adrenaline's moving through me like electricity. I'm barely on my feet again before I'm bouncing on my soles and he's lunging for me. Wayland's lunging back, faster than I've ever seen him move.

Wayland grabs the guy by the arm and pulls him in. The knife he took from the park's in his other hand. Without hesitation, without fear, without it even registering in his focused expression, Wayland shoves the knife through the guy's eye.

The attacker collapses instantly.

Wayland steps over him. His foot braces itself against the guy's back. His hands are so tight at taking the handle and he yanks the knife back with more force than he probably needs.

"Holy shit, Cross," I say.

Everything about the bar changes in that moment. The radio doesn't make sense anymore, it's noise and vulgarity and torment. The air's gone sour, not with blood, but the smell of sulfur. Signs that should say BUDWEISER say BUT WHY NOT; that should say HEINEKEN say NO HELP; that should say OLD MILWUAKEE say FUCK OFF.

Wayland's lips pull back, replacing the worry or panic or attempt to hide either of those things with a snarl of disgust. "Deadman," Wayland says.

A glass cracks.

KC and Ralph are not behind the bar anymore, they're not anywhere I can see. Everyone has dropped what they're doing. The two guys who'd been playing pool are knocking each other out, the stronger of the two making the other guy eat the felt of the table. The guys who'd been

53

in the corner of the room are fighting those from the other side while the living stand with their backs against the walls, some with their phones out, recording what's happening while others look on like every other Baltimoron.

Look the other way, don't get involved, even standing in the same room, pretend you don't see it happening. You got a story to make up for when the badges show up if you're slow enough to get caught by them on your way out. One of the cameras is pointing at me. "Fucking light off!" I say. The LED is blinding.

A bottle's cracked over someone's head. Blood floods down some guy's face before whoever smacked him with the bottle is grabbed to bash his head into a table or chair or whatever the hell is nearest. It's a race to see who can be the most deadly as frenzy takes over. I'm at the bar, grabbing my abandoned bottle and knocking it over the head of whoever's closest, so long as it's not Wayland. My vision's so dark, I can't make out much, I just see a body and think *break him open, make him fucking suffer. Not enough, not enough, not enough!*

I laugh as the glass shatters and I reach for the next thing; Wayland's bottle maybe. I don't know whose drink I've got in my hand, but I'm taking it to the nearest person. Something hard smacks me in the back of the head. I fall to the ground. Roll onto my back. Some guy's over me, drawing his hand into position.

"Jo!" Wayland says. Rage works like fuel inside of him. The guy on top of me's bigger than him, but Wayland pulls him off like nothing and punches him in the face, then again and again. I'm hearing Wayland's knuckles crack. The guy punches Wayland back, but it's not like with Jag, it doesn't drop Wayland; he's panting through his teeth, punching harder. This one grounds the banger, and Wayland's on top of him, going again and again and again as his voice fills the bar.

I'm standing up again. "Way—" A hand goes around my throat. Another's got my shirt. I'm walking back, stumbling, feet off the floor. My eyes water, my vision blurs, I'm gripping the hands holding my throat, fingers digging into the skin under my nails. I can't breathe, but I'm trying through a cough and a laugh. Wayland's gasping somewhere. I try to say his name, but nothing comes out. "Fuck—off!" My back hits the ground. I gasp for air; pain runs through me. The groan turns into a half chuckle. My arms shake as I push myself up.

Amber bar lights catch on the tip of the blood-stained knife falling from Wayland's hand. One of the guy's from the pool table swings a pool cue at his head. Wayland falls. The guy towers over Wayland and without so much as a pause, he drives the pool cue into Wayland's head.

"Cross!" I focus on where the knife fell. If I can grab it, I can cut them all off. I lunge for the knife. Someone grabs me by the back of my shirt and throws me again. I land on top of a table. It flips. The glasses and baskets and food fly off. The back of my shirt's sticky and wet and smells like alcohol. A long, red line runs across my forearm while shattered glass lays on the floor beside me. I'm getting up. A foot slams into my side and I'm rolling over from the speed and power and force behind it until I'm laying on my back. The overhead lights are darker, too dark to see more than the shadow of a big man standing over me. It's not my dad doing it this time. My teeth clench; I can't hold them there. My jaw goes slack. It's a big guy. Is that the bastard that killed me? I can't see his face, but the neon bar lamps light the back of his head like they're a running monologue of his thoughts.

He slams his foot into my chest again. My voice is an unfamiliar scream. I can't breathe. I'm already dead, but I'm still trying to breathe and everything hurts instead.

The air's starting to smell more like water and smoke, like rain and burning wood and I don't know where it's coming from, but it's overpowering the alcohol and sulfur and spite. I open my eyes. Not enough to see anything but the vague shadow of the big guy standing over me. His foot comes down hard on my chest, picks up, drops again. Each time it strikes, it's harder. I'm gasping. He slides his boot up my chest until he's pressing it into the crook of my neck. I try to keep my chin down, but his foot's stronger. He pushes my chin until it's up and his heel's on my neck.

Snorting laughter staccatos. He crushes me. My hands grab at his leg, now trying to dig into his skin in the same way Val digs into the chests of the dead to get their hearts. His pants are too thick, my fingers are too weak, everything's so heavy. I can't. My fingers curl into his pant leg. He picks his foot up, my hand drops away. He stomps into my chest again. "Say you like the pain, bitch. Maybe I'll stop, maybe I'll do it how you like." He spits on me.

Suddenly, the guy's sounding familiar; he's sounding like my dad. Everything else is distant and muted like my head's underwater. My vision's spotty, mostly black, but I feel where the guy is on top of me. My hand's reaching down my thigh, finding my pocket and my lighter at the bottom of it. My thumb presses the plunger down once, then twice.

I know what the flame feels like.

The foot's bearing into my chest. I'm coughing, gasping, trying to catch of breath of anything, but feeling liquid hit my lungs and something sharp thrusts into my side. I'm not sure if my arm's moving, but I'm willing it toward the guy's leg. The flame catches on his pant leg, small, but it's there. The smell of burning cloth starts to fill the room.

Wetness is on my face. Not spit. Not tears. It's warm. Forcing my eyes open, crimson stains the big guy's shirt. The pressures off my chest and the guy's stumbling back, grunting and snarling and turning around fast with swinging arms. I try to breathe even though I don't want to. Everything hurts too much.

Another crash. Another table flips over. Chairs follow, and then shattered glass. I can't hear words, but his hatred's clear.

Familiar black hair stands over me.

"J…?" I don't have a voice, but I feel his name in my throat.

"I'm here, Jo."

His voice doesn't sound right. "Wayland?"

A hand reaches down. It grabs my arms and pulls me up. Another hand goes to my chest and gets me to my feet. Closer now, there's no cigarette smell or his cologne or the grease and shop or the burnt smell from the shitty toaster he has that's always overcooking everything. My eyes fall closed again. My feet are moving, mostly dragging, and the arms around me are the only things keeping me up. I can't get *those words* out of my head. The gratitude from every time he makes me not feel so alone makes me feel pathetic and helpless and like a joke if they get closer to my lips. What it really means is that I'm a loser for thinking them in the first place.

Wayland's arms are gone. "Jo!" he says. My legs crumble. I knock my head on a step somewhere, bite my lip, my teeth chatter. I'm tasting blood.

"What the hell?" The thug's heavy steps stagger away.

I roll onto my back.

Bad idea.

It hurts—It hurts so goddamn much I'm holding my breath and rolling onto my side. Still, more pain. I can barely open my eyes, but it's enough to see the fire moving up the thug's leg; its light is brighter than anything else in the bar. A couple of glasses fall over. He empties a pitcher onto himself, making it look like he's pissed his leg. He's yelling something that doesn't make sense, a string of curses, mutters at a loud volume. Maybe it's not even him making them gibberish, but me.

Then Wayland screams. A thud follows. He's laying on the floor next to me. His eyes are wide, blood mats his hair to his head and puddles underneath him.

"Holy shit—Way—" I gasp, reaching for him. My ribs try to pierce my stomach with every little movement. My skin's coated in sweat and I'm dizzy to the point Wayland's on the ceiling now and the words plastered on the walls are flying around me like they're being said to me from every direction. My hand touches his.

A foot meets my stomach.

I roll over a couple of times.

The thug's standing over me with a sneer on his face. His burnt foot lifts, hanging over me. "Goodbye, bitch." He stomps down on my head, and everything goes black.

FOUR.

I'm hearing drumming in my ear, slow, morphed, someone's pretending to play some kind of somber party anthem. The guitar's gone. It's not drums, it's me. The ceiling comes in dark. The strips of light across the ceiling are dim amber and the neon signs read what they're supposed to instead of glowing rage like a new kind of Baltimore graffiti. Red, white, and blue lights reflect off the windows and flash between the thick window bars, somehow penetrating the slits where the daylight couldn't. The air smells like blood and sulfur, spilled beer and chicken wings, broken wood and fresh rainfall. The iron smell of blood feels heavy to breathe in, like sucking in mud instead of air. My jaw's tight, my head's throbbing, my eyes keep closing, too heavy to keep open. I can't will myself up. The quiet acts like reassurance that it's fine if I don't move for a while longer.

I let my arms drop over my face to block out any light that might try to penetrate them, even while closed. Something wet splatters against my cheek. I wipe it away, examining my arm. It's too dark to tell what it is, but the color looks almost right to be blood. I wipe my hand on my pants. My arms are still shaky, but I push myself up to sit.

My head bumps into something, not hard, but warm.

"Val?" Charon's monotonous voice says from across the room. "What are you doing?"

Beside me are a pair of black pointed boots, black jeans going into a black jacket and tee. Val's standing over me, part of a human heart in his hand. Blood drips down his chin from a bite already taken. He looks down at me. Well, maybe not at me, because the way he's looking, it's like he's seeing through me instead. He scans over the room. "I dunno," he says. The heart's back at his mouth. He's eating it like it's an apple. Though the first bite is a little more normal, after it touches his lips, he's shoving it into his mouth, eating it as fast as he can like it's going to disappear or someone might take it. Three more chomps and it's gone. He licks his lips, then his fingers. I'm not sure if his nails had always been that long and sharp-looking before. Like talons. Desperately, he's sucking the blood off his fingers. "I feel like there's something over here."

"It's useless, Val," Charon says. "Whatever you think you feel over there, if it's not human…"

"Yeah, yeah, yeah, but like, there *is* something here…"

"Probably." Charon approaches Val. "You don't keep a fetish around unless you're trying to hide something."

"Doesn't smell like the usual rot," Val says.

"Yes, well, who knows what that *medium* is housing here." There's a mild hiss in Charon's words. He turns around. "If you're done, we can go now."

Val shoves his fingers into his mouth again, licking what remained of the blood from each digit, one at a time. When he's finished with his hands, he wipes them on his pants, but whatever's left behind doesn't come off. His nails are black, either painted to hide the blood probably under the polish or they're stained forever from how many times he's ripped a body open to pluck the heart out. Though it seems stupid for a bird to paint his nails, let alone the bird of a guide for the dead? So maybe he doesn't paint his nails. Maybe they're just black because he's a black bird and that's how they look when he is a bird. The remains of his meal smear around his lips. He turns around. Charon says, "Clean your face," and Val quickly complies. Though some of the blood comes off then, most of it just smears and he has to wipe with his hands a couple of times before the mess is mostly gone. Then he lifts his shirt and uses it against his skin to get the little that remains.

"Val," I say. "What the hell are you doing?"

His dark eyes turn sharply back down at me. My body goes stiff. I'm holding my breath. He leans down. He squints, going side to side like he's searching for something. He doesn't see me. He reaches a hand toward me.

"Val," Charon says. "What *are* you doing?"

Val straightens. "I dunno. I just feel like there's something over here and it's bugging me."

"Forget about it," Charon says. "Are there any more bodies?"

"Yeah." Val sniffs hard. His hands tuck into his pockets. He steps over me. "There's one in the back too. Uh, this way." Val steps around the counter, over a broken chair, past a flipped table, and down the bar. Charon follows him, clothing still white, still spotless in this dodgy, now bloody bar. Even the light from the neon signs hardly touches him, muting and being absorbed, leaving his coat, sweater, gloves, and shoes mostly white and glowing. There's no dirt, grime, or contamination. With his hands in his pockets, he pulls his coat closer. He walks past me without so much as a sideways glance or a feeling of being ignored. It's more like he doesn't even know I'm there.

I wait until I can't see them anymore before I breathe.

The memories come back then, fast, sporadic, like a film in fast-forward and with sections cut out, but enough of them remain to paint a picture of what happened right before that moment. At least what I was awake for. I push off the ground. My legs are wobbly, unstable. I grab a nearby barstool to help me balance. There's gore on the floor where I laid, but I pretend it's spilled chips and bread and chicken wings because if you move fast enough, anything looks like food in the dark. "Way?" I say. "You here?" My voice is low in case Charon or Val might hear.

I'm looking around too fast. The throbbing that had died down is coming back and the dizziness is like a blender, spinning the room faster with each turn until I have to close my eyes and lean against the bar or smack into the ground. I choose to sit back on the ground, just because I'm already tilting and I don't want to risk knocking my head and Val finding me, if, for some reason he was faking my invisibility. I lay down, close my eyes, press my hands to the floor just to feel like I've got a body and something keeping me grounded. A throb pounds at the front of my head where the thug had dropped his foot on me. A couple deep breaths. I open my eyes. The spinning's still there, but at least it's slow now and can see again. "Cross?" I mutter. "You here?"

"Yeah, Jo. I'm here." He exhales. A thud. I turn my head. He's just stood up. Staggering back, he catches himself on a nearby table. He grabs one of the chairs tucked under the table and sits down. He wipes his eyes, then leans forward so his head can fall into his hands. His hair's sticking to his face. His fingers are dirty. Blood's chipped under his nails, against his fingers, his shirt's fabric. I look away like it's gonna give him some privacy and some time for me to come up with a good excuse for why he looks the way he does and it's got nothing to do with a fight.

"You remember what happened?" I say.

"Yeah…"

"Do you believe it?"

"I can't believe anything right now, Jo."

"Yeah…" I'm going through the last things I remember, what I heard, what I felt, what happened to Wayland, and whether my brains really are splattered on the floor behind me somewhere. I saw what happened to my dad when I put the gun to his temple both times. It wasn't fake like the alcohol in Mortem; what was left behind didn't get absorbed into the surface of the couch. Being dead apparently doesn't mean you don't leave behind gore and I guess it doesn't mean you don't feel pain either. I'm kinda struggling to understand what it even means to be dead if I still have a body. There's the anger, yeah, but what else?

My throat's dry. I swallow hard and it hurts. I get off the floor carefully. Everything's straight enough for me to get back to the bar and grab a loose drink off the counter, somehow it survived the carnage and I'm too thirsty to question whose lips might've been on it before everything went down. More than half-empty, it's lukewarm, but it's better than nothing, so I drink it.

I set the bottle down and turn around, taking in the room. We're the only people still here, but the dead guy Wayland stabbed in the face and a few police markings. The dead guy looks bad, shirt ripped apart, ribs are cracked open while his chest oozes onto his clothing where his skin's been pulled apart by what looks like sharpened knives. Having seen what does that, I can't help but think of Val's nails and then my own body torn open for him to feast on.

I grab at my pocket, looking for my phone. It's not there. I scan the floor. It's sitting near an overturned table a couple feet from me. I check the position of the badges, where their attention is, and gauge whether they'll notice me or not if I move.

I take the chance.

Whatever they're muttering about pauses when I lean down but continues a second later. I back away before even daring to breathe again. I press the button on the side of my phone. The screen lights up. The cracks on it aren't any bigger than they've been. I've got four missed messages and a call from Jag. My foot bounces as the guilt comes in.

"I'm sorry," Wayland says.

"For what?" I shove my phone into my pocket.

"For... this." He looks up at the body. His eyes drop again. He holds his head in his hands.

"I've had it caked under my nails for worse reasons, Way. It's fine." I knock him in the arm as I walk past, this time, going for the bar. A voice from the corner of the room echoes in a soft mutter; badges coming in, talking, three of them. I stop moving, waiting for them to talk some more before I continue.

They haven't noticed us.

I climb onto the bar step, then pull myself onto the counter. With my legs still in the air, I turn around and jump off on the other side.

Wayland's watching me. His eyes meet mine. I smile.

"Jo—" His lips twitch with the start of a smile, but they sink back into a straight line. He looks toward the door, badges lights flash in the open cracks. The door swings open, then closes without anyone coming in. Wayland runs toward the bar.

"Yeah?" I'm walking along the shelf, touching the glass of each bottle as I walk by them, looking for something good. I lean back, check over the bar again, this time not looking for the badges or death, but Ralph or KC. I see neither, so whiskey goes to one hand, vodka to the other. Cider's nice, but never strong enough when you want to get blasted so hard you can't remember yesterday and you're looking forward to the headache in the morning.

"Pick your poison." I turn around, lifting the bottles one at a time.

Wayland's fingers curl against the counter. He keeps glancing between the badges and me, but he's watching them way closer.

"We're fine," I sing softly, putting the vodka back on the shelf. I grab something else. "You really think they're gonna do something now if they haven't already? I mean, they checked the body, but they left us alone? I could get it if they only ignored me, but you're not the same kinda trashy—"

"You shouldn't talk about yourself like that, Jo." Wayland's facing me again.

I suck in a breath through my lips. I put the whiskey back too, grab another bottle from the shelf, still whiskey, just a brand I've never had before. Looks expensive. "How about this?" I hold the bottle up for Wayland to see.

"Hey—" one of the badges says. I don't know he's talking to us until his voice gets stiffer and he says, "You're not allowed in here," while approaching the bar.

My hands lower. "Sorry?"

"I thought you said no one was in here," the badge says, turning back to one of the guys he came in with.

"There wasn't. Must've snuck in," a different badge says. He's stopped at the dead guy's body.

The one officer's still coming toward us. "What are you doing back there?" he says. It's only as he gets closer that his vagueness becomes familiar. Short dark hair, a sad kind of facial hair, patchy, he looks young, and his voice sounds like someone who just got out of academy. You know that thing when you're not totally corrupt yet, but just coming into power and maybe you have a little hope that you can do something good in your community?

That's only what some guys go into the academy for, obviously, until they discover their first taste of power by telling someone to stop skating on those stairs or get off the grass at the park or, "It's midnight, what are you doing here? Go home or I'll cuff you and put you in my backseat. Then you can give me real lip, you know what I mean?"

Give him six months. That's how long it takes to lose faith in the strangers you thought you wanted to serve. Then, one simple smack to break someone out of *hysteria*, and you're done for. It's always that first taste of power that turns it into an addiction.

"I—" Light catches on his badge. The words Officer David Garrett light up, taking me back to the interrogation room a week ago. Rocky's fluffer. He never got to any good questions, but he was annoying enough it almost made me want to talk to Rocky just to complain. "Garnet?" I say. "For real? It's you?"

"What?" Garnet says.

"I thought you were a paperwork and office kinda guy, personally. I just don't see bangers being afraid of you, you know?"

"Are you trying to steal from a crime scene?" Garnet eyes the alcohol bottles in my hands.

I look at them too. "Oh—Oh no. I work here." I turn around and put them back on the shelves. "Sorry. Didn't realize something was going on. Might be a little tipsy. It's practically part of the job."

"You didn't realize you were the only one standing in an active crime scene?" Garnet says.

I stare at him for a minute. "Nope. Sorry, musta missed last call. Was busy playing the knockout game, you know?"

Garnet's lips straighten. His muscles tighten. He pretends he's not reaching for something like his gun or his walkie-talkie, but I don't know what he's reaching for, so I just think he's doing it for show. "I'm gonna need to ask you some questions—"

I walk out from behind the bar, empty-handed. "Sorry, G, I don't talk to badges." I walk past him, fast, expecting him to grab my arm or stop me or demand answers while asserting his authority for the first time outside of an interrogation room, but he doesn't. I don't know why, but I'm not gonna slow down to ask. I grab Wayland by the arm and pull him for the door while saying, "Let's go."

"You can't—" Garnet says.

"Sorry, what?" I say. We're running by the time I push the door open because I don't want to be stopped and I know if I take much longer, the badge'll run and jump me and his friend at the corpse will tackle Wayland or something and that's just the kind of escalation I don't need right now. Broken glass crackles under our feet. The badge at the body looks up as we pass, but doesn't grab either Wayland or me. Maybe another newbie who hasn't learned force is the only way to get what you want in this line of work.

Wayland and I are out the door and running across the lot toward his car. Maybe we shouldn't be going toward his car since it's stolen, but there's enough going on that maybe no one around the bar will notice. Badge cars and an ambulance light the front of the building. Ralph and KC are standing with a badge who's got a recorder out. What looks like a white string is wrapped around Ralph's right arm, somewhat curled between his fingers. His rings are gone and his skin looks blacker beyond the tattoos, like the ink's spread further through his skin. He doesn't even pretend to notice me, though KC's eyes meet mine. I think he's gonna come toward me, but he doesn't move from his place beside Ralph.

A small group of people stand around, but not as many as I remember being in the bar before I blacked out. Then you've got at least three mics standing off to the side with their cameras. A local station and two people belonging to some national outlet.

We get to Wayland's car, but just keep going. Better than the badges catching up. A mic says, "Were you inside?" to us as we walk by, then another says, "Do you know what happened here tonight?" and another says, "Can we get an interview?"

I don't stop walking, I don't look at them, I don't even pretend to notice them. Though since I'm still holding Wayland's arm, I slow down. He's muttering, "Sorry," but at least he's not stopping as we keep going until we're a block down the street.

The racket in my chest is back and so are the rattling chains. A click in my head. They weren't there at all in the bar, but since stepping out, they've been getting louder and louder and the dizziness is coming back. Everything around me heats up and I'm sweaty, hot-skinned, my hair's stuck to my head and I'm not sure if it's sweat or blood. I bring my hand to my lips like I'm still holding a bottle, but my hands are empty. I bite my thumb instead and let my teeth comb the top of my thumb and exhale a "Fuck."

I turn back to look at the bar, just to make sure none of the badges or mics are following us. They aren't, but Charon and Val are. A pulse goes through my body; everything's trembling. The emergency lights in the distance go dim, really, everything fades around Charon and Val. Wayland looks back to see what I'm looking at. Spotting them, he visibly startles.

"Where did they come from?" Wayland says.

"I dunno. Last I saw them they were in the bar," I say.

Something's pulsing in my face and I don't realize I'm having trouble focusing until I step toward Charon and Val and my foot's wobbling. Wayland grabs onto my arm saying, "I got you, Jo," and I say, "Thanks." The bare trees outside look like crackled lines breaking the sky apart.

I straighten up, putting as much weight as I can into my feet to balance me, like that works. I blink a couple times, trying to focus my vision enough to see if Garnet's come out of the bar looking for us, but I don't see him. I take a solid step forward, then another, this time, I wave.

"Hey, Char. What's up?"

"Was that you at the bar?" Charon says.

"What?" I say.

Val comes up behind Charon. He slides his arm around Charon's shoulders and leans against him, head to the side, black against white while his dark eyes go from watching me to avoiding looking at me for too long. It's less like he doesn't want to look at me and more like he's disinterested or can't see or unable to focus. The same way the birds the other day didn't care to look at me. His head's turned, peering in the direction of the badges and bartender.

"The mess," Charon says.

"Oh." I suck my lip in. "...It was a lot of people. Ghosts. Apparitions. Whatever."

"There were two deaths, Josephine. You're supposed to collect the already dead, not create more."

"Yeah... Yeah..." My voice cracks. I'm reaching into my back pocket for my box of cigarettes. "I don't know what happened. One second I'm dancing and the next thing you know, a knife's going through someone's head. We didn't even drink that much, so, like, it wasn't our fault."

"Do you understand the volatility of the spirit?" Charon says.

I look past him to Val, hoping his face might give me answers even though I know better. "Not exactly, no."

"Spirits are sensitive to the emotions of others." Charon's standing in front of me. His pale, blue eyes watch hard to the point I feel like I should run. Chains rattle in my head, like thunder purring in the clouds. I tighten my legs so I don't step back the closer he comes, though I look past him toward the bar, using it as a distraction. "With little to anchor them to reality, they will be inspired by what others around them feel. This is what makes spirits much more dangerous than humans. One spirit can turn twenty into a mob of nothing but violence, thirsty for destruction they do not understand. While the first spirit to anger may have been led there by a residual response or memory, the others typically are not, thus, they have no means to resolve their escalating response. They feed on each other, getting worse and worse until the object of the haze has been destroyed. Generally, there are few ways to stop a frenzy such as that once it's started. All it can do is burn out. Fortunately for you, it took place in the presence of a *medium* who could end it."

"Wait, what?" My tongue flicks over my lip. I light a cigarette and breathe to give myself a moment to think. I close my eyes and let the flavor of nicotine focus me, take away the heat, the beating brain, the confusion. I need another hit before I open my eyes. "What do you mean a *medium*? Are you talking about Ralph or KC?"

"Everyone here knows *the medium*. It's not a position you come into secretly," Charon says.

"They're kinda freaky." Val shivers. "The guy collects dead ravens."

"You're one to talk about freaks," I say.

Charon looks sidelong at Val. His expression is the closest thing I've ever seen to emotion. Displeasure? Disgust? Annoyance? I'm not sure. "A *medium* is something that exists between the two extremes: life and death. They have the uncanny ability to speak with those you cannot and the skilled medium can manipulate the soul. Though he is fairly young. He does not have complete control." Charon's sharp eyes turn onto Wayland. "The other is nothing short of a *siren* everyone would be better without."

The rattling chains get louder in my ear, like a threat coming closer. My skin's on fire, bubbling under the surface and I'm feeling the acid wash of regret and Charon's chains pressing into my skin, constricting me, reminding me of the feeling that goes with being collected. "How do you know that's what happened here?"

"You will know a medium by the sigils they wear. The markings left on their skin are the contracts they've made with death," Charon says.

"Wait… Is that why you couldn't see me inside of the bar?" I say. "I was right in front of Val and you didn't even notice. Is that what a medium does?"

"What you're speaking of is a fetish," Charon says. "As you can see, the *medium* here is able to manipulate death. Upon entering his territory, all we can see are the souls to be collected that are tied to a heart. It is no sooner that Val removes the heart that he can no longer find the body and I can no longer expunge the soul."

"You can't collect souls in there?" I say.

"If they are without a body, they cannot be traced," Charon says. "That is one of the reasons I recruited you. Flush the souls out of Terra Santas."

"Yeah, yeah. I know. I'm just working on something else right now." I grab at my cigarettes, light one, and pop it into my mouth. I'm pinching the filter between my lips, using it as an excuse not to say anything yet. I'm looking for Ralph in the distance, but he's not there. At least, not where he had been. "So… mediums hide the dead? They help ghosts?"

"They can."

"What about with the rage stuff? The violence?"

"Regret is only the start; horror is the transformation." Charon's still staring at Wayland.

Wayland's stepping back, his arms are tight at his sides. Looking close, he's trembling.

"That's crazy," I say, watching the bar now, looking around the crowd gathered outside and trying to spot Ralph, but we're either too far or he's not there. Maybe it's a little bit of both. I shouldn't be buying into all of this so easily. Religion, spirituality, and con artistry all have a tendency to look the same, but I know Ralph and while he's kind of weird, he's never come off as anything short of honest. Besides, how else would you explain KC's being there? "Are mediums dead?" I say.

"No," Charon says. "But they have a foot in both worlds. Through preparation of the soul and desire, they offer themselves as a sacrifice to the *Cogs* in hopes of being granted the ability to manipulate the dead. Few are granted the ability; few among your kind have what's necessary to work within our system."

"What do you mean sacrifice?" I say.

Val licks his lips. "There's another one, Charon." He breathes out hard before pushing off of Charon. He's stepping back just as fast, turning around, throwing his head back to smell the air. He turns around, sharp. "That smell! Charon! We need to go!" He licks his lips again.

Charon's attention turns to Val as he paces up and down the sidewalk, moving fast, turning, looking everywhere like a bird trying to get out of a cage. Though there were no visible barriers, it's like he was unable to get too far away before coming back, springing across the street, and pacing again. He had never seemed so energetic before. Ravens gather like an audience to watch him from the sides of the road, rooftops, and anywhere else they can find a place to sit. Their eyes nearly look like they're glowing red, though some appear white when at a certain angle. All the landing birds have glowing eyes. Charon sighs. His bright stare goes back to Wayland, then it comes to me. "Do not let me catch you in this situation again, understand?"

"If you're so concerned about the mess we'll make, why don't you just collect us now?" I say.

"Do you see the bird?" Charon barely gestures to Val. "Broken creates broken, death creates death. As you can see, your kind are plenty and getting worse, yet you somehow still have your wits about you enough to not be entirely driven strictly by destruction. A wandering soul is more typically inconsolable, corrupt, and worthless. You are not automatically rescued of the same fate by my permission to remain. We had an agreement and it did not include permission to conduct yourself in the manner that destroyed another. Your job was to track down the dead me. That was the deal. Do you understand?"

"Yeah, I get it…" I use the nicotine to force relaxation back into my muscles, at least partially. I don't look at Wayland, I can't, not with the way Charon's watching at him. Another puff. An idea. Charon turns away. Val's transforms into a bird and takes flight while a couple of ravens sit off to the side. I look back at Charon. "Can the medium help us with the sensitivity thing?"

"Every medium is different depending on intentions and abilities enabled through their contract," Charon says.

"So… That's a maybe?"

Charon's facing away. He's watching Val now, who's disappearing into the darkness in the sky in an unnatural way, like black mist has devoured him. "That is a maybe," Charon says, then he's walking and the dark mist eats him too after a couple of steps. It's not really a mist because I can still see the bar in the distance without disturbance, but it was like Charon was walking into something washing him away the further he went until he was no longer there.

"Do you really think he can help?" Wayland says from behind me.

I'm scanning the outside of the bar again, looking for Ralph or KC in the crowd, talking to someone at the front of the building, but he's not there. Maybe he's inside walking them through things like I had to do back at the shop for Wayland's car. If he's inside with the badges, then there's no way Wayland and I can talk to him now. My foot's tapping and I'm taking puffs on my cigarette so fast it's like an obsession to breathe. "I don't know, but it's worth asking him about, yeah? If he can stop us from going crazy, make us go back to normal, and put things back to how they were, it's worth it to ask."

"I don't want to go back to how things *were*, Jo," his voice is slow, pushing through the usual hesitation he has, he sounds more certain of himself and the slowness is deliberate.

I stop walking. I should feel so much worse than I do hearing him say that. Maybe I've just lived in Baltimore too long. All those times of saying the status quo here is bleeding on the pavement, I don't know how much I actually believed it, but now I don't have much of an argument against it. The expectation of finding a body isn't horrifying anymore and neither is thinking that every time I see Wayland, he'll have blood on his hands because that's just how it is now and that's how it's always been, right? But I don't feel anything about it, I just know we need to stop because we can't keep doing this; we'll get caught, but more, I don't even know how to tell Jag about what happened today. I don't think I should. Not if I want to keep him.

But if you've gotta lie to someone like that, doesn't that just mean the end is coming?

"You don't want to keep killing people, right?" I turn to Wayland.

He shakes his head. "No, I don't."

"Okay, then that's what we're gonna fix and we'll figure out what's next after that." I'm going back to the bar, thinking maybe Ralph will be more obvious when we're in the parking lot, but not only are the badges and ambulance still there, but there's another badge pulling in. Out of it comes the last person I want to see at a crime scene. Tall, broad shoulders, graying blond hair, and the facial scruff like someone who hasn't been home in two days. Rocky.

I make a b-line for Wayland's borrowed car. I'm pulling at the door handle repeatedly with my head down until it clicks unlocked because this car's got a remote. I climb in, nearly throwing myself into the seat, and pull the door shut. My head's still down, though I pull the sun visor mirror and watch the bar entrance through the back window. Rocky greets some officer standing outside, Garnet comes to the door, and then both of them disappear inside.

Wayland gets into the driver's seat. "Where should we go?" he says.

"How about your place?" I stare out the windshield. The buildings across the street blur. "Have you been there yet?"

"When would I have gone?" He laughs, it does nothing to hide his discomfort.

"Theoretically, last night."

"I haven't been home."

"Then I guess that's where we should go."

Wayland starts the car. I check the mirror again. Ralph's not there. The crowd around the bar's thinned. Flashing emergency lights bleed into the car. Wayland adjusts the rearview mirror so carefully, it's impossible to imagine those hands doing anything violent like slamming a knife into some guy's skull or cutting a rando into pieces. The care he takes in adjusting his seat is just as careful, like he's afraid to break something by pushing even a little too hard. The hesitation turns Wayland back into the person I've always known and things are feeling a little less messed up than before. The radio comes on low, but it's so irritating that I feel like screaming, so I flick it off.

"I haven't been home in a while," Wayland says. He's looking down at his lap. His jeans—Jag's jeans, are stained from the fight. His own, someone else's, maybe some of mine.

My tongue flips my lip ring. "It's gonna be fine," I say.

"Okay," he says with a little more confidence, then we're pulling out of the parking lot and heading down the street, out of the center of Baltimore and toward his suburb.

The graffiti's more plentiful in this neighborhood, ranging from images of eyes to trees to clowns and nuns. I don't remember seeing rivers on the buildings before, but there's no way to explain the sweep of blue running through them now, where a fish like a ghost is jumping out. It's orange and white and almost see-through while its fins are wavy and more like angel wings. The words SHE WILL MAKE YOU LOSE YOURSELF look sunken in the water. CLOSE YOUR EYES AND COUNT TO FIVE is accompanied by a pair of eyes, bloodshot, with bullseyes where the pupils should be. We turn another corner and there's another pair of eyes, a black blob on the wall. A raven sits on the stoop next to it.

I take my phone out of my pocket as a distraction to keep me from looking out the windows. The screen flashes that I've got messages from Jag waiting. My thumb's hovering over the messages; guilt weighs hard on me. My teeth clench, mashing the filter of my cigarette until it's unusable, so I open my door and drop it outside.

I'm seriously thinking of turning my phone off again. Don't look, cause as long as you don't look at something, you can pretend you never saw it and if I never saw Jag messaging me, then he can't be mad when I don't answer, right?

The lie is so bad, I can't pretend to believe myself for even a second. It doesn't matter how long I put off looking at the messages. They've still been received, he's still assuming I've read them, or at the very least, that I've seen them, and most of the time, he's right and I'm a jackass if I don't answer him. Feigning ignorance doesn't work when someone knows you well enough; it's one of the reasons you should never let yourself get close to someone. By the time you start picking up on their habits and favorite things, they've picked up on yours too and that's when shit gets dangerous.

My screen goes black. My thumb falls against it. Relief and dread mix as the screen refuses to light up. I press the power button on the side and the screen does what it's supposed to do. I tap the messages on impulse. The clock in the corner reads it's after eight. The first messages came in three hours ago and they read:

JAG	Grabbing dinner. What do you want?
	nvm. Picked already.
	Guess it's a surprise.

Then, two hours ago he sent:

| JAG | Where the hell are you? |

My response is harder to write than it should be.

JOEY	With Cross
	Spending the night at his place.
JAG	Are you fucking serious?
JOEY	He's having issues rn, J.
JAG	We're having issues rn, Joey.

My fingers hang over the keyboard. I have to read the line a couple of times before it registers. It's not that I don't understand it, but it's like I read it, I know what it says, my head flushes it, and I need to read it again.
I can't deal with this.

My face is hot, my heart's racing so hard it's in my ears and my visions going black. I rub my eyes trying to make it stop. The thing that makes me the most nervous... Jag saying *we*. Up until a couple days ago, this stuff with Jag's always been easy.

I bite the inside of my mouth. Toe-tapping, I come up with a dozen things to say back, but they're all wrong.

JOEY	Different kind of issues.
	You wouldn't understand.
JAG	Try me.
JOEY	I can't.
	or you'll be like
JAG	Explain.
JOEY	Just
	It's like he's burning out, J.
	I can't let it happen.
JAG	I know what burning out is.
	You can't let him pull you down
	with him.
	No offense,
	but you're not very stable either rn.
	There's nothing you can do.
JOEY	You gonna help him?
JAG	He kill someone again?
JOEY	…
JAG	…
	Did he fucking murder someone,
	Joey?
JOEY	I told you that you wouldn't
	understand.
	I'll talk to you about shit tomorrow.
	I have to be with him tonight.
JAG	You guys dating now?
JOEY	No.
JAG	Couldn't tell.
JOEY	We're not fucking.
JAG	Tonight the night?
JOEY	He's my best friend, J.
JAG	So fuck him.
JOEY	I don't want to fuck him.
	I want
	You're
	FUCKING Christ

	J
	I'll talk to you tomorrow.
JAG	You chose the guy who wants to kill me
	over me.
	I get it.
	Just say you're out.
JOEY	I'm not fucking out.
	Holy shit.
	J
	PLZ
	He's not trying to kill you
	I can't do this right now.
	Good night.
	And I'm not fucking him.

I turn my phone off and shove it into my pocket. I don't need to save battery, I just need to mute the temptation to check it every five seconds by tapping on the screen or feeling the buzz against my leg because something else has come in and I need to see how much I messed everything with Jag up before attempting to save it for another couple of days.

Heat's in my face. Tears build in my eyes. I rub them like I'm tired and let my head drop back. I wish I'd brought a bottle from the bar. I need something to drink, getting blasted really would've helped, at least it would've let me relax for a couple hours and maybe I'd come up with something better to say the next time Jag talked to me.

If he'll talk to me.

We were never supposed to be more than a couple of coworkers working out stress together sometimes. I don't know when sometimes turned into often; I don't know when I started going to him for more than that. I don't know when I started *needing* him.

I knock my head against the seat again. Wayland's

saying something. I don't catch any of it, but I say, "Yeah, yeah, yeah." Not a good answer, because he follows up by saying, "Jo? What's up?" and I say, "Nothing," but after a second, I can't keep it to myself either and I say, "I pissed Jag off and I don't know how to fix this kind of shit." I rub my eyes again. This time, I catch them in the sun visor mirror. I almost don't recognize myself between the darkness of night and how empty they look.

How could Jag even look at me when I look like this? Like I'm dead? I look down at my hands, smudged in black, blood, and dirt. I slide them under my thighs so I don't have to see them. I watch out the window. At least we're out of the city, mso most of the graffiti's gone now. "It's probably better like this anyway…"

Wayland looks sidelong at me. His hand reaches, but stops halfway and returns to the steering wheel. "He'll either come back and talk or he won't, Jo, and if he doesn't… then whatever. That's him and you'll still have me."

"Yeah… Thanks, Way." I glance at him. He smiles, briefly. I close my eyes. The car is quiet for the rest of the ride and I don't really mind it. I try to focus on what I'll say to Ralph tomorrow so I don't have to think of anything else and I can push everything I'm feeling back down like the fear that comes along with the thought, what if Jag really never talks to me again?

I don't think I can live with that, but I don't know how to fix it.

FIVE.

We park the car a block away from Wayland's house so we won't have to explain where it came from. The neighborhood's so unlike mine with grass still clean cut from the last mow of the summer. No garbage on the ground. Living rooms, kitchens, and bedrooms all light the windows of warm homes, families who don't worry about being abandoned every time someone goes through the door and don't treat you like a bad person for wanting to go out.

The problem with living in a neighborhood like Wayland's is that everybody knows everybody, like in the chat-on-the-porch-every-day kind of way; give-Christmas-cards-every-year kind of way; know-when-the-grass-is-half-an-inch-too-long-so-Harold-must-be-in-the-hospital-for-cancer-again kind of way. Everyone knows what to expect in front of everyone else's house and the car wouldn't be there long without someone asking questions and eventually calling it in.

The closer we get to Wayland's place, the more he slows. He's dragging his feet, he's stepping off the sidewalk, swerving like he's gonna turn around, and I'm grabbing his arm when he's trying to cross the road.

Wayland eyes move down from my face to my shoulder. He raises his hand, his arm shows signs of discoloration, bruises forming. The creases in his hand are filled with dried mud, a mixture of gore and the elements from Leakin. If you look close enough, his dark shirt shows stains from the bar. His hair's matted and the color under his eyes seems too prominent, but that's just sleeplessness, I'm sure of it.

"I don't think I'm ready for this," he says.

"We'll get inside so fast, no one will notice," I say.

Wayland exhales; it's trying to be a laugh, but it sounds hopeless. "I think it's impossible not to notice, Jo… How much do I smell?"

"No worse than any teenage boy ever. Don't think about it."

He laughs again, but this time, a little more genuine.

"I just… I know what it's like to worry about what will happen when you go through the front door, what your parents have been thinking since you've been gone." My eyes blur. I hear my dad's suicide echo in my ears like it's coming through the door.

I exhale hard and shaky. "Maybe my being gone was never a couple of days, but you know, I wondered what my dad thought while I was sitting in school or smoking or whatever. I couldn't focus on anything but that and what he'd say when I got back. I guess maybe I was obsessed with what my dad was thinking when I was gone because it was when I left that he *reacted*. Maybe I didn't remember upfront, but it was always in my head when I wasn't home. How much was he saying he hated himself? How much was he saying he hated me? How much of it was actually from worry that I wouldn't come back and he'd be alone and how much of it was just pure hatred because every time I was gone, he thought it was because I hated him and I was like my mom?" Tears burn in the back of my eyes.

This isn't what I was supposed to be saying. My fingers curl hard into Wayland's arm. His free hand drops down to mine and he grasps it. I push out a sigh like a chuckle. It doesn't sound right coming through clenched teeth. I look down the sidewalk toward his house.

Wayland's legs are stiff. A couple more steps and he's still dragging. I turn around so I'm stepping back, still holding his hand. He's still resisting as I tug him forward, but less than before. He keeps looking behind me and every so often, his grip pulses, grabbing me tighter, then letting go, looking at me like he's embarrassed, then back at his house.

"What I meant to say is I get the fear, but I don't think you have anything to worry about, Way," I say. "Your parents love you and they'll be glad to see you home... Assuming the badges's let them move back in."

He nods.

My steps stutter, but I don't fall. I let go of Wayland's hand and he lets go of me back. I sink to his side as we reach his house. He pauses again at the start of the walkway while I'm making my way to the door. I wait for Wayland to catch up, then ring the bell. He's stepping back, saying something to himself mostly, saying maybe he should walk around the block one more time and is it dark enough while the porch lights hang overhead and his hands are shoved into his hoodie pocket now. I grab him by the arm. He's moving more with a push than I'm expecting and I drag off the steps with him. The front door opens. Wayland's mom is standing on the other side. What was a polite smile fades into something of fear, disbelief, sorrow, joy. My skin prickles.

"Hey, Mrs. Cross. You're here," I say. I'm kinda surprised she even opened the door. "I, uh, I brought you something."

Wayland clears his throat. His face is red. He's pulling

against my grip, though it's more like he's leaning now and he's staring at his mom. "Hey, Mom," he almost whispers. He's coming back from the pull, his eyes still on his mom while she doesn't even look like she sees me anymore. Maybe she doesn't know who I am like the last time Rocky saw me. The look he gave, the way he spoke—It was like I was someone new to him. You wouldn't think anyone could forget the face of a suspect.

Mrs. Cross runs out of the house and wraps her arms around Wayland while I let him go. A sob catches whatever she might've been trying to say. Wayland's stiff, hesitating to take his hands out of his pockets. His mom mutters something to him that sounds like, "I was so afraid," and "We haven't heard anything," and "I love you." Wayland's hands come out of his hoodie and carefully go around his mom. I'm reaching for my cigarettes, turning away, because I've always been out of place in Wayland's house and near his family, but it's never felt more obvious than right now.

My foot bounces. I close my eyes and knock the lid off the box and back just to give my hands something to do. The back of my hand brushes against my closed eyes. I mutter, "Fuck," before I realize and then I'm hoping neither of them heard me.

"Where have you been?" Wayland's mom says.

I turn around and Wayland's holding his mom just as tightly as she's been holding him. "I've been scared. I'm sorry."

Wayland's mom ends the hug. She's stepping back. Wayland's hands are back in his pocket before she's far. He's looking down her shirt where his hands had been, searching for fingerprints or grime he'd left behind. "What happened?" she says. She reaches for his face. His eyes draw up to hers. She wipes away some gunk staining his cheek with her thumb.

"I have... I was..." He looks sidelong at me.

Straightening, he meets his mom's gaze again, this time, his voice more sure. "I got lost on the way home from that retreat, you know, for the thing I've been doing."

"I didn't know you had something like that coming up," Wayland's mom says.

"Yeah, I don't really—Haven't really talked about it." Wayland steals a glance at me, then he's pulling back from his mom, not running off the steps, but making moves to walk around her and slip in the door past her. He blindly reaches for me, catches my arm, and pulls me through the front door with him as he doesn't stop. "I'm tired. Jo's spending the night. Everything's fine," he says.

"People have been looking for you, Wayland," his mom says.

"I know," Wayland says.

"Your father wants to know what's going on—"

"I know—But I can't talk. Not right now, Mom. Sorry." Wayland says. Faster, we're going up the stairs and to his room, he's using more force now.

I only catch a glimpse of his dad coming out of the kitchen with a towel in his hands. Wayland's mom turns to him, confused and concerned. I say, "Hey, Mr. Cross," before I can't see him anymore. They're talking, but we're going down the hall. It's surreal to be here again when it was only a couple of days ago that I'd been here with Jag, looking for hints of where Wayland was while avoiding badges maybe sitting outside the window. The discolored carpet's gone and now I'm wondering if that'd all been in my head before. Something really weird had been going on that day. The sounds, the smell, the air in the house. It was like someone had been watching us, but it wasn't the badges.

We're in Wayland's room before he lets go of my arm. I'm standing in the center; he's pushing the door shut and locking it. Again, I'm getting déjà vu from when Jag and I had been here. The laptop's not sitting on the desk, probably nabbed by the badges after I sent the email.

I turn back to the shelf Jag had gone through. The books he'd touched stick out a little more than the others. I walk over to the shelf and push them each back in while trailing my fingers along the books' spines.

Wayland says something. All I hear is his voice. I turn back to him going, "Hm?" and he says, "Did you want to shower?" He's wiping his hands on his hoodie.

"No, it's fine. You can go first."

"You sure?"

"Yeah. You look pretty cruddy. It doesn't suit you."

His movements are kind of jerky, turning away like he's not fully committed to the steps he's taking. He grabs clothing from his drawers, pauses, leaves them open, steps back, pauses again, looks at his hoodie, his hands, and the dresser again where he'd touched it.

"Nothing's there, Way. You're good."

"I'll help set up for bed when I get back, okay?"

"Okay."

Wayland's too focused. Door opens and shuts when he leaves. Seconds later, the shower's running.

My heart's throbbing. I cover my eyes, push my hair back, laugh.

It's all so goddamn ridiculous.

I go to Wayland's stereo and turn it on. The last CD in the player is singing about fixing a broken heart. I turn around and stare at Wayland's bed. It looks so comfortable, a contrast to my stiff hair and the clinging tightness of my shirt drenched in beer and dried blood. I really do smell. Maybe I should've showered first.

My lips move along with the words coming out of the radio and I'm back in time, sitting on Wayland's bed with him, switching between flashcards to quiz him for the SATs and telling him he doesn't need all the extra work.

I grab the sleeping bag out from under Wayland's bed and roll it out. I'm taking my shirt off. It's over one arm when I stop and roll it back down because maybe this isn't the time for that. Not after what happened earlier, at least. I lay down on top of the bag. My fingers slide down my thigh, biding their time until I grab my cell phone from my pocket. My thumb caresses the power button and I'm thinking of all the things I'd say to Jag the second I turned it on and it showed me his number. Whatever he's said at this point doesn't matter. He's pissed; maybe he won't even give me a chance to mess up trying to fix it. Would it be enough if I said "Please don't be mad, I don't want you to leave me"?

The screen's not lighting up. Either I didn't hold the button long enough or the battery's dead. I lay my phone on my chest before I'm tempted to press the button again. I look at the nightstand where Wayland keeps a charger for me when I spend the night. I should get up. I'm gonna get up in a second when I open my eyes again. The sound of the shower's gone. The radio's fading out. I don't know when I got in the sleeping bag or when my jeans got to the floor next to me, but I can't keep my eyes open anymore.

SIX.

I'm feeling antsy. It's not much different from the nights I ran away from home. I worried about dad, but sometimes I needed air, you know? Sometimes, even when you know something bad's gonna happen, you still have to go out to get the air so you don't suffocate. You've gotta have enough air to hold on through the worst of it.

I don't know when it started getting so bad I wished my dad would just die and then I hated myself for thinking it. Sometime after his death, but he wasn't always the worst. I've gotten so familiar with the feeling of his hand around my neck that it's not that weird to feel suffocated anymore and I know just how bad I'll look the next morning based on how long he held me down. He never *kept* me down though and that's the part I never understood.

I reach for my phone; it's not on my chest. It's not on the floor beside me. I'm sweating and the blanket's sticking to me. I kick it off and roll over. I don't know what time it is, but the lights are all off and the music's not playing anymore. When I open my eyes, Wayland's back is facing me from the bed. There's a crispy smell in the air.

The floor's hotter than it should be.

Wayland rolls onto his back with a soft groan, then his voice is a half-sleeping mumble when he says, "Jo…?"

"Yeah?"

"Are you… smoking?"

"No?"

"Then why do I smell smoke?"

"I dunno."

"Do you smell it too?" His eyes are open now, staring at me through the darkness.

"Yeah."

Something's out in the hall, shaking the house. Wayland's mom's voice carries. At least I think it's her, but she sounds like she's underwater. I'm off the floor, Wayland's out of bed. The thumping's so hard, a framed picture bounces off Wayland's shelf. The glass case cracks, hitting the floor. The picture's of Wayland's premed graduation from a year ago, maybe two? I don't know anymore.

In the picture, my arm's around Wayland's shoulder and his arm is around me, his parents stand behind him, and now a fissure of broken glass cuts us apart.

The bedroom doorknob rattles, twists hard, and the door flies open. Soot covers the left side of the man's face and his clothes are burned on the same side his skin is seared and raw. He's still got a knife in his hand. The hallway's lit too much behind him. A fire shouldn't be that big, that fast, but it illuminates whatever's left of his face. It's the shaved head, the grimace, the bloody, jean jacket and red patches on his arm. All of it identifies him as the guy Wayland stabbed at the bar.

"You're supposed to be dead," I say.

The guy's attention drops from Wayland to me and he's swinging his knife at the same time he's coming through the door. He throws an arm back, pushing the door closed while he lunges.

I step back in anticipation, reaching behind me for anything I can use as a weapon. A bat, a board, a lamp—something, but Wayland's room is so tidy, everything's big furniture or books and the lamp's on the other side of the room. The knife misses. The guy lunges again, closing the space between us as he aims the knife for my chest. I grab a book off the shelf and chuck it at him, then another and another, reaching for everything I can. He blocks the books with his arm, still coming toward me. The next book hits his head while he's lunging.

The guy grabs my arm. In a second, I'm on the ground, my forearm hurts, my knees crack. I roll onto my back. The guy's coming down on top of me. His knife grazes my arm, he hisses, a sneer on his face. He draws the knife back. I slam my feet into his stomach. The knife falls from his hand. In its place, he's catching my hand and pinning me to the floor. Another kick. He moves further up my hips so my feet can't reach him. "Fuck off!"

My arm pulls against his grip. I swing with my free arm. He catches it and pins it down too. Each tug, I'm not strong enough to make a difference.

The floor's hot against my back and I'm sweating and swearing and cutting Wayland's name into all of that while pulling against the guy's hold until my arms hurt and the more I move, the more sound I make.

"That all you got?" I say, twisting with a yank. Again, I kick at him. He lets go of my hand to pick up the knife. I shove my palm into his face, going to bash his nose while I yell. He growls or laughs or says something, I can't tell when half his face is burned and his lips aren't moving— Or maybe he's just wincing in pain. My mind's racing, but it feels like too much time's passed since the knife's gone up, since the guy said anything, like I'm in slow motion, but racing at the same time. He chokes on something. The knife falls out of his hand again. Thick blood builds in his mouth, dribbles down his face, and falls onto me.

Standing behind him is a black figure, lit only by the minimal light making it through the bedroom curtains. Part of the silhouette glows. A hand draws a knife out of the man's body and slams it into the back of the guy's skull next. There's only a second of resistance maybe, the skull fighting the blade, but Wayland's force overpowers it and the knife slides through the guy's bone like it's going into a sheath. The guy's blood's draining onto me, making my shirt stick to my skin. Wayland shoves the guy over, hard, almost throwing him, and is on top, following him to the ground with the knife in hand to stab him again. This time, he leaves the knife in the guy's head while reaching for the other knife on the floor. With the same moves, he grabs it and stabs it into the guy's neck. Blood puddles on the floor, picking up in the wool of my sleeping bag and on my pillow.

I'm on my feet; Wayland's pulling the knife out and thrusting it in again and again and each time it goes in, it's easier. I put my hand on his shoulder and say his name. I have to say it a third time before it's like it reaches him and he stops stabbing the guy. He's panting through his teeth. He turns, swinging hard, looking at me over his shoulder with the knife held tightly in his hand.

"What's up, Jo?" he says. It's like the grunting rage from a moment ago is not even registered or he doesn't remember it or something. I look at the dude underneath Wayland. I should feel something, but all I can think is *this is fine, bastard's already dead anyway*.

"You good?" I say.

Wayland looks down at the corpse. "Yeah. I'm good."

I go to the bedroom door and turn the room light on. The air in the room's getting thicker with smoke that's starting to burn my eyes. My own breath's shallow and I'm feeling lightheaded from it. "I think we need to go, Way." I grab my pants from the corner of the room and pull them on.

"Yeah. Okay. One sec." Wayland draws his finger through the dead guy's blood. Across the floor, he writes 21-1-12, then he's standing, reaching for my hand, and going for the exit. He opens the door and smoke fills the room. I pull away from him to grab my phone off the nightstand, it's laying beside his. He must've picked it off me when he came to bed. I stick Wayland's phone in my pocket too. Wayland grabs a hoodie from his clothing basket and pulls it on, covering the new bloodstains in his shirt and giving him a pocket to bury his hands in.

Sirens and yelling are coming from outside, but I don't know how far out they are. The stairs at the end of the hall are lit with the warm colors of fire. Smoke fills the hallway and flames lick the walls in a pattern where the guy splashed gasoline on everything while he ran. Chains are rattling now too with a whistle, a caw, Charon and Val arriving for the soul. The walls are fire and the floor's burning too, all except for the places where footprints from the other side of the River Styx have been. Wayland grabs my hand. My skin chills. I laugh and say, "Holy shit," to suppress it. Wayland laughs too and says, "I know." Then we run down the hall, down the stairs, past the fire, and through the front door.

The night sky's lit by the colors of emergency blue and red, feeling more at home than the typical white moon. But maybe that's the point. The moon's not even out, hidden behind a cloud along with all the stars, leaving Baltimore to deal with itself like it always has. Wayland and I keep running until we're past the emergency vehicles in the street and beyond the gathering crowd and voices saying something sternly to us like we should stop and hey or whatever, it doesn't matter. It's a tone I can't listen to right now.

We reach the dark side of the street. It looks dark, anyway, until we turn around. Wayland's house is burning away too eagerly; the first floor's engulfed with flames coming out the busted windows. How did it move so goddamn fast?

A car I don't recognize sits in the grass between the front door and the garage, its hood is banged in and there's a dent in the garage door.

How did we not hear that?

Wayland's house lights the neighborhood, trying to transform it back into something familiar to my city: rubble or a relic made of anger,. Fire reaches for the fence, tossing out greetings to the neighboring houses like saying *join me*.

The colors and words bounce around my head until none of them make any sense anymore and it's all just noise with the red and white and water and hissing and a caw from somewhere until my heart slows down again and the neighborhood doesn't look foreign anymore. A black figure appears in the window on the upper floor. It pulls away too fast to give it form, but it shouldn't have been that blurry. A voice is saying something. I come back from looking at Wayland's room window to a badge standing in front of us saying, "Do you live here? We'd like to ask what happened," but just as soon as I hear the words, they don't make sense again, like I'm hearing them and they're going right back out of my head.

A hand touches my arm. I turn around, step back, swinging a punch to protect myself. The badge's too close, got his hands in the air now, acting like it's to show he's not a threat and he's saying, "Is that your blood?" and "Do you need medical assistance?"

"No," I say. "But I wouldn't mind if you left me alone, you know?" My fists sting. I shake them off to get the buzzing out of my fingertips. It doesn't help. It's only the pacing away, putting space between the badge and me that gets my head to shut up. "Sorry," I say too loudly, just to make sure he hears it. "Can I just get, like, five seconds before you ask all your stupid questions?" I'm pacing down the street, moving fast enough that apparently, the badge isn't following me.

"Stay close, don't wander," the badge says.

"I know what *stay close* means," I say, turning around.

Wayland's walking off with the badge, heading to where his parents are standing with more, looking back at me. He gives a little nod that tells me, "I'll try talking to them." He stops mid-step. "Do you think they'll recognize me?"

I shake my head. "They haven't yet." I comb my fingers through my hair. "I don't know what it is, but it seems like they really don't have any idea who we are. Even if you say your name."

"Okay." Wayland nods. With a deep breath, he continues toward the house.

I turn away and keep walking. My tongue flicks over my ring. I'm eyeing porches and trees and everything, looking for any sign of the birds that've been following me for days, but the fire doesn't betray any black feathers hiding in the leaves left behind by fall.

When I get down a couple of houses, I turn back and my pacing becomes laps to put the chill on whatever's going through me and telling me to bring Hell to the badges. It's just being close to them and I know I never liked them, we've had issues in the past, you could maybe even call it *trouble*, but it's ridiculous how much they're filling my everything with an impulse to destroy. *The dead are sensitive* is hardly a strong enough sentiment to cover this.

The fire's going down, but I still feel it against my skin. My shirt's stuck to me, even in the cold. I try to run. Two, three steps in, I stop, body heavy, vision going blurry.

The burn in my eyes is making Wayland's ember of a house turn into an oil painting against the night sky. My hands are shaking as I pat down my pockets for my cigarettes, thinking maybe some nicotine will bring me down. My cigarette's lit and in my mouth. Maybe I should just run. My hand glides across my phone. Before I think too much, I'm taking it out and pulling up Jag's number. Tears go down my cheeks. I pull up my hood, wipe my eyes, and type.

JOEY	I'm sorry, J.
	I'm so
	Fucking stupid.
	I don't know what I'm doing.
	Someone lit up Cross's house.
JAG	u ok?
JOEY	Yeah.
	Probably.
	Everyone got out.
JAG	Good.
	You call someone?
JOEY	You think badges would show up if I did?
JAG	The world isn't against you all the time.

The messages go cold. My foot bounces. I take the cigarette out of my mouth because I'm tempted to chew on the filter and ruin it, but then I pinch it between my teeth so I can use both hands.

| JOEY | Badges are here tho. |
| JAG | Good. |

The messages go cold again. I'm trying to figure out if he'd been staying up or sleeping and I want to pretend he'd been smoking and watching TV with the leftovers from the dinner I wasn't there to eat, thinking all night about changing the locks because he's not sure about telling me to my face that he doesn't want to see me again. I'm too unpredictable, reckless, crazy, selfish. I already got his answer earlier. Or he'd say I gave him mine. I'm holding the phone too hard. My vision blurs again. I wipe them with my hand so I can see the screen again. My mind's racing so fast, I can't think of basic words.

JOEY	You
JAG	?
JOEY	I'm sorry.
	I need you, J.
JAG	I'll be there.

I sit on the curb at the house across from Wayland's. My cigarette's lit. The fire's pretty much out while the emergency team stands out front and firefighters walk through the building carefully. The house door hangs open, flaunting the charred insides. My vision goes blurry and red and I suck back the tears with another drag from my cigarette. All I can think about are the bright halls and family pictures and rooms I'd spend so much time in that aren't there anymore. I have a whole sleeping kit under his bed, it used to happen so often when we were in school. When I dropped out, it became less and when IJag and I started messing around, it changed again.

I suck on my cigarette like I'm using it for air, hoping that enough of it might bring me down so I don't snap at the next person I talk to. I don't know if it's the nicotine or the rocking or the sitting away from everything else that's working, but my head's coming back under my control. I just try not to catch the badges for too long when I'm looking for Wayland. It's nearly impossible since he's standing next to them, talking to them like I never could.

"Hey."

Jag's voice is low, soft, too soft to be talking to me. I

look up, wiping at my eyes in the same movement I'm grabbing my cigarette from my mouth to cover what I'm doing. Jag's coming toward me. He leans down, grabs my arm, and pulls me up by it. I drop my cigarette. His arms go around me and he brings me to him. My hold on him's tight. I don't try to breathe, but when I finally do, his smell is comforting and I bury my face in his chest and shoulder just to get more of him. His lips are so close to my ear, I feel his breath. We sway slightly with his lead. Everything's so quiet, getting so far away. I'm not sure where I am anymore, but that's fine. I let my eyes close knowing he will keep me safe.

A bird caws.

My eyes open. I jerk back to look for it. Jag's hold loosens, but he doesn't let me go, hands staying firm on my arms. "You okay?" he says.

"Yeah." I take a breath, trying not to look. Don't make him panic too.

"Need a hospital?"

"I don't know what I need."

"Probably medical assistance. Did the EMTs check you out?"

"No."

"Why the hell not?"

"Because I can't be over there right now, Jag. There's too much… too many badges." I pull away. I look down to where my cigarette's fallen and pick it back up. The end's still bright, seeping slowly with smoke. On a spotless street? I don't care it fell and suck on it anyway.

"I'm getting to the end of how much of this I can put up with, Joey. I need you to stop jerking me around if you're fucking serious about what you said."

"I'm not trying to jerk you around. I just—I don't know what you want me to say—"

"Tell me what happened," Jag says. A light flickers. Looking over my shoulder, Jag's lit a cigarette. His voice is tired, hair lopsided. Maybe he fell asleep on the couch, watching something.

"I don't know—"

"Bullshit."

Another caw comes.

The hair on my arms stands. My jaw clenches. I can't move. A subtle rotting smell's been building and it shouldn't be in this neighborhood. I prefer anger over the nervousness I've got now. It's almost like experiencing it for the first time. I swallow hard, but my throat's so dry, it hurts. The smoky air burns my eyes. I wipe them with the back of my hand. From the crowd of cars and the neighbors and the badges, Wayland's looking back at me. His parents stand around him, talking to the badges, but he's like a statue. Then he's moving between the crowd and sliding past the cars, coming toward me. "Be right back, J," I say and I'm already going toward Wayland, hoping Jag doesn't try to follow me.

"Hey, what's up?" I say to him. The closer Wayland gets, the more I notice he's not watching me, but Jag. I grab Wayland by the arm and turn him so his back's to Jag, guiding him to walk with me down the street. "Hey," I say again, tightening my hold on his arm. He resists me a little, but after the first couple of steps, he gives up. "What'd they say?"

"What?" Wayland says.

"The badges. They tell you anything? About the fire, the mess, the blood upstairs? They have anything to say?"

Wayland shrugs. "They mostly asked questions." He slides his hands into his hoodie pocket.

"Oh—Here." I break contact to reach into my pocket. I take his hand, placing his phone in it. "Grabbed this for you."

Wayland's eyes drop to the phone. He slides it away into his pocket with a quiet, "Thanks." His hand falls to his side. His fingers brush mine as we keep walking, then he reaches a little further until he takes my hand. His fingers are colder than mine. His skin's so pale, bright blue veins show through thin skin. I look up to meet his face. His hoodie's over his head. Black bags create hollows under his eyes. "In an emergency, you're only supposed to grab what's on your way out or really important."

"This is important. It's the only way I can keep up with you when I'm not here."

Wayland's feet drag. "Where are you going?"

"I have to go back… with Jag."

"What about spending the night?"

I laugh, but it's tight, strangled with tension. "You guys aren't staying here either."

"You can come with us."

"I don't think that's a good idea, Way. For a couple of reasons."

"Like he's gonna get mad?" Wayland leans away from me.

My nose is on fire, the burning smoke mixes with the smell of decay.

"Let him. If that's what he wants to do, let him walk. You won't lose anything."

"I don't… I don't want to do that, Way."

"Even if he did, you wouldn't be alone. You'd still have me."

"And you've got me too, alright? But I gotta take care of Jag too. I don't want to lose him, you know?"

A caw comes from above. A fat raven sits on top the nearby ambulance. Blue lights bounce off its feathers. Its eyes are pointed, attention focused on something in the distance. I look over my shoulder. It's staring at Jag. I put a hand around Wayland's waist and keep walking the other way, saying to myself, "Don't look, don't look, don't look." We're only a couple steps in when Wayland's slowing down again, now feeling like he's fighting against me to move. His hands slide out from his hoodie pocket.

He picks his fingers. He wipes his hands on his pajama pants. They leave streaks of flaky red against the dark blue fabric.

"I don't know what to do, Jo." Wayland's voice is an exhale, low, intimate. That's not what he wanted to say, but the breath before the words is the pause that stopped whatever he's thinking. "I don't think I can do this without you." The words are too tense to feel like anything that should be said out loud.

"Way." The night air feels silencing over my voice. The chatter of nearby neighbors, whispering, a badge radio coming in and out, the heavy boots of the firefighters packing things up or running checks or doing whatever it is they're supposed to be doing, and a stray alarm alternates between echoing roar and instant silence. A clattering beak enters with little black bird feet moving down the sidewalk. The other raven's still on the ambulance. That makes this number two. Up ahead, another raven's sitting on someone's doorstep. A caw comes from behind me. I don't want to look; I don't want to count another one; I don't want to see seven of them and I don't want to see them all watching Jag. "I'm not abandoning you, so don't think that's what this is."

Wayland's jaw goes tight, his muscles go tighter. His body's stiff, but he's walking faster, pushing ahead of me, dragging me with him. His arm twitches in a way that doesn't look natural, but like he's trying to keep control of a body that might go rogue against him. "How long?" he says.

"What?" I try to laugh, but my chest's too tight.

"How long are you gonna be gone?"

"I don't know what you mean—"

"You're gonna go with Jag. When will I see you again?" Wayland takes his hood off. The red lights from the nearby emergency vehicles assist the street lamps to show the start of a bruise under his eye.

"Tomorrow. Daylight. I'll be back."

Wayland lets me go and keeps going until he's at the sidewalk. He sits on the edge, then, he's rocking slightly, squeezing his eyes shut, taking slow, deep breaths that try and shake out of his control. It's not distress. Whatever feeling I'm getting from him, it's not fear, it's not... something I've ever associated with Wayland. The push is strong and angry and takes me back to the room where he was plunging the knife into the ghost's head and the way he turned back to me without anything showing in his face like he knew what he was doing. "Okay." He breathes out.

I come toward him. He stands up. His hands are on my arm, squeezing slowly. He's not holding me still, but holding himself. His fingers loosen, hands moving up my arms, up my shoulders, up my neck. His eyes meet mine. Even now, he's without his glasses. I don't even know if he can see, but he's been driving, so he must be alright, yeah?

His fingers tickle the back of my neck, under my neckline. He steps forward. Unprepared, I step back.

"Can someone give me the short of it?" Rocky says. There's no reason he should be so loud, but his voice is too familiar, it cuts through everything in a supernatural way. He's yelling and quiet at the same time. My jaw's tight. I'm hoping the voice is just in my head, but it's not. The jacket, the badge, the dark hair, stubble, height and broad stance like he's not afraid of anything coming at him. Too many years, too much stress, probably three heart attacks already at the ripe old age of thirty-nine. Rocky's standing with the badges in front of Wayland's house. "You the family?" he says to Wayland's parents. Then, "Glad to see you're alright. Was there anyone left inside?"

"Jo?" Wayland says.

"Sorry, Way—" I pull away from him.

Wayland's hands fall, dropping to his sides, finding

their way to his hoodie pocket. A couple steps around him, I'm looking at the house, the yard, the lights are too bright even when the street's black and I'm feeling exposed every time the lights from the badge car or ambulance hit my face. They're spotlights of red and blue bouncing off my skin, telling Rocky to look at me and ask questions and cuff me to take me away. I probably know something, right? I look like I know too much, really.

I step back. "You've got your phone now, yeah?" I'm patting down my pockets to make sure I still have it. I take my phone out. My cigarettes. Everything from the last couple of hours is a blur and I'm not sure what's been in my head and what's been real. Even the fire doesn't seem real even though I can still feel the heat against my skin.

"Yeah." Wayland pulls his phone out of his pocket. His fingers are dark, all I can think is blood, blood, blood, and what'll Rocky do if he sees Wayland's hands looking like that. He's already got a thing out for Wayland. It doesn't matter—It doesn't matter, right? He can't see the dead? I know this, but I still don't want to test it, risk it, wait around to be recognized.

"Good." I keep going, glancing over my shoulder. My foot catches on the concrete. I catch myself with a couple of stumbling steps.

"Jo—"

"If I stick around here, I'm gonna—Do to the badges what you did to that poor asshole we left at Leakin." I laugh.

Wayland doesn't. "Okay," he says.

Rocky turns away from the house. His eyes meet mine—Or at least I'm sure he's looking at me. "Sorry, Way—I gotta go." I spin on my toes. It's not really a run, but it's a skip and my heart's dragging behind me. I close my eyes, trying not to imagine Wayland's face, but then opening them, I'm looking at Jag standing just on the other side of the crowd with a hand in his pocket, cigarette in his mouth, and irritation stressing out his face. He's trying not to show it. He turns away and takes another drag.

As I get nearer, I slow down, but only so much so I can walk past him swaying my hips more than I usually do, look back at him to see if he's following, and then keep going. One of the police cars in the background squeals its short, choppy scream. A bird caws. I turn around, still stepping back, now looking for Wayland. I don't see him and his family's not with the badges anymore. They're not anywhere I can see. "Shit," I mutter.

Rocky turns again, this time it's like he heard me. He's looking right at me. I turn back around and walk faster.

"Why are you running?" Jag says. He's behind me, but not as close as I thought he'd be.

"I'm not running."

"Hella sus, Joey."

"Hella lame, J." I slow down; he does the same, so he doesn't catch up.

"What were you and Cross talking about?"

"What's it matter?"

"He was really close."

"We're always close."

Jag's footsteps stop. "Closer than that." His voice is hard. My heart's throbbing in my ears so hard I'm deaf and dizzy and feel like I just can't. "He looked like he was gonna kiss you."

"Don't tell me you're jealous, J."

"Jealous? No. Questioning why the hell I came out here to watch Cross put moves on you? Yeah. You told me nothing was going on."

"It's not like that—I'm here with you, aren't I?"

"And making me second guess every decision I've ever made."

"You're welcome."

"Not a compliment."

"I'm gonna pretend it is, though."

Jag sighs.

I turn back around. "Sorry."

My walking slows; Jag's moving fast until he catches up. The badge lights are in the distance now, four blocks down. I scan the trees. Not much in the way of cars. A white sedan in a driveway, nothing in the road that shouldn't be there. This neighborhood's always been good about that. No trash, the only time cars are parked in the driveway is when someone's having a party, then lights are flashing and laughter fills the air with the smell of barbecue so good, I don't know how every party's not crashed. It's the weirdest thing to walk through some place you've grown up in, look at the buildings in the suburbs, and think just how foreign it all is.

I slow so much, I'm almost not even stepping back anymore. Jag catches up enough that a step forward and I can hook my fingers on his hips. My hands clip to his sides. "Where's your car parked?"

"Around the corner." His hand goes for my shoulders.

"Thanks." I act like I'm going to smack his ass, but I grab the cigarettes from his pocket instead. I run for his car at the end of the block. It's hard to miss, even in the dark, bright red and all.

Jag mutters something, probably, "Fuck," and then his footsteps are echoing after me. He's letting me get away. He runs faster, he's got longer legs; we've done this before, and he's caught me every time. He doesn't catch me now until we're back at his car and then he's still running until he runs into me. I'm pressed into the side of his Mustang. Jag's hips pin mine; his hands go down my arms and press them into the car too. He grabs the cigarette box from me and slides it back into his ass pocket. Slick, his hands are going back down my arms, stroking my skin until he's at my wrists, then my hands. He laces our fingers together, my hands are over my head, reaching back. He leans in, closing what little space there might've been between us until his feet are on the outsides of mine. My back arches so I can look up at him.

"What's up, J?" I say.

"You kill somebody?" he mutters.

I try to twist. Jag won't let me. My back's against the car and my shirt's sticking to my back. I pretend it's all sweat. I arch my back more to thrust my hips a little more into his. "You know... we should probably get out of here. Your car's not exactly inconspicuous and I bet our favorite guy would get a kick out of finding us here..."

Jag's glance flits toward Wayland's house. The look isn't long. He steps back, letting my hands go, already walking around the car when he says, "I told you before: if anyone asks, your body will be bouncing off that bus so damn fast."

"That's what I like about you, J. I can always trust you."

He opens the driver's side door. I open the passenger; unlocked as usual. I'm inside the car. I can't think too much or it'll feel like I'm abandoning Wayland. But if I stayed with him, then I would've been abandoning Jag and I don't know what I'm supposed to do, but I feel like if I told Jag no this time, it'd be over for real and I don't think that I can deal with that. The texts were bad enough; I didn't think he'd come and I still don't know what to say. I close my eyes and hope Jag doesn't want to talk.

In the rearview mirrors, Wayland's house stands out against all the other perfect homes, two or three stories tall, the bright fences wrapped around each yard, mostly left unmarred, somehow the fire kept contained, and outside the house is the busted glass, firetruck treads, and the average look of Baltimore burnout. Give it twenty-four hours and I bet it'll be covered in graffiti too; someone just passing through to give a final parting message.

I wonder, given a new canvas in a squeaky-clean

neighborhood, what would the Baltimorons do?

I've already seen some of that with Wayland, right? He had never been a bad guy or corruption incarnate. He was one of the few in this city who was going to make something better for everyone else, who didn't spend his time trying to escape or destroy or fall into the mix of what he could get away with or who he could take shit from. He followed the rules, being told if he did everything right, he'd get whatever he wanted and he'd get out of the city alive.

I hate this goddamn city so much for taking him from me, for staining his hands, for making him feel like he failed. I knew Baltimore was hungry, but I thought there were at least *some* it'd leave alone. Trailer parks and prisons and shitty neighborhoods like Cherry Hill are filled with potential meals for the blood lust. Wayland should've been safe. He should still be alive.

"Hey, Joey," Jag says.

"I never asked you to care," I say.

"You didn't have to, but I can't keep doing this."

"I know." My hand finds his; I give him a squeeze. It squeezes me back—A reminder that maybe everything isn't fake, sometimes just fleeting and that makes it scary since it's a promise that someday, the high will end. "Sorry about the trouble."

"Sometimes, I wonder if I'm just being dumb to go through it."

"And I wonder why. Like, am I really worth it, J?"

He grunts but doesn't add anything more. The only time he lets go of my hand on the way to his place is to change gears. Fingers laced, I don't say anything else and for the first time in a while, I can almost pretend there's nothing else going on; things aren't as bad as they are like nothing outside of this moment's any different than it ever has been.

SEVEN.

We're walking into J's house. He tosses the keys onto the counter, I'm closing the door. It slips from my fingers and shuts a little too heavy. Jag turns around. "Sorry," I say.

He turns back around. His jacket's off, thrown over the side of a chair, then fingers running through his hair as he strokes the back of his head. He gives a heavy sigh. The house smells like the day-old pizza mixed with fresh cigarette smoke still lingering. The kitchen window's open. Jag's Marlboro's and lighter are on the kitchen island. There's a single butt sitting in the ashtray on the coffee table, the tip still burning a little bit. I grab it to give it a try, but there's not enough heat left to give me any payoff. I go to the fridge and grab a beer. Jag says, "Me too," so I pick one up for him too. Cap off, I hand it to him. "Thanks," he says, but keeps walking past me to the living room. Cigarette caught between his lips, he knocks a knuckle against the countertop.

Jag sits in the living room. His sigh's the only sound, then everything's quiet. Not even the neighbors or someone coming down the hall too loud. There's nothing.

"You wanna tell me what happened?" he says.

I pick up the cigarettes from the counter, but instead of taking one, I tape the box between my hands. "I told you, some asshole broke into the house and lit it up. I think he was from the bar."

"Not what I meant." Jag's head drops back against the couch.

I'm still standing in the kitchen. My legs feel heavy, but restless. I walk around to the other side of the island so I can lean against it, facing Jag.

My shirt's sticking to my skin and my hair's clinging to the back of my neck. I meant to shower at Wayland's so Jag wouldn't see me like this. Black dusting my fingers. Sulfur, ash, maybe a little of both? I wipe my hands on my pants. Most of the black dust rubs off, but my fingers still look too gray and I can't help but wonder if Jag sees me like I saw those guys in the bar, looking ragged and gross and dead. I run my hand up my neck. Stiff pieces of clumpy hair smack the skin between my fingers. My hand comes away dry. I try sucking on a cigarette again. Nothing because I didn't even want to light it, so I chew on the filter instead.

The silence of Jag's apartment is uncomfortable and makes me feel like I don't belong. My life's never been a quiet place and when someone's pissed at me, the right response isn't this. He should be angry, yelling, calling me every dirty name he can think of, and maybe smashing me across the face because I'm just a little too mouthy a lot of the time. I get it. I'm not really that fun to be around and that's why I wonder why Jag still comes when I call.

I close my eyes. The burn builds in them. The room's cold. There's not a ticking clock anywhere in his apartment, but I'm still hearing the soft click of the changing second hand.

Every time I'm here I wonder why he ever let me in. Something's pulling me toward the door, telling me I need to go home before I make shit worse and because my dad's gonna flip his shit if I don't get back before he realizes I'm not in my room, but then I keep reminding myself that he's actually gone and he's not coming back. The memories of his death are still so blurry. All I can remember is the blast of the gun going off after stepping out the door for the first day of first grade. I told myself it was the TV being too loud, even though it didn't sound anything like the TV and the clunk of the gun hitting the floor when it fell from his grip didn't sound like the TV either, but it was soft enough that maybe it was his foot or my dad tripped when he got up to take a piss. I still went to school thinking he'd be there when I got back.

I wasn't entirely wrong.

He was still in his chair. It just… He'd finally lost his mind and it was all over the cushions. The house smelled like beer and piss and rot and death; I still say that's what made me throw up, not seeing my dad's lifeless arm hanging over the chair or just how blown out his face was. I tried saying, "Dad," once, but I didn't want to say it a second time and confirm what I knew, so I locked myself in the closet in my room and covered my ears, listening to the TV on blast and thinking of him staring at it with his usual beer in hand and who-gives-a-shit attitude. I bit into a pillow I was holding against me, fabric wet from crying. I couldn't breathe; I couldn't think; I couldn't come up with what *tomorrow* meant and every time I bit down, I got dumb enough to think, "Mom," because I knew she wasn't coming back. No one was coming for me. No one cared.

I had the phone in my hand and I don't remember what the operator told me. I don't know how they even figured out what was going on because I couldn't say it. I couldn't do anything but stare at his chair and cry and say, "Why is he gone?" and "Why did he go?" and "I don't have a mom. I don't have anyone. What do I do?"

At least I remember the discomfort of the operator.

She didn't know what to say; I don't blame her for it.

Then, the first people who knocked on my door weren't even the badges. It was a small sea of microphones and people too pretty to be standing in Deadwood looking for their next paycheck at my door with peeling teal paint. Mics made to look like plastic dolls stood next to anemic and broken trees, a tire swing, and trash stuck to our stairs like we were sideshow attractions or Halloween decorations, no different than the homeless people they stepped over every day getting to work.

So many places in Baltimore look abandoned, even with peoples' livelihoods and homes put inside. It's a different world to them in the same way the nice-looking buildings don't look like they belong to my hometown when I see them.

At that moment, the only thing familiar to me was my own face reflecting back in the camera lens, and that was the last face I wanted to see because I was responsible for killing my dad. The other day was just me finally pulling the trigger myself.

"So," Jag says. "You gonna give me an answer or what?"

"I said I'm not fucking off," I say. The cigarette filter's flat. I should've just lit the damn thing.

"Also not what I'm talking about," Jag says. "You want to tell me what kind of fucked up shit your *friend* did now? I can't keep getting involved with this—"

"Then leave." That's not what I wanted to say. "At least then I can't take you with me." My breathing is choppy. "I don't know how to make this stop, J."

Jag's got his cigarette out of his mouth. He's straight, looking more serious than even a second ago. "Is that what you want, Joey? Should we call it?"

Everything hurts. I can't breathe. Those words never should've come out of my mouth, but I don't know why I can't stop myself from saying shit I don't mean and I can't say the things I want to. The answer to his question won't come out. Part of me knows it's because if I tell him what I *should*, he'll have all the power to wreck me, then what? But I don't want him to go. I want to be selfish; I want to keep him as long as I can.

I will my head to shake, but it doesn't move.

"There was blood on the washing machine." Jag puts his cigarette in the coffee table ashtray. His fingers tighten around his beer bottle's neck, then loosen. His gaze holds mine until I look down at my hands. I wipe my face, grab at my shirt like it's a towel, and laugh at myself.

"I'm tired, J." My fingers are buzzing with what feels like the soft jolt of electricity and the white noise from death keeps interrupting my thoughts so I don't get too far into them.

"Did you bring him here?" Jag says.

I'm barely picking my feet up, making my hips sway more than a little, tapping my fingers against the counter. I let them drop off the edge. They find the bottom of my shirt, finger the fabric, pull it over my head, and toss it to the floor. I meet Jag at the couch. My knees press into the cushion between his legs.

Jag sits up. His eyes meet mine. "What's he trying to do to me, Joey?"

I smile. My head shakes gently. I take the beer from his hands and place it on the coffee table behind me. Then, I'm crawling onto his lap, straddling him, sliding my hands up his chest. He's got a hand on my hip, steadying me, while the other goes around the back of my neck. He pulls me in close. It feels like nothing else in the universe exists. "He hasn't said anything about you… but there's a hellova lot *I* want to do to you, *Jagger.*" I lean in, bringing our lips together. I mash his head against the couch while I'm pulling at his belt, tossing it somewhere, then going for his shirt.

He breaks our lips apart. "You taste like blood." His breath tickles my lips. He's panting, chest rising fast. His heartbeat throbs in the fingertips I'm twisting in his hair.

I kiss the corner of his mouth. "Sorry I'm a little scrappy… What else can I say?" I pull his shirt over his head. Then, my lips capture his again.

Jag's hand slides down my thigh, the other's on my shoulder, and in an instant, Jag rolls me over, my back presses to the couch, and he's over me, between my legs, guiding my hands over my head. His lips caress the bruises my dad left on my neck the last time he choked me a couple days ago. Back arched, heat's gathering everywhere Jag's hands go. His strength pins my wrists to the armrest while his free hand moves along my bare stomach up to my breasts. He pushes my bra up. "What happened yesterday?" His exhale warms the nape of my neck. "Who did Cross kill?"

"Please don't ruin the moment, J…"

"Joey… What did *you* do…?" Jag's hand slides down my stomach, tickling my skin, driving me crazy and I want more. My back arches, trying to get more from his hand. His fingers find my fly, pop the button, pull the zipper down.

I lick my lips. My eyelids flutter, eyelashes trying to hide me from the way he's looking at me. The pity, sincerity, sadness, whatever it is. My heart's racing and I feel weighed down by guilt. I shouldn't be here. I've never been good enough for Jag and every time I'm around him, I risk dragging him down to my level. I just… I don't want to let him go either. Sometimes I let the grease stains fool me into thinking he's as dirty as I am, but he's never been like that. He's never looked at me with the same contempt the badges always have or the dismissal of the teachers or store clerks when you make it out back with a box of Pall Malls and a bag of Doritos.

When death didn't stop my dad's shipwreck of a life, I should've known it wouldn't stop mine either. "Nothing. I didn't hurt anyone."

Jag catches my neck between his teeth. He pulls, sucks, kisses down my collar, toward my breasts. "Where'd the blood come from?" he mutters into my skin.

"We got rid of some trash at Leakin. I met him there…. That's all." My legs wrap around Jag's waist.

"Really?" He presses himself against me. His lips hover over mine.

"Really…" I lift my head to meet him. It's a match being lit; Jag presses my head into the couch, hard, and he's pushing my skinnies down my thighs in the way that says he's done this so many times before. It's one of the things I always liked about Jag. Maybe he doesn't always want to give me what I want, but he gives me what I need when all I want is to run and find someone who'll give me not just what I'm used to, but what I deserve.

"Joey, you're into something really bad…" Jag says.

"I know… I don't know how to make it stop."

A couple of harsh knocks rock the door and I'm back in my house and Dad's standing on the other side saying, "Keep it down," while he's smacking the door again and again and again. The wood's cracking, hinges screaming, ready to snap apart at the next blow and my bruises already hurt in anticipation. He smacks the door again, says he's coming in, the fight's in his voice and I say, "Fuck off, Dad," into Jag's lips.

The knock comes again, harder.

I'm not at my house.

Jag's breaking the kiss. I'm leaning up, trying to follow, but my hands are still pinned and I can't go far. He's looking at my face with the same kind of surprise I'm probably giving him.

"Baltimore PD," a voice says from the other side of the door. "Anyone home?"

"Shit," Jag says, pulling back. He's off the couch.

"Ignore them." I sit up, too late to grab him. He's picking up his shirt from the floor and pulling it on.

"Rhetorical question," the BPD says. "I know you're home. I followed you here."

"Awesome," Jag says. His foot catches on something

on the floor. My soiled shirt. He kicks it to the corner. "Fuck." He rubs the back of his neck. His face's red, he looks back at me again, rubs his face, goes for the door while saying, "Shit." He circles back from the door to pick up his belt at the foot of the couch. I reach for him. My fingers catch his shirt, but he pulls away too fast. He's trying to put his belt on as he walks, but gives up and holds it folded in his hands instead while he grabs at the door. "Put something on."

I pull my bra back down and shimmy my jeans up my hips, zipping them. "You don't talk to badges, J. They don't help you."

"Not everyone's out to get you, Joey."

"I'm not talking about everyone. I'm talking about the BPD. There's nothing good that comes out of talking to badges, ever—"

"And what would you have us do instead?"

I don't have an answer. My jaw's tight and I go to the bedroom before I say something worse. The sound of someone's car stereo's leaking in from the downtown streets outside. All I hear in the lyrics is someone going *kill him, kill him, kill him, kill him yah* to drums and all I can think is someone got paid how much to say that for a track?

Jag opens the door.

"Good evening," I hear from the living room, not Jag. "I'm—"

"Detective Grant," Jag says.

"Right," Rocky says. "Have we met before?"

Jag doesn't answer.

Rocky clears his throat. His voice becomes serious, but doesn't lose the friendly tone, the *buddy* tone, the kind bad guy badges only use with male suspects because they think they can build a friendship and squeeze cute little secrets out of them with the right words. With me, they prefer to act like they're my dad, thinking disappointment will make much of a difference at this point in my life. It's hard to care about a badge's disappointment when you've been looking at your own life for twenty years going.

"You have a moment to talk?" Rocky says.

"What about?" Jag says.

"There was an incident in a neighborhood tonight," Rocky says.

"Sounds like typical Baltimore," Jag says. "What's that gotta do with me?"

"Right." Rocky laughs. "The difference is that your car was spotted on the scene." Rocky's quiet, maybe waiting for more of something from Jag, but Jag doesn't say anything. "Obviously, you don't live in that neighborhood and it's pretty out of the way for you, isn't it?"

"I've kinda settled in for the night." Jag shifts his hand, gesturing to his belt. "How do you know it was my car?"

"You drive a red '67 Mustang, fastback?" Rocky says.

"Yeah."

"Nice car."

"Thanks."

"You work on it?"

"Yeah," Jag says. "A project I started with my dad."

"Nice." Rocky nods.

"You didn't answer how you knew it was my car."

"I saw it in the neighborhood, ran the plates. It looked familiar, now I know why," Rocky says.

This is the worst part. If you don't know any better, you'd think the badges actually cared about you, wanted to know your life story, wanted to give you sympathy and answers for everything you're being haunted with. They'll find something you have in common or at least something they know enough to bullshit with you about until you're comfortable and jabbering and thinking maybe you're friends now because you're laughing and the badge doesn't seem as judgmental as badges typically should be and so why should you be defensive? After all, they're the good guys, right? As long as you're non-violent, you get the treatment: build rapport.

Once you've got a better relationship with someone, it's easier to manipulate the answers out of them under the guise of *helping them remember something*. You drop your guard, let your lips fly looser than you meant because a second ago you were laughing, and you didn't think that *I don't know* was gonna come back and bite you in the ass, but the badges pretend *I don't know* is code for *I'm guilty and won't tell you* so they work it until they get the phrase they need to use against you in court.

"Wow," I say, coming out of the bedroom, swaying my hips with exaggeration. I get to the end of the couch before I cross my arms. "You sure got here fast." I look Rocky down. No blood on his shoes, they shine black. His slacks fit too well, they don't drag so the cuffs aren't dirty either. No stains from greasy lunch or spilled coffee. He's got some darkness around his eyes. Not death, just tired. Sometimes it looks the same though. "Slow day on Creep Street?"

Rocky's head twists to the side to look at me. He laughs. "Unfortunately." He clears his throat fast like he thinks I won't hear it. "It's never a slow day in this city."

"Right." My lips curl into a brief smile. "Someone's always gotta be fucking up someone else's day, yeah?"

Jag rubs his temple. "Would you put something on?"

"What?" I glance down. I'm not expecting to be hanging out. The dark crust of mud, cuts, and dried blood stand out more on my pale skin, but maybe not as much as the purple bruises that formed where the thug from the bar kicked me. "It's just a bra," I say. "We're fine. Right, Rocky? You don't mind, do you?"

"That's not what I mean," Jag says.

"Sorry if I'm interrupting something," Rocky says.

"Always," I say.

Rocky comes into the house further, using his hand

sticking out for a shake like it's permission. He keeps his hand out when he's standing in front of me, even when I don't take it, he's waiting, staring, smiling. Finally, he lowers it to his side, tucks his hand into his pocket, first his pants, then his shirt and jacket. He withdraws a card with gold lettering on the front. "My name's Detective Stone—"

"I know who you are, *Rocky*," I say.

Another laugh slips from his lips. He clears his throat, looking surprised. He puts the card back into his wallet. "Rocky?" he says.

"That's your name, yeah?"

"Stone," he says.

"That's what I said."

"You…" Rocky's tongue moves inside his mouth, pushing his lip from the bottom. His glance flickers past me to Jag, but it's not long before he's back at me. His lips flatten and he's looking harder now, leaning forward. I'm stepping back, even though my legs tell me not to. My skin's getting hot, my fingers curl, and I'm thinking he's gonna fight me. He's doing the detective thing like he's memorizing my face. A hum vibrates in his throat. His hand slips into his pocket again, pushing his jacket back. "Do I know you from somewhere?" he finally leans away. "You've got a face."

"I'm sure you say that to all the *good girls*." My arms tighten across my chest. "Making a profile?"

"Knock it off, Joey," Jag says.

"Joey?" Rocky says. "You're the second girl I've met recently named Joey."

"*Second?*" I take a step forward. My head cranes to the side. "Are you messing with me, Rocky?"

"I don't know what you mean by that," Rocky says. "What'd you say you do for work?" He's talking to Jag now, turning away from me.

"I didn't," Jag says.

"Sorry," Rocky says. "What do you do?"

"I work on cars," Jag says.

"That's right." Rocky snaps his fingers. "That's where I've seen you before. Bodymore Body Shop, right? Actually brought a body in a week or two back?"

"You been drinking on the job?" I step closer even though my body's telling me to keep away. My hands are fists, blood running, my vision's turning into a tunnel framed by red, waiting for a chance to smash him against the counter.

"*Keep yourself level,*" Ralph says in my head then the scene at the bar plays again in my memory, the waking of the dead, and Charon's warning that losing your shit ignites every ghost nearby. I take a couple of deep breaths trying to push the rage back down. I resist the urge to pace away thinking it might look like guilt. Light catches on the cuffs hanging from Rocky's hip. In that moment, I'm already feeling them on me. I touch my wrists. Different from how Jag's hands felt on them just minutes ago. A shiver goes through me.

"I'm not sure what you mean," Rocky says.

"A body. You're talking about a body," I say. "You forgot about a murder from, like, a week ago."

"I didn't forget," Rocky says.

"It's fine if you say you don't care. We already know," I say.

"I understand why you feel that way." Rocky watches my hands, my wrists, then looks at Jag. He licks his lips. All that tells me is he's got a habit. Tobacco, booze, something worse. He's looking for a trace of it on himself to take the edge off or give him something familiar to chew on when he's uncomfortable. I know the feeling; I've got it in my mouth right now and when I'm not smoking, I play with my lip ring. "There is corruption in the department," Rocky says. "But there are many of us who do care."

"Right… Yet you forgot about a couple of stiffs from only a week ago," I say.

"It's unfortunate with all the bodies, all the crime, all the paperwork stacked in the inbox, they can blend together," Rocky says.

"That's one way to talk about the dead," I say through my teeth. I turn away, go to my bottle of beer sitting on the kitchen counter, and finish what's left of it. Bottle in the trash, I'm grabbing another from the fridge.

"Speaking of which, I'm sorry about your loss," Rocky says to Jag.

"What are you talking about?" Jag says.

"That girl from your shop. We found her body a couple blocks away from the precinct."

"You sure about that?" Jag's attempt to suppress his defensiveness fails.

"Pretty sure. Looked just like her—"

"You have anyone confirm yet?"

"Eh, hunting down family has been a bit of a task. We might call you in a couple of days though." Rocky's searching his pockets for something. Front, back, side, jacket, but he comes up with nothing. More of that habit the badges try to hide. Fingers flying along the flask he knows he can't dip into while he's talking to someone, lest he should lose any mild sense of legitimacy he may have left. I'm watching him close to see if he licks his lips again or if he looks a little too long at the beer in my hand or the one in the living room. Maybe he'll stagger his way over to one of them thinking I won't notice if he's talking and keeping us on our toes, but he doesn't move. "Sorry to bring it up," he says. "I didn't realize you didn't know. At least I figured you would've noticed her missing from work." Rocky laughs weakly.

"She was fired last week for missing work," Jag says.

"Well, damn," Rocky says.

"Donny's got a business to run without babysitting a

hooligan, so whatever." I sip at my beer. It's not enough. I need something in my mouth because the beer's not doing it for me. Lighting up in the apartment isn't an option with a badge here, though. They don't keep any kind of secrets but their own.

I drink down half the bottle I'm holding, but it's unsatisfying, empty-feeling, irritating. My foot's bouncing. I'm leaning against the counter, swaying my hips with a little head bob and running my fingers through my grimy hair, trying to chill since walking away would leave Jag alone with this jackass. The other half of the beer is gone in seconds, so I'm grabbing a third already, popping the cap on the edge of the counter.

"You alright?" Rocky says to me.

"Peachy," I say.

"What's all over you?"

I look down at the bruises on my arms, the sealed cuts mixed with the long scars down my right arm. Remnants of my sixteenth birthday might someday be invisible next to all the other damage. My body feels like an extension of Baltimore; covered in graffiti left by those who I've come in contact with one way or another. I pull away from the counter. "You're getting pretty bold," I say.

"You get into a fight with someone?" he says.

"You got a warrant?" I say.

"I'm just asking a couple of questions—"

"And answers cost you a warrant." I'm turning away while I talk. The beer's loosely in my fingers and I think I'm gonna drop the bottle, but I don't. I pause to set it down on a nearby end table so I can reach around and unhook my bra, letting it drop onto the floor. Facing away, nothing should be visible to him from where the detective is standing. I pick up the beer again and wave with my fingers. "Good night, *Rocky*," I say, continuing to Jag's room without looking back.

The door's half shut. I should be able to hear them still,

but the other room's silent. My heart's throbbing in my ears, pounding in my head. I feel like I'm losing it. I set the beer down on the dresser and grab out my cigarettes to light one. I close my eyes; my hands are trembling.

The nicotine feels like I'm breathing for the first time in days, it's that good.

"She's something," Rocky says.

"It's been a rough couple of days." Jag sighs. The way his voice deflates, I see him rubbing the back of his neck, then his eyes, exhausted, wondering what the hell he's still doing with me. "Can you just... tell me why you're here? I have some shit to deal with."

"Right." Rocky clears his throat, straightening.

I use the wall to prop myself up. My back presses into it while it holds all my weight and I slide to the floor. Goosebumps form on my arms. The smoke seething from my lips warms my face.

"You said you were in the neighborhood," Rocky says. "Why?"

"My..." Jag pauses. His voice shifts like he's looking toward the bedroom. "Roommate is friends with someone who lives there."

"Roommate?"

"Yeah... We're not really the type for labels and even if we were, *girlfriend's* stretching it right now."

Rocky laughs. "I hear you. Relationships are... something."

"They're a little more than that." Jag snorts. His knuckles tap against something. He's got the box of cigarettes in his hand again, replacing his belt as the buckle hits the counter.

"So, you were in the neighborhood for her?" Rocky says, his voice a gesture toward the bedroom.

"Yeah. I was picking her up and that's it." Footsteps. Jag's going for the front door. It opens. "If that's all you came for... it's been a night, so I'd like to end it."

"Of course." Rocky chuckles weakly. He's walking too. "I appreciate your cooperation. My apologies for interrupting."

The heat's building under my skin again. My hands are so tight, my knuckles turn white. I push off the ground. I'm watching for the bedroom door, just so my fingers touch the knob. Before I do anything, I pull away and go to the bathroom instead. Shower's on, pants off; I'm in.

The water's hot.

My foot's bouncing and I'm muttering something, but the words come and go so fast, I'm not sure what I'm saying. I just know the words go together. I smack my hand against the wall. With the water, they splat. I'm trying to calm down, but everything's looking too red, redder than before. Red like when I killed my dad and the thoughts are flooding back with the need to feel something fighting against me, hitting me, holding me down and making me scream.

My fist hits the wall again. The burning water runs down my back. It's not the first time I'm really feeling whatever cuts are there. I'm trying to remember what happened at the bar, but it's only making the anger worse. I hit the wall again, then again, harder. My knuckles crack. I pull my hand away, shaking the light throb. I laugh, cover my mouth, make it stop. I step under the water. Close my eyes, hold my breath, hope the wash takes me away from whatever's pulsing inside of me calling for violence.

Fuck, I want it to stop.

"Hey," Jag says.

My head jerks up. I turn around. I slip. My back hits the wall. The fresh bruises make me hiss.

Jag's tossing his shirt off. His body morphs through the glass shower door, making his form jagged and uneven, a work of art where a wire has gone through wet paint and pulled him sharply in both directions. His remaining clothing falls away, kicked between the toilet and the sink cabinet. The glass door slides open. He's standing in front of me now and I'm pressing myself into the wall. The cold tile feels so good against my skin. His arm presses into the wall over my shoulder while he's leaning down, craning his neck, coming in close. His eyes hang partially closed. He tries to smile. He's tired, irritated, stressed, but he's trying. "You're acting crazy, you know?"

"Sorry." I meet his eyes. There's too much compassion in them, I can't keep hold. "I'm dead. Please don't hold it against me?"

Jag leans down saying, "You're not *dead*." His lips brush against mine and keep going, moving off my jaw, down my neck, over my shoulder, toward my breasts. He pins my hip.

"You heard the badge. They found me."

"I don't know what game you're playing…"

"It's not a game, J…" The words catch in my throat. My breath's a solid object. My head drops back and I let the wall take on most of my weight.

"Then why do you keep saying that? You're standing right in front of me."

A laugh bubbles in my throat. "What if I told you ghosts were real?" My eyes water. I blink rapidly to push back the threatening tears, glad he's in the crook of my neck, so he can't see my face, but my nose's getting clogged and I close my eyes, hoping the water will help.

It doesn't.

Jag's lips are gone. I open my eyes; he's looking into them and I hate him for it. My chest hurts, body pulsing with adrenaline and fear and anticipation that he'll see everything I'm thinking, and the dirt under my fingernails from the last couple of days will be the final straw where he says *fuck this*. I want him to read my mind, to know everything I've been through in the last twenty years like it'll help him see I'm not so bad, but then I don't want him to know me like that either because then when he walks away, it won't be from the sarcasm or who he thought I was, it'll be every intimate detail that makes up who I am that he's rejecting.

It's better to be left behind for what people *think* of you instead of everything you are.

The warm water, clean tile walls, spotless shower, bright lights, and quiet remind me I don't belong here. Jag's hand moves up my hip, my chest, and hooks under my chin. He's tilting my head back, making me meet his stare. I press into the wall, willing myself to disappear, but apparently, that's not really how ghosts work. "Whatever happened with you, we'll get through it together, Joey."

The pain stings. I laugh it off, but a tear still makes it out, runs down my cheek. "What if I needed you to bury a body?"

Jag chuckles, but it's short. His eyes stay on mine. "I'm not helping you bury your dad."

"I didn't kill him, J. I just... I put him to rest."

"What does that mean?"

My throat tightens again. J's hands are the only things keeping me in place. The racket's building in my head, telling me to run, get out, don't look back, it's too late for any of this. I wrap my arms around Jag's neck. My fingers lace with his hair. I pull him down, closer, while I stand on my toes so my lips can better reach his. My head gently shakes. "You wouldn't believe me if I told you."

His hands are on my thighs, lifting my legs around his waist while he presses me into the wall. Every one of my senses is going crazy, but the need to run is muted under our panting breaths. When we're done in the bathroom, we don't get dressed and continue in the bedroom.

It doesn't feel right to lay in bed with him at the end. For years, it's been 'leave when you're done,' sneaking out while he's sleeping, never because Jag told me to, but because I had somewhere else to be, someone else to see, a responsibility to take care of. My dad. Maybe that's not all there ever was to it.

Jag's arm is over me; his chest is pressed to my back; I'm scared by how comfortable I feel, how much I don't want this to end and panicking at the thought of what I'll do when it's over. I hate how much I need him and I keep telling myself to shut up, don't say that, you knew this was temporary when you started it, but God, I want this so bad, please don't take it away.

I'm not even religious, but I think God left Baltimore a long time ago when he saw just how fucked we were and I don't blame him for it. Deadwood's just one of a million neighborhoods showcasing every kind of trash broken families have to offer. Everyone worth anything lives in the suburbs and they don't come here unless they have to.

The city's graffiti will tell you the same thing. It's all warnings for the curse that'll hit you if you stay too long and the hopelessness that haunts us:

RAGE IS KEROSENE;
      LIGHT UP YOUR LIFE.
           LET THE STRUGGLES BLOW AWAY
   LIKE ASH IN THE WIND;
     FUCK THIS WORLD.
          BEGGARS CAN'T BE CHOOSERS;
STOP BEGGING AND TAKE WHAT YOU WANT;
     FUCK EVERYTHING.
       I WISH DAD WAS HERE.
THINK I SAW HIS BODY BEHIND POE'S HOUSE.
   DON'T EAT DICKS LIKE LYDIA.
     PLZ HELP ME, SUM1.

You get used to the yelling and abandon and fear and waiting for the day your boss gives you the pink slip and everyone forgets your name. The only proof you exist is how miserable you feel, but no one else can see it; no one sees you, except for once you kill yourself and put your writing on the walls next to the last basket case or criminal.

I still can't believe Jag's not gone yet. What we had was easy, but I don't think it'll work anymore because I'm not easy anymore. Someday, he'll have a girl come into the shop with a tiny car from Europe; she won't need the oil change she ordered, she just wanted an excuse to say hi because she's been watching him for a while now. She'll have nice, long hair and hands that are soft and clean and probably've never touched grease. She'll smell like peaches and sugar and skin glitter and since her dad loved her, she'll have no trouble telling Jag she loves him.

He'll finally see what he's been missing out on and then he'll go the way of the badges and forget me too.

EIGHT.

I wake up to a caw.

The room smells like coffee and cigarettes. Blankets are pulled tightly to my body, but everything's cold and the bed's empty. The air's too crisp; one of the windows must be open. I don't see Jag in the bedroom. I don't hear him in the other room either. I sit up, push my hair back, and rub the crust from my eyes. My phone's plugged in on the nightstand. I didn't do it. I grab it and look for any messages from Wayland or Jag. There aren't any. I open a text to Wayland and say, "Staying out of trouble?" Laying back down, I drop my phone. My arm lays over my face. A couple minutes pass with nothing happening. I send another text.

> JOEY   Hit me when you get this.

The clock in the corner of my phone says it's ten in the morning. "Shit." I'm pretty sure it's lying, but there aren't any other clocks in the bedroom to check it against. There's no way Wayland's still in bed if it's that late already, but if I slept late, maybe he did too, so I pretend that's the reason he's not saying anything. Last night was a shitshow, so I can't blame him, yeah?

I drop the phone onto the nightstand.

I was hoping he'd tell me where his family went last night. I refresh the messages to see if maybe my phone was just lagging or busted or something, but no messages appear before or after what I'd just sent. I shouldn't be so worried about him, but I can't stop thinking about how I left him at my trailer and the bags in the woods and what if it happened again, but this time his parents were around? I know he wouldn't do anything to them, but they wouldn't understand.

I get it; they don't need to.

But I mean, what's there to get about killing someone in a blood lust and chopping them to pieces? A small laugh slips out of my lips. Excitement trills under my skin. I smack myself in the cheek and get out of bed.

I've got one of Jag's shirts from the laundry basket.

The damn bird caws again.

I go into the living room. The window behind the couch is open. I go over to it, lean out. The bass from someone's car is too loud, distorted, bouncing off the outside of the building and the parking lot, disappearing into the distance. I close my eyes and breathe the cold air.

That's what it had been.

Wasn't a bird, just someone's radio. My teeth pull at my lip, begging for a cigarette. The thumping bass disappears. A caw comes. I open my eyes. Three stories down, four ravens are lounging on the ground, spread between the entrance, the sidewalk, a tree, and the parking lot. "There's nothing here for you!" I say. I lean back inside and close the window.

"Hey," Jag says.

I turn around. He's standing in the kitchen, cigarette in the ashtray on the center island and a cup of coffee in his hand. The Mr. Coffee on the counter's still half full and warm. "Hey." My face is burning. "Don't you have a job you're supposed to be at?"

"After yesterday?" Jag sets his cup down. "I got the day off. What was that about?" He nods his head, gesturing toward the window.

"Hm?" I pretend I don't know what he's talking about.

"Someone hanging around outside?"

"You could say that."

"Should I check it out?"

I shake my head. "No."

"So." Leaning against the counter, he crosses his arms. He doesn't believe me. He keeps looking at the window. "What are your plans today?"

I don't think long enough before I speak. "A quick trip to the bar, then I need to find Cross."

"A bar? At ten in the morning? No." Jag's stare locks with mine. "There's a limit to my patience, Joey."

"What do you think I'm gonna do?"

"Not to be an ass, but I know your dad—"

"I'm not my dad!" I push whatever's near me off the counter. It's only a half empty water bottle, but it doesn't matter. I never wanted to be like this or like him. Shame fills me and I can't hold Jag's look. My ears are hot. I pace across the kitchen, past the island, and into the living room. My fingers comb through my hair, pressing hard against my scalp as I move. "Fuck. Sorry. I'm not trying to be a bitch, J. I just—"

"You're on a crash," Jag says. "I get it."

"For the millionth time, I'm not high."

"I don't care to argue about this anymore. You're coming down from something. Check back with me in a day or two and we'll see if your shit's in a box, alright?" Jag picks up his cigarette from the ashtray and takes a puff.

I groan into my hands. "I'm not trying to chase you off—"

"You're doing a shit-ass job at that." Jag wipes his eyes. He turns away from me, bringing his coffee to his lips again. A ring of coffee remains on the counter where the cup used to sit.

"I'm sorry, It's just—Wayland's saved my life more times than I can count. The least I can do is try and have his back."

"Fine. We'll go to the bar."

I pop my lips. My skin's hot. "I don't need you to come with me."

Jag half laughs, making it bitter. "I'm not letting you go alone. If you're not going to tell me what's going on, then I need to see it."

A caw comes through the glass. It sounds like the bird's in the room. I turn around and around, scanning the couch, the living room, the kitchen, going for the bedroom.

"Hey," Jag says.

I keep turning, keep looking, push the bedroom door open too hard.

"Hey, hey, hey." He's behind me. "What's up?"

My vision blurs. The room zooms out of focus. I shake my head. I realize I'm not breathing when I try to speak and don't have air. "You don't hear that?"

"Hear what?"

"Nothing." I turn back around, going to the kitchen now to grab a cup from the cupboard and pour some coffee. If you pretend you didn't see it, if you say you didn't hear it, then it's like it's not there and the birds aren't following us. More, they aren't following Jag. "I'm gonna get dressed so we can go."

Jag's driving without saying anything. The radio's turned up. I knock a cigarette out of my box and offer it to Jag. He takes it, lights it, keeps driving without a word and without looking at me, though he's muttering softly to the radio. I put a cigarette in my mouth, but instead of lighting it, I chew on the filter. My foot's bouncing so hard, the vibrations going up my leg with the beat. I'm feeling heavy and exhausted, but I can't stop moving. I want to go back to Jag's place, fall onto his bed, have him fall onto me, and turn into oblivion for a couple of days or maybe a couple of weeks. I don't know. I want to stop thinking and feeling and wanting for anything, but being still's making me annoyed and I'm afraid every time I open my mouth, I'm gonna say something worse to J that I don't mean and he doesn't deserve.

I know I've never been good at controlling what I say, but it's gotten so much worse. I don't even feel like myself anymore sometimes. When I'm not thinking of all the bloody messes I'd like to make with whatever's comes into my line of sight, I'm thinking, "Sorry, J," on repeat.

We pull into the BAIT's neighborhood; during the morning, I almost don't recognize it. The light hitting the trees almost makes them look purple and black in the shadows. A couple lines of graffiti run across the side of the brick wall we pass. Most of it is illegible neon writing wrapping around itself. Then one wall says, WHERE'S YOUR GOD?

The next says   OOPS, SHOT HIM, MY BAD.
And the next,   I'M NOT SRY;
                       GOD'S A BASTARD.

The image of a raven's head with no eyes holding a string of guts in his mouth covers the side of BAIT's. Above it in blocky, black letters reads HAPPY again and again and again in different angles and sizes.

Jag turns down the radio and asks if he should park in front of the bar and am I sure anyone's even here. Seems kinda stupid, yeah, what bartender is usually their bar this early on a weekday anyway?

"I texted him before we left. Plus, he just lives in a backroom. I really don't think he leaves the bar much," I say. Even if I hadn't texted him, it would've been a fair guess he'd be here. I mean, he's the kind of guy who lives in his bar. I know he lives here because I've shown up at eight in the morning before and had the same question. Parking in front of the place is a sketchier question. Not because of Ralph or the bar. Jag's car being in the neighborhood, in general, puts it at risk, but whatever ghosts might be watching the bar also make it worse. I don't want to be responsible, so I tell him, "Park wherever you want. We'll figure out what happens after that."

"Yeah… I don't wanna play that game if it means my place gets lit up next," Jag says.

"Then park four blocks away and we'll hope we don't get murdered walking back—"

"Always the optimist, huh, Jo?" Jag dabs his cigarette out in the ashtray.

His use of the name catches me off guard. With Jag it's always been Joey, with Wayland, it's always been Jo. "I gotta be." I put my cigarette down next to his. "If I'm not optimistic, what do I got left?"

Jag doesn't say anything, but parks a block away from the bar. It's not that far. The cold doesn't bother me as much as I thought it might. It felt so much sharper in the car, but standing in the actual air doesn't feel like much of anything. I'm walking fast until we reach the parking lot. Then the feeling I had last night sets in like a soft murmur and my impulses go quiet. A chill runs down my spine. I look around the bar's entrance for the ravens that've been following Jag. None of them are here now. At least maybe that means they've been following something else.

I'm not expecting the door to be unlocked when I pull on it, but it is. Jag takes it out of my hand. I walk in saying, "Thanks," and he follows.

The lights are low, setting the mood to 'evening, after work' even though it's early. A little yellow, brighter than the other day. Some other set of lights is on, not the amber ones. The neon alcohol signs are all turned off. The place feels like a broken illusion and the tension that's been in me for days is mostly gone. The bar's half-empty, the broken tables last night are mostly gone. Glass chards, loose wood, and staining give the floor more character than it usually has. I approach the bar counter quickly and stand on the step beneath it. Neither Ralph nor KC are visible.

"Ralph? You here?" I knock gently against the counter.

Despite being alone, I keep my voice down. It feels like I'm going to be found by someone I don't want, another dead man hiding in the corner of the room, waiting for me to come in so he can bash my face in and take Jag on next so Charon will pick us up.

I remind myself there weren't any ravens outside. No one's gonna die. Or we should be good for now at least.

"Ralph?" I say again.

"Who comes for a drink this early in the morning?" The bar acoustics camouflage Ralph's position. "You an alcoholic?"

"You left the door open. You're kinda asking for trouble in this neighborhood."

Ralph comes around the bar shelf, stepping behind the counter. "I warned you." His appearance is the same black feather, fitted black jeans, black t-shirt with a culty-looking eye on the heart, though today he's got a black bandanna tied in his hair. He leans against the counter in front of me. He surveys my face, my body, down to where the counter cuts me off, then to Jag behind me. "You don't have much experience with the dead, do you?"

"It's been, like, two days. Gimme a break."

"Escalation hits fast."

"I noticed."

Ralph tap the counter slowly. He's got on so many rings, one of them's jade, one of them's a silver band, and one of them's gold. Around his neck is the same pendant he had on last time. Thick, oval gold frame embedded with pearls and at the center of the necklace is a long, semi-transparent red stone with specks of black and gold floating in it. It's so unique, I don't know how I never noticed it before. It doesn't seem to go with the rest of his style—except for maybe one of the gaudy rings. Something he picked up in one of those new-age shops or at an estate sale by a weird old lady. "You live in Baltimore. You've grown up around ghosts and they don't change much."

I purse my lips. I'm sweating. I wipe my hands on my pants. "That's why I came to see you. A friend of mine tells me you've got a fetish. Not the blackmail kind, the magic kind."

"How much do you believe?" Ralph looks between Jag and me.

"Well, I didn't believe anything two weeks ago, so… call me malleable." I stare at him. "What exactly is a fetish?"

"Your friend didn't tell you?"

"Reapers aren't exactly forthcoming with information about the afterlife. Actually… I don't think anyone from that side is," I say.

"Mmm… Yeah. You're mostly right about that." Ralph steps away from the counter. He turns to the alcohol behind him, fingers gliding along the shelf edges until he reaches the Hennessey.

"You know the reaper?"

Ralph laughs. "Which one?" He comes back to the counter. He's got a couple of shot glasses in his hand, one for each of us and himself. "You want?"

"Not really." I lick my lips. I'm watching the bottle pour a second shot too closely. As much as I'd like something to take the edge off, I don't think I can do it with Jag around. Thing's are bad enough without him thinking I've got a drinking problem too. "So, what's a fetish?"

Ralph tosses back one of the shots. "It's a contract, a symbol of a deal you've made with the keepers on the other side. The Cogs and Judge—You talk to them, make them a little promise, and if they believe you, they give you a fetish. Pending on what you ask for and what all you put in, you might get less than you asked for or nothing at all." He throws back the other shot. Next, he's getting a glass from under the counter and filling it with ice and water. "What are you searching for?"

I exhale, release the counter, back off the step. My foot lands on someone else's, a hand catches my side and shoulder. My back falls into someone's chest. I gasp, close my eyes just as I think it's Jag.

"Watch it," Jag says.

"Sorry." I pull out of his hold. Something clicks. I turn around. KC's at the door, locking it now.

Ralph looks me down again. There's something in his eyes that makes them look glossed over, distant, different than how they should. The way he looks is like it goes through me, evaluating every part of me from the things I feel to the things I've seen and thought and dreamed and even things I can't remember anymore, but somehow, he's getting access to them. "Let me start with an easy question: Do you know you're dead?"

I laugh. "Duh. I don't know how I wouldn't... Aside from how unbelievable everything is."

"You'd be surprised by the number of spirits who don't realize they're no longer experiencing life, but the world through the lens of regret." Ralph wipes his nose. His rings click on his icy glass. He looks at Jag, then back to me. "I'm still not sure if *doomed* is the correct word, but it is what it is. You've seen the types of souls that return."

"And because of that, everything's bad?"

"Yes."

"Why? Is it because the world really is a shit show, but the living just can't see it?"

"It has more to do with the state of your soul than the world itself. You ever wonder why most people couldn't see some of the things you believed were obvious and obscure? Strange or vulgar or obscene? That's from the regret seeping in before your death. Regret's not even the right word. Anguish? Contrition? Heartbreak? I don't know if there's a way to capture what's happening in any human language. But certain people will see two layers of things: the world of the living and the world of the dead— on a variant spectrum. Some people think it's just depression or psychosis, delusion or hallucination, but no, it's your soul rotting and changing the way you see things. And as you'd expect, once you experience the rot, there's no turning back."

"What all happens when a soul rots?" I say.

"Sometimes it looks like persistent pessimism. At worst, you live in an inhumane version of the world, surrounded by hatred, brutality, and corruption; you seethe with the desire for destruction as protection for yourself and punishment for presumed offenses against you. Everything's an insult when your soul is bankrupt," Ralph says.

"And that's why the dead are so angry?"

Ralph nods. "They can't help it. Those who refuse absolution often don't perceive themselves as having caused their own end."

"Nice poetry, but what the hell's this have to do with anything?" Jag says.

Ralph looks Jag down, back up, and for a moment, it appears as if his eyes softly glow. He takes a step forward, Jag steps back saying, "Don't."

Ralph turns his attention back to me. "He doesn't know?"

I glance at Jag, back to Ralph, and shrug. "I've tried to tell him. He doesn't believe me."

"Normally, I'd say that's reasonable—But when you've

been this close to death?" Ralph chuckles softly. "Cynicism is just a way of evading the truth a little longer."

"What do you mean?" I say.

"Death changes how you see things, but you don't respond with destruction until a trigger is pulled, an insult is made, a grudge is turned on. Then you can't think of anything but putting an end to the insult. Unfortunately, anger begets anger, pain begets pain, destruction begets destruction. It's a vicious cycle and all it takes is one soul's insult to activate the others nearby." Ralph's eyes lock on mine. "What kind of fetish are you looking for?"

"I don't know. What can they even do?" I look at Ralph; he's watching me closely. "Maybe something that'll help slow the snap or stop the rotting before someone completely loses themselves in the worst of it…?" The words catch. I don't want to think about the worst that could happen; you could almost say it's already happened except Jag and Wayland's families are fine, but I've already seen where he's ready to go. The body in the trunk, the one in the woods, the couple at Armistead, and the way he went after the guy in the house and at the bar. I don't hold any of it against him; I know what it feels like to lose it. I've done it—at least, I've looked at bodies now without feeling anything at all. I might not know what's going on in Wayland's head specifically, but I know what he's feeling when he's taking someone down.

Ralph leans back. He sets his glass in a bin under the counter. "KC, stay out here?"

KC says, "Yeah."

"You two, follow me," Ralph says, stepping out from behind the bar. He leads the way down the hall in the back of the building. They look unreasonably long for how small the place is. Blank walls with no doors, wooden paneling, and picture frames with nothing in them. At least, the frames look like nothing but black squares to me. At the end of the hall is a wide, wooden door, leading to a much smaller office. Immediately outside of that is a smaller door leading to a bathroom and a storage closet. "Come in," Ralph says.

I do.

Jag's close behind me. The office has an old metal filing cabinet, a small wooden desk stacked with papers and letters and bills, a bottle and an ashtray. More empty bottles lay on the floor beside the desk. On the walls are photographs of a band, album cover art, a signed CD that looks like it might've been burned on a computer, a pair of drumsticks and an old base. A couple of guitar picks are framed together with KC's signature underneath in silver. In the corner of the room hang several bones, feathers, and a bird's skull connected with black and purple strings. An amethyst crystal connected to a chain lays in the papers on the desk next to a straw doll shaped like a person. There's another bird's skull on top the filing cabinet. Outside of science class and the couple of times we went to the museum, I've never seen so many dead animal parts.

I look closer at the pictures on the wall. One of them has all four band members in it. Bass, synth, drums, singer. The top corner reads BAIT. The bottom has four signatures. Band memorabilia is all over the room, including a band t-shirt containing a black circle reading HYLE on three sides. Another band tee has an eye in a triangle on an ornate golden circle and a variety of white leaves. The line before the outer edge of golden laurels reads BADASS IDIOT TRAIN: AGAPE TOUR.

"It really is hard to give up on an old life, huh?" I say. "Dead or living."

"Sometimes human nature is really illogical. Whoever chose sentimentality for our design wasn't really thinking, huh? It's caused more destruction than probably anything outside of idealism, and you know what happens when you put the two together? Unimaginable disaster." Ralph laughs. "It's almost funny things meant to be so positive and good can cause so much mayhem."

Without looking, I hear Jag walking around behind me, surveying the pictures on the wall. It's hard not to look. So many bones, so many eyes, so much memorabilia taking us back to a time that doesn't exist anymore with people that don't exist anymore. Not in the same way. Weirder is all the eyes. Metal, painted, distinct, artistic, the eyes are on almost everything. I didn't even realize the I in BAIT's was dotted with an eye or that the small shapes on Ralph's bandanna aren't the typical things you'd get printed in white, but a more obscure take on eyes. Has it always been like that?

"You guys were really into the occult," Jag says.

"It's been known to save a life from time to time." Ralph grabs at twine hanging from the ceiling. A black feather hangs off the bottom. His small flip makes a bell ring gently.

"Right, but at what cost?" Jag laughs.

"That's always the question, yeah?" Ralph says. "How can anyone outlive this life? Is there a way to avoid the fates once they've been revealed? Is there even such a thing as choice if we live to fulfill a destiny?"

"I try not to think about that kind of shit unless I'm four beers deep," Jag says.

My jaw tightens, my foot's tapping fast, but it's more the usual uneasiness and I can't grab onto any of the questions I had before coming here. All I want is a bottle of something hard and a seat in the corner where I won't be bothered and don't have to think of what's coming next or the cost of stopping a disaster. My phone buzzes against my thigh. "How do I get a fetish?"

"Depends on what you want." Ralph walks around to the other side of his desk. He pops open one of the drawers, finds a tin with an eye on the front. Inside is a couple of rolled cigarettes. He pulls one out, but doesn't light it.

"What do you keep on the bar that makes things quiet?" I say.

"That's a sanctuary fetish. Almost like a blessing; that's why it works within the walls of the bar and where I live, but not the parking lot or any extension outside," Ralph says.

"So, you've basically made a retreat for the dead?"

"A cantina, yeah."

Jag lets out a hard breath. Arms crossed, he licks his lips. His eyes train on Ralph while his fingers tap against his bicep. His lips twitch with a tightness of something to say, but he's figuring out what words to use. "I thought this was about Cross, but... Joey, are you in a cult?"

"What?" I laugh. My hand covers my mouth. I turn to Jag. "No. I'm not in a cult, J."

Ralph's laugh is harder. Mixed with cigarette smoke, it turns into a cough. "He doesn't know?"

"He knows, he just... doesn't believe me," I say.

Jag's head drops forward. He's looking at the walls again, the framed pictures, CDs, retired instruments, busted stereo in the back. "The guy worships a dead musician."

"That's a pretty weird thing to say," Ralph says. "You worship your dead friends, buddy?"

"I don't put up a shrine," Jag says.

"Look a little harder." Ralph lights his cigarette and takes a drag. He stretches his arms out over his head. The light hits him just right where scar lines reflect off his forearm, hidden between the black ink and skin paled by time. His forearm, elbow, outside of his bicep. All of his exposed skin's got it. Scars from cutting, needles, surgery maybe, and things that look deliberate. Rituals? No. But it's more than I've seen on any person before. "There are two kinds of people around here: those that live in shit and those who shit every day, but pretend they don't. The filth is hard to ignore, even when you live on the bright side. Leave your cushy suburb, and you're bound to see something you never asked for. Profanity painted on the side of a building, someone imitating gore, a robbery you don't feel like you got any business stopping or how about a *domestic dispute* that's *their problem*. If you turn up the music and don't hear the calls for help, you can pretend you never heard them, never saw them, and you didn't do anything wrong for ignoring it all, yeah?" Another puff of smoke, he lets this one out slowly, smoke comes through his nose.

"Broken windows, broken bottles, rusted cage doors, and stripped cars. Abandoned houses and shut-down businesses make this city look like a crash-landed dream. Picture success and the promises the world makes you; we're what you get when you see through the illusion. We're not here because we suck on following through with an escape plan, it's just for some reason, we love this goddamn city that hates us." Ralph sets his cigarette in the ashtray on his desk and opens the drawer nearest to the floor. "A shrine to the dead."

He's at the end of his seat, reaching into the back of the drawer for something. Sitting back up with a smile, he's got a half-empty bottle of Hennessey in hand. Ralph throws a leg over the side of armchair's armrest while he twists the cap off the bottle. "What is it exactly? I dunno. Sometimes I think it's a death wish, but other times, I just think it's because it's what we're used to. I visited Virginia on tour. Couldn't fuckin' stand it, Richmond was the worst. Bunch of bougie assholes. Didn't belong there and I didn't need anyone to tell me that. I felt it." He brings the bottle to his mouth. "KC got it. This is our city, part of our identity. It's madness out there and when he doesn't..." Ralph laughs into the bottle of Hennessey, this time, he leans back, taking a long drink. He smiles into the bottle's lips again, mutters something, then shakes his head gently. "We can't stop the killing, but maybe slow it down a little. You talk to the Cogs? Humans are pretty fucked, you know?"

I'm biting my lip. I'm pretty sure the radio's playing in the other room—Maybe it's the one in the corner, but all the lights are off and I'm hearing too much bass. "I know," I say. "Worse when we're dead."

"Everything's worse when you're dead. But people still choose to come back." He gestures to me with the bottle. "It's an addiction."

"Unfortunately…" I glance at Jag. "There's always a reason to come back."

"One reason too many," Ralph says.

I swallow hard. My throat's so dry, it hurts. I'm close enough to reach over the desk and get the bottle from Ralph's hand, so I go for it. He lets it go, smiling out the side of his mouth while he reaches for his cigarette as a replacement. I take a shot of Hennessey. No one says anything. I put the bottle back down, take a step back, trip over Jag's steel-toed shoe, and fall into him. Since when was he so close? I stand upright. His hands are on my shoulders. They move down slowly as he lets me go.

"There're a lot of reasons to not check out," Jag says.

"Talking about Post Mortem?" Ralph says.

"No," Jag says.

Ralph picks up the bottle from his desk. He holds it in his lap, his hand tight around the neck. He takes the cigarette from his mouth and dabs it into the tray. Then, both his hands are on the bottle's neck, turning it in his lap and it's like I'm feeling those hands on my neck too. The bruises pulse with memory. I pull my head back, turn away while closing my eyes. Feelings and pain come from my insides, causing panic. Squeezing my hands, I hold back a hiss. "I want a way back to normal," I say.

"Resurrection?" Ralph says.

"A second chance. A little peace. Whatever. Can you do that?"

Ralph lowers his legs from the armrest. His head rolls, his eyes go with them and the liner around his eyes make the blue look brighter, almost supernatural in the same way Charon's eyes glow in the dark. For a second, that feeling of something strange seeps into the room. I don't know how to describe it. The eyes in the walls are coming out more, multiplying, living where I didn't see them before in photographs and shapes in the wooden desk, and the little hangy things made of string, even on the spines of books stacked behind Ralph. "The Cogs don't grant that kind of thing, really."

"What did you get for KC?" I say.

"Hm?"

"He's dead, yeah?"

"Yeah."

"What'd you do for him?"

Ralph purses his lips. He looks like he's thinking as he looks away. He takes a drink from the bottle. His lips curl up, he mutters something to himself that doesn't sound like English—and actually, it sends a chill down my spine, making me think of the gibberish I heard in the bar in Mortem. His fingers are long and slim. He sets the bottle down to pluck the bandanna off his head. With his hair free, he runs his fingers back through the black waves. The feather hanging from his ear grazes his neck from how low it hangs. His fingers drum against his thigh, he nods, and mutters something again like he's talking.

Jag mutters, "We should probably go before this guy loses it."

"That's everyone in this town, J. We're always one meltdown away from witnessing the worst moment of someone's life," I say. Even though I laugh, I'm looking for Jag's hand, slipping mine into his as tension builds and the impulse to run rams itself into my head with pain and pressure and insults I can't understand, but I feel in my heart. A weight drags my face down and I don't want to keep my eyes open or stand or everything about me says sit on the ground, rot, end, hope you disappear.

My hand tightens around Jag's. My legs wobble a little. Feeling him next to me might be the only thing keeping me standing. "Can you help me or not?"

Ralph flicks his tongue against his teeth. His lips purse. He stares over the desk at me; his eyes are definitely glowing, even if it's low, it's like there're white lines drawn around his irises, slits through his eyes that stop near the whites. His expression reads distant, and looking at him, a part of my head is telling me I don't know who I'm looking at anymore, that talking to him is dangerous while the normal part of my head reminds me this is my usual bartender, Ralph.

"Yeah." His tongue flicks again. "You're gonna need a heart to satiate the blood lust." He covers his eyes with his hand. Bottle on the desk, he leans forward, arching his back, pressing his hand harder into his face. "And for that, you'll need a couple of things. No promise, but bring me them and we'll see what the Cogs say, yeah?"

"Yeah." I exhale a slow, uneven breath. "What do you need?"

Ralph's hands slide down his face. The liner around his eyes drags with his fingers, looking more like blackened, wet tears than smears brought by touching. He looks past me, meeting Jag's glance. He chuckles, shaking his head. The chuckle fades. "Four things…"

"A virginal sacrifice one of 'em?" Jag says.

"Ah. You've done this before?" Ralph laughs.

"Every cultist wants blood," Jag says.

"Or semen." Ralph winks. "But blood is the oil of the heart. Unique to you, keeps you alive, and can bring back the dead. I know it's easy to forget just how important blood is when you throw yourself at the pavement, prefer scrapping, or give it away for free for some *karmic* goodwill—but that one, at the very least, should tell you there's a little more value in it than vital control. When you give someone your blood, you share your life with them," Ralph says. "Talk about borrowed time."

"So then blood *is* a requirement of your *ritual?*" Jag says. "How much?"

"We'll talk about that later," Ralph says. "For now, bring me these: feathers from a valravn, a vial of Lethe, and—"

"What's that? I say.

"In mythology, it's the water from the river that runs through Hades," Jag says. "The souls of the dead are forced to drink it which makes them forget what they've done, said, or suffered when they were alive."

"Pretty accurate, I'm impressed," Ralph says. "It smells sweet, but yeah, don't drink it."

"I'm supposed to go to Hades?" I say. "Where the hell is that in Mortem?"

"Sol might have some, but maybe she won't," Ralph says.

"And if she doesn't?" I lean against the desk with both hands. "Then what?"

Ralph shrugs, half-smiling. "Ask Sol."

"I fucking hate Sol," I say.

"That's an overreaction," Ralph says.

"Seriously?" I say. "Everything about her's fake. Everything she says is a lie and it doesn't matter how many times you ask, she pretends you don't know any better and waits for you to give up."

"But," Ralph raises his finger. "She says it in a nice way. So, there's that."

"That almost makes it worse." I don't know what's happening. A wave of something goes through me. My eyes blank out. I go off balance. I'm reaching blindly for anything to keep me standing while I'm stumbling back. Jag's hands are on my shoulders, then I'm sitting. My chest is tight and it's hard to breathe and my vision's going in and out and the room doesn't look like how I remember. It's dark and velvet and red and pulsing all at the same time. It can't be the sigils in everything. They mean something, right, but they shouldn't be affecting me. They've been there the whole time and I didn't feel anything before. Ralph never said they did anything like attack people either. A couple of clicks. I'm barely able to see it, but Ralph's tapping his fingers against the desk again. Muttering. The black tattoos on his arms almost look like they're moving or glowing black or something.

"Joey, what's up?" Jag says.

"I just had…" I exhale. "I think I'm hungry." I wipe my face. My hair sticks to my forehead. My fingers comb away the sweat. I wipe them on my pants. "What else do I need?"

Ralph licks the corner of his lips. "Ashes of lost time."

"How do I get that?" I say.

"Bring me a treasured memory. I'll do the rest."

My jaw tightens. "What is with the dead and cryptic shit?" I stand up. My vision goes spotty. I step forward and use the desk for balance. "First it's drowning in regret and now it's ashes and memories. Can you just be straightforward about what I need?"

Ralph shrugs. "I'm just translating what I'm told."

My skin's suddenly hotter than before. My face feels like it's on fire. My shallow breathing make the throb in my head worse until I'm sitting back down in one of the chairs before Ralph's desk. I swallow hard, give my head a small shake, hoping it pushes back whatever feeling's in my skin now making me feel dizzy. Its feeding the soft, foreign whisper deep in my ear. "When I've got everything, how long does it take for something to happen?"

Ralph's lips purse. He looks to one side, shifts to the same side of the chair, stacks his legs on top of each other, knee to knee. "It depends on how the Cogs feel—"

"Oh, great. *Feelings* are involved," I say through my teeth. "You know, people don't really like me much. Say I've got an attitude, rude, *immature*, whatever. 'Should've outgrown that angsty shit in high school, yeah? You're an adult now; act like it.' You don't want to know what the badges say to me."

"You are kind of standoffish," Ralph says.

I wipe my eyes. Look up at him. He's got a smile on his lips. He brings a new cigarette to them, still smiling as he takes the hit. When did he light up another one and can I get one too? "It's part of my charm." I lean back.

"I don't think *charm*'s supposed to chase people away." Ralph laughs; he stands, grabs the bottle of Hennessey off his desk, and tucks it into one of the drawers.

Suddenly, the room feels much smaller than it was. Crowded with smoke and booze and occult shit and band memorabilia, it should've always felt this way, but now it's feeling like something that's keeping me in place so Ralph can read me in ways I hoped Jag never could. I've always worn long sleeves and jeans to hide my skin like it'll betray the story of my life. Hood up, head down, I've wanted to avoid risking people seeing the shit I don't know how to hide. I'm backing away. Jag's hand's on my hips, which prompts him to step back with me until he hits the door and I run into him.

"The Cogs are evaluators. They stick with what they say and don't shift things often, especially for a dirtied soul. They... You'll want to keep your hands clean," Ralph says.

"What does that mean?" I say.

"Don't do what you did at the bar the other day. You might be dead, but your story's still being written to them. They're still watching, they're still—"

"Judging?" I say.

Ralph's lips purse again, but it's brief and twists into a smile. He pats down his pockets, looking for something.

149

I'm thinking cigarettes, but he stops looking when he finds his phone. "Not judging. They don't do that. They just… keep records, pass notes."

"So… Judging, but you say it prettier so you don't have to say it at all," I say.

"Still wouldn't call it judging." Ralph's eyes meet mine. The blue looks like it mixed with some red from something else and they're turning purple. "When you get those three things, feathers, Lethe, and memories, gimme a call and we'll do the next step. With something like this, the sooner we reach the Cogs, the better. Got it?"

My heart's throbbing, hurting my chest, waiting to burst. I put my hand on Jag's where he holds my hip. My fingers curl around his. "Got it," I say.

Jag's got the office door open. He's pulling me out gently, but just as soon as we're out of the office, I feel like running. Jag's hand's in mine. We run through the bar with KC watching from behind the counter. Jag's not dead weight, but keeping up the moment he feels me going and going and even when we get out the door, we're still running until we're down the street because I don't want to stop, even when we've already passed his car.

"Joey," Jag says.

My fingers loosen on his. I'm going to keep running without him. His hand won't let go of mine though. He stops. His strength is enough to pull me back. His arms go around me and I'm brought to his chest. The fall air feels much colder against my flushed cheeks.

"You told me you weren't involved with a cult," Jag says.

"I'm not in a cult," I say between pants. "Ralph runs a bar."

"And a back door business of, what, waking the dead?"

"I didn't know about this shit until, like, two days ago," I say.

"You're getting into some really bad shit, Joey. Cross,

the murders, now this? I need you to tell me what's going on."

I close my eyes and let his warmth wrap around me. I take in his smell, the cigarettes and musk and oil and 2-in-1 shampoo that smells like grass and granny smiths. How do you even get started on explaining something again that wasn't believable the first couple of times? When every explanation just leaves you looking crazier and crazier like you should be shut in a hospital and ignored for the rest of your life?

Nearby sounds from the highway echo. His breath makes my skin tingle. There shouldn't be chirping bugs, but that's what I hear and I'm thinking my mind's playing tricks on me. Then there's a loud caw. It echoes all around, hiding the direction it came from. Heat rushes to my face. My eyes open, vision already blurred with building tears as I think, *he's going to die*. I wipe them away before they can come out, acting like I'm tired instead. A chuckle covers whatever else threatened to come out in my voice. "Sorry, J… It's too late to do anything but something crazy. If it's too much for you, I understand. You don't have to stick around."

Jag doesn't say anything for a while. He also doesn't let me go. His slow breaths help slow mine and at that moment, I wish nothing would change. My heart goes from pounding to a gentle roll. I reach around him, looking for something to grab. That becomes handfuls of his shirt as I press my face into him. "I'm sorry," I say again.

"You don't have to be sorry." Jag strokes my back. "You just need to tell me what's going on and what the hell that bartender's talking about."

I step back. Jag's hold on me loosens, though he holds on as long as he can until I step out of reach. Two steps away and I'm turning on my toes to face him. "To be totally honest… I don't know. I don't know anything about fetishes or the Cogs or anything Ralph's talking about. I just… I don't know what else to do, but I have to do something for Cross and… I have to make sure that nothing happens to you."

"Nothing's going to happen to me, Joey."

I slowly shake my head. "I'm not sure about that, J."

"What did Cross say to you?"

"He didn't say anything. I just… There's a feeling."

A caw echoes off the street. I turn around. I have to find that stupid bird. It shouldn't be hard during the day. It's not dark, though it's cloudy. We're in a small residential neighborhood with a handful of random corner stores throughout. A bar, a salon, a liquor store three blocks away. Brick buildings, wires, an almost empty parking lot down the street. I turn around again. Jag's Mustang stands out so hard against the faded colors of the buildings in this neighborhood.

Another full circle.

I can't see any black birds.

I turn back to Jag, then it's there, standing on the electrical pole above Jag's car. Another fat one hangs on the wire coming off the electrical pole. Both stare down at Jag, one with its head twisted to the side. A black light moves through the sky like a wave from a lighthouse. It catches on the raven's eyes, turning them into rubies for a second. "You see that, J?" I point to the top of the electrical pole.

"What?" Jag follows my gesture.

"The ravens," I mutter like the birds will react if they hear me.

"Yeah."

"Really?"

"Yeah… Am I not supposed to?"

"You just had the hardest time seeing any of them last week. I felt like I was going crazy."

"To be fair, I didn't see any birds last week, but I'm

definitely seeing them now. Why?"

I close the space between us so I can run my hands up the front of Jag's shirt. My fingers barely catch in the fabric. I open my hand and grab again, getting a better grip on his shirt. "We need to go, J." I glance past him, checking on the ravens to make sure they didn't move or multiply. There are three of them now. Two on the electrical pole, one on the ground a few feet behind him. "And you need to go home."

"Yeah?" Jag says. "And where are you gonna go?"

"The fort."

"I don't understand—"

"And you don't have to come with me. In fact, it's probably better if you don't." My eyes lock with Jag's, but I'm not seeing totally straight. I'm not even thinking straight. Ralph's words echo in my head with reinforcements of impossibilities. Everything in my body's telling me to run so if something happens, I don't drag Jag down with me. My fingers itch from the cigarettes not in my pocket and I want to feel the bump of the skateboard under my feet while I fly down the street, music set to trash my ears while the cold stink of Bodymore wraps around me.

Jag scratches the back of his neck. He's looking at the sky, exhaling in exasperation with a groan. His lips part, he starts to say something, but stops too soon to know what. He rubs his eyes, then sighs again. He reaches for his ass pocket. He's got a cigarette and lighter in hand. The warm, red dot at the end of the stick feels like the only bit of warmth there is right now. Everything else is muted and distant.

A siren rattles through buildings blocks away. Jag comes to me. He grabs my wrist, lifting my hand. He slaps the cigarettes and lighter into my palm. "I told you, whatever shit you're going through, we'll figure it out together." He lets my wrist go and walks past me, making a beeline for his car.

I watch him, thinking I should start something with him so he drives off without me. I should run in the other direction; I shouldn't put him in the crosshairs of whatever's stalking him. The birds around us are four now. They follow Jag's every movement as he goes down the street. One jumps out of a tree and slowly follows him down the road. It's a blur against the pavement as my eyes water, turning into a streak of poorly smeared finger paints where the road marks should be.

"Joey?" Jag says. "You coming?"

"Yeah…" I pop a cigarette out of the carton and run to catch up. He's inside the car before I get there. I climb in. The Mustang's engine roars, then purrs. Jag puts the radio on low, filling the space where we don't say anything. I roll the window down a little, giving the smoke somewhere to go when I pluck the cigarette out of my mouth.

"I hope you know what you're doing, Joey," Jag says.

A chuckle bubbles in my throat. "Me too."

Jag laughs briefly. His hand leaves mine to go for the stick shift. Just as I'm thinking of slipping my hand between my thighs to keep them warm, he comes back. Somehow, the daylight's not doing him justice. The overcast and red blots out his features, turning his face almost into a blur of an outline like a ghost in the bar below. Water pools in my eyes again. I close them and sit in silence as I wait for us to hit the fort. I have to make sure I get into Mortem this time. Not just for Wayland, but to show Jag I'm not totally insane.

I need him to see the world of the dead and understand me when I say I'm one of them. I don't know what I'll do if I can't get us there because I don't think I can ask Jag to put up with me anymore if I'm actually totally insane.

NINE.

We got to Fort Armistead almost an hour after leaving the bar. The road's pretty clear, but it takes forever to get over the bridge. The sun's dipping, so the sky's turning red and blue and purple. It's that time of fall that when the sun starts going down, it's dark ten minutes from now—If that. There's only one sketchy car in the parking lot, bumper hanging, tape over the passenger side taillight. It's always a wager whether to park under a light or not. Without the spotty lot lights, there's a chance no one will see Jag's car and try to break in, but then the darkness hides any attempts that're made. Put the car under the light and it's easier to spot but it'll highlight when an asshole's trying to find something he can resell. Jag parks partially under the light. He leaves his doors unlocked because there's nothing of value in his car and he'd rather someone just open the doors instead of breaking a window or worse.

I check my phone for any messages from Wayland. Still nothing. I send him a message telling him I'll come see him as soon as he gives me a location. "Need to hear from you, Way," then my phone's back in my pocket.

The lights around the fort aren't that great. There are a couple spread out on the platform just patchy enough to make some of the graffiti look like demons hiding in the gaps. The wall that read HORROR IS WHAT HAPPENS

WHEN EVIL OVERTAKES THE HEART is now struck through with a red line. Underneath it reads, STFU SHAKESPEARE and I HATED THAT BOOK and GOD. Beside it reads BALTIMORE IS THAT HORROR SHOW, whatever that was referring to is gone now, washed over with gray and scribbles of other graffiti. Beside it reads WHEN'S IT START? And FRIDAY, MATINEE and THE FUCK DID YOU JUST CALL ME?" with a crudely drawn blood-dripping knife next to it.

Over each of the catacomb entrances, there's another single light, though the likelihood that they work is always a crapshoot. The one we're heading for is on, though it's buzzing with the threat to go off at any moment.

I'm going down the stairs to the catacombs holding Jag's hand. The trees rustle with soft clapping in the wind. I stop at the foot of the stairs. An energy pulses through me. I should go back to the car, drive off, don't look back. Something's telling me *you go in, you never get back out* and something else's competing by saying *you're not gonna get in. Doesn't work like that.*

I hold my breath to find the source of what I'm hearing. There's only the sound of nearby mumbling from someone in the brush. I keep holding my breath, then close my eyes to see if maybe I'll hear anything else. Something lands, a caw nearby, then another, then another. A small chorus of chuckling birds. My hands are clammy. Wiping my head with the back of my hand, my forehead's sweaty too.

Graffiti over the entrance reads TURN BACK in dripping neon green. Along the sides reads MISTAKE MISTAKE MISTAKE MISTAKE in black, sideways, framing the door from bottom to top and covering over old graffiti. My mind's racing. I'm sure I'm already hearing the organs that play in the tunnel to Mortem.

Something touches my shoulder. I jump, squeak, say

"fuck" under my breath. I turn around. Jag's standing close behind me. His lips pull back with disbelief. "We're not going into the catacombs, Joey," he says.

"You said you'd come with me."

"Right. But I didn't agree to a suicide pact."

"This is how we get in."

"Get in where?"

"The city of the dead." It sounds too crazy; I don't believe I even said it. "This is where you find the shit that's haunting Baltimore." I take his hand and try to pull him through the threshold of the entrance. The mud's wet. My feet sink a little into the leaves covering the mud. I keep going until I hit the concrete landing outside the door.

"It's not ghosts hiding in here." Jag follows my steps at the same pace.

On the ground beside the catacomb entrance is a mixture of trash. Needles, a plastic spoon, lighter, a used condom, an old bottle of Gatorade with something yellow in it. Not clear enough to be piss unless it's old, mildewing piss. The smell of soggy garbage, human stink, and decay blow through the doorway on an invisible breeze, accompanied by the mild scent of sulfur.

I can't stand still; I'm walking faster and faster, only held back by Jag's caution, so I nearly bounce in place to keep moving. I step back until I run into Jag. He's closer than I'm expecting. I turn around to face him. My free hand finds his and then I'm stepping back, tugging him deeper into the catacombs with me. He doesn't come, but stands firmly in place.

"I know I've been saying this a lot lately," Jag says. "But I don't think you're getting how insane you're being."

The inside of the arch reads TRUBEL over a mess of other graffiti. Shape over shape, a battle of Baltimoron brains trying to scream over one another to stake their claim on the cement. The anxiety quickly turns into laughter in my stomach. My fingers tingle from the rush and it's going through my arms, into my head, out my lips in short chuckles. I meet Jag's eyes. "Do you trust me?"

Jag looks at the sky. A deep breath, a sigh. "I'm not sure I do anymore." Still, he steps forward with me now, even though the tug's lighter than before.

"Trust me one more time then decide?" I say. "You're already here. What do you have to lose?"

Jag looks down my face then away. His lips pull to the side, pursed. "A lot, actually." He looks back at me.

There's another caw. A raven sits on a branch in one of the trees outside the fort, directly behind Jag. Fort lights catch on it; somehow, its form is little more than the shadow of a bird, but its eye glows red. It cocks its head to the side, looking like it's sizing Jag up, thinking of his flavor.

That's my sign. Go. Don't wait around to count seven of them licking their beaks and waiting to rip Jag's heart out. "I'll keep the dark away from you if you do the same for me."

The water fills my shoes the second we're through the threshold and with each step, my feet sink further into the muddy path.

The ground squishes even though it shouldn't, even though the floor's made of cement. Someone's bringing mud or there's too much garbage floating in the water that it acts like a second floor in some places. I take out my phone and turn the light on. Jag's holding his phone up too, flashing the light in front of us. The original pale cement seeps through breaks in graffiti. TURN THE FUCK BACK stands out against the colorful scribbles too messy to read. Dick jokes, dick drawings, boobs on women with horns and no faces, the random Bible verse countering the calls for oblivion, murder, destruction. REPENT. The random 666 next to HE'S COMING FOR YOU and someone else's GLOCKED AND LOADED BITCH, TRY ME. A pair of bloodshot eyes with bullets for pupils accompanies the phrase. The sound of water rolls off the walls, almost making our steps echo like tides moving in. Metal crackles underfoot. Something slim rolls up my ankle, catches in my shoelaces.

"Whoa!" Jag's voice echoes. His arms are around me. His chest bumps into my shoulder while his phone hits the ground with a crack, pop, at least it's not a splash, right?

I brace myself against him to right myself. "Thanks." I pat his arm. His leather jacket's smooth and cold and I wish he wasn't wearing it so I could feel him instead.

"This is pretty damn bad, Joey," Jag says.

"It could be worse," I say.

Jag's cellphone landed face-down and the light fills the corridor we're in. It casts shadows along the floor until it cuts off with a sharp right turn. On the wall in front of us is graffiti like a crime scene; a chalk outline in bright yellow of a body in a mangled shape, blood splatter in the head, and a box of matches lying outside the line. The phrase LA LA LA LA wraps underneath the body tape. A little further down the wall reads, I CAN SEE YOU DYING.

Jag grabs his phone from the ground with a quiet, "Ugh. I think my phone just got Hep B." He points the phone at the ground. By his feet is a needle head and a used condom, blue, thick at the end.

"Gag." I say.

"How many junkies you think are hiding down here right now?

"I'm hoping none. It's kind of cold tonight."

"Yeah... but realistically, how many you think? There's no way this place's empty."

"Realistically?" I glance back at him. "Maybe three. But don't worry. The compound's pretty big. We'll probably never run into 'em and if we do... You can shove me their way and run."

Jag chuckles, fast, short. "Do I sound worried?"

I laugh softly. "Not at all." I'm not sure if I'm actually hearing something in the water. Memories from the last week flash through my mind. The couple disappearing into the catacombs, the thing chasing me through the darkness, running, the labyrinth, the corpses waiting for me outside. Now that I know it was Wayland, I shouldn't feel like this, but he's just one ghost and at this point, I almost assume half the population of Baltimore's already dead. We'd be better off otherwise, right?

I'm careful going around the corner. Jag bumps into me. Not hard. He flips the light around the corner and looks before I do.

"Clear," he says.

On the wall's a crudely drawn bathtub, bloody handprints run down the side, across the ground. Real handprints. Bold words read LEAVE BEFORE THEY HARVEST YOUR CORPSE next to a poorly drawn version of BPD insignia and the words YOU'RE WORTH MORE DEAD wrapped around the badge.

My feet are cold, my skin is freezing. I'm shivering under my hood. At least that's how I excuse the shaking. I'm reaching back for Jag until my fingers find his arm again. My hand slides down his sleeve until I get his hand. It's so much warmer than I'm expecting. His fingers curl around mine in response. "Scared?" he says.

I laugh again; my breath catches in my throat. I look away. "Will it convince you to stay if I say kinda of a little, yeah?"

Jag snorts.

The corridor opens into the larger fort room with the long slab in the middle of it. A table. A shelf. A sacrificial table where any poor fuck too unfortunate to be pulled in here by themselves and forgotten might end up. The light's not enough to show if the water's pooling under the bottom of the slab has a tinge of red. It's dirty and stains drain down the sides unevenly, but still, it could be mud or shit or piss or wasted refinements left from someone's last bottle.

Jag's light sweeps the room. A puddle in the corner looks silver for a second. My body's immediately hot. Memories of the pain of the river strike through me and that pain quickly turns to rage, gripping Jag's hand tighter. I'm breathing harder, pulling him along now and I don't know where I'm going exactly, but I need to be moving.

"Fuck," My voice echoes again. "Fuck." I kick a crushed water bottle down the hall. It wasn't empty and its contents spray down the soil and cement. The smell of rancid piss is strong.

"Joey—"

"Sorry," I say. "It's just… I don't know how to explain it right now." I laugh to release the tension. "I thought maybe it was just MP, but it's here too." I'm stuttering over my words when I shouldn't be, sometimes my thoughts go completely out of my head and I'm forgetting where I am. The air smells sweet now with the sulfur. At least a little. "You smell that, right?"

"The sewer?"

"No." My foot slips on something like I've stepped on ice. I catch myself against the wall.

"You okay?" Jag turns to me.

"Yeah. Fine. It's just… algae or something." My phone illuminates the wall behind me. My fingers press against the bloody handprint so much bigger than mine. It smears brownish-red over otherwise gray cement. Nails scratch desperately into the stone in an escape that shouldn't be. Beneath it is the phrase NEVER SATISFIED written like it was finger painted. I pull back; my palm stings, searing with a soft burn. My heart pulses in my fingertips. "Let's keep going. I think we're almost here."

Further down the corridor is the phrase BLEED MORE, BODYMORE painted in red. Underneath it says CRY MORE, BITCHES and beside that PLEAD, BABY,

PLEAD. There's a painted building, broken in half by the second story with jagged teeth tearing out from where the windows should've been and a pile of bodies is hastily going into its open mouth.

"I didn't know people came in this far to paint," Jag says.

"You'd be surprised how deep it goes…" I say.

Still, the graffiti's getting less and less the deeper we go. If the path to Mortem is the same every time, then the lesser the paint, the closer we are. I just don't know how to break through. If there even is a way to break through without trying.

A chill goes down my spine. It snakes under my shirt. My skinnies are columns of ice against my legs. I'm running before I'm thinking. The light bounces around the corridor. I'm pretending I can see better than I do so I can keep running while J's like, "Whoa—Joey—Where—" and instead of fighting me, he's coming along. Misfit puddles splash under my steps. Ahead of us is a dead end created by a collapsed passageway. Around the bottom edge of the stone is a couple attempts at blue fire reading HOME OF HADES, NO ESCAPE, and DEVOUR \ YOUR CALM where a crack runs between the words.

I don't remember any of that from the last time I was here. I guess maybe I wasn't looking hard enough. I was running. Or maybe someone else has been down here since. The broken stones look right, though the entrance looks smaller than the one I escaped through before. I'm letting go of Jag's hand to climb inside, shimmying to fit. I can get through, but I'm not very big; Jag might get stuck.

"Joey," Jag says, the implication in my name is, "Don't fucking go in there. Christ, what the hell are you doing?"

"Follow me and find out." I press into the wall. "I need you. If I say that, does it help?" The stone mutes my voice this time. No more echoing, but flattening. It disappears, gone the second it hits the stone, and almost muffled coming out of my mouth. I'm on the other side of the rocks. It's elevated and jumping down from it, the water's halfway up my calf. The chill's climbing up my thighs. There's no scuffling of shoes or swearing and J's not saying anything anymore. I reach for my cigarettes, popping my lips, giving me something to do to try and calm my nerves. I take my phone out instead. Light on, I point back at the rocky entrance. "J?" My teeth chatter, my hand shakes, making the light bounce. The scattering illumination makes my nerves worse. My hair's clinging to my forehead. Hot and cold at the same time. I step back into the entrance. "You there, J?"

I don't see him.

He should've been obvious.

The tunnel's not *that* long, but looking in with the light, it's acting like it goes on a while, like there's a sharp turn, like that's not what I went through. I check the water at my feet. It feels so much higher than it is. My pant legs are wet up to my thighs. Something splashes behind me. I spin around. Light reflects off the flooding water. It's more black than brown. Another splash comes from behind me.

I spin again, step back, grab my mouth. "Holy shit, J."

His foot hits the water as he comes out of the hole, carefully moving to fit through the passage. His lips curl. "Shit, that's cold," he says.

"Glad you made it." I pat him on the shoulder. "For a second there, I thought you got lost."

"Don't be so sure we aren't."

I turn back toward the corridor. "We're fine." My voice is weaker than it should be. "Probably." The spill from Jag's phone light betrays nothing, but a long, straight path and pale walls. There're no turns, no trash, no graffiti except a simple YOU WALKED IN THE CORRIDOR in black on the left. A little further down, the wall reads YOU CHOSE THE DARK on the right. The flooded path turns to complete darkness where you can't tell the floor from the walls from the water from anything else; the light becomes meaningless. I look over my shoulder to find Jag, but the dark's even taken him from me. I reach back to find him with my hands. My fingers bump his arm. I latch onto him, telling myself it's so he can't get lost again, but knowing it's for me and I need him.

Then there's a soft whisper; I'm not sure if it's in my head or if something from the water, Mortem, and whatever connections this place has to the afterlife. I exhale hard. A smile curls on my lips. My grip on Jag tightens. "You trust me, yeah?"

Jag looks down at me. In that barely lit space, I can make out his face just enough to see that his eyes aren't soulless when they meet mine. He smiles, laughs, both fall flat. "Would I be here if I didn't?"

"You were always a good sport, Jagger."

He looks like he's going to say something, but he doesn't and I'm stepping back, pulling him forward with me. I turn around. Run. The water splashes hard and fast. The glowing dots in the distance become clearer the closer we get. It's not a figment of my imagination.

"The hell is that?" Jag says.

Laughter bubbles in my throat before the word comes out. "Fear."

Fuck.

I'm becoming like them.

Cryptic.

Fear doesn't make sense, but it's what the wall says. Though the graffiti outside the fort's changed, the inside hasn't. I don't know how long we're running until the gray corridor reads FEAR in glowing green paint. More water's dripping around us, coming down the sides of the walls like there's a leak somewhere. With the mild glow, it's not black. It's got a red tint to it, not thick enough to be blood though. The paint catches in the slim streams coming down the walls, amplifying the glow like radioactive tears.

Fear trails down in green, red, blue, orange, and yellow. Everything's glowing spray paint until the corridor's lit.

"What the hell—" Jag's panting. "How—How are we—Where are we?"

"*Hollow Death.*" I laugh. The words make my skin tingle. We're still running. Now, I'm not even sure my feet are touching the ground, though I feel myself moving.

The corridor's never-ending. The walls are almost entirely covered with tears from fear.

The temperature drops so much, I can see my breath, but the water's not turning solid.

I slide on something in the water. Jag pulls me into his body. He's slipping too, but I'm held against him now, arms constricting tightly as we fall back together. The ceiling reads FEAR FEAR FEAR FEAR and over it in black are the words LONELY? and WELCOME HOME. The cold water hits my back, fills my shirt, and makes my clothing stick to my body like a frozen layer of skin. My head's throbbing. Jag's heat burns through my clothing, too hot to touch.

The pounding throb is so much harder than before.

It's not mine.

I hold my breath.

Darkness surrounds me.

Then, there's the dead. Skulls and bones stare from the sides as we fall through an abyss too wide to touch the walls. I couldn't, anyway, even if I wanted to. Jag's arms only grow tighter as he mutters, "I've got you."

It's not like the first time I came. I'm not screaming, but chuckles snake out of me. My body can't choose whether it's hot or cold as everything freezes and burns at the same time. Organ music plays in the distance. Soft procession. Church music? A grinder? A circus? None of it made sense last time. Then there's the chanting.

Monks. Prayer. Latin. I don't know.

My vision goes blurry. I'm not sure how or when it

happened, but I'm facing Jag and my arms are around him too. I bury my face in his chest, eyes closed tight. His head presses down near my crown. My head fills with a voice that's not mine, thoughts I can't hear beyond the panic coming through their feelings. I'm overwhelmed with things I can't process. Cackles surround me, echoing from one side of the abyss to the other. They build and build and build until my ears blast out and then all at once, there's nothing.

Like a bubble popping.

Pain, guilt, fear, anger.

It's all gone and there's only absolute silence left.

TEN.

My head's throbbing when my senses come back. The soft sound of organs and drums sing a lullaby in the distance. I'm trembling and cold, my body's so heavy, I don't know if I can even move. My eyes open slowly and shut again before I see much beyond the dark, purple sky. I force them open a second time. Black spots threaten to blind me again. Everything feels like I've been woken up too early after staying up too late drinking and I'm not sure where I am or what I'm doing or if I'm still in a dream or having a hangover so bad, my house is literally upside down. Touching the ground, my fingers slide against something hard and warm. The tendon between the bone-like walking path. I find a firm place on the stone and enough strength to push myself up.

A riff of a distant electric guitar sends a shiver down my spine.

The revitalized version of Old Town Mall stands around me with Post Mortem on my left and the glowing Cavae Mortem sign on my right. Faceless ghosts filter in and out of the surrounding buildings like they've got somewhere to be. Maybe it's just this foreboding feeling of *get it done now because your chance ends soon* and without being able to think of what that means, they run between Kaufman's and FIT and WATCH THIS and disappear in Lodgings across the street.

"Holy shit…" I press my hand to my head. "I can't believe it worked." I get to my feet.

A deeper groan grabs my attention.

Jag.

Sitting up, he rubs the back of his head saying, "What the hell happened? And "Joey, you okay?" and then "Where the hell…?"

"I'm fine, J. Good, even. You?"

He's already on his feet. Even when standing, he falters back half a step, catches himself, and stands upright. "I, uh… I don't know." He looks around, spending decent time taking in each building with a mixture of suspicion and confusion until he's rubbing his eyes, looking again, and growing a more confused look on his face.

The feeling I had the last time I was here is back. The mute and hollow party of Mortem takes over. My throat's dry. I lick my lips. The thirst for unending alcohol is coming fast, accompanied by a mental invitation to the bar.

I draw my phone out of my pocket. The screen's black and it won't turn on no matter how many times I hold the button down. I'm not sure if it's dead or waterlogged, gone for good or blocked by whatever walls try to keep the dead underground.

"Where exactly are we?" Jag says.

"Hell." I tuck my phone away, trading it for my soggy cigarettes. Doesn't matter. The water at least doesn't ruin them once you get here.

"Funny, Joey, but I'm being serious."

"Me too." A flame licks the end of my cigarette and I take advantage of the first hit while holding the box.

Jag eyes the Old Kaufman's, the Salon on the corner, and the lighthouse where the fire station should be. The black light swings through the sky, spreading the purple and glowing red around the beam.

"*Where are we*, Joey?" Jag says. The way he walks, he's

barely picking up his feet, legs stiff.

"*Cavae Mortem.*" I point to the sign at the entrance of Old Town Mall. Strings of working festival lights flash around the words.

Jag looks the sign over, then me, then the sign, then me again. "I still don't know what that means."

"Great, right?" I rub my eyes. "Pretty much the same kinda welcome I got the first time I was here."

A kid who doesn't look old enough to even be in middle school steps through the courtyard, jumping from stone to stone, avoiding the cracks. A ponytail, jeans, pink shirt with a horse on the front. She makes her way out of the courtyard and toward lodgings, laughing and talking to someone no bigger than she is. The worst thing about this place is knowing everyone's dead, but at least there's a silver lining in that everyone's done with the worst life's got to offer, right?

"You know how when you die, you're supposed to go somewhere, J?" I say.

"You mean limbo?" He looks around again then back at me. "When you die, you go to Old Town Mall? Really?"

"Sort of." I follow his glance this time. "Apparently. They told me this is the rest of forever when I got here, but then a reaper told me judgment's over there." I point down the street to where the festival lights of Old Town Mall can't reach, where the mist eats the smaller businesses, broken concrete, and what used to be Peter's. I'm pretty sure I'm hearing drilling come from somewhere. A distant high-pitched scream.

Almost a scream.

Distorted by something in the air.

It's horror, not a scream.

There's no other way to describe it.

"Who exactly is *they*?" Jag says.

"The bartender." I turn toward the bar.

Jag stuffs his hands into his pockets.

Another puff from my cigarette and I feel like I've taken some kind of drug. My head's swaying gently. I look at the sign for Lodging's, thinking it might be nice to turn in for a bit. I wonder if the room would look like Jag's or mine back home.

The courtyard air smells like alcohol and something a little sweet. Nothing's on my mind, but wasting time. I feel like I came here for something, but if I think too much, it's like a bucket of water washing off the sidewalk chalk.

My sneakers squeak, turning against the warm, bony ground.

The sign for POST MORTEM hangs from the building with columns made of arms and rib cages. Fingers hold the patio roof up. The reason I'm here comes back.

Pinching my cigarette between my lips, I grab my phone to try the power again. Nothing.

Without saying anything, I make a beeline for the bar. I've got to get in before everything's kicked out of my head again. It wasn't that long ago that I was here, but it feels like I've got holes in my memory, some of the recent past is wiped already. "Shit…" I mutter into my cigarette. "Jag?" Even his name feels foreign to me.

"Yeah?" he says.

I jump. Turn around. He's standing behind me. It's only seeing him that gives me the meaning to his name again. Then, everything about him comes back and so is the phrase Baltimore, the house, my dad, Wayland.

Something's wrong with me.

"Sorry—Was having a moment," I say.

"How hard you hit your head?" Jag takes me by the arm and pulls me to him.

I won't look him in the eye. He won't let me turn away. Fair.

"I don' think I bumped my head," I say. "You're not having trouble remembering anything, though?"

"I don't know where the hell we are, but that's pretty

much it."

"It's Cavae Mortem, the city of the dead… or the holding cell, I guess. Limbo. Whatever you want to call it." I pull away from Jag and make my way through the bar. Sol stands behind the counter, filling a glass. The foam reaches the top, the liquid's clear, amber, bubbly. She sets it right in front of me as I climb onto the stool.

"Welcome back, Joey," she says. "How many times is this now?"

"You got a punch card to stamp?" I sit down.

"What's that?" Sol says.

"Prizes after so many visits." I reach for the mug.

"Oh." Sol laughs. Short, forced, fake. She's just as bad at this now as she was last time I was here. "The Cogs don't want to encourage repeat visitors."

"Dad?" Jag's voice comes from behind me. He comes up beside me fast, his focus on Sol.

"That's not your dad, J," I say.

"It looks like my dad—"

"But she's not. She's just some spirit bitch whose only purpose is to lull you into a false sense of security by wearing the faces of people you know until the reaper. Comes. Her favorite methods are alcohol and small talk—which sounds pretty sketch now that I say it out loud."

"Would you let me do my job?" Sol says.

"He's not dead," I say.

Jag's not paying attention to me. He takes a seat at the bar, still watching Sol. My jaw tightens; I'm almost tempted to tell her to make herself look like Jag's dad for me too, just to give me a chance to see what Jag sees, who he misses, what he thinks of when he thinks of his dad. I never got to meet him. Jag said he died in a car accident, drunk, but not much more than that. He doesn't like to talk about it beyond saying his dad was a good guy who struggled to take back his life sometimes.

"What are you doing here?" Jag says to Sol.

"Well," Sol says slowly, "and I really hate this part…" She leans onto the counter. "But you're dead, Jagger and this is the rest of forever—"

"He's not dead!" I slam my hands onto the counter.

"What do you mean he's not dead? He's here—" Sol says.

"Same song, different chorus. We cheated the system, Sol." I lean back, crossing my arms. "You guys need to get that little glitch fixed if you really don't want this to keep happening."

"I don't know what you're talking about," Sol says.

"You're such a goddamn liar. It would actually be kinda funny if you weren't so fucking obvious." A growl comes out. "You know this isn't the rest of forever. Stop telling people that."

Sol reaches under the counter for a mug. She fills it and sets it in front of Jag. Immediately, I grab it and toss it at the shelf behind the counter. It disappears into nothing before it can collide with anything. I tip over my glass sitting in front of me. The liquid spills out; the counter absorbs it. Sol looks at the nothing mess, crosses her arms, and lets out a sigh. For the first time, there's some fragment of emotion. Irritation, annoyance, 'I'm so done.' She wipes it back into a smile, but crosses her arms too. "What else am I supposed to tell people?" she says. "Oblivion? I'm not gonna tell anyone they're going to judgment soon. They'll run, they'll cry, they'll beg and resist. If not here, then when the reapers come and then you just make everything worse."

"After, judgment…" Jag's saying slowly. He leans back, looking at Sol again. Down, up, down. "And you're not my dad?"

"I am whoever you need to see right now," Sol says.

"What do you see?" Jag says to me.

"I look like her mother," Sol says.

"Shut the fuck up, Sol." I slide off the barstool. It's

fine. I'm getting antsy anyway. I reach for Jag, grabbing onto his arm to urge him off the seat. "We came here for something specific. You know someone named Ralph Reagan?"

Sol purses her lips. She turns away, grabs a rag from under the counter, and wipes it down furiously. There's nothing on it, but she's walking down the bar to get away. I follow her. "You know it's not in my authority to speak of other souls. Death vengeance and all is pretty messy, you know?"

"He isn't dead," I say.

"That makes the questioning worse," Sol says.

"It's not anything bad. Probably. He's into culty shit, runs a bar on the topside with a ghost friend from his band who definitely died a couple years ago. Murder, suicide, I don't know—"

"You'd be surprised at how consistently musicians are here," Sol says.

"Overdoses?" I say.

"Misery's got a lot of ways to kill." Sol tosses the rag over her shoulder. Her head dips to one side. "Musicians die violently a little more often than the average, one way or another. Self-imposed deaths are brutal, though. Makes the regret higher."

"Torment makes artists, right? What's new there?" I sigh. "I'm not here to talk about that though. I only bring him up because he told me to get Lethe from you and something tells me that if I don't name drop, you'll pretend you don't know what I'm talking about again."

"Lethe?" Sol says, suddenly looking startled. She steps back from the counter. "I'm not sure what that is."

"You're not doing this to me again," I say.

"What?" Sol says.

"Did the *Cogs* program you to do anything other than lie?" I say.

The smile on Sol's face falters. Maybe, for the first

time, she looks more human than the approximation she tries to portray. There's still something in her face though. Her eyes are glossy, wide, too focused, too bright and blank. The smile comes back. "I don't know why you insist I'm always lying—"

"Let's start with how you're always wearing someone else's face and end with you telling me I was dead when I wasn't. From the start, everything with you's been one fabrication after another," I say.

"I'm making you more comfortable in your circumstances," Sol says.

"Yeah. By *lying*."

"Everyone else down here accepts it." Sol's hands flatten on the counter. "Why don't you?"

"Because I haven't given up yet." I climb back onto the bar step. My hands slap into the counter to get Sol's attention. She complies and doesn't say anything. I step away from the stool. I reach for my cigarettes, but stop after feeling the box through my pocket. "I'm not trying to be difficult or cause a problem, Sol. I just came for some Lethe. Tell me where it is and I'll leave."

Sol slowly leans against the counter. I swear her lips are moving. She's muttering something to herself, but it's so quiet and I don't understand any of it. Her head drops forward. She pops her lips. "I don't have any Lethe. Sorry."

"Okay, then where do I go to get it?" I say.

"You can't get it," Sol says.

"Why not?"

"Because it's hidden in Caedis Silvis. One direction leads to judgment and the other to…" Sol stares for a moment, expressionless, like she stopped working, Sol ejected from her body. "The only way I receive it is from *messengers* passing through. Souls can't traverse the forest without a guide. So, sorry, but you're not getting any." Her voice kicks up again with optimism. She shrugs.

"Not good enough," I say.

"I don't know what you want me to say," Sol says.

"I need Lethe—"

"I'm trying to help you—"

"No, you're fucking not."

Sol takes a breath. The smile's gone again and it's not coming back. Her face isn't replacing with the customer service look she's been wearing all this time. The music in the bar changes. The soft rock shifts to something off-key and flat. It's not that they can't play very well, it's that whoever is playing knows how to play in a way that hurts to hear. The guitar's picking goes high-pitch, fast, and screeching off-key notes at scattered intervals leave me feeling anxious. "Stay out of the forest. Forget about the Lethe."

"Thanks for the tip, Sol, but that's not gonna work for me." I step back, looking for Jag without *looking* for him. My back hits his chest; I step on his toes. He grabs my shoulders, stabilizing me.

"You okay, Joey?" he says "You look like you're gonna be sick."

"Sorry." I wince. "Do you hear that?"

"The band?" Jag says. "They're pretty good."

"That's not what I'm hearing." I hold onto his arm. The sound's making me dizzy; it's harder to keep my eyes open or move or feel motivated to do anything at all. "Sol. Outside." I let go of Jag to stumble my way toward the door. I can't stay here anymore. I don't realize how hot it is inside until I get outside and the cool air in the Mortem courtyard slaps against me. I turn around to Jag saying, "Your face is hella red, Joey."

I reach for my cigarettes. "Yeah, yeah, gimme a minute." I take one out and light it while I'm looking for Sol, but she's not in the door, not mixed into the tables, not anywhere behind me. I continue to back away from the bar, watching for her, trying to get far enough away that the shitty musicians inside can't affect me anymore. My head's throbbing, not enough to hurt, but enough to break off anything I'm trying to think. I keep going until I've stepped out of the Old Town Mall courtyard and am in the street between it and Lodgings.

Like stepping through a portal, all the noise from the Old Town Mall courtyard is gone. The movement's gone. The people walking from building to building are gone and it appears as an empty, but brightly lit courtyard. I sigh. Another nicotine hit. A cackling caw cracks through the silence. I jerk back around, scanning everything from the courtyard to the streets to the darkness toward the forest for any sign of Val. Building to building, window to window, roof to roof, there's nothing. Static light from the wig shop-turned-glass-window full of TV screens distorts the storefront in black and white pixels. Something in the back of my head's telling me to go to bed, wait it out, have a good time. What's sex like in the underworld? The sign outside of Lodgings says WHY ARE YOU SO ANXIOUS?

"You'd get it if you were me," I say.

"What?" Jag says.

"I don't know. I think I'm going crazy. Do you see Sol anywhere?"

"No."

I'm not waiting anymore. I lock onto the forest down the street, where the bleeding town lights turn off and turn into the beaten up, rusted metal door of Peter's. The purple mist disturbs everything past that, trying to hide the trees of Caedis Silvis and the sharp roots breaking through the cement. Slowly, I'm getting closer and the compulsive feeling to get away presses into my back, urging me to stay back. The air's thick, like walking through water. A soft bell rings in my ear the closer I get to the trees. Signs hanging in the abandoned strip read DON'T and STOP, becoming more frequent the closer I get until they turn into voices in my head talking over each other incomprehensibly.

The voices aren't mine.

I can't help but think it's some other creature like Sol, but not her. Something made of the feelings that hide behind the words in the way you don't have to understand what someone's saying in another language to feel their raw emotion.

This place likes to use perception as a toy, keeping everyone under control. Baltimore's enough of a mess, but can you imagine if the bloodthirsty, vengeful, full of resentment dead of Baltimore fell out of their slumbering state and knew they were dead already? If they were aware they were murdered by some other fuck who slithered his way out of judgment and the powers that be just let him go? There'd be fuck-all anyone could do to stop the rage that fueled the screams of, "How the hell did I turn up here?" Every buried Baltimoron isn't gonna need to jump into the river to turn Mortem into the average Baltimore neighborhood we're used to. All it would take is to shut off whatever's in the air that mutes our emotions. Maybe if you got worked up enough, you could overpower the thing holding this place together. I go through a catalog of shit that makes me angry to try and work myself up, but everything I think is pulled from my head before it makes me feel anything. My body turns into a mixture of panic and contentment, never fully giving in to either.

BURN IT UP is carved into the side of a tree. FALL IN thinly shows on a neighboring tree. Then, one at the front of the forest reads DADDY and LET ME GO, more desperately cut into the bark than the others.

Something inside me's acting like a magnet hitting a negative. My body feels propelled from the forest and I'm fighting against the current to get closer. My chest throbs louder; my vision spots black.

"Jo, I'm here," his voice comes, no louder than a

whisper.

"Wayland?" Goosebumps form on my skin.

"What?" Jag's suddenly beside me and I don't know where he came from. "Cross is here?"

"You didn't hear that?" I say.

"I didn't hear anything that sounded like Cross," Jag says.

I don't know if I believe him because the sound was so clear, it was like he was standing next to me. Something tickles my arms. It feels like a hand. "Wayland?" My voice goes flat. I turn around to look for him. He's not in the streets. Back in the forest, I search for him, between the trees, but I can't see that far—or that well. "You in there?" I step off the concrete. A root grabs my foot. I step into the squishy forest ground. My foot sinks and the wetness in the mud quickly seeps through my canvas shoes.

Jag grabs me by the arm. "Where are you going? You heard what that thing that looked like my dad said." He pulls me back, but just as fast as he's got my arm, he's letting go, shaking his head, and rubbing his eyes. "What the hell?" he mutters.

"What?" I don't want to hear him say what I'm thinking.

"I'm... not sure." He grabs my arm again and keeps pulling me back, hard and fast, dragging me with him. With a bit of distance, he releases my arm and refocuses on the trees, searching from one to the next like something's hiding from him. "But the closer I get, the less I can see and it's hella cold."

"That's the Liquor," Sol says.

"Shit," Jag says.

He and I turn around. Sol's standing on the sidewalk across the street. Her arms cross like she's trying to make herself smaller, shoulders pushed in. She's not looking at either of us.

"What about the voices?"

Sol nods toward the trees. "Those are the echoes. They come out in the Liquor."

"Okay…" My voice is sharper than I mean for it to be. I can't help it when every goddamn creature in the godforsaken afterlife can't be bothered to say things straight. Everything's coded language you're expected to already know. I'm standing in front of Sol, tossing my lit cigarette to the pavement. Stepping on it to put it out, the butt's already gone. Disappeared. I rub my eyes. "But what does that mean, Sol?"

"It…" Sol glances behind her, to the abandoned strip, then to the forest. Her expression melts into observation of the trees. "I don't know how to describe it to you. Echoes just live in Caedis Silvis. I think the Liquor brings them out. Both are meant to keep spirits from wandering. I don't know what else they would be connected to."

"How do they do that?" I say.

"Inebriation on antiquity," Sol says.

My hands curl into fists. The slight build of anger's strangled out instantly, leaving me feeling restless instead. I pant through my teeth. "Can you be direct, for, like, once, Sol?"

"I really don't know what it means," Sol says. "Inebriation is outside of anything I understand and I can't go anywhere nearer than this—"

"You operate a *bar* and *inebriation is outside of your understanding*?" I stare at her, waiting for an answer. Nothing comes. "You're such a shit liar." I turn back to the forest. A couple steps toward it, I stop as the current from it presses against me again. "You said *something* brings you Lethe from here? When do they show up?"

"Whenever they like," Sol says.

"Great…" I rub my face. "I don't have time for this." I'm going back toward the forest, walking faster this time so the momentum's harder to stop by whatever force is trying to persuade me to turn around.

"Joey—Stop." Jag grabs me by the arm. "You're being an idiot."

"Sorry—I don't know how to be anything else, J." I laugh, pulling my arm away from him. I turn on my heels, step backward so I can watch him as I go. "But hey, sometimes idiots get shit done, yeah?"

"Yeah, sure, but if something happens to you, what about the people that care?"

Heat goes through my body. For the first time, I'm grateful to whatever creature's out there muting things so I can't second guess what I'm about to do out of shame or embarrassment or fear. "That's why you gotta wait here for me. Send out a body crew if I'm not back in forty-five?" My lips curl into a half-smile. My eyes are stinging, the mist wraps around me and darkens the streets of Mortem rapidly. I'm barely on the sidewalk by the forest, but I feel so far away.

"Why forty-five minutes?" Sol says.

"Lucky number, I guess." I turn around and make a run into the trees, hoping to get ahead of Jag enough that he can't try to stop me and he doesn't dare follow.

"Joey!" He's coming toward the trees. I know it when the Liquor hits him because he groans, curses, and steps back again.

"Don't go in there," Sol says. "I don't... Echoes do not return the living. Really... they don't return anything."

"I can't let her go in there," Jag says.

"Without a reaper, there's nothing we can do. If you go in unguided, you will become lost."

And that's the last I hear from them before the absolute darkness of Caedis Silvis takes over, turning the air mute, burning my nose with sulfur and sweetness, and chilling my skin so much it hurts like I'm being pricked by a million needles. Everything around me's black. The ground's sinking under my steps, my feet get deeper and deeper, like I'm being pulled into the earth and it's harder to lift my feet. My hands are my guides, feeling a branch or tree and taking me around it. The longer I go forward, the fewer the trees become.

ELEVEN.

There's nothing left of Jag or Sol or Old Town Mall. The cawing birds hiding around Mortem are silent and still. My panting doesn't make a sound. There's no bubbling mud or splashes from the muck sinking under my feet, even though it crawls around the edges of my shoes and dampens my socks and climbs my pant legs. The trees have come back as purple outlines against a black backdrop, often still only half visible. The twigs on the ground aren't the right color and they look more like bones, discolored from age. The discolored sky's visible through fans of branches and leaves, giving spotlights of red streams, cutting slits in the darkness.

The air's become so thick, I can't breathe. I have to force it. Every exhale is too heavy and makes me feel sick and light-headed. God. I choke when the breath finally comes through. My arms are throbbing. It feels like Dad's hands are still on me. My face's throbbing too. I think he punched me, I don't know, maybe thirty minutes ago?

Fuck.

The sound comes back first. A soft river brook mutters down the road. Then one of the faulty streetlights buzzes, buzzes, buzzes... coming on forever down the street. It flickers with optimism that it's somehow going to make it through the night. "No, dude. You're gonna get punched out, as per usual," I say.

I stop walking.

I wasn't expecting to hear my voice.

The winding street's slowly taking form. Then the shadow of bushes and long branches blocking off the metal dividers separating the street from the path. My eyes are throbbing and wet. My left knee feels like I smashed it into something. I'm holding my board in my left hand and a six-pack of Natty Ice in my right. One of the bottle's is already gone. I kick a plastic bag. Squishy. Surrounded by flies. I tell myself it's a bunch of nasty clothing and trash and the nearby water's bringing out the mosquitoes so I need to keep moving.

When I get to the road, the sky's there again. The stars mix black and white on a purple and blue canvas. I put my board down on the road and follow Franklintown until it intersects with Dead Run so I can cross the bridge, onto the walking path.

On the other side, there's a chance for distraction. I kick hard and step on the deck at just the right time to throw myself onto the pavement at the other end. I'm hoping to hit my head or bite my lip or break my arm, but I've fallen so many times before that my body knows how to catch itself so I don't get hurt. The Natty Ice bottles clatter. One of them's fizzing.

My forearm burns a little. The moon gives me just enough light to see the new scrape, but it's shallow, meaningless, not even bleeding. My face hurts worse. My wrists pulse with the feeling of hands being around them, crushing the veins, feelings, me. My ears are ringing. I pull my legs in, hold them to me, and close my eyes.

"What the fuck?" my dad's voice echoes. "You really think you're better than me now? Was it because of that little prick? Tell me!"

I'm pretty sure he's in the trees, but I'm not sure where he's coming from. I curl into a ball to cover my face for when the next blow comes. I already feel it, throbbing against my back. I hold my jaw tight so my teeth don't clatter.

"I'm not, dad! I'm fucking not!"

"You're not what, Josephine?"

"I'm not anything!"

"Damn fucking right!" My head jerks like someone's grabbed my hair.

I swing back onto the pavement, someone invisible tossing me. Eyes closed, I scream. I grab at my head and wait to feel his foot somewhere. Face, stomach, legs, stomping me while I say, "Dad—Please—Dad—I—I didn't fucking mean to come in late, okay?"

"You want to be like your fucking mother? Then leave already."

"I don't want to hurt you, dad."

"It's too goddamn late for that."

My eyes are wet, but I don't know if I'm actually crying. My voice doesn't sound like it belongs to me. I clutch my head, waiting for a strike that doesn't come.

"Shit, Josephine… What did I do to you…? Goddamn it. Goddamn it! I'm sorry, I—I don't know what's wrong with me. Josephine, I didn't mean to do this—Goddamn it!"

Slowly, my eyes open.

The sky's above me, not the trailer ceiling.

The beer bottles come into sight, laying sideways on the pavement.

Beer's spilling onto concrete.

I can't tell which one's cracked.

Maybe they're all cracked.

Not shattered though.

Nothing's ever broken enough for you to see it at first glance.

Let it get ruined first.

I'm breathing hard, getting onto my feet, reaching for one of the bottles. I pick one up and toss it at the ground as hard as I can. It smashes to pieces on contact. The fizzing beer is so loud now. I pick up another bottle and do the same thing. Then, I toss a third.

The smell of alcohol shouldn't be so strong, but it's like he's breathing in my face and the drunkenness is mixing with the piss he can't wash off and the dead buried in Leakin Park. Out of the corner of my eye's another black garbage bag, sitting off the side of the trail. Flat at the bottom. Its stink crawls through the mud and branches and dead grass and broken glass just so it can wrap around me.

I'm not breathing.

I don't know when the tears started down my face.

I wipe my cheeks with the back of my hand, but they're still wet.

Why couldn't I be the one in that bag?

I grab one of the remaining bottles off the pavement.

Cap off, it hits the ground. I press the bottle to my lips. I choke on the beer trying to drink and breathe at the same time.

Something caws somewhere.

Party.

My head's fuzzy. I turn around, looking for the audience of this morbid show.

There's nothing visible in the trees, on the path, hidden between the branches. Moonlight catches on glossy, black eyes and a long, black beak. The bird's the biggest I've ever seen. It's not alone. At least six others sit in the trees with it. Am I going to die? Are they waiting to eat me? I don't know why I think that. My lips draw into a sneer. "What the hell are you looking at?" I pull my hand back. "Stop looking at me!" I throw my bottle at the biggest bird.

It misses.

The thing caws. Laughter.

"Fuck you!"

My vision blurs with tears. I'm going for the last bottle.

Light catches on something else. Shattered brown glass lays on the ground beside me. Fuck. I can't feel anything, but the building pressure in my head, throbbing face, his hands grabbing my wrists and throwing me across the room, into the wall, my spine cracking, another smack, another scream, and all the goddamn hatred I don't know what I did to deserve.

I can't do this anymore.

Instead of the bottle, I pick up a shard of glass. My hand's shaking. My skin puckers with goosebumps from the cold nipping at me. I try to breathe, but snot strangles me.

The glass is cool against my fingertips. I'm not thinking of anything but how to make all the noise stop as I press the tip to my arm. It's just a prick at first. Not deep, but enough that a bubble of blood comes out of the incision. Beneath it, the bruises are already darkening.

"Do it." His voice overlays mine. "Do it, *you bitch*, and don't come back."

"You've got the guts to leave, don't you?" he says on his own.

I press the glass back to my arm. A sob shakes my body.

"At least tell me you hate me first," he says.

"That's the problem, dad." Tears stream down my cheeks. I suck in hard, trying to make them go back inside. The glass draws a line down my arm. "I don't hate you. I wish I did, but... I don't. I just—I want you to fucking stop!" Red springs eagerly from the gash. My fingers close on the shard. The stinging carries into them, turning my fingers red and bloody too.

My phone buzzes against my thigh.

"Shit." Startled. The glass goes deeper than I mean for it to, then falls out of my hand.

The feeling's there that someone's watching.

I kick the glass into the grass and turn around. The

birds aren't where they sat before. Every last one of them's gone. Or maybe they were never there. The path, the trail, the bridge, the trees. Nothing. They aren't there.

My phone buzzes again.

I take it out of my pocket. The screen's cracked from a fall I don't remember. My thumb slides along the cracks, going up to the notification window that says 2 MESSAGES: WAYLAND CROSS. I wipe the tears from my eyes with the back of my hand. My arms sting; the cold air nips at the fresh cuts. "Fuck." I breathe in through a stuffy nose and wipe my face again like he's gonna see it when I open his messages. My bloody fingers wipe on my jeans before I touch the screen.

WAYLAND	Hey Jo—
	Happy Birthday! :partyhat: :cake: :confetti:
JOEY	What are you still doing awake?
	School tmro.

He doesn't answer immediately. I pass a small section of the paved walkway, stopping at the bridge when I feel light-headed. Each time I turn toward it, the broken glass appears as if it's almost glowing. After the third time, I lean down for it, but pick up the unopened bottle of beer instead. Cap off, I sit down by the bridge, facing the water, letting my legs bounce with my phone on the wood in front of me. It buzzes, screen lighting up with Wayland's name again.

| WAYLAND | I wanted to be the first to tell you happy birthday. |

It's so stupid.

Tears build in my eyes again.

I wipe them away. Smile, laugh. It doesn't last.

JOEY	Thanks
WAYLAND	Why are you still up?
JOEY	Bullshit
	I mean bullshit's why I'm up
	Fuck
	I can't breathe, Way
	I can't think
	I'm doing stupid shit
	I don't know what the fuck to do
	I

Can't write the rest of that message. I can't say what I'm thinking or what I want to do. My hand's shaking so much I can't read the screen. My mind goes blank every time I try to type anything else and I just stop. What if he says "good" or "it's about time"?

WAYLAND	Jo?
	Where are you?
JOEY	MP
	Bridge
WAYLAND	I'm coming.
JOEY	Don't
	Don't tell your parents.

It's been five minutes and he hasn't responded. I'm laying on the ground with the beer in my hand, half gone, laying with the glass out of reach because if I wasn't, I don't know if I could stop myself again. The cold's seeping into my shirt and under my skin. I close my eyes and just try to breathe.

A bird caws again.

Sitting on the bridge railing, the big one's back. I wipe my eyes to make sure I'm seeing right. He's still there. "I'm not dead," I say softly. "Not yet." I swallow. Pant. "Sorry."

Close my eyes. I'm not sure how long it's been, but the bottle's been empty forever now. I keep putting it against my lips, thinking something's gonna come out, but it's empty and now it's feeling like there was never anything inside to begin with. My eyes flutter shut, but any time I start to relax, I hear crackling under someone's weight, I feel like I'm falling, and I gasp, thinking my dad's found me and I'm not ready to see him again.

Light bleeds over the bridge from the street on the other side.

Jo?" Wayland's voice echoes off the trees.

It's worse than the sound of badges. It's worse than the neighbor's tossing around glass and screaming at each other because *he did what again*. It's worse than Dad's sobbing, asking for forgiveness he doesn't really care about when he says, "I fucked up," and then, "I can't believe you made me fuck up like this again, Josephine."

"Jo?" Wayland says again.

I raise my hand into the air. "I'm here." I'm still laying on the ground at the end of the bridge. Blood trickles down my forearm from the cut. I bring it back to me and try to wipe it off. My black shirt's a towel to hide my shame.

Wayland runs across the bridge.

"Watch out for the glass." I gesture in the direction of the broken bottles, not too far away on the concrete.

Wayland's at my side, sitting on the ground next to me saying, "Why are you laying down?" and "Why aren't you wearing a coat?" and "You're bleeding," before I can sit up.

"I left the house kinda fast, I guess." I'm trying not to look, but I can't take my eyes off the blood seeping through the cut again. It's coming out so fast and won't stop. I'm trembling. I can't tell if it's the cold or adrenaline or something else. At least the cut doesn't hurt that much. I let my arm fall to my lap.

Wayland straightens. He reaches for me, but stops halfway. He can't choose whether to look at my face or my arm and keeps going back and forth. "What happened to your face, Jo?"

"You like it? Birthday present from my dad." I try to laugh. A sob sneaks out instead. I tighten my jaw to catch it, but the trembling worsens. My eyes water. I blink a couple of times to stop it. That doesn't work either. Tears blur my vision and run stripes down my cheeks. My hands curl into my thighs. I close my eyes, hoping to avoid his expression of pity or judgment or whatever's coming. It's the same look everyone at school's been giving me for years before turning away and pretending they didn't see anything. "No one gives a fuck, Wayland."

The warmth of his fingers over mine startles me. I jerk back, suck in a gasp, and open my eyes before I remember it's him.

"I do," he says, looking right at me, leaving me exposed instead of forgotten.

The words fill my head. I can't keep from crying. My hand tightens on his. "I don't know what's wrong with him. He hasn't always been like this. It's not always this bad. But, fuck. Wayland, this is normal, right? Families fight and it gets better? I don't know if I'd even care if he didn't fucking remember what he did long enough to pretend he cares sometimes."

Wayland's thumb strokes the back of my hand slowly. It's so simple, it's enough to make fresh tears roll down my cheeks. "You want to come to my house?" he says. "We can get breakfast on the way to school."

I hate that question. It doesn't matter what I say, it feels like a lie to answer. Every decision I make is the wrong one. "I can't, Way... My dad..." I suck in a hard, trying too hard to breathe. "If I don't go home..." The laugh hurts. "He's gonna drown in his own piss. He's gonna... You know... It could kill him."

"Fuck your dad," Wayland says.

I pull back, surprised. I've never heard him swear before; I don't think I've ever even heard him say *crap*.

"I mean… it's your birthday. You can do whatever you want and your dad can just… figure it out."

"What if I want to skip school tomorrow?"

"Then I'll skip too, okay?"

"Okay."

Holding my hands, Wayland helps me to my feet. When he lets go, I wipe my face again. My hand's smeared with runny eyeliner and blood. Fingers, the back of my hands, my arm's got Dad's fingerprints on it too. Christ, I don't even want to know how much is still on my face with probably none of it around my eyes anymore. I lower my hand, sticking it into my pocket. Wayland's staring at my arm with questions I don't think he knows how to ask. He's already got the answer, maybe afraid I won't tell him the truth.

Maybe more afraid of what he'd do if I did.

"I won't get blood on your mom's car, okay?" I pluck my skateboard from the ground.

"I don't have paper towels or anything," Wayland says.

We're at the side of the road, standing next to his car, a white SHO Taurus with a number lock on the door. I set my board down. My fingers hook around the hem of my shirt and I pull it over my head. In the same motion, I wrap it around my bleeding arm.

"Jo—"

"Just tell me we're not going to the hospital," I say.

He won't look at me. He's biting his bottom lip, swallowing. He walks around to the driver's side of the car. "How bad do you think it is?"

"Do I look like a fucking doctor?" I wait for him to open the driver's side before I climb into the passenger. He starts the engine. The park doesn't look so hopeless with the headlights on. "You can look at it when we get to your place if you want." I stare at the window, watching him in the reflection, waiting for the disgust, his change of mind, the face he'll make when he says, "Oh shit, I was wrong this time."

Instead, he says, "I'm not a doctor either," with a laugh.

"Yeah?" I turn to him. A small smile pulls onto my lips. "Doesn't matter. You're the only person in the world I trust." My skin prickles from the cold coming at my bare skin. I'm trembling; my foot bounces. "With everything."

Wayland's trying not to look at me. Both hands firmly grasp the steering wheel and any move's a quick side glance he's trying to hide. I don't think he knows I see him. His hand goes for the heat. I turn to him. He pulls his hand back like he's been caught doing something wrong. The heat's already coming through the vents, though. He laughs and says, "Sorry, I was cold."

I sink into the seat. My bouncing foot slows. I don't think I can keep my eyes open for the ride back to his place. The warmth is only making it easier to pass out. I don't know what to say other than, "Me too. Thanks."

TWELVE.

I open my eyes and the car's parked. We're in the driveway of Wayland's house and he says, "We'll go in through the garage so my parents don't hear us." He unlocks the side door and waits for me to go in first. I cross the threshold and the lights-off darkness is all there is anymore. It smells too much like oil, burnt coffee, cheese microwaved too many times and soggy ramen noodles tossed in the trash maybe a week ago.

"Wayland?" I say.

A tinny radio that sounds like the one at Bodymore Body Shop plays the same oldies station Jag has on every hour of the day he's at the shop. They like to spin the same twenty-five songs on rotation between repeated commercial breaks that are always too loud. It's thanks to his obsession with the channel I know the lyrics to all these songs made before I was even born. The music's accompanied by metal on metal, a tool hits a hood. I open my eyes and my hands are around the rim of an open hood, a blue Toyota I started working on maybe twenty minutes ago. The garage's too warm; sweat's sticking my hair to my face. We're closed, so the doors are closed too.

Jag's on the other side of the garage, at a hydraulic holding a silver Dodge truck, muttering along with the Bee Gees about night fever. I lean back with a groan. Oil changed, filter changed. Tires? No, and something's going on with their electrical. Someone dropped this shit off thirty minutes to closing and thought they'd get it back before five. This is why I hate the fall. Everyone's coming in just to get their tires changed for the snow, but then they're reminded of all the other shit they already knew was wrong and just tack it on, thinking the wait time will be the same or sometimes even *less* after adding twenty million jobs onto their initial appointment. You know what's not fun? Getting twenty calls from the same person within a day because they thought you'd be done by now. "I need my car in the morning. I have work, you know? Can you be at least kind of considerate and actually do your job? 'Kay, thanks."

I dunno. "Maybe bring it in earlier," never seems to be an option so all you can say is, "We'll do our best."

Donny's said the customers have more patience since he hired me. "You're cute, you're young, you're female... Customers don't want to yell at that... unless they're women. Never understood it myself, but the female mind is... No offense, but there's a reason I'm divorced." He says it with a laugh, and as stupid as it sounds, that's what makes me want to believe everything he says.

Electricity burns my fingers, sparking loose power against them. I step back, shaking my hands in the air with a soft, "Shit," hissing through my teeth. My pocket vibrates, a text from Wayland asking if I'm ready to go. I use that as an excuse to step away.

JOEY   Gimme 45
              Gonna finish tires.

I slide my phone back into my pocket. I turn back to the car. Just looking at the battery makes my fingers tingle again. Fuck. I was working the wrong connector. Negative, then power. I'm too tired to work on this shit right now. They day's been too long, my brain stopped working an hour ago, my body's not far behind.

I checked the clipboard paperwork for the tires bought, then head over to the storage shelves. I locate them by brand and purpose. I grip the first one, tug, it's stuck, another tug, harder, slanted, the tire comes off the shelf and falls to the floor. My muscles are nothing. I can't pick it up, so I lean it and roll it out to where the car's waiting. In the shop, there's no sound of work anymore. I look over to the truck Jag was working on. He's not there. Probably in the break room, slacking off. I return to the tire rack and go for the next tire. A yank. I don't know what the hell is holding onto it, but the tire won't move. I fix my grip and pull again. My arms weaken, my fingers snap off. I land on my ass.

"You're supposed to disconnect the negative first, Josie."

I line back up with the tire. Deep inhale, deep exhale, grab it. My fingers slip again. The tire's not moving.

"Hey, Josie?"

The next time I grab it and pull; there's no momentum. My fingers can't grip anything, my arms are shaking, tired and weak.

He whistles. "Can you hear me, Josie?"

"It's not *Josie*." I turn to Jag. He's got a Styrofoam cup in his hand. Steam rises out. The smell of cheap coffee joins the rubber from the tires.

"Sorry, didn't realize it was a touchy subject, *Josephine*." He brings the cup to his lips, looks away, takes a sip. His fingers leave black oil smudges all over the white. He's wearing jeans, also smudged in a mixture of stains from different car fluids and his gray tank's not much better. A couple scrapes on his wrists tell me he's either had a hard day or he's been too careless. He's a little older than me. Twenty-four maybe with black hair, short on the sides and longer on the top. He knows what he was doing, but I never liked him. Everything about him screams asshole and he's used how good he is at fixing cars to get away with it.

"Don't call me that either. Only my dad uses that name and believe me, you don't want to be him."

"Daddy issues too?" He laughs. "Why am I not surprised?"

"Did you want something?"

"Well, first, what am I supposed to call you since my two guesses are apparently wrong."

"Joey. Next?"

"Joey?" He laughs again. Louder this time. Feels like a surprise, more than it's at me, but I still don't like it. "Trying to be one of the boys now? Those daddy issues go deeper than I thought."

"You can call me whatever the hell you want, but if it's anything other than Joey, I'm calling you *Micky*, Jagger. Got it?"

"Funny thing about that is… I don't really care. Not even half as much as you do, apparently."

"What the hell do you want?"

Jag nods toward the tire rack. "Did you want some help with that?"

"Just because I'm a girl doesn't mean I'm weak or I can't lift tires and fix cars on my own, thanks. I wouldn't be here if I didn't have what it takes." I turn back to the rack. My arms are already shaking, hanging at my sides. I don't want to grab the tires again just to hear him laugh when my arms snap and the tire's still there.

"You ever build a car?"

"Part of your interview process?" I turn back around. Jag's leaning against the wall, his cup's held close to his lips, but he's not drinking; he's only watching me. "Maybe if you took off the douchey aviators before you walked in, Donny wouldn't've needed you to prove you're not a thoughtless prick."

"Aviators are not douchey—"

"They are the *douchiest* sunglasses in existence."

"No."

"Yeah."

"What do you have against aviators?"

"You caught me. It's not the aviators I'm judging." I lean against the tire rack. "But if you can question why I'm here, then I can do the same to you, yeah? Sounds fair."

"Sure." Jag finishes the last of his coffee. He crushes the cup and drops it into the trash can on the other side of the door. "Donny said when you came in, he had to start you on answering phones and changing oil. The latter of which you didn't know how to do anyway."

"Sounds like Donny needs to learn how to talk less," I say.

"Look, I get it. There's a helluva learning curve for even the simplest things around here, huh?"

"Oh, fuck off, Jagger."

Jag's footsteps echo through the room. It's not that he's stepping hard, but his shoes are heavy. Steel-toed. He can't help the clatter. His gait's slow, deliberate, and focused. His hand presses into the rack over my shoulder and he leans in. When he speaks, his voice is loud, but close and intimate. "I just wanna know, *Joey...* What's your story? Why are you here?"

"What makes you think I've got some kind of story, huh? Because I work here? It's a job." I cross my arms. "What about you? Or do you not *have* to have one because you *belong?*"

"I used to work on cars with my dad. He loved 'em. Race cars especially. When I was thirteen, we started rebuilding his old Mustang. When I was eighteen, he gave it to me."

"Why?"

"Safekeeping mostly. Plus, it meant he didn't have to spend any money on a birthday gift that year."

"Aren't you worried he'll want it back someday?"

"Nah." Jag shakes his head. "He died."

"And that's not tragic?"

"Sad? Sure. Tragic? Nah." Jag shrugs. "I just call it life."

I try not to laugh. Nothing's funny about how much I want to tell him about my dad because it feels fair, but I don't want the pity. I don't want the judgment. I don't want it to be ignored again and made to feel like I don't matter. "I dropped out of high school," I say.

"Yeah? Me too. Then what?"

"Then I ended up here."

"That doesn't sound so bad."

"I'm kind of a fucking idiot. Everyone says so." I'd come in, not prepared for the test, not prepared for *any* test. Even when I studied with Wayland, the stuff just didn't stick. Dates and history and random chemical combinations weren't important and who cares if I don't know the things you know? I bet I know a lot of things you don't know too. Like how to stop bleeding fast or how to get stains out of clothing when they've been sitting for a while or the best way to hide bruises and pretend you don't have alcohol on your breath at nine in the morning or how to get out of a parent-teacher conference when your dad can't get his ass off the couch because he's so fucking drunk, he doesn't remember his own name, but you can't say that. So, you make up excuses teachers will pretend to believe so they don't have to get more involved.

It really didn't matter what you say. They had all the reasons in the book. Ignore the bruises and cuts. The bad attitude is just childish rebellion *she'll grow out of*. Falling asleep at my desk means I'm either too challenged by the work or not challenged enough, depending on who you ask. They made it easier to skip class because they'd give me so much shit if I came in late, but when I skipped entirely, they hardly said anything. I was in the seat. I preferred the snarky, "Felt like coming in today?" over "Tardy means detention. Try leaving a little sooner,

Josephine. Try not to miss the bus. How about messing around less and thinking about your future more?"

It would drive my dad crazy every time I got detention. He'd think I finally left him. Then he'd say I was being vindictive by coming back late. Then he'd resolve to beat me so I *couldn't* go and cry so I *wouldn't*.

It worked every goddamn time.

"That count as a story?" I say.

"You don't sound like an idiot to me."

"Sorry, I wasn't ready to be put on the spot. Didn't realize a tragic life was a requirement for being a mechanic."

"I think it's more the attitude you've got that says you've seen some shit, but read into that however you like—"

"I don't have an attitude." My hand presses into his chest, giving him a push. Not hard. He doesn't move.

"Oh, excuse me." He laughs. "What do you call it?"

"Protection."

"Alright. From what?"

Shit. Wrong answer. I don't know how it got out of me. He's quiet, staring into my eyes. "Why do you care?" I say.

"Because you look like someone who needs it." The smile's faded and he steps back, giving me room to walk away and I take it, feeling exposed when I wasn't before. Where his hand was so close to my neck, I still feel the heat from his body and I want it closer.

I cross the room to the door, get back into the garage, the cool air, breathe. I keep going until I'm in the break room at my locker, grabbing out my hoodie. Jag stops in the door. "Did you need something?" I say.

"You might try being a little less scrappy. The voice might work on the phone, but working the front desk looking like you cage fight on the weekends isn't gonna get you anything extra."

"Solid advice. If only I didn't live in the cage. Got

anything else?"

"Yeah." His voice makes me turn to look at him. Arms crossed, leaning against the door frame, Jag's got a smile like he knows something I don't.

"What?"

"Escape."

I'm moving across the break room. My hand goes around his neck, his goes to my hip. I pull him down and our lips come together. He's backing me up so fast. His hands slide over my ass and down my thighs. He lifts my legs to wrap around his waist. He's strong; he doesn't slow down or falter. My fingers stroke the hair on the back of his head while desperately I seek refuge in his mouth. My ass hits the counter or the breakroom lunch table. I'm not sure which and I don't really care. The cold air hits my skin as soon as my shirt comes off. I grab at Jag's clothing with just as much urgency, tossing his shirt to the ground. Everywhere he touches goes hot and all I can think is how much I want his hands all over me. My belt slides loose. His lips move down my jaw, my neck, my shoulder. As quickly as it started, it all stops. His heat's pulled back and nothing's happening anymore. His hand sits on my thigh, so I know I'm not imagining his being here.

I open my eyes. "Why'd you stop?"

Jag meets my gaze for a second, then he's looking down my body, slowly. First, I think he's checking me out, but the pause goes on too long and he's not trying to take my bra off or kiss me or pull down my skinnies or tell me what he thinks. Instead, he's stroking the bruises on my stomach from where my dad kicked me last night or the prints going down my arms. I know the marks around my neck are gone, but I'm getting more nervous the longer Jag stares and it's feeling like he can see everything that's ever happened to me, even the shit my dad didn't do.

I grab both sides of Jag's face and redirect his eyes to mine. My heart's beating so hard, so fast, so loud. I don't know if I'm even able to talk. My face's hot. Embarrassment, shame, waiting for the disgust to show in his expression. I'll beat him to the punchline. "Scrappy really doesn't do it for you, huh, Jagger?"

"Your boyfriend do this?"

I laugh. Tears well in my eyes. My head drops back, letting the laugh go louder than it should. My tongue rolls over my bottom lip, catching the taste of dried blood, left somehow from when it busted yesterday. I cover my eyes with my hand like it's just that damn funny. "If it was my boyfriend, you know I'd just fuck off, right?" My hand slides away from my eyes only when I'm sure I can see straight again and the tears are pulled back. I meet Jag's eyes to assure him I'm not lying. He's waiting for me. Another laugh struggles out. "What's another bastard out there if he's not mine?"

Jag's hand slides down my thigh. The other unhooks my belt, pops open the button on my fly. He pulls my hips closer to the edge of the table I'm sitting on. The break room around me comes into view. The air's stale, spilled coffee, gasoline, and microwaved leftovers. The sticky table holds onto my jeans. The clock ticks loudly between our breaths. "You're really not seeing anyone?" Jag says.

My hand slides around Jag's neck. I pull him closer to let my voice lower, making sure this moment is a secret that only he and I share. "You think I want anyone seeing me like this, Jag? I don't even want the lights on right now…" I reach for his lips with mine. A peck. "Help me escape. At least for a little bit."

Jag squeezes my thigh. His hand presses to my chest to urge me back onto the table. Strong, but not forceful. His muscles don't scare me, but make me feel safe for every second he's against me. It's a comfort I can't remember ever experiencing before and I get lost in every sensation. For the first time in a long time, shit doesn't feel so hopeless. Maybe I'm dumb thinking that. It's just sex, right? I know he doesn't really care, we're doing each other a favor, but for as long as it lasts, I want to think of the escape he's helping me make, a home that's not broken, a future I can pretend to have.

The body shop bell rings. Jag startles at the same time I do. He pulls away from me saying, "Shit," while he looks over his shoulder like he'll be able to see the lobby from inside the break room. My head's still spinning from the flurry of feelings begging the moment to continue and make me so drunk I forget what day it is. I wipe my face with the back of my hand. The blurry clock comes into view.

9:30pm.

"Fuck. It's Wayland." I push myself up, sliding off the table to sand. My legs wobble at first.

"What?" Jag steps back. He grabs his shirt and pants off the floor at the same time. He holds my jeans out to me.

"Wayland." I take my pants and put them on.

"Who?"

"My ride." I pull my shirt on, then grab my hoodie. I'm trying to catch my breath. My skin still tingles everywhere Jag's lips had been while greasy handprints darken everywhere he touched me, washing over my dad's anger like something that never happened.

I pull my sleeves over my arms. Grease from the day's work blend with the chipped black nail polish. Jag's tightening his belt. I walk past toward the break room exit; he grabs my arm. "What?" I turn around.

Jag looks me down a moment. I press my hand around my neck to work out my hoodie collar, thinking maybe it's still showing something bad.

"You don't need to go with him, Joey," Jag says.

"It's just Wayland." I pull my arm away. Turning on my heels, I step out the door backwards. I wipe my cheeks with my hoodie sleeve. I don't want to know how bad my makeup probably looks now. "My best friend."

"I thought you said you didn't have a boyfriend."

"Not boyfriend, best friend." Jag's following me.

"Does he know that?"

"Yeah." I open the glass door to the lobby. Jag takes it out of my hand when it's open. Wayland waves low at me through the front door. It's clear the moment he sees Jag. He stops. Straightens, his hand falls to his side, and he looks away. I unlock the front door and pull it open. He comes inside, slow and unsure. A peek up catches me, then Jag, then back to me and the sitting area. "Uh, sorry... Am I early?"

"No. You're good. I'm just so fucking tired, I'm pretty much useless. I couldn't even get the tires off the rack." I laugh. "I'll just have to finish shit tomorrow. Let me grab my board and we can go." I'm back in the break room. I grab my skateboard from against the wall, check the clock again. When the hell did it get so late? I didn't think it'd been that long. My hand runs down the back of my head, patting down my short, black hair. When my head drops, the edges of my hoodie threaten to pull over my wrists. A large bruise sticks out next to a cut.

Jag saw all of that just now. What the hell is he thinking?

My tongue flicks my lip ring.

"Hey, you okay?" Jag comes into the break room. I turn around, taking a deep breath. I barely nod. My hand goes into my pocket, looking for my cigarettes. They aren't there. Somehow, he knows what I'm looking for. His hand touches the counter. When he pulls it away, he's got a box in his hand. He holds it out to me.

"Thanks." I take the cigarettes.

Jag looks like he wants to say something, but I don't want to give him the chance to ruin the moment. I slide the cigarettes into my pocket. I check the other side to make sure I still have my wallet. I turn on my heels, keep walking backward toward the break room door. "See you tomorrow?" I say.

"Probably," Jag says.

"What shift?"

"I come in at nine."

"Me too."

Jag's keeping pace. His hand catches mine. "Hey." He stops. So do I. "If you get into trouble, gimme a call. You got my number?" His voice is low, it's almost eaten by the tinny radio still playing in the back of the garage.

My eyes go blurry. I smile. "Thanks, Jag."

"You got my number, right?"

"Yeah."

"Don't lose it."

I pull my hand back then turn away. A lazy wave over my shoulder. "Good night, Jagger." I don't look at him anymore while I'm walking to Wayland, standing awkwardly in the waiting room by the front door. That's where he always waits, and I never figured out why. For years, any time he's come to pick me up or wait for me, he's always stayed by the front door, never coming in further, never sitting down, never getting comfortable. It made sense to stand outside my place because that's where I told him to wait. The further from my place he was, the better. He couldn't smell my dad from the sidewalk, couldn't see my dad from the other side of the door, and couldn't hear the shit my dad said about him when he wasn't around. Not that my dad cared. He wanted Wayland to hear him. He wanted to scare him off, to make sure there was never anyone I felt like I could go to if I needed a break from him, ensuring his home was my home too, forever.

Stranded, you'll take whatever you can get so you're not alone, right?

They say family's all you've got at the end of the day. Everyone else can choose to leave, but not *family*. Shows what they know, right? The only way I'm stuck with my dad is I know he won't leave me; he needs me and Dad was stuck with me because I wouldn't kill him like Mom did. But Jag and Wayland and anybody else? As soon as they see how fucked up I am, the door can't close fast enough.

Loneliness is the worst killer you can't see.

It makes you scared, delusional, angry, drunk.

When you're alone, you don't know what the hell you're doing anymore because there's no one around to call you dumb for pissing yourself; no one's there to tell you to stop screaming, it's scaring the neighbors; go get a job or run to the gas station. When you're alone, all you've got are your thoughts, the voice in your head telling you everything you've always worried about is true. I've heard it before. Maybe not the same voice as my dad. I understand why he keeps the TV on blast though. The voice knows what's gonna get to you the most. When I'm skating around Baltimore, the echo across the walls in graffiti looks like the attempt of others to subvert their own demons. Everybody's got a voice in their head, whispering the sweetness of destruction, maybe telling them to rob a bank, shoot someone, get yourself off.

Escape this miserable plane of existence by any means necessary.

I wonder what my dad's voice says the most.

Does he repeat what his voice says about me?

Wayland's holding the front door partially open. Since when? I don't know. "Joey?" he says.

I shake my head a little, coming back to the body shop lobby. "Yeah?"

Wayland's hesitant. He only half glances over his shoulder, then back at me. "Who was that?"

I look back toward the garage. Two more tires sit next to my Toyota. He's walking up with the fourth to stack next to the lift. He catches me looking. He gives me a smile. My chest weighs down with guilt. I brush my hair back while I blow out. "That's Jagger."

Wayland turns back to the garage again. He tries to do it fast, but it doesn't go unnoticed. "*That's* Jagger?"

"Yeah." I chuckle, patting Wayland's shoulder as I walk by him. "Don't look so concerned. He's kind of a jerk, but he's alright."

"Joey?" Jag says.

I'm not even out the door yet. "Yeah, Jag? I turn around.

"Can you hear me?" Jag says.

"I said yeah. What's up?"

Wayland's close, but still just standing behind me, holding the door, watching me carefully. His lips are flat, sadness reflects in his eyes. Worry. I never noticed it before. My heart races. Why do I feel like I'm about to lose him? "Way?" I turn to him. He lets the door go. I touch his shoulder. His eyes meet mine. The whites are red. His irises are black and bigger than they should be. "Are you okay, Wayland? You look... You look a little—"

"Yeah, Jo. I'm fine." His voice is flat, hard, sad. Through his modest smile, a tear slides down his cheek. It's not the color it should be. It's closer to red.

"Way—" I cup his face. My thumb wipes at the tear. Another one comes. "What's wrong?"

"I don't want to lose you, Jo."

I wipe the next tear. It's discolored, red. "You're not going to lose me. I'm right here."

"That's not it." His body tenses.

"Joey?" Jag says.

I glance over my shoulder toward the garage. He's standing in the doorway.

"Say something." He sounds desperate.

"Sorry, J—I'm kind of in the middle of something. Can we talk later?" I turn back to Wayland, but he's gone. My hands are empty. But still hanging where they had been and he's just gone. The auto shop waiting room's empty. Outside the windows, it's pitch black and there's nothing beyond the cement sidewalk. No parking lot, no lights, no cars, no Wayland. Jag's in the lobby. His hands go around me. His fingers burn against my skin. Suddenly, I'm freezing. The garage is gone and the lobby lights are fading.

My legs go weak. I can't hold myself up anymore. Jag's saying my name again and again and again—Or he's saying something and I can't make out the words, just that his voice is soft and he's the only thing keeping me standing. His voice fades into the background. The tinny radio's gone too. How did I not notice?

Slowly, everything around me's disappearing and I can't stop it. My fingers close weakly in Jag's shirt. I try to say his name, but my lips won't move. Everything around me's gone. Tears leak from my closed eyes, leaving burning trails on my cheeks. I feel like I'm drowning, an anchor's pulling me down and I'm too weak to swim against it.

My throbbing heart overpowers my senses, blanking out everything in my head. All I can do is think Jag, help me, please… I don't want to die.

THIRTEEN.

The thumping isn't music. Under my skin, it's making my body jitter. Hands are burning heat against me. My eyes shoot open. There's a figure above me, staring down, focused and watching and surprised at the same time he pulls back.

"Joey?" he says.

The name doesn't register. Nothing around me registers for a while. It comes first as a gentle bubbling brook, the smell of sulfur and shampoo and cigarettes and mildew, the whistling and a familiar caw. I reach back, looking for the ground. My hand sinks into the mud, too wet to be ground. I yelp with a panic that shouldn't've been there.

"It's okay," he says.

His blurry face becomes clear. Next, it's everything behind him. A forest, a small river going somewhere, huge, thick, square walls shooting straight into unending darkness above. Blocked off windows and archways lit by pale sigils scatter across the sides of the tower. The dark woods of Caedis Silvis are to my left and above is the purple sky, clear and visible with the distance from the trees. Spots of black stars, the large dark moon, and a beam of black shoots through the sky like a cut in the air. Everything reminds me that somewhere through the trees is the party, the afterlife, and I'm at the end.

Something burns the back of my throat and nose. I lean over, coughing, heaving, and gasping. I roll onto my knees, holding myself up on all fours. My palms sink into the mud, but it's not much this time. Water finds its way out of my mouth. A hand slides gently along my back, even after I'm done spitting up water. I wipe my mouth with the back of my hand and wait for anything else to come up. Once I'm sure it's over, I sit back.

"Can you breathe alright?" he says.

"I'm fine, J. I'm just… I… I'm a fucking idiot."

"Yeah, you really are," Jag says.

My eyes sting; my lungs hurt. I have to breathe slower, but I can't and the short, sharp breaths are making me dizzy. I look back at the large, square building on the other side of the water. No doors, nothing to see through, no noise coming from it. Unlike the Old Town Mall, there's nothing familiar about the never-ending tower of stone, shape on top of shape. Instead of feeling the warm embrace of invitation, this structure tells me to take my chances running back into the woods before it can get me. "Where…" I'm forcing the word out of my raw throat. My hand slides along my ass pocket, looking for relief while the other bounces against my thigh. I don't know what I need, I just know I need something. A cigarette hangs in my mouth, unlit. I can't find my lighter.

God, I hope I didn't lose it.

"What did I tell you about wandering into the Liquor?" Charon's voice surprises me.

My vision blurs again. I wipe the fresh tears from my face. Charon's, fortunately, not hard to find. The tall building is well lit and its light bleeds onto the shore on our side of the brook running around it. Charon stands further away from the water with the dark trees. By contrast, his white clothing nearly glows against the backdrop, barely affected by the darkness waiting behind him. Val, as a raven, stands on a branch above him, blending into the shadows and trees but for his red eyes that give shape to his face. He's not so much hiding as he's part of the forest.

"I didn't wander," I say.

"If you truly wish to end it, you only need to say so," Charon says.

"Good thing that's not what I'm going for," I say.

"Then your actions are counterintuitive. When will humans evolve to have reason?" Charon looks at the tower. His glowing blue eyes quickly come back to me. Jag's hand's on my shoulder, giving it a squeeze, reminding me I'm not alone. "The Liquor will guide you to *its* end if you have no respect for its boundaries. If the blindness of the Liquor's first warning does not ward you back to the courtyard, it will consume you, delude your senses with visions of the past, and deliver you to *Poena* where you will no longer cause trouble. Disobedience of the order comes with consequences and you are not given warnings for anyone's benefit but your own."

"What is *Poena?*" I say.

"Pain and punishment for eternity. Godless wrath, destruction, and callousness without pause. The creatures inside have no purpose, but lust, anger, and a hunger for causing pain. If you dislike the restless spirit, you will like the creatures who make Poena their home even less," Charon says.

"Sounds like Hell," I say.

"Yes," Charon says.

"Lethe is the water that runs around *Hades*, Joey," Jag mutters in my ear.

A chill goes down my spine. Everything up to this point has been symbolism. How was I supposed to know this time it wasn't? I turn back to the massive building. Archways carry up the side of the otherwise smooth surface, opening the wall to nothing but more stone the color of sand. It doesn't look like there's a way inside but for the solid gold door on the front that doesn't look like it opens. Tall. Ten boxes holding pictures of something too far and finely drawn for me to read from this distance. "Is my dad in there?"

"Yes. Rotted souls are placed in Poena when returned by a reaper. Now, tell me what exactly are you doing here?"

I can't stop staring at the tower, knowing how close I am. Does he feel like I'm close too? Is he inside saying, "*Why, Josephine, why? Where are you?*" to anyone who will listen? "I came to get some Lethe," I say.

"Did you not consider asking Sol before embarking on the equivalent of a suicide mission by running into Caedis Silvis alone?" Charon says.

"She told me she didn't have any."

Charon sighs hard. "Lethe is laced into every consumable in the courtyard. You drink, you eat, you forget. Even at Lodgings. The purpose of Lethe is to make you leave everything behind. Forced into your being, it will fill your lungs, stomach, and mind. You will forget everything you have said, done, suffered in both life and death. Everything in Cavae Mortem is designed to put spirits at ease. As you've noticed, it can be quite the task for some, so calming distractions are woven into the fabric of this place. There is a tap of Lethe in the bar, alongside everything else Sol serves."

"Wait." I take my cigarette out of my mouth. "So, not only has Sol been drugging me, but you're saying that bitch lied and tried to get me killed for real?"

Charon stares at me, his expression unchanging.

"You gonna lie to me now too? Just say it." I stand up too fast. I'm not ready for the ground to give out or be as squishy as it is or my legs to be so weak. Jag grabs hold of me to help me balance. I put my hand over his, mutter, "Thanks," and look away from Charon to the river. A cold sweat washes over me. My shirt's sticking to my skin, soaked from what I was pulled out of. I'm breathing hard, getting dizzy just staring at the water and at the same time I want to run away, I want to fall in and dunk myself in memories of whatever else it's willing to show me. "Is this at least what we came for?" I say.

"Yes," Charon says. "The Lethe in Sol's courtyard and the river are the same."

I slip out of Jag's touch to edge closer to the river. I slip my unlit cigarette behind my ear, but keep the box in my hands, making them find busy work by popping it open and closing it again. The closer I get, the more I feel the push and pull on both sides of my body. It's hard to explain. Closer to the edge, the forest turns into sandstone paving, matching the ground and the tower jutting into the sky. The water's clear, without even a little fogginess and it moves without waves. At the bottom of the shallow water is the same tower paving. In the light, dust like gold washes through the undisturbed water, being the only thing that shows it's moving. A large, translucent black fish like a shadow of a koi with fins like wings swims past with purpose. The fish splashing along sounds more like a soft whisper that pulls at my chest in a way I've never felt.

Dive in.

"What makes this stuff so different?" I say.

Val laughs. Human, but bird-like. I turn back to Charon just as a raven crosses from the tree branch and lands beside Charon, turning into a person. The trick is so flawless, there's no visible change, but my mind stops seeing a raven and starts seeing a person as if he'd never been an animal. "Don't you know anything?" Val says. "Styx is regret. Lethe is nothing."

"I don't understand."

"Like *you* become *nothing*," Val says. "It's over."

Something wraps around my ankle. A yank.

A hand grabs the back of my hoodie while another goes around my waist. "Watch it—" Jag says.

I stumble back from the edge of the brook. When did I get so close? I swallow; my throat's dry. "Sorry." I press my palm into my eye. My fingers brush back through my hair. I grab the cigarette from my ear and put it back in my mouth. My lighter's not hard to find this time. "I'm... having trouble thinking," I say after a hit.

"Yeah, duh," Val says. "That's what Liquor does. When it's in a puddle, it's Lethe. When it's in the air, it's Liquor. Get it?"

Charon moves closer to the brook, stopping on the sandstone near me. He looks down. Another black fish swims by, fast, then slow. The gold sparkles in the water and the stone floor are visible through it while its fins are so long, curving like ruffles as it propels forward. The surface of the water breaks slightly, but nothing shows above it. The shadow of something long and thin like a vine or tendril casts over the sandstone. It reaches for me.

Charon puts out his hand, extending his finger toward the water, and the shadow of the tendril sinks back into the water. The fish disappears down the stream. "The Liquor's job is to capture runaway souls," Charon says. "You are not the only human who has tried to stray from the path, become impatient waiting, or sought the way out of your ultimate end. Some have reached *Finna* and Styx, but preferred the forest to the river. As I said before, everything has a structure, a system by which we all abide. There always has been and there always will be. Those above not only favor order, but they only create in a structure of order."

"So, everything's about making rules for the personal satisfaction of punishing people when they break 'em?" I say, suck in another hit of cigarette. The nicotine's not doing anything to calm my nerves. My hand's trembling, my teeth chatter, and my foot bounces. I keep switching my weight from side to side, hoping for more effect, but it does nothing. An arm slides around my waist.

I pull away with a gasp, gritted teeth, and a "fuck," at myself for being startled again when it's only Jag. "I've talked to enough badges. They do the same thing. Don't need laws if you've got a dark room, though. If they say it, it's the law and what the hell are you gonna do about it?"

"Without order, the system of creation would not exist," Charon says. "Chaos can only destroy."

Another fish swims past, this one without slowing down, without the tendrils, without the tempting threat of being pulled back into the past.

Charon turns away with a sharp, but brief look. "I do not believe there is a way for you to fully grasp it. No human can. As *creative* as your kind may be, there are limitations to understanding what is beyond humanity. You *kill* each other in argument over who will be *rewarded* in the afterlife. Ultimately, your arguments are about *who is right*, while none of you reflect upon the bigger picture that perhaps every last one of you is wrong because the truth is beyond your limits.

"Good and evil, life and death, action and reaction. Everything in the universe has been created on a system of give and take for a benefit and purpose even I do not understand. It does not matter. If the system of order is disrupted, it will overflow into absolute destruction in the same way water builds to a flood or fire grows until there's nothing left to feed it. You have seen what happens when you reject your path and return to the plane of the living. If there was no natural order, it would not be one or two or three escaped souls rotting, it would be all of them, dooming the living."

"And everything's an insult to the rotting soul, huh?" I stare at myself in the reflection of the clear water. I'm nothing but a ghostly outline. I know I shouldn't, but I can't help myself. I drop my cigarette into the water. The moment it touches the surface, it's submerging and disintegrating into absolutely nothing. Panic strikes through my body. My skin tingles in memory of being submerged too. Bile burns the back of my throat. I cover my mouth and take a step back.

Charon stares at me for a while. "Regret creates anger and anger turns into wrath; the sole way to expel wrath is on an external target. Not all humans suffer from this flaw, but it is unique among your kind. Failure above means failure below. You wander because you cannot forget. You disobey because you have never been able to relieve yourself of your human suffering. Yet, you will perform ridiculous tasks if it makes you believe you will have some control over your outcome. Moment by moment, you choose, you find another path, you affect others, however, you cannot circumvent death."

"Speaking of…" Val says. For the first time since he appeared, he moves away from Charon's side and makes his way toward Jag and me. He watches Jag as he comes closer, looking him down, back up, and licking his lips. His back arches, his head cocks to the side. "You smell pretty good. Feeling weak? Maybe like dying soon?"

I step in front of Jag. Val keeps coming, moving around us. His eyes never leave Jag. "You're wrong," I say.

Val comes closer so that he's standing beside me. He leans over, taking a deep, slow breath. His smile grows wider. It's like he's hypnotized. "No, I'm not." He licks his lips again. "Your death's not even days away."

Jag's hands go to my hips. He pulls me closer to him and urges himself between Val and me. "Look, buddy, I don't know what you're smoking, but I'm not planning on dying any time soon."

"That's not how this works." Val laughs.

"You're wrong," I say.

"How?" Val says.

"Time of death isn't as certain as you think—I just saw it." My skin's going hot. The weight of Jag's hand on my hip's getting worse. I'd never mentioned this to him. Obviously, he'd always been aware of the kind of shit my dad did. Sometimes, he'd even heard me repeat it, but I tried to keep that away from him like if he knew what justified my dad putting his hands on me, Jag might agree and maybe even laugh before walking away.

I've waited for Wayland to dump me for the longest time for the same reason. Instead, every time I fell, every time I wanted to throw myself off a bridge, he's come running, catching me every damn time. Charon condemns humans for clinging onto lost causes, but that's the only reason I'm still alive.

I step away from Jag, getting away from his hold and the constant reminder that he's standing there, judging me. "Back then, I didn't get it, but... when I was sixteen, I almost killed myself and I was right there at the door. I know it now because there were enough of you watching me. At least seven. That's the rule, yeah? Seven or more and death is coming any minute."

"Something like that," Val says. "A heart about to stop lets out a smell that goes for miles. It's so good, you don't even know and if you don't get there fast enough, they'll pick the bones dry before you even land." Eyes flicker to me, but not for long. On Jag, he licks his lips again.

"If you don't stop looking at me like that, I'm gonna pop you," Jag says.

My skin's crawling. I'm going to throw up. Tears blur my vision, but against Poena's sandstone surface, Jag can't hide. I lunge for him and grab at whatever I can get. Two handfuls of shirt. I pull him toward me, keep stepping back, keep going and going and going until my feet are sinking in the mud and his arm's around my waist again and he's not following me anymore because he's saying,

"You'll go back into the woods."

"I don't fucking care, as long as it's away from here," I say, but he won't move anymore. I wrap my arms around him instead and pull myself to his body like if I let go, he's going to disappear and I'm going to be alone and everything else will just stop existing too. My fingers curl into his back, holding onto his shirt as tightly as they can. "One choice can't determine everything," I say through gritted teeth. "The fact I didn't die back then is evidence that fate can change—if it even exists."

Maybe that's the problem. People see the magic in the world because it's not that subtle. Everything we think's ridiculous or doesn't make sense gets shrugged off because to believe the impossible would break the control everyone thinks they have or the punch-drunk vision that things can get better, so long as you put enough effort in. If you close your eyes, you can pretend the impossibilities you see every day are fables believed by idiots and that makes it so you don't have to acknowledge we live in a never-ending dream where everyone's punished in the end anyway.

"To some extent, you are correct," Charon says.

"Then even if you say Jag's going to die, it... He doesn't have to and whatever you're smelling's a false alarm—So stop following him." I take a deep breath. The exhale falls out faster, harder than I mean.

"Sorry." Val shrugs. "I go wherever smells best and lately, that's been him. I don't wanna miss my chance, you know?" Val returns to Charon's side, though he can't keep himself from looking at Jag. As much as he tries, his stare's as obvious as Donny's when a hot woman comes into the shop.

"That medium up top told me I can get a second chance if I bring him some stuff," I say.

"There is no rescue for someone who has already given up," Charon says.

"And if everyone believed that when they looked at me, then I wouldn't fucking be here either." I'm staring at Charon much harder than he's looking at me.

He takes a breath, sighs, and turns toward the brook. He reaches into an interior pocket on his jacket and withdraws a small glass vial, not too unlike the one he captured my dad in. He leans down, dipping the glass into the Lethe. At the touch of his skin, the water hisses, but does nothing to change him. Shadowy curls graze his finger as a fish passes through the water beside him without stopping. He twists the cap back onto the vial and brings it to me. "Your passion will be your disappointment."

"Yeah, well, I'm used to it." I take the bottle and hold it out to Jag. He takes it and puts it in his coat pocket. "But thanks…" I offer a smile, somehow, thinking stupidly, that he'd change his face and maybe give one back. He doesn't. "For giving me the opportunity to be disappointed."

"A creature struggling to its death only lashes out until it can no longer move," Charon says.

"Maybe that's why I've never been able to avoid scrapping." I laugh. Weak. Short. "It's always been a fight, you know?"

"I will never understand human reason," Charon says.

"I don't think I want to," Val says, a chuckle breaking his words.

My foot bounces. I run my hand through my hair a couple of times, switching to rub my eyes. "Oh." I look at Val through my fingers. "Can I get some feathers?"

"What?" Val says. "Why?"

"They're for Ralph," I say.

Val looks sidelong at Charon. His expression is something more confused than cocky, asking for permission while asking, "What the hell is she talking about?" without saying it.

"How many do you need?" Charon says.

"He didn't say."

"Val." Charon holds out his arm as he speaks. Val's posture straightens, his eyes lock with Charon's, and, within an instant, without any other words needed, he understands the expectations given to him. It's strange, but loud in the way his posture shifts, his expression changes from questioning to firm obedience, and he crosses behind Charon. A man in black turns into a big raven that lands on Charon's arm. Previously obsidian eyes reflect the light from Poena. Charon reaches for Val, plucking a couple of feathers, hard, but careful. He holds them out to me. I give the feathers to Jag, again, they go in his coat pockets, much bigger than the ones on my jeans.

"Thanks," I say.

"If there is nothing else, I would prefer to move along. I do not know if you noticed, but when a soul stands near the Lethe, it calls. You have been leaning toward it and trying to walk back into it as we have stood here. You are lucky he keeps putting an arm out to stop you." Charon gestures to Jag with a nod.

My face goes hot. "Yeah, well... Jag's always stopping me from doing all the really stupid shit."

"Perhaps if you made better decisions, your circumstances would not be so loathsome," Charon says.

"I've been telling her that for years," Jag says.

"I'm trying, okay?" I don't stand around the tower anymore because now that Charon's said it, I notice when I'm leaning or stepping or tipping and when Jag's arm grabs at me again. Then there are the voices in my head that I don't remember being there before. They're not loud enough to find words, but it's enough to hear the spite and anger, resentment and destruction.

My skin's on fire, prickling from the freeze of my wet hoodie. I rub at my arms.

Charon leads the way back into Caedis Silvis while Val, human again, follows behind Jag and me. The forest's Liquor is kept away by whatever is around the two of them that propels it.

"You doing okay?" Jag mutters over my shoulder. He's not looking at me, but watching Charon's back with a glance behind him to check on Val every so often. The light from Poena disappears quickly without having to go far and the sound or lights from Old Town Mall never comes back. "Joey?" Jag says.

"Yeah." I didn't realize I didn't answer him. "What about you?"

"Still not sure I'm not tripping the hell out right now, to be honest." He chuckles.

"It's… a lot to take. I know." My hand finds his swinging between us. Our fingers lace. He gives my hand a squeeze.

Before long, we're back at the dock. Charon's boat illuminates the water under it with a soft, cool glow. The black searchlight from the firehouse beam flashes through the sky. While it's overhead, the lantern on Charon's boat glows brighter, simmering down again when the light's passed.

"This is…" Jag looks over the water. The lake continues in the distance until it's covered by a purple-gray mist that keeps beyond hidden.

"Crazy, right?" I ease toward the dock, the boat, urging Jag with me by our connected hands. My shaking comes back the closer I get. I fight off a wave of light-headedness. On the boat, the water's calm, silver, a mirror. Jag sits on the bench next to me.

"What did you call this again?" Jag says.

"*Finna* is where you dock on the River Styx," Charon says. "And this will take you to *Iudicium*, judgment."

"Judgment?" Jag says.

"Not for you," I say. "For the living, it's the exit." I

wink.

Val laughs, closing the boat door. We're moving fast. In the distance, the house like Orianda is already forming. I didn't see it happen last time I was here. It's taller, like it's stretched, but not to infinity like Poena. After seeing the tower, though, they're made of the same materials. Carved sigils line the dock, the archway, there are fake windows on the house, glowing dim blue and white light where the glass should be. The closer we get, the more the feeling of *run* nags at me, making my heel bounce.

"So, uh, Charon…" I wait for his glowing eyes to find me. "If this place is judgment for me… how do I get out?"

Charon turns into the boat from facing out. "How did you escape the last time?"

Pain boils to the surface of my skin. I never thought I'd forget the pain or smell or feeling of being swallowed by Styx until I got to the other side of death and all I could think of was capping my dad. Being near the water brings it all back. The sulfuric burn in my nose. My eyes burn too, threatening to close. I don't know if I can do it again. I stand up; the shaking worsens. I look over the edge of that boat again and sit back down as nausea hits.

"What's that mean?" Jag says.

My throat tightens trying to stop me from swallowing. I look for the shoreline that's no longer there. I don't know why I'm hoping to see it or Wayland on the other side, even knowing it wouldn't really be him if I did. I grab my phone from my pocket. The screen's still black and it won't turn on. "You know the hole I fell into at MP when we were looking for Cross?"

Jag nods slowly; he doesn't remember what I'm saying at all.

"This is the same stuff. That's why it burned." I shake my head. Exhale hard. "Doesn't matter. You're gonna have to pick me up on the other side, okay?"

Jag's hand's on my knee. He looks into my eyes. I can't

keep the connection. Embarrassment? Shame? I don't know. My jaw's too tight. "It feels like you're skipping a lot of shit, Joey," Jag says.

I'm rocking, smiling tight to hold back the building panic. "I just don't know if I have time to explain—Or convince you of how far this shit goes. I mean, I'm going through it and I barely believe it." I laugh, short, almost like a gasp. "Just... follow these guys out. I'll see you on the other side at MP. Text me when you get there, okay? Maybe my phone'll work. If it doesn't, I'll be at the bridge over Dead Run." My face's hot, anticipating what's coming before I jump in.

"I don't understand," Jag says.

Standing, my legs threaten to give out. I put my phone back into my pocket. "Just... don't try to follow me, yeah? Promise." I wait for an answer.

Jag doesn't give one.

I take his hand. His fingers closed hard around mine.

"Last time you said that, you almost died," Jag says.

"It's this, or I never see you again, J. For real." My skin pricks cold. I turn back to the water. My face blurs in the reflection. My cheeks are covered in smudgy, black fingerprints. I try to wipe them away with my sleeve. Mostly, they smear further. My skin crawls; my fingers curl at my sides, my entire body's stiff.

"Remember, Josephine," Charon says. "You chose the dark."

I want to ask what that means, why it keeps showing up everywhere around me, but I'm afraid of the answer, so I don't. Never ask questions. That's the rule. So instead of asking anything, I say, "I know, but at least that's what I'm used to."

I try not to think as I throw myself over the side of the boat. The pain's immediate, burning everything, erasing every thought I had and making it worse as it forces its thickness into my throat and melts my clothing to my skin.

I can't think of anything but *Wayland* and every little thing about him that I've ever overlooked. All the shit that's happened to him because he got involved with me. While the last time I jumped in the river, I couldn't think of anything but getting away from my dad, I can't get away from every bit of "Fuck you" I say to myself for dragging Jag to Mortem and Wayland to death.

The searing pain hurts more than anything I've ever felt, intensified by the river. I'm screaming, delusional, someplace that shouldn't exist. The end finally comes with a feeling of nothing and peace that lasts only for a second.

FOURTEEN.

My phone's in my hand; I'm alternating between pacing and standing still with a bouncing foot. I'm on my third cigarette in thirty minutes; they're burning faster than they probably should. Granted, they probably shouldn't be burning at all. They're fucking soaked, but my phone's back on now, so I'm not asking questions. I've tried sending messages to Wayland, but he's not saying anything back and every time I try to call, it's immediately cut off. I don't even know if the calls are going out. The text is messed up sometimes. It's probably Styx in the circuits; it doesn't work like water, it just likes to get in the way. Last time I jumped in, my phone eventually came back to functional, so it should be fine, right?

I check again, looking for Wayland's number. This time, his messages are gone completely.

Then a message from Jag comes down from the top saying, "On my way."

At least it means my phone's not broken. I send BRIDGE back to Jag. It's misspelled, there's a number in it, but my hands are shaking and I don't care enough to fix it as long as he knows that I'm here. The pacing's getting worse and I'm on my fourth cigarette now, throwing punches through the air and at small branches I know I can take.

It's twenty more minutes when Jag's Mustang pulls up

at the side of the road. He leans over to unlock the passenger door.

I climb in.

He's turning the radio down.

We get out of the park without him saying anything.

I don't know if it's all me I'm feeling. Nervous.

"You look like shit," Jag says.

I catch myself in the side mirror. My hair's hard, like it went through something sticky and I look like I've got a fever. "I've been through shit." I laugh and rub at my eyes. "You don't want to know what it's like to drown on regret."

Jag doesn't say anything to that.

Out the window, the words GOD, LOVE ME are painted on the side of a brick townhouse. A couple of eyes, a fire, then some random gang tags in different colors, painted one over another in a pissing contest to reclaim territory. The next wall reads WORDS HAVE NO POWER TO IMPRESS THE MIND inside of a mouth with no teeth. The head doesn't have eyes. Around the jaw, it reads WITHOUT THE EXQUISITE HORROR OF THEIR REALITY. Next is a large, black orb meant to be reflective with a creature in a black robe saying DON'T TRUST THE REAPER. THE BASTARD WEARS WHITE.

I laugh bitterly. My whole face hurts, so I groan, press my hand against it to make it stop. Somehow, I'm congested and my nose is a faucet at the same time. "So stupid… The reaper doesn't even look like that." I wipe my nose with the back of my hand. I'm still trembling. Jag slides his hand from the clutch to the center console. Maybe not an invitation, but I pretend it is and take his hand.

"*That's* supposed to be a reaper?" Jag finally says.

"Hard to believe, I know." A laugh bubbles up and chokes out immediately. "I'm not sure I even believe it yet."

Jag exhales hard. "You doing okay?" The way he asks says he knows the answer and knows he shouldn't be asking, but he did it anyway and there are so many things I want to say, everything more honest than the natural, "Yeah, J, I'm fine. Thanks," that comes out first.

Habit.

Bad decisions.

I catch him giving me a side glance. He squeezes my hand, then slips it away to take the clutch. As soon as he switches gears, my hand's back in his.

"When you jumped into the water," he says slowly, working his stiff jaw. "I didn't think I could stay there. Joey... I almost jumped in after you. Your friend said not to, but... I didn't think I'd see you again."

"At least... they did that." A strong throb tightens in my chest, goes through my fingertips, up my arm, and into my head where I think I'm going to explode.

"I couldn't listen to you scream like that." His teeth clench. His hand's squeezing mind so hard it hurts. "I've never heard anything like it. You... didn't even sound like yourself and fuck, Joey... I can't... The way you've sounded before when you've been asleep doesn't even compare. You're seriously gonna tell me you're fine?"

"Yeah." My foot's bouncing faster. "Yeah, yeah, yeah, yeah." I'm not looking in his direction. If he looks into me, maybe see something I don't want him to see. I draw my hand away from his. My own hands meld together, pick at my skin, lace around each other to pretend it's some consolation. My feet alternate now and I'm still saying, "Yeah, yeah, yeah." I press into the floor just enough to get my ass off the car seat. The seatbelt at my hips keeps me from going too high. Still, I've got my cigarettes in my hand. There're only three left inside and I'm wondering where the hell the rest went. The box was full this morning. I roll down the window before one's lit and in my mouth. The long, slow drag isn't enough to fix me, but it's a start.

The stop sign on the street corner has a pink and black fist painted on it. The wall behind it has CHOSE DARK and LOOK BACK and REGRET with bleeding eyes drawn separately. I take another drag, faster this time. "I've gotta be, right?" I steal a quick glance, give him a half-smile. It's gone by the time I turn away again. "I chose this."

"If something happened to you, you didn't *choose* it."

"I do a lot of stupid shit," I say.

"Yeah?" Jag says. "What's new there?"

"Nothing." I snort. "I just think it's finally catching up to me. Sorry I pulled you into this with me." I laugh into my cigarette.

"You've gotta stop blaming yourself for shit you didn't do—"

"But you've gotta admit, I bring a lot of it onto myself, right?" I grab my phone again and find Wayland's name back in my contacts list. I send him a quick, "You dead?" and "Where the hell are you, Cross?" then drop my phone again. I sink into the car seat. I put my cigarette out and turn the radio up. I can't keep my eyes open. All that's there anymore is the soft sound of oldies rock while everything else sinks away. Jag's muttering lyrics when he thinks I've fallen asleep. His thumb strokes my hand intermittently when he's not shifting gears. It's nice, but it's not enough to stop the building panic and this feeling like the birds really are all around the car, even when I can't see them.

When we get back to Jag's apartment, the light's on inside. We're still in the street, pulling into the garage when he says, "What the hell...?"

It's not just that the light's on, it's flickering and dark and the curtain's pulled back in a weird way. You can't see furniture from here, but there's something smeared across the glass.

The engine's barely been cut when Jag's almost running toward the building. We take the stairs. The moment we hit his floor, the smell hits. Sour stink, mud, rot, and blood. The carpet's stained with fast shoe prints, spread far like sprinting, red and fresh-looking. I crouch beside one and touch it. The blood's still wet and gooey, though it's cooled. A path of crimson smears along the hallway while fingers trail along the walls. There's more blood dripping between footprints. We're not even at his place yet but where the prints stop is obvious.

311: Jag's place.

No one has been bothered and there's no hesitation in the steps to make it look randomly selected.

Jag runs the rest of the way down the hall. His front door's hanging open, the latch torched, the knob busted out from blunt force bashing it until it snapped.

"What the hell," he says through his teeth.

Inside, the couch's turned over, the cushions are pulled out, torn apart, and foam lays on the floor in front of the cracked television screen. The end tables are knocked over and pulled open with the drawers hanging out. The lampshades are bent while glass from the bulbs littering the wooden floor. Not all the lights in the unit work; half of the overhead lights in the kitchen are busted, and the bedroom is mostly dark. Glass sits on top the counter; the metal lamps are banged up like someone brought a bat. The fridge is hanging open with much of its contents spilled onto the floor. A couple of beer bottles lay broken behind the kitchen island. In the bedroom, the windows are knocked out while the room's split apart, sheets scattered and mixed with loose clothing. A couple of springs litter the floor along with foam from the pillows and a spread of clothing from the drawers and laundry basket. The bathroom's the least destroyed with only the contents that had been on the counter tossed. On the mirror, the words SORRY and I CAN'T TAKE IT BACK are written.

Returning to the bedroom, the wall behind the door says LOOKING FOR A WAY OUT and the living room wall says HELP, trailing off, all in the same color: crimson.

I take a picture of everything with my phone. Back in the living room, Jag's got his phone pressed to his ear and he's giving someone his address.

"We'll be here," he says, then hangs up.

"Jag…" I say.

"What else am I supposed to do, Joey? Ignore our place's been busted into?"

"Realistically, what do you think the badges are gonna do?"

"They'll put this on the record."

"Right." I cross my arms, turn away, take another picture just to give myself something to do. I push the remote across the floor with my foot. "All you're doing is giving them another chance to see your face and where you live so it can bite you in the ass later." I pace toward the kitchen, but halfway there, the busted bottles on the floor become visible and I remember there's nothing left to drink. I keep going anyway to close the fridge door.

"Don't do that," Jag says.

"What?" I say.

"I know *you* don't think it's a big deal, but disrupting a crime scene kind of fucking matters."

"Right." My tongue runs along my bottom lip. I need to put something in my mouth so I don't say something stupid, but all I've only got like three cigarettes left and the badges coming will make me put it out anyway since we're not supposed to smoke in here. I pull the fridge door back open, moving slowly, careful to adjust it as I bring it back to where it maybe once was. "How's that look, J?"

Jag rubs his eyes. "Just stop touching it."

I pull the fridge door open just a little bit further.

Instead of walking with it, I lean forward, thrusting my ass out behind me while I grab the shelf with the other hand. "Why don't you come and make me?"

Jag's pursing his lips; he rolls his eyes and comes across the room. There's not as much of a smile as I'd hoped for. Still, he comes up behind me. His hands slide from my shoulders, down my arms, and to my wrists. His muscles move against my body; his grip is strong and comfortable. I let him pull me away without resistance. He's stepping back into the living room, tugging me with him. His hands slide back up my arms until he's wrapping them around my shoulders. Both arms are tight and he pulls me to him. The pressure builds inside me. My legs are weak; I wrap my arms around him too. If it wasn't for him, I don't think I'd be standing right now.

"I know it's hard," he says, "but you have to accept that your friend is a lunatic, Joey. He's acting like someone who's burning out."

"That's why I can't let him go, J."

"He's gonna take you down with him."

"So? Why don't you let him?"

"Because I fucking care about you."

"I don't know why." Stepping back, I push against Jag's chest.

"Sometimes, neither do I." He lets me go.

"Shit. I'm sorry." My fingers lace; I press them to the top of my head. "Fuck." I turn away, walk fast, glass crunches under my shoe. "You have no idea what it's like—What the river does to you—how it goes through every corner of your head and just—Ugh—I lived with a dead guy for fifteen years, Jag. What's going on with Cross isn't that bad."

"Yeah? Who'd your dad kill?"

The impulse is there to grab something—anything—and chuck it at Jag, but everything's knocked over and harder to reach, so I end up with nothing but a hand-thrown through the air, then fists balled up at my sides. "Don't you dare say my dad is better than Cross!"

"I'm not saying your dad was a good guy, but how long's Cross been dead? How many people've followed after him? And his house? What about his family?"

"What happened to *you don't choose shit that's done to you*, huh?" All I can see is Jag and the thoughts screaming GO FOR THE THROAT on repeat like every time my dad came after me. I turn around so I can't see him anymore and go through the living room. Jagged glass punctures my sneakers' rubber soles, but I keep going, hit the fridge door shut, growl, and swear at myself for not being able to stop the impulse. Glass makes it through my shoe and digs into the bottom of my foot. I step back, grabbing at the counter. More loose glass from the bulbs cut my hand.

"You're losing it, Joey—"

I push off the counter.

"Watch where you're going," Jag says.

"I'm trying!" My blood's pulsing harder under my skin, maybe not blood. I don't know. I'm dead. Nothing should be pulsing, but I feel it, you know? The rage, bursting under everything, burns me from the inside. The voices are getting louder. It's the same lust I felt at home with my dad, the same shit from the bar, the same thing I felt around Donny for cutting me loose. The voices seethe in my ears, *knock him out, give it a try*; they're drowning all of my thoughts, stalking me around the room and getting louder the further from J I get as I think, "Shut up, shut up, shut up," so loud I'm saying it.

"Slow down, Joey." Jag's coming toward the kitchen and I'm stepping back. The faster I move, the faster he moves; he's trying to catch up.

"Stay the hell away from me, Jag. Alright? I need a minute. That's all I just need a fucking minute to breathe." I'm covering my eyes with my hands. It's not the tears, it's not the room spinning, it's that I know this has to be what

Wayland felt leading up to every one of his mistakes. Turning out the lights should help. My heart's pounding in my ears again, fighting for control over the voices. I feel sick; I'm gonna vomit, fall over, faint if I don't sit on the floor. I'm panting and all I hear is the hissing of busted lights and I think J's saying, "Goddamn, she's crazy." At the same time, it doesn't sound like him and I can't tell who is talking to me anymore, but who else could it be when it's only him and me here right now?

The anger's not subsiding and I don't know what to do with it; I reach for anything I can find on the floor. A handful of glass. I throw it onto the kitchen floor, hissing again as it cuts into my hand. A light flickers.

Jag doesn't say anything, but goes into the bedroom. I lay on my back, letting my arms drape over my face while I breathe hard, panting harder, deeper, trying to relax. My tongue flicks over my lip, my teeth grab at my ring, trying to find something to do other than swear or echo the things going on in my head.

Breathing's not doing anything, so I switch to hold my breath. I thought meditation was supposed to help rage. They sell it on TV; they sell it for thousands of dollars at college; they sell it as weekend packages or things to do with your girlfriends *to reset your internal clock*. Who would've thought that *selling breathing* was another goddamn scam?

I let out a heavy breath. It's shaky. The dizziness threatens to throw me through the floor. I'm not sure how. I exhale again, harder.

"You done?" Jag says from the bedroom.

"I could use a beer." I drop my arm back over my face.

"Should I come back later?"

I lower my arm. The ceiling's blurry, the jerky impulse comes back strong. I'm never ready to hear his voice, but for the last couple of weeks, it feels like I haven't been able to shake him off. "Probably," I say. I wipe under my eyes in case there might've been something there. Then my fingers go to my jeans. A couple of red stains stripe my thighs where my fingers have been.

Rocky's standing in the hallway on the other side of Jag's busted apartment door.

"What, you the only badge working Baltimore nowadays?" I say.

"Sometimes, it damn sure feels like it." Rocky steps over the mess of crumpled rug by the door. He scans the floor, going to the living room, and stops on the word ESCAPE, which I hadn't noticed before. He moves carefully, coming further in, but goes no further than the kitchen island.

Jag's standing at the bedroom door. The detective eyes him.

"We should stop meeting like this," Rocky says to Jag.

"Two times is a habit, right?" I say.

Rocky's focus on Jag breaks. His head drops to the side and something flashes across his face. Confusion? Familiarity? Suspicion? His eyes go a little wide for a second like he's found something and I'm thinking, *oh shit, does he actually know who I am?* I don't know what the point of faking amnesia with me would be when he remembers Jag. We're kind of a packaged deal under the circumstances.

Rocky's head twists to the other side. His eyes narrow. His lips purse and he makes a soft 'hm' sound.

"Can I help you?" I say.

"I'm not sure…" Rocky draws his notepad out from his pocket. His pen clicks. He pauses without writing anything down, though the pen's tip presses to his paper. "Something felt familiar just now, though." He laughs.

"I'm sure it did," I say.

I close my eyes again and drop my hand over my face. I pretend it's because I'm nauseous. My face is fever-y anyway. I turn onto my side, putting my back to Rocky to make myself feel better. The room goes quiet.

I shouldn't hate it so much.

I shouldn't be wishing for Rocky to say something just so I don't risk hearing a raven's laugh from somewhere, so I'm not thinking about how they're following Jag and how sure Val is that he's going to die soon and what I can do to stop it. If it's not Jag they're following, maybe it's Rocky. That'd be better, right? I wouldn't need to feel bad if they took Rocky away.

Fuck. Why doesn't he say something?

I roll onto my back.

"Why exactly are you here?" Jag says. "Aren't you homicide or something?"

"At the moment, I guess *or something's* about right," Rocky says. "Saw your number come up in the emergency calls. Figured since we've become somewhat familiar with each other, I'd check it out. You'd be surprised at how many murderers are caught during innocuous interactions. Something small goes wrong and, well…" Rocky gives me a brief look, then he's surveying Jag where he stands in the doorway, then me again, and then around the house. "So what happened here?"

"We don't know." Jag comes into the living room. "Joey and I were out together and when we came back, the door was busted in and the place looked like shit."

"Did you notice anything missing?" Rocky says.

Jag scans the room. "I haven't really been through everything, but maybe…" Jag's loud steps make me sit up. He moves into the kitchen, careful where he steps as he looks over the counter, the floors, pulling open the cabinets, and even the microwave. He goes back to the bedroom. "Shit," he says. Back into the living room, he's looking around the floor again, picking up pillows now, the blanket, the couch cushions.

"What are you looking for, J?" I use the kitchen island to help me stand up.

He's still moving things. Another trip to the bedroom. He comes back. His lips press into a line. "Shit," he mutters again. His hands rub the back of his neck. He crosses his arms with a half shake of his head.

"What's missing?" Rocky says.

Jag looks at me. He holds his breath in, gives the room another scan, sighs. "A gun."

My skin goes hot.

"We had a gun," Jag says.

Rocky writes something on his notepad. "What kind of gun?"

"A handgun," Jag says. "Joey, you know what kind it was?"

"No," I say.

The dizziness is back. I lean against the counter for stability.

"Do you know anyone who might've known you had a gun or do you believe it was taken at random?" Rocky says.

"No. It was brought into the house, like, two days ago," Jag says. He walks along the backside of the couch. He stops, his attention on something, the cabinet holding the washer and dryer. His eyes follow the blood along the floor, the print on the cabinet's folding door. "Maybe."

"What are you thinking?" Rocky says.

Jag combs his fingers through his hair. Another sigh. "Her friend, Wayland Cross," he says.

"Or maybe it was a random robbery and they broke in, saw the gun, and took it," I say. "Things don't have to be that complicated."

"That's not funny," Rocky says.

"I'm not joking," Jag says.

Rocky's weight shifts, his expression doesn't. Briefly, his glance flickers to me. "We haven't made it public yet and I shouldn't say anything to you either." He glances between us. He taps his pen against his notepad, shakes his head a little, and takes a break. "But Mr. Cross is a person of interest in a current murder investigation. We've been looking for him for about two weeks. We haven't found much about him, but we think he might be dead or have fled the state."

I laugh quietly, turn away, go for my cigarettes.

"You don't seem surprised," Rocky says.

"That's par the course in Bodymore, *Rocky*." I put an unlit cigarette in my mouth.

"You know, not everyone's so casual about death," Rocky says.

"Yeah?" I pretend to take a drag. "Death doesn't seem so real if the fuckers come back and haunt you after the fact."

Rocky stares at me, analytical, familiar, but again, confused. My face is hot. I put the cigarette back in my mouth and turn away, though still leaning against the kitchen island, my back's not to Rocky. The apartment falls quiet again, except for the noise from a neighbor down the hall.

"So," Jag says, "do we make a statement or how does this work?"

"I'd like to talk to you separately—"

"Fuck," I breathe into my hand. "Sorry."

Rocky takes a moment before continuing. "If that's alright…" He's looking between the two of us.

"Yeah," Jag says.

"Party," I say.

"Then we'll keep this information on hand with our current investigation and let you know if we find anything substantive," Rocky says.

He takes Jag into the hall and they go far enough down I can't hear them from the apartment. I'm pacing the living room, looking across the counters, under the overturned tables and the couch, thinking maybe the gun fell somewhere when the asshole wrecked Jag's place or maybe I moved it while being half asleep. I check the drawers in the bathroom. I don't know why it would be there, but I'm hopeful it's not *gone*.

The gun's not there either.

I know I left it on the kitchen counter. I'm still hoping I'm wrong and Jag's wrong and that everything Jag's said is out of some kind of insecurity he pretends he's never had.

Jag and Rocky come back in. It feels too soon. My hair's sticking to my forehead, matted down with sweat. Rocky waves me over and with everything I've put Jag through tonight, I don't feel like I can refuse this.

I put my unlit cigarette on the counter before leaving the apartment. We go into the hall by the elevator and Rocky asks me like five times, "Has he ever hit you?" and "What are the bruises around your neck? They look like hands," and I tell him, "Those are from last week and maybe two days ago. I'm a little scrappy and that's about it. Jag's not the kind of guy you're thinking of." I laugh at how absurd the image of Jag being like my dad is. "You really think I'd be here if he was?"

Something changes in Rocky's face. He smiles a little, but his lips press flat.

Pity.

People dole it out in buckets because it's easier to give than actual help.

"You'd be surprised at the kinds of things I've seen people forgive," he says.

"I don't put up with that bullshit," I say.

Rocky laughs.

"What's so funny?" I say.

"Nothing. Just... I've heard that line before, God knows how many times. Broken spouses fearing the unfamiliar. Sure, being in the house isn't great, but it's better than the unknown of stepping out the door, wondering who would ever want you again after rejecting the only thing you've ever known. *He's not always that bad,* right? And he'll do something nice sometimes, it's small, but it's enough to make you rethink everything you've ever felt because right now it doesn't feel *that* bad. You think you're being over-dramatic; things are finally getting better; he's just in pain and if you step away and something happens, you'll blame yourself," Rocky says.

He glances down the hall like he's heard something, maybe he's checking for someone in the doorway of 311. "A lot of *dysfunction* continues that way. If not by the same person, it's someone else who treats you the way you're used to. Maybe you get mad when he beats you, but it's been happening for so long that when it doesn't happen, you wonder how the hell you messed up your usual. I've seen people become anxious when they weren't getting beaten. The expectation grows; either you've found something unsustainable or the coming mistake is going to be worse than anything you've done before. Things might be good now, but how long until *you ruin everything*? Once subjected to enough abuse, some people can't help but repeat every bad thing they've ever heard about themselves like it's the truth, you know? I've seen it so many times, even after being taken out of a bad situation. But what can you say? Once routines are mare, they're hard to break."

"I've noticed," I say. "That's why we keep bumping into each other, yeah?"

"What's that?" Rocky says through a laugh.

"I said, sounds like a sad existence."

"Some people really get stuck in the mindset. And it's... a horror show." Rocky acts like he's not watching me, but he's not good at it.

"Fits right into Bodymore, then." My fingers sink into my pants pockets. I'm reminded of the bloodstains running down my thighs from the fresh, stinging cuts on my hands.

"Please, don't hold back how much you hate this city." He laughs again, this one's more honest than the others.

"I wouldn't say that. It's the only thing I've ever known and it's part of who I am. Sometimes the misery around this place just gets... a little tiring." I turn away on my heels. Looking down the hall, Jag's door still hangs open. The bloody trails look so wrong here, like they did at Wayland's house, like the horror show that was my house. I got rid of my dad, but it hasn't stopped the destruction from stalking me, no matter where I am. My fingers graze my phone. I haven't felt anything come in, but I wonder if maybe I missed a signal when I was fighting with Jag. I turn back to the detective. "Are we done here?"

"Sure thing," Rocky says. "Just confirm for me one more time what happened."

Back to the badge tactics; he's trying to catch me in a lie. It's what they do, even when you're the one that puts in the call, even when you're supposed to be assumed innocent. Badges really don't think that. Instead, they think *what did you do*, if not this time, then what are you hiding? He's waiting for me to forget something or contradict myself because he thinks I'm gonna get overly sentimental after his story. I'm supposed to trust him now and he did it so well that I feel like I actually should, at least a little. Maybe I'm just tired.

I tell him the same story he got the first time, the same story Jag told him when he came into the apartment. He asks me more about the gun, like if it's registered and where I got it and when I say I don't want to talk about it, he says, "It wasn't yours, was it?" just confirming to me how they're always looking to catch you on something.

I don't want to answer, but not answering is worse. "It belonged to my dad. When he passed, he gave it to me. Is that illegal or something?"

"When did that happen?" Rocky's writing without looking at his notepad.

I don't know what the city knows. I don't know if they have his death certificate from when he died or if it only showed up after his soul went away. I don't know if I'm the only one that never registered he died back then or if everyone was just as fooled by his ghost as I was. So the best answer I have is, "I was eight."

"Sorry to hear that," Rocky says.

"Don't be," I say. "He was a piece of shit. After the speech you just gave, you'd be glad he's in the ground."

"Then I'm glad you're in a better place—"

"I don't know if I'd say that. My—" The words catch in my mouth. What was I about to say? My house? My boyfriend's house? Both feel scarier than lying. "Jag's place got broken into and this whole gun thing—"

"Don't worry about that right now." Rocky slips his notebook away. "You were a kid."

My lips pull into a small grin. My head cocks to the side. "Are you saying you're gonna *cover* for me, Rocky?"

"I'm saying we'll figure something out. I'm not totally heartless, you know?" He laughs.

"Maybe," I mutter, too quiet for him to hear.

"Do you and your *boyfriend* have a place to stay tonight?"

The word catches me off guard. I'm not breathing. My jaw's tight and my brain's telling me he's not talking about Jag. Maybe I told Wayland we were kind of doing something casual, but by something casual, I meant *just fucking*, right? And even that's probably over after this. I can feel it. As much as I call him an asshole, Jag's actually a good guy—too good for someone like me. I wipe my face, feeling the heat and sweat on my skin again. The tears in my eyes. I'm tired of crying. I'm tired of questions. I'm tired of everything but his quiet off room, his smell, and his body against mine, keeping me sane for a couple more hours while the rest of the world fades away.

"Yeah," I say. "We'll figure something out."

Rocky pulls out his wallet. He withdraws a familiar card. Recycled cardboard, thick, gold lettering. His pencil clicks and he writes against the hard surface of his wallet, then hands me the card. "If anything else happens, feel free to give me a call."

I take the card because Rocky keeps holding it without moving and I know it will make him get lost faster. I don't think he believes that Jag doesn't beat me. He keeps looking down the hall and looking at me in a way I know he's checking out the bruises he can see again, wondering how far down they go like he didn't get an eyeful the last time he saw me.

"Thanks." I slip the card into my pocket and pull my hoodie over my head. "We done now?" I'm already stepping back.

Rocky pats down his pocket, pulls out his notepad, writes something. He nods to himself. "We are... What was your name?"

"Joey."

"Good night, Joey."

"Good night, Rocky." I turn around, making my way back to Jag's apartment as fast as I can. My phone's in hand. Still nothing from Wayland. I curse under my breath. The elevator dings. It almost sounds like a whistle. "Oh." I turn around on my heels. "Rocky?"

"Hm?" he turns to me.

"If you see a murder... run the other way, alright?"

"A murder?" he says. "Do you know something I don't?"

"Probably." I laugh. Look away. Don't let him catch my eyes. The laugh stops, caught on something like a cough. At the sound, Rocky's coming toward me now. "But I'm talking about *ravens*. If you see a *murder of ravens*, run. You know what a murder is, right?

"Actually, a group of crows is a murder; a group of ravens is an *unkindness*... or a conspiracy," he says.

"Figures." I roll my eyes. "That what a group of badges is called too?"

"Nah. Usually, that's a squad or a unit."

"Oops. My bad. I've been calling it 'bullshit.'"

"You really don't like the BPD, do you?"

"How could you ever have guessed?"

"I get where you're coming from. We don't have the greatest record—"

"You have a *shit* record—"

"But we're not all bad."

"That's the glitz of the badge talking."

"'*Integrity, fairness, service.*' Every day I put in the work to be worthy of wearing the uniform."

What a dork. I can't help the smile, but I push it back down just as fast as it comes. "You want to earn some cred? Start by finding Wayland Cross."

"I'll see what I can do."

"I'll look forward to the call." I turn away again. A couple steps down the hall, I stop again, turn back. "Do you remember my name?"

"Joey, right?"

I smile. "Sounds about right." I turn back around. My hand raises in the air. "Good night." I wave over my shoulder. The elevator dings again by the time I'm at the apartment's threshold. Jag's got the cushions back on the trashed couch and a couple of bags stacked on top of it. "Where're we going?" I push the door shut. It won't stay closed until I hit the lock on the knob; even that's sketchy though. I don't think it'd hold if you knocked on the other side.

"Mom's house," Jag says.

I groan. "I don't want to go to your mom's house, J."

"We're not staying here and we're not going to your place."

I always feel bad when I see J's mom, like she's disappointed that he hasn't brought home someone better yet; that he's settling; that maybe she thinks she's a failure too because her son hasn't nabbed something better. The bruises make it worse. If Rocky noticed, Jag's mom'll notice.

"Maybe you should go there and I'll just go home." I peel open one of the bag's on the couch to see which one's mine. Jag's clothing is in this one. I zip it shut and grab the other bag.

"Yeah, that's a great idea, Joey. Sounds super safe."

"Nowhere's safe, J."

"No offense, but my mom's house is better than your place."

"You say that like I don't know it already—"

"Then why the fuck are you fighting me on this?"

"Because I don't belong there!" I toss my bag back onto the couch. Hot. I'm not seeing clearly. Tears. Frustration. Exhaustion. Anything that's less pathetic than what's actually going around in my head. Jag's taking too long to say anything.

"You dragged me to Hell, you're spending the night at my mom's."

"So you believe me now?" I say.

He's staring at me. "I don't know what to believe, Joey. I saw some shit, I'm working it out, I'm tired, and I don't want to deal with any more of this tonight, alright? That's pretty much where I'm at. So, grab whatever you still need from the room; we're leaving."

I grab my bag off the couch and take it to the bedroom. Jag's picked up most of the clothes, though I never really unpacked when we got here the other day. I open the top dresser drawer where my stuff usually is. Jag's clothes are tossed in now, not folded, mixed. It doesn't matter. I never brought much to begin with since Jag's house was never supposed to be my home. I don't need anything else, but I walk into the bathroom. I'm scanning the shower for our soap, my toothbrush, a comb. I turn back to the bedroom. Jag's standing in the door.

"What are you looking for?"

My jaw's tight; I have to work the answer out. "I don't know."

"Why are you afraid of my mom?"

"I'm not afraid of your mom, J."

"But you're stalling."

I cross the room to him. My fingers press into his chest. Electric. Heat rushes through my body. "You're not supposed to call me out like that." My hand slips around his neck I stand on my toes to lean in closer. My lips graze his; Jag turns his head to make me miss.

"Joey," he mutters, arms around my waist. "We need to go."

A caw comes through the broken window. I let go of Jag and step back. "Yeah." I pick my bag up from the bed, shut the dresser drawers, and slip out the door past him. "How long are we gonna be at your mom's?"

"I'll call the landlord again first thing tomorrow, alright?"

It's not really, but I don't have an argument. I dragged him through so much, I can't tell him I won't stay at his mom's place unless I don't want to see him ever again and… I don't think I'm ready for that. It's only one night. Another caw comes and I feel like if I leave, it'll be my fault if something bad happens to him. The same way it was my fault when my dad died. Jag's gotta be the one to walk away so I know I didn't pull the trigger.

I grab his bag from the couch so I'm carrying them both out the door. He shuts the apartment, locks it, but the crack around the hinges makes it obvious how easy it'd be to break down again. Jag's close behind me, going down the hall and while we're standing at the elevator, he takes his bag, offering to take mine. "I've got it, J. Don't worry, but you look like you're gonna pass out. You sure you can drive?" I say.

"I'm fine," he says.

"Can I at least carry your bag?"

"If you really want it."

"I do, J. It's the least I can do."

He's hesitant, but he gives his bag back to me before we're out of the elevator.

We're at the car and I'm kind of surprised nothing's happened to it. Busted out windows, dents in the door, something. Jag would've lost his shit if Wayland had been waiting around here somewhere. Would've been worse to not be Wayland, but a bunch of angry ghosts looking to get revenge on me.

My foot's bouncing while Jag drives. He's keeping both hands on the clutch and wheel and not looking at me at all. I'm holding my cigarette box. I need one, but there's only one left, so I don't take it. The radio's on low and Jag's muttering along. He doesn't know most of the words, so he's making some up and slurring them together. He does this when he's tired, to keep himself from falling asleep. We get to his mom's house and the porch light's on. His brother's bedroom light's on too. The driveway's empty. Jag's mom lives in a small place, not as nice as Wayland's, but it's not trash either. It's made of old, faded bricks that look gray in the dark, with a short, wooden fence, and a white door. Jag unlocks the front door and waits for me to go in first. He locks it behind us.

"Lane," Jag's voice echoes off the thin, plain walls.

A door opens at the end of the hall. Lane comes out of his room wearing gray basketball shorts and a black tank. He doesn't play any sports—At least, I don't remember Jag telling me he does, but he mixes music. He's fifteen, was an accident, though Jag's told me his mom doesn't like to say that. Lane glances between Jag and me. He's got the same color eyes and the same shape jaw as his brother, just less developed and boyish. His body's lanky, like he hasn't grown into his arms or legs yet. His dark brown hair is just barely long enough to tie back out of the way.

"Mom's working tonight," Lane says. "Did she know you were coming?"

"I texted her," Jag says. "My place was broken into, so we're spending the night."

"Who'd you bring?" Lane says, looking back at me, but only for a second. I've only met him a few times, but he's always been like this. Maybe it's the unfamiliarity, but he can't even look at me for long. The couple of times Jag's had me eat dinner here, the kid's never tried talking to me. He just sort of talked to Jag or his mom about whatever he wanted and I'd just be there, but it's like I wasn't. I don't know. I don't care. It made me feel better that he didn't really acknowledge me, you know?

"Joey. You've met her before." Jag drops his bag on a living room chair. He takes the cushions off the couch. Underneath is a foldout bed.

Lane briefly looks at me again. "Another Joey?"

"Same one," Jag says.

"She looks different," Lane says.

"It's been a rough couple of weeks." Jag tries to laugh; it comes off deflated. With the bed pulled out, he goes to the hall closet and grabs a couple pillows, a blanket, a set of sheets. I'm still standing in the entryway when he walks by again. "Take off your shoes, Joey. Or are you gonna run?" He drops the blanket and pillows on the chair.

"Would you chase after me if I did?" I say.

Jag unfolds the sheet for the bed. He tucks it under the first edge of the mattress. "Haven't you noticed? I'm always chasing after you." Another tired chuckle. He wipes his face, groans, looks at me through his fingers.

I slide my shoes off. My face's burning. I say, "I need some water," while walking toward the bathroom. Door closed, locked, I sit on the toilet for a minute. My heart's racing. The water's on as cold as I can make it go and I'm leaning down to drink. Coming back up, my reflection stares at me like I'm a stranger. Smeared, black eyeliner paws down my face and somehow, there's still enough around my eyes to turn them into pits of nothing. My irises and pupils are the same, but instead of being green or black, they've got a kind of red shine to them. I wash my face and lean back. The image doesn't change.

The red marks around my neck look darker. Have they been this dark all night? Is this what the detective saw? I'm lucky he didn't think I was high and lying about a fight.

I slide my phone out of my pocket and sit on the toilet again. I'm in Wayland's texts. There's still nothing there.

JOEY   I need to know you're ok, Way.
              Message me.
              Call me.
              Something.

I set my phone down. My foot's tapping. I shake my head to try and get the throbbing out of my ears. I feel like my brain's going to explode. The sink's still running. I pick up the phone again.

JOEY   Were you at Jag's house?

My hands are sweaty. I wipe them off over the blood streaks. I'm staring at my phone, not sure if it's blurry because I'm tired or it's the adrenaline. The phone buzzes. I almost drop it. The screen reads:

WAYLAND   NO.
              WHY?
JOEY   Someone broke in.
              Stole some shit.
              You ok?

Too much time passes without Wayland saying anything.

JOEY	Ralph at the bar.
	You know him?
	He said he could help us.
WAYLAND	HELP?
JOEY	With the ghost thing
	He knows some stuff.
	Where are you rn?
WAYLAND	JO
	I

It's minutes and he still hasn't said anything.

| JOEY | Tell me what you're thinking, Way. |
| | I can't help you if you don't talk. |

Still nothing. I try calling, but the phone's ringing's distorted, then it disconnects. The second time I call, electricity comes through my hand and goes down my arm. I drop the phone with a yelp.

"Joey?"

"It's fine, Dad—I'm fine." I reach for the door to check it's locked. I push on it a little to see how much give it's got. It's firm. That doesn't matter if he starts hitting it though. I turn the light off, close my eyes, and press my hands to my ears. My feet are on the toilet and I'm making myself as small as I can. "I was just startled, Dad. I'm fine."

"What are you talking about, your dad? Joey—Do you know where you are?" Jag's voice echoes down the hall. The doorknob shifts. The lock holds it back. "Joey?" I pull away with a gasp, then curse myself for thinking I'm at home, for turning the lights out and pretending that this would save me.

I turn the bathroom light back on. I pick up my phone from the floor between my feet. My hand's trembling. I put my phone back into my pocket. "Yeah, yeah, sorry. I'll, uh, I'll be out in a minute, J." Standing up, my cheeks are wet with red trails. Not blood, but I don't have time to question it. I wipe them off with the back of my hand, wash my face, and turn off the faucet. Unlocking the bathroom door, Jag's stepping back when I push it open.

"You okay?" he says.

"Yeah." I wipe at my eyes like I'm tired, hoping there's nothing left in my face to make the lie more obvious. "Fell in. Someone left the seat up." I laugh, walking past Jag. He goes into the bathroom after a moment and I'm grateful for the chance to be alone. I'm at the side of the fold-out bed, looking down at the pillows and pulled back blanket waiting for people to cradle. I glance at the front door, the keys on the counter, my skateboard against the wall.

I slip into my shoes. My hand's on the doorknob and I've got my skateboard in my other hand. The voice in my head's saying, *go, go, go, go, go* and my phone feels like it's burning my thigh. I set my skateboard down to wipe my sweaty palms on my pants again. Breathing out hard, I'm getting lightheaded. I think that's what's causing it. I slide my shoes off and kick them toward the armchair. My jeans go next and take my socks with them. I'm hot, sweating so much my shirt's clinging to my skin and I can smell myself under the cotton, but I don't want any more skin showing. I go through my bag until I find my phone charger. I'm laying down once I know the battery won't die. It's not long before Jag's back.

The light goes off, the mattress springs squeal under his weight, then his arm's around me. His body curves around mine and his warmth makes me feel safe. He mutters, "Try to relax, Joey. Nothing's gonna happen," and his breath warms my skin, trying to coax me to sleep.

My eyes keep trying to close; I should let them, but every time I get comfortable, I panic. There's a sound, shrill, it has to be a caw, then another. My eyes open wide;

everything's tense. Jag's hand finds mine. Our fingers lace with his on top. His lips are near my hair, burning into the back of my head.

"Whatever you're thinking about we'll solve tomorrow, alright? You're not gonna do anyone any good running yourself out until you're busted. Cross is probably sleeping too," Jag says.

I don't want to leave it there, but I can't fight anymore. My eyes close, my heart slows down, the weight of everything hits me fast and takes me away from everything.

FIFTEEN.

When I wake up, I'm cold. I reach for my hoodie's hood, but it's not there. My hands glide down my bare arms. When did I take my hoodie off? The house smells like coffee. The toilet flushes down the hall. Jag comes out of the bathroom wearing grease-stained jeans and a t-shirt. "What about Freddy?" Jag's saying, his phone pressed between his shoulder and his ear as he tightens his belt. He stops in the hall. His eyes catch mine. He turns away. "Yeah, yeah. I know, it's just shit all around."

I climb out of bed, grabbing my hoodie from where it hangs off the couch armrest and pulling it over my t-shirt. My jeans come off the floor next.

"What if I sent my brother in for me?" Jag steps into the kitchen. A wall separates us now, though there's a cutout between the living room and kitchen. "Calm down, Donny. I'm only joking."

I pull my jeans on. Tight. I lean down to pull them past my knees, one leg at a time. Jag's watching through the kitchen cutout. I turn away from him and lean forward slightly. I'm pulling my pants on a little slower now, letting the waist catch under my ass, then, all in one pull, they're over the hump. I click the checkered belt, clipped with a seatbelt head.

"Sorry. Repeat that, D?" Jag rubs his eyes. "How backed up are we? Shit. Yeah, well... Everybody's crazy right now. So one day's too much? Yesterday didn't count. Look, D, I appreciate you trying, but what the hell's there to do in spring? You know this isn't about time off. What about half?" He looks at me again, but immediately, he turns his back and leans against the counter. "Fine. Fine. Yeah. I get it. Yeah. I'll be there soon." He hangs up. The phone's in his pocket the same moment he's sighing. The next second, he's pouring himself some coffee. There's another cup for me. He sets milk and sugar on the counter even though he doesn't use them.

"So…" I walk around the wall into the kitchen. "Your girlfriend need you today?"

"It doesn't help we're overbooked to hell," Jag says, followed by a curse under his breath. He's already digging out his cigarettes, though he puts the box and lighter on the counter. He doesn't smoke in his mom's house, but he usually has a cigarette after his coffee. Doesn't matter where or when it is. "And down a person."

"If I had a job, maybe I'd understand," I say.

"You should talk to Donny about that."

"I don't think he's interested in having me back, J."

"Maybe. You were kinda nuts the last time you were in. You're pretty lucky he didn't see your little outburst though. But you'd be surprised what an apology can do."

"Apology for what?"

"Missing work, the badges, threatening to kill him…"

"You telling me that's not the *normal girl shit* he's gotten used to?"

"Maybe only that last one." Jag chuckles, takes a sip of his coffee. "Just make sure you emphasize how much you appreciate him and how much better your phone answering skills are compared to the rest of us."

"What's that supposed to mean?"

Jag sets his cup down. He's walking toward me. "You know, sometimes you make it sound…" His hands go around my hips and he pulls me to him. "Breathy, maybe a little pitchy when you pick up—"

"Don't make it sound dirty, J. I don't flirt with customers."

"I'm not saying that, I'm just describing what I hear, you know?" He leans down. His lips press to my ear. His voice hitches up, soft. "Hello..? This is Joey... for Bodymore Body Shop... Of course I can handle *really big tools* like a pro—Oh... Oh no, sir... This isn't *that* kind of *body shop*..."

"I do not sound like that." I press my hand into his chest, pushing back. His grip tightens to keep me against him.

"When I said *oil change*, sir, I meant your *car*." His voice is hot and overly erotic.

"I don't sound like that." I lean back, pulling my ear from his lips. "And I'd *never* call any of our customers *sir*."

"Mmm... Pretty sure I've heard it."

"You're not a customer, J. By the way, didn't you have somewhere to be?" Stepping back, this time he lets me go.

"Right." Jag picks up his coffee and finishes it off. The cup goes into the sink. He grabs his cigarettes from the counter. One's out of the box, the rest are pocketed. He pats his other ass pocket to check for his wallet, then grabs his coat off the back of a dining room chair. "I left a message with the landlord. I'll call him in a bit to double-check the locks get replaced before tonight, alright?" He pulls his aviators out of his jacket pocket.

"Yeah."

Jag passes me. He opens the door, pauses halfway out. "Joey?"

"Yeah?"

He glances out the door toward his car, takes a deep breath, and turns back to me. "Try not to do anything stupid while I'm gone, okay?"

A smile tugs onto my lips. I purse them to stop it. My arms pull tightly to my chest. My head drops. "You're kinda asking a lot of me, J."

"I know, but I'm hoping you'll take some special consideration this time around."

"I'll think about it."

Jag chuckles, but it feels more like a sigh. "Thanks." He turns back around to leave, pulling the door shut. Again, he stops, saying "Wow!"

"What?"

"There's just… a big ass raven, like, right out here." Jag's staring.

I come to the door. The thing's sitting on the grass off to the side of the driveway and Jag's car. A caw comes from another direction. There's another raven sitting in the trees at the end of the driveway. Then, there's another one on the roof of Jag's house. Four of them. My heart races. "I thought I told you to stop following us, Val."

"I don't care what that guy said, Joey. I'm not dying and if there's something up with the birds, it's nothing but superstition," Jag says.

Jag's not as comforting as he might think because I know what it looked like when I died and when I almost died and every time I've seen someone die. I'll still make excuses like I did at the trailer park, like there's an actual choice. So many of us hang on the borderline every day with death not actually being that far off. It's just a question of accident, malice, or self-imposed. If my neighbor couldn't pull herself off the ground for sixteen hours, the birds thought she was gonna die when it only meant everything hurt and she didn't care enough to get up. Or maybe they're here for someone else and the death Val smelled had rubbed off on Jag.

"You should talk to your mom," I say.

"Why don't you?" Jag lights his cigarette as he walks to his car. "I mean, you're not doing anything else today, are you?"

"Right."

"Good."

"So, J…" I step onto the stoop.

"Yeah?" Jag stops, door to his Mustang open.

"Promise me that… if you see a bunch of ravens, you'll go the other way." My throat tightens on the words. I bite the inside of my cheek. With arms crossed my foot bounces and I'm watching the fattest of the ravens stuff its beak into the dirt. I didn't even know they did that. I thought they plucked at bodies, hearts especially, not earthworms. "And while you're running, don't cross the street without looking both ways. They might try and getcha." I give him a pair of finger guns. My tongue clicks. My chest is so tight, I don't know if I'm breathing. I squeeze a smile onto my lips. It doesn't stay long.

Jag's expression changes to concern. He takes the cigarette from his lips. "Okay. I'll watch out for the birds, but you've gotta promise me you're not gonna do anything crazy. Hang out with my mom, chill for a little while. I don't want to get a call later saying you're in a prison cell, it's a little cold, but the food's not bad, alright? We'll go looking for Cross after I get off," Jag says. "Afternoon. It's not that far away."

"Yeah." It comes out too slow. I know the quicker I answer, the sooner he'll leave and I need him to leave. Get away from the birds; get away from the danger; get away from me. If he's gone and the birds stay, then at least I know they aren't tracking *him* anymore. But how fast would they move if they were?

Jag takes a minute to get into his car. I stay outside, watching him round the corner at the end of the block. The autumn air pricks my skin. I run my hands over my arms and step back inside. I drink my coffee while standing. It's cold now. I text Wayland:

JOEY   Hey.
                What are you doing today?

By the time I finish the cup, Wayland still hasn't responded. I can't shake the possibility that I've pissed him off, leaving him the other night. Maybe he blames me for what happened to his house, so I type, "Sorry Way," and put my phone away.

I fold the blanket sitting on the bed Jag and I used last night. Setting it on a nearby chair, I stack the pillows next. Once I've got the bed folded back into the couch, I wash the few dishes in the sink. My phone vibrates. It's not Wayland; it's Ralph saying, "You still alive?"

JOEY	You know something I don't?
RALPH	You were urgent yesterday.
	Then quiet.
JOEY	You send me to Sol to die?
RALPH	No. Why?
JOEY	Bcuz she's a fucking lying bitch.
	who tried to kill me.
	Don't ever send me to her again.
Ralph	…
	Yeah
	You know
	Servies really don't mesh with souls.
	They don't *get it*.
	Forgot about that.
	lol
JOEY	What?
	That's it?
	How do you forget that?
RALPH	They don't talk to me the same way?
	You get what you needed tho?
JOEY	Without your help.
	Getting the ashes now.
RALPH	Bring a memory.
JOEY	So like a picture?

RALPH	Preferably, yes.
	Otherwise
	As long as it's personal.
	Picture's just better.
JOEY	Why didn't you say that yesterday?
RALPH	¯_(ツ)_/¯
	I translate.
	Easy to forget sometimes.
JOEY	…
	I'll be by later with everything.
	Be ready to work your magic.
RALPH	I deal in absolutes.
	Not magic.
JOEY	What the hell's that mean?
RALPH	Yes or no.
JOEY	Whatever
	I'll be by the bar soon.
RALPH	Party.

I put my phone away. On a chair in the living room are Jag's and my bags. I empty the contents of my backpack onto the chair and put it on. I go through my things, looking for the feathers and the Lethe. They're not there. I go through Jag's bag next. Not there either. "Shit." He must have them. Probably still in his car from when he picked me up last night. I grab my skateboard and I'm out the door. No matter how late Jag's mom came in last night, sticking around's making me anxious for the moment she decides to wake up and find me. What if she doesn't remember me like Lane? It's probably better off like that anyway.

Board down, I'm going as fast as I can until I'm jumping burbs, stairs, and sidewalks to get to Wayland's neighborhood. His house looks like a nightmare mixed in with white picket fences, fresh paint jobs, and the homey SUVs in the driveways. It's the image of a violation and it doesn't feel like it's just a house, but more it's tied to what Wayland is now too, a crisp ghost of his former self.

Something that's not only gone, but has been purposefully destroyed with malice. Against the green lawns and bright fall sky, the house is a shadow made of ash. Not totally, but enough. Corruption from the inside snakes out the busted windows and melted front door. I only assume that's how it works. I never paid much attention in science class, even when we were playing with chemicals and fire. It's either that or the bastard who came around knocked out all the windows on his way upstairs.

I don't see that as a possibility though because how did none of us hear it?

The closer I get to Wayland's place, the less I want to be here. None of it's right. His normal laughter, awkward, trying to be calm and relaxing and welcoming, isn't there. In fact, it's almost like there's no sound at all. No birds. No neighbors. No cars. Nothing. It's like walking into a void. The grass turns grayer as I walk down the sidewalk. Ash catches on my pant legs, apparently waking at my entrance and turning me pale too. Yellow police tape goes over the door that doesn't look latched. I reach for it. From the outside, the door's a little darker red than it should be. It feels crisp to touch. It doesn't want to move, but it's unlocked.

It creaks when I push it a little harder. I do as little as possible to get in, turning to my side and shimmying in sideways. I put my board against the wall behind it. I'm not ready to look at Wayland's house. It's only been a couple of days since I found out Wayland was dead. It didn't feel so real when I could look him in the eyes and hear him and hold him, but this…

The spot in the living room where the fire started is darker than the rest of the carpet. The couch and chairs are worse off too, probably doused in gasoline. It still smells like it. Blackened wood moves toward the stairs, like it was caught on footsteps, caught on the ghost. His movements from that night are seared into the carpet. His partially burned face flashes into my mind. Then the knife going into his head and Wayland stabbing him again and again and again until I said his name and just... he turned to me like it was nothing. "Everything's so fucked," I mutter.

The weak wood creaks under my steps. It shouldn't hold me, but it does. Fire like it came from fingertips drags along the walls. I press my hands against the lines and pull my fingers along the marks. Behind me, I hear Jag saying, "Put your DNA on everything? Really? It's like you want to get caught." I pull my hand back once I'm at the top of the stairs.

The stitched pictures marking the births of Wayland and his sister are gone, laying on the hallway floor with burned frames, cracked glass, and everything charred to the point where all you can read is ND, none of the decorations, his birthday of December 23rd, or his size.

I move past the windows on the second floor, past the bathroom, and straight to Wayland's room at the end of the hall. I've come this way so many times, but now I'm scared to go in, like I'll see him laying on his bed, dead and unmoving and these last few days will have been make-believe and he really is gone and I'll never get to talk to him again. Tears build in my eyes. I take out my phone to check for messages. Nothing. I send Wayland a quick, "Talk to me, please," then I say, "Shit," to myself and text, "Does that make me sound desperate? I don't fkn care anymore. Talk to me, Way."

I slip my phone away. My fingers tingle. I'm thinking maybe I'll go outside and smoke and come back, but fuck, that's dumb and it won't make this any easier. "Wayland?" My hand hovers over the doorknob. "You in there?" I gently touch the knob, more so I can feel it move if maybe someone is on the other side and they try to grab it. My heart's pounding in my ears. I don't know if I want him to be on the other side or not. "Wayland?"

The knob's misshaped in my hand. Metal melted and reshaped by the last hand that twisted it. I push the door open. Wayland's bedroom isn't his anymore. Bed sheets are pulled back, burned spots litter the floor alongside the bloodstains in his rug and between the ridges in the floor. There are chips in the wood from where the knife missed once or twice or maybe went too far through the guy's body. Burns ransack the bed, put holes in the blankets, and desperately crawl up the walls to escape through the windows. A gust blows through the broken window.

That couldn't have been caused by the fire, right?

Not when the floor hasn't broken out under me?

Or maybe the house won't snap because I'm not really here?

A chill goes down my spine.

I take out my phone and text Wayland:

JOEY	I'm at your house if you want to hang.
	or don't
	I've always been more of a loner anyway.
	:p

I slip my phone back into my pocket to resist staring at it, waiting to see if he'll send me anything when it's been quiet since yesterday. My nose burns from the lingering smell of smoke and caustic remains of the fire. The blood's fermented and ammoniac. Then there's the sulfur. It's not right that Wayland's house smells like a burial ground.

Black, ashy marks burn trails over the floor, hide blood, and climb up the bookshelf. Some of the books have burnt spines. Laying on the floor before the shelf is a mint-colored journal. The cover's dusted with ashy fingerprints. Somehow, it's not charred. Papers haphazardly hang out the sides. Something thicker sticks out the bottom. A photograph. The one Jag showed me last week when we were here. I pull out the photo and hold it against the journal. I look like shit, but Wayland? He's a stranger compared to now. Downcast eyes watch me from the side, his elbow bumps mine, and he's got this small smile, bashful and unburdened. The edge of the photo's darkened from a lick of fire, but it's not much. My eyes water. I wipe them with the back of my hand, slide the picture into my pocket, and tuck the journal into my bag. I'm at the bedside table Jag dug through last time we were here. Opening it, there's a small, black box sitting on top of what little else there is in the drawer. It looks like a ring box. My chest's tight. My fingers graze the velvet. I draw my hand back, close the drawer, open it again, hoping the box isn't there. I dreamed it up, please, I don't want to be the worst fucking friend that ever existed. I open the drawer and the box is still there.

My heart's throbbing. I can't breathe. I can't tell if that was a caw, some car driving by outside, or a neighbor shutting a door. None of those sound the same, but I'm sure I heard something. I just can't remember what the hell it sounded like.

My thumbnail sticks into the upper lip of the box. I close my eyes. My hands are so sweaty. I wipe them on my pants then slip my nail back under the lip. I push the box open. A silver ring wrapped around itself sits wedged in the slit of a velvet pillow. Small diamonds fill the band while a slightly larger square diamond accents the top. My vision blurs. Tears slide down my cheeks. I wipe them again with the back of my hand while snapping the box closed.

Jag knew. Jag saw this and I've been the biggest fucking idiot to both of them. The way Jag looked at me when he said, "Nothing," and knew Wayland's password said it. The way Wayland stood beside me through everything *said it*, but somehow, I never noticed, I never picked up the hints and I don't know how I missed *all* of it. I don't even know how he doesn't hate me because of what I've done to him.

I take the ring from the box and put it in my pocket. I wipe my eyes again and take out my phone to text Wayland. My fingers hang over the screen, the buttons, moving slowly along the cracked lines over my keyboard. My skin's hot, sticking to my hair. I brush it back. I drop my fingers on the send button, trying not to think about it. The screen goes black. I tap it to wake it up. The message sends.

JOEY   I found the ring.

"Shit," I mutter.

JOEY   I'm sorry, Way.
              I'm so fucking sorry.

I exhale hard. My cigarettes replace my phone. I can't light up in Wayland's room. Even if the place is torched. All I can think of is passing out on his bed while listening to *Motion City* and craving a cigarette. I leave the room. The door closes louder behind me than I mean for it to and it bounces on the frame. I don't turn back to see if it stayed closed. I'm going down the steps, grabbing my board off the wall, and moving out the door with the last cigarette from my box in my mouth. My hand's looking for my lighter.

"Forget something?" Rocky says. He's standing two squares down the front walkway. His car sits in the drive, his hands are in his pockets. He smiles like this is a coincidence. *How funny we both come to this bar after work on*

Tuesday, huh? kinda smile. "I didn't know you lived here."

"Oh yeah?" I take the cigarette out of my mouth. "Practically a second home."

"That so?" Rocky's coming closer. He stops when he's standing in front of me.

I set my board down. My foot presses on the deck. I cross my arms. "Yup."

Rocky mirrors my posture. He nods toward the door. "You read the tape?"

I glance back at the house. The badge tape across the door hangs a bit limp, pulled looser by my intrusion. Irritation bubbles in the pit of my stomach. The badges never came back to my house once they put the tape up. They never went back to the park once Wayland went missing. But of course, they're here. Badges can't catch the real criminals that break windows and beat out neighbors and leave bodies in the streets for kids to find on their way home from school. They only know how to follow nobodies who can't fight them off, the ones who don't have the time or money or friends to beat off the city. And I mean that in the grossest way.

Take the plea bargain.

Pretend you're guilty.

Suck off the state.

You'll get out fast and the judge will like you more for it.

That's what they always say, just so they can claim they've caught another criminal and they're *just doing their job to protect the city*. You agreed, after all. If you didn't think you were a criminal, then why the hell did you ever take a plea? It had nothing to do with the prosecution and your own defense attorney, borrowed to you by the city, telling you that if you don't take the plea, you're gonna rot in jail for the rest of your life. It's like I want to believe in the myth that badges are meant to do good, but every time I see one, I realize I'm just desperate to believe things aren't as bad as they look.

"I told you, I practically live here." I turn back to the detective.

"Hm. I don't believe you."

"Sounds like a personal problem to me."

"You don't look related to the Cross family."

"Wow. Way to racially profile someone."

"That's not how that works."

"We're living in a modern era, Rocky. For all you know, this super nice Asian family took pity on my poor soul. It's not really a problem, right?"

Rocky purses his lips. "Fine. Forget I said anything about that." His hands move to his hips. "A building in this condition is dangerous to be in. What would *your family* think if something happened to you?"

"Probably nothing since they're all dead."

"All of them?"

"...Probably."

"Probably?"

"Except for the ones who live in this house, of course." I uncross my arms, copying Rocky's posture now. "Wouldn't you know it? Apparently, you can't trust a dead bastard to stay dead once he shoots himself in the head." I turn my hand into a gun, point my finger at my head. My hand bounces back, pretending to recoil as an invisible trigger is pulled. "You'd think if someone was miserable enough to take themselves out, they'd fucking stay that way."

"What do you mean?" Rocky says.

I pop my cigarette back into my mouth. My hands run down the back of my head. I find my lighter. Cigarette lit, I take a drag. "Did you come here because you wanted something or because you're stalking me?"

"I was in the neighborhood." Rocky casually pushes his jacket back. Light catches on his handcuffs.

I pinch my cigarette between my lips, stifling a laugh.

Stepping on the tail, the head of my board lifts into the air and I pick it back up. I go down the stairs. We're arm's length from each other. My legs urge me to run, but my mind's telling me to fight him with a million bloody images of my board on his face. I close my eyes, shake my head, try to think of anything. "So… stalking it is then?"

"I don't think I caught your name," Rocky says.

"Barbara," I say without thinking.

Rocky stares at me. Eyes narrow a little. I know what he's thinking: *You're a piece of scum lying to me, but I can't call you out. It'll ruin the long game.* "Something about that doesn't feel right," he says.

"What?"

"You don't look like a Barbara."

"Oh. Name assessment is part of your job now?"

"In a way, it always has been." He lets his jacket go. Reaching into his pocket, Rocky withdraws his card and offers it to me.

I don't take it.

"A lot of bad things have been happening recently. As you can see, even in a neighborhood like this one. It's probably in your better interest to keep a number like this on hand." Rocky waves the card a little. "And avoid going into places like this."

"I already have your card, Rocky," I say. "At least two of them?"

"Do you now?" He lowers his hand.

"Yeah. I mean, can we cut this shit? You gave me another one last night." The words come out before I can stop them. It shouldn't have worried me so much to speak, but everything this badge has been doing since day one has felt like a setup. When he came to the garage, the questions he asked, the tone of voice, the continuation of how he's seemingly followed me everywhere I went, just like the bodies. He's familiar enough, though I don't think I ever interacted with him until the stunt with Wayland's car. Though, to be frank, all badges look pretty much the same when they don the suit. They serve the same power and the uniform just helps erase anything that might make them stand out.

Rocky cocks his head to the side. "Where have we run into each other before?"

My jaw tightens to stop the words from coming out. His stupid face looks so genuine, I hate it. "My friend's house was broken into last night. You came. You asked if he beat me."

Rocky's eyes narrow. Not mad. Thinking. He's looking at my face carefully, maybe looking for a lie. "Really?" He reaches into his pocket. A small notebook comes out. He flips through the pages, glances at his notes, then back to me. "I remember following that call, but not you."

"Oh please, stop the bullshit. We stood in the hall by the elevator. You kept looking at the apartment and acted like I was lying when I said Jag's a good guy. I told you to watch out for ravens and you told me they're called an unkindness and that not all badges suck. Just admit you know who I am and you're trying to back me into a corner. I get it." I hit the cigarette. Turn away. Watch down the street at the end of the block for his backup.

"Excuse me?" Rocky says. "How do you know all of that?"

"Because I was there!"

Rocky steps toward me. "Who *are* you?"

"You've only been chasing me around for, like, two weeks now—"

"Why would I be chasing you?" Rocky says. There's no hint of malice or cocky condescension in his voice. Genuinely curious, genuinely confused. So unlike a badge. He glances over his notepad.

My chest tightens, foot bouncing. I watch him. He steps closer; I take the cigarette out of my mouth. I meet Rocky's eyes, then go down to his broad chest. He's relaxed, but engaged, ready to move if I try something. You always hear the stories of trigger-happy badges looking for the next freak to gun down. There's aggression in the air; I don't know if it's coming from him, the burnt house, some dead guy haunting one of the other McMansions in this neighborhood, or a banger hiding in the bushes waiting to finish me off. I pick up my skateboard and put a little more space between us, going further down the walkway.

Puff of cigarette.

I turn back to Rocky. "You really don't recognize me?"

"No." He laughs a little, not at me. "I sort of feel bad. You almost seem desperate to be recognized."

"Never." I still don't believe him, but he's too good at looking honest, at putting on that face of *not being such a bad guy*. I've talked to him too many times already that I've become too comfortable and maybe if it was some other day, I'd answer his questions. "I just think it's probably a good idea for you to know who I am, but I'm not gonna say more than that."

"Why's that?"

"Because…" A slow puff gives me more time to think. "I don't talk to badges."

"Personal policy from experience?"

My lips pinch my cigarette. I shake my head. "Nah, Rocky. You know the drill." I smile crooked.

"I don't think I do." His eyes lock on me.

I put out my cigarette, mashing it into the walkway, then I'm stepping back, going through the grass, making it to the sidewalk. He's following me, even if at a slower pace. My heel catches on something. Rocky lunges. I catch myself and keep the space between us. He straightens. "Am I being detained or something?"

"By all accounts, you should be for breaking and entering."

"I told you, *you can't break into your own house*. Go ahead, call the owners. Ask." My throat tightens at the last word. What if Wayland's parents don't actually remember me? I didn't actually talk to them the other night. Shit. I told him my name was Barbara too. They definitely won't know what's going on. Now it's either I tell Rocky I lied about something or have him find out by making the call. Great.

"Pretend I believe you. What excuse do you have for disrupting a crime scene?" Rocky continues toward me, slow, methodical, like a man trying to catch a feral cat without scaring it off.

The bottom of my rubber sole meets pavement again. I stare for a while. The blackened house in the background's getting to me. I don't want to be here anymore. My eyes water. I take a deep breath to push back the tears. "Just… looking for the ashes of lost time."

"You want to come to the station for a bit? Answer some questions?" His steps speed up, his voice is more instant. His hand's going for his cuffs.

"Nah, fam. I said I'm good." I almost trip again stepping off the curb. The voice in my head's begging for Rocky to grab me so I can smack him with my skateboard. I taste blood in my mouth and don't know why. I lick my lips and wipe them with the back of my hand thinking maybe there's blood on them, now, but it's all saliva. "Last time I came for a visit, I got killed."

"You did, did you?" More steps forward, faster this time. I'm stepping into the road, backing up, turning so I don't run into the sidewalk across the street, the houses, the dead end. Rocky says, "Watch it. You don't want to get run over."

I laugh. "Would it really matter at this point?"

His expression changes. Concern, pity, disgust. Eyebrows furrowed, lips down-turned, his hand's nowhere near his belt anymore, but partially reaching out. "You're not thinking of hurting yourself, are you?"

A laugh catches in my nose. I turn away, but realize

quickly how much of a mistake that is and I face the detective. "You think you could do something if I was?"

"Desperate situations cause people to do desperate things. I get it." He's coming fast now, his legs are longer than mine. I'm nearly jogging backward to keep away, but he's still gaining. I think he's speeding up. I pass a stop sign at the end of the block. Keep going. "Whatever's happened, there's always a way out that doesn't have to be desperate—"

A glance over my shoulder. I just gotta see where I am. Look away for too long and Rocky will jump me. It'd be two seconds to hit the ground, roll onto my stomach, arms behind my back.

A laugh sneaks out of my throat. My fingers grip my board. Rocky makes a sudden dash to get closer. I propel away, turn around, dash, and he slows down again. "Sorry, I just think it's funny… that we can sound so alike, but mean something so different."

"Care to elaborate?"

"Not really." I shake my head. My foot catches on jagged concrete. I'm expecting Rocky to lunge for me, but he doesn't.

"You're not alone, Barbara."

I laugh. "Fuck. Now you sound like Jag."

"Are you in trouble?"

I'm shaking my head again. "You keep asking questions I don't want to answer."

"They say if you keep asking, eventually, you'll get an answer."

"What if it's a lie?"

"A lie holds more truth than you might think."

I chuckle. Pass an intersection, a yard. "Yeah… Why do you think I don't talk to badges?" Now's my chance. I put my board down. Instantly, I'm on it, kicking down the street. The plastic wheels chatter underneath. Kick again, I'm pushing off as fast as I can, hoping it's enough to outrun Rocky. A few blocks down, I jump the sidewalk, pick up my board, and pull myself over a wooden fence surrounding someone's house.

The detective's behind me, running. His head twists to the side. I only get to see him while I'm throwing myself over the top of the fence, but don't slow down to watch if he follows while I cross the yard. My chest hurts and I'm breathing hard before I'm back on the street again. I'm blocks away and keeping near the houses, ducking between them when I hear a car coming in case it's him.

Thirty minutes go by and I never see Rocky's car.

After another thirty, a badge car passes, but it either doesn't see me when I duck into a yard or they just don't care anymore.

The air's cold. I pat down my pockets to make sure I've still got everything. Phone, lighter, ring. I just have to go to the body shop now to grab what Jag's got without him seeing me. I put my skateboard down and head in that direction. I pass by a bus stop just as the right line's going by, so I get on that and take it most of the way. The side of the building where I get off reminds me YOU CHOSE THE DARK in white.

I don't remember seeing it there before, but everybody's gotta have an opinion nowadays.

A caw comes overhead. A mutter of judgment. I've gone all day without seeing a raven, but the second I'm closer to Jag, there's one sitting on the sidewalk. The smell of sulfur hits. I pause to approach to the raven. When I don't move, it lifts its head to look back at me.

"You really need to find something better to do," I say. "I'm not letting you take him. I'm not letting you take *either* of them."

The raven lowers its head without so much as a chirp of acknowledgment and I continue toward the Bodymore Body Shop.

SIX TEEN.

The parking lot at the shop looks pretty normal for a Tuesday in the fall. Four cars are waiting to be serviced in the lot while the garage doors hang open, a vehicle parked at each lift inside, even if not being actively worked on. I go around back without crossing the large, glass storefront and open garage. I can't risk being seen. I already hear Jag if he sees me saying, "Thought you were talking to my mom today."

I don't have an excuse for him except, "Sorry, I'm dumb," but I think he's getting tired of hearing it.

Donny's car is parked in the back next to Jag's with one space between the both of them. Then there's some green SUV to the right of Donny's car, another space between them. They said they don't park next to each other to make sure there's room to open their doors, but I'm pretty sure it's a holdover from urinal habits.

The door to Jag's Mustang's unlocked. It always is. The radio's pulled out from its usual spot in the dash. Jag's always been really good about removing the valuables because this car really isn't hard to get into. The space between the window and the hole is more than enough to comfortably jimmy something in and once you've got the car open, you can get into the trunk through the backseat. Convertibles have it worse. You'd be surprised how many people are willing to cut open a soft-top rather than bash in a window. Though, I guess you might be surprised to know how many people are willing to break into a car for an outdated CD player radio and a couple extra speakers if they know where to look.

It means he probably didn't leave my stuff in here, but I'm hoping he thought the feathers and water were dumb enough that they didn't need to be taken inside.

I run my hand along the cupholder, looking for the bottle and feathers. There's not even a spare lighter or plastic wrap from a new box of cigarettes. I slide closer to the passenger seat, climbing over the center panel, cup holder, and stick shift. I close my eyes and let the smell of the car get into me for a second. Nicotine, leather, Jag's familiarity. My fingers curl into the seat. My heart speeds up, slowing down with my exhale. I reach for the glove compartment next.

Nothing but a couple of brown, paper napkins from various restaurants.

I lean back. Yelp.

A raven's sitting on the hood, staring at me. There's a caw and another one's sitting on the ground by the dumpster not far from Donny's car or the shop's back door. I brace myself with the seat and peer around out the back of the car to look for more. Nothing in the grass outlining the parking lot. I turn back to the door. Yelp again. A body fills the open driver's door. I jump back, suck in a breath, and swing a punch with closed eyes.

"Gonna throw the wheel at me next?" Jag says.

"You forget to bolt it down?" I open my eyes, tug at the wheel knowing it's not going to come off. I smile, lean back, trying not to show how much he really startled me, but I'm already breathing hard and it's not from the run here. I check the raven in front of me; it's staring at Jag.

"You know, if you missed me, you could've just called and said so," Jag says.

"And pull you away from Donny for a few hours?" I turn back to him, now leaning against the wheel.

Jag leans into the car. "You avoiding my mom?" He presses his arm into the spot over the door.

"Probably." I hang my legs outside.

"She's not *that* bad—"

"I never said she was bad. I'm just not great at talking, so I'm staying out of her way—"

"I dunno. I think you're pretty good at talking… *most of the time*. Isn't that the whole reason Donny hired you?"

"He hired me because he pitied me."

"Okay, fine, but the customers still like you."

"And dealing with customers is different than me being *me*. I'm not customer-serving your mom." I stand, pulling myself out of the driver's seat. He steps back to give me enough room to walk away, then closes the door.

"What are you looking for?"

I pace away. Across the parking lot, a fat raven hops from under the trees in the grass. There's still a raven by the trash. The one on Jag's car is gone. I turn around and now there's a raven standing closer to the front of the store. Another hangs off the roof. One of them caws.

"Joey?"

I turn back to Jag. "The feathers and drink from downstairs. I forgot about them last night. Do you still have them?"

"Oh." Jag crosses his arms and leans his ass against his car's window. "And you were just gonna sneak in, take your shit, and run off without saying hi?"

"Well, I'm getting kinda tired of making a fool of myself." I'm trying to keep my cool, keep my foot from bouncing, keep from breaking the contact that makes it look like I'm ashamed or trying to hide, but I can't.

Jag comes to me. He puts an arm around me and pulls me to him, hard, tight, suffocating in a good way. First, my arms are at my side and I'm holding my breath. He presses his lips to my head. My arms snake around him. His grip loosens but remains on me. "You know, Joey, no one thinks as poorly of you as you."

"I don't wanna go inside, J."

"Why?"

"For starters, I'll have to look at Stache's stupid face and I don't know if I'll be able to keep my cool knowing he took my job—"

"His name's Felix."

"Mmm, Stache seems more fitting." I pull away from Jag. My fingers flick over my upper lip, pretending to outline a mustache. "It's kinda thin. Is he seventeen or twenty-five and already balding?"

"He's not a bad guy," Jag says.

"Oh, you guys fucking already?"

"Joey, please…" Jag's smile is in his words. "He doesn't even shave his legs."

"That what does it for you, J?"

"That… And he doesn't change the filter when he makes more coffee."

"Have you tried smoking his pipe out back to see if he'd reconsider?" I snort.

"You're really mad."

I don't want to be this mad, but it's coming back. The adrenaline, the rage, the whispers from the grave that say hurting someone a little more will make the pain go away, free up the job, make me feel better. It's all so convincing and I can't argue against it. "He took my job, Jag—"

"He didn't take your job. You were already let go—"

"And what if Donny hates me now and won't let me come in?"

"You're afraid of Donny hating you *now*?"

"I'm not afraid." I exhale hard to release the tension. I

step back. Another deep breath. My mind's racing me telling me to leave and come back when I can try and sneak in again. "Where's my stuff?"

"Break room. My locker. Jacket pocket. Go ahead and get it."

I go around the front of the shop. A raven sits on the sidewalk in front of the store entrance. I step over it; it doesn't move. Jag walks around the bird to grab the shop door. The raven still doesn't move, though it tracks where Jag goes.

"You need to be careful."

"They're carrions, Joey. They don't eat what's living." There's one on the sidewalk, standing by Jag now.

"That's the problem." My hand looks for his arm. I can't think of anything but a murder scene of J's head broken open, stabbed, beaten, and lifeless like the dude on Wayland's bedroom floor. "They're waiting for something to die." I go into the shop, if only for the reason of putting space between the ravens and Jag. He follows me in, close behind.

I go through the lobby only focusing on what I came for. The front desk's empty. Felix is in the garage. Probably in the back corner where I used to work most, where my toolbox should be. I open the glass door to the garage. Jag takes it from me. Donny's office door is open, the light's on.

"Jag," Donny says. He comes out from behind the blue Beamer on a lift, steps back, looks up at the fender or maybe toward the suspension. "What'd you see out there?" He turns toward us, visibly straightening when his dark eyes land on me.

"Nothing unfamiliar," Jag says.

"Donny." My throat's tight. My body jerks forward as I tell it to keep going for the break room and not to start something. My legs won't listen.

"Joey." Donny nods, smiles quickly. "I thought you

were dead." He laughs.

"Only for a little while." My eyes wander to the corner of the room where my toolbox sits. Used to sit. Someone else's grease rags hang on the outside. I can't see it well, but light catches on a couple of tools laying out on top, scattered. Then Felix rolls under a mounted Jeep. "You moved on quick.

"Not because I wanted to," Donny says.

The sound of metal meeting metal fills the room. The junk radio in the back corner crackles. Jag's channel's playing.

"Were you in jail, Joey?" Donny says.

"Not once."

"She lying, Jag?" Donny's focus moved from me to him.

Jag shakes his head. "No. Not in jail."

"Wow, Donny." My eyes roll. "I appreciate the trust you have in me." I turn away, biting the tip of my lip ring so I can't say anything else I'll regret. I was supposed to apologize, not throw more gasoline on this dumpster fire while Jag watches me burn down every opportunity I have left.

Before entering the break room, the mess is blatant. Trash spills over the edge of the bin by the door, someone's left a dirty paper plate on the table and why the hell's one of the chairs on the floor? The room smells like burnt beans while the coffee pot isn't even dark enough to be fresh. It looks like someone put water in a used filter and tried running it again. Styrofoam cups lay scattered on the counter, a couple of them stick together, most of them are stained on the outside with splashes of old coffee.

I pick up the chair from the floor and shove it back under the table a little harder than I mean to. Without even touching it, I know how sticky the table's surface is. Someone spilled something a couple of times and never wiped it down. I re-stack the Styrofoam cups. The counter's just as sticky as the table from spilled sugar and the leftovers of paper sugar packets clinging to the mess of spilled coffee water. "Holy shit." I run a hand along the counter to sweep up the paper packets. Almost none of them come off, choosing to stick to the sugar instead. I grab a handful of paper towels, wet them down in the cold water Donny still hasn't fixed, and wipe the counter off. "Jag... Are you serious? It's been, like, four days."

"It's been, like, a week." He leans against the door, a smile on his face, too entertained while I grab another wad of paper, dip it under the water and hand soap, then wipe down the counter a second time.

"Oh, my god." I toss the paper towels away. "This is you guys after a week?" The smell from the trash hits me. Old, mildewing coffee filters. I open the coffee filter shelf on the coffee maker. It's growing white fuzz. "You guys are so gross." I toss it in the trash bin, pick up the spilled pieces from the floor, then knot off the bag. I'm not the cleanest person either. I never have been. On weekends, I skip showers sometimes, even when I smell and the easiest place for me to find clothing is usually on the floor in one of my bedroom corners. I don't make my bed; there's no point when no one comes over and bedsheets pushed down to the foot or against the wall just makes it easier to climb into at the end of a long day. But work is different. Work isn't supposed to be like home and it's at least not supposed to smell like forgotten candy, sweat, sour milk, and mold. I grab a plastic bag out from under the sink. I toss the tied-off bag at Jag, then put the new bag in the bin.

I go to Jag's locker. "You know, I've seen your place. You don't let it look like this."

"Yeah, well, I've actually gotta impress somebody over there. Make it look like I got my shit together, right?"

"You do pretty well most of the time." I pull Jag's locker open. The feathers are in a small, plastic bag on the top shelf, sitting under the weight of the Lethe bottle. I unzip my backpack and stick both items inside. Locker closed, I turn around. Jag's standing behind me, coming closer. His hand bolts to the closer locker door; he backs me up until he's craning over me.

"What's next?" His breath is so close, it's hot on my skin. The adrenaline from before is turning into a desire for a distraction, my lips mashed against his, close the door and push me down on the table, no matter how sticky it might be. It's gonna get worse.

My hand goes up Jag's chest and catches on his collar. My fingers tighten with a handful of fabric. "Ralph's waiting." Take a deep breath, release both it and his shirt. "I'm not trying to cause problems. I just want things to be normal again... At least a little bit."

"Hate to say it, Joey..." Jag leans in. His voice lowers. "But one of the ways back to normal..." He presses his mouth to my ear. I press harder into the locker. "Is to apologize to D and ask him for your job back."

"And what if he says no?"

Jag pulls back, shrugs. "Then you'll be where you are now. Isn't it better to say you tried?"

"No... It's not."

"If he says no, we'll figure something else out."

"I hate asking for shit, J." My voice is going whiny again. I don't want to hear myself talk; I know I sound bratty and I look like a kid saying shit like that. It's not being told no that I hate. I get that plenty and have never had a problem doing whatever the hell I want anyway. What's worse is having to give the power of my life over to someone else that I actually kinda care about. I don't value too many people, but the one's that I actually consider important have the ability to wreck my life just by telling me to fuck off.

I'd never tell him because God knows how hard he'd laugh at me, but Donny's meant more to me than my dad for years.

The job at Bodymore's been the only one I've had since I left high school. All I did was walk in and ask him for a chance after seeing the sign out front. I didn't think he'd actually say yes or keep me around after learning I knew nothing about cars. He taught me everything I know and never lost patience with me when I struggled or went slow.

I get why he told me to fuck off a couple of days ago. If he said it now when things have boiled down a bit though, it wouldn't be for the same reason.

"Try it," Jag says.

I push against his chest. He steps back. "Donny!" I say, making escape of break room. I'm already too aggressive, like I'm yelling. "Sorry!" I say, but that's not what I mean. Sorry for yelling, for being a bitch. This isn't the real apology. I'm going into the garage. I don't expect him to be standing right on the other side of the door. Felix is a couple feet away.

They had to be gossiping, like, five seconds ago.

I attempt to force Felix's existence out of my mind. I shove my hands in my pockets. My fingers graze my phone and the ring at the bottom of my pocket. I clear my throat. "Look, Donny." I exhale, hard. My foot's bouncing. I glance toward my corner of the shop. "I'm… I'm sorry." My lips purse. Another breath. "For acting crazy the last couple of weeks and snapping and bringing in bodies and badges and Hell. It's just been… really fucking fucked and your call last week when everything else was falling apart… It felt like my life was over. I died and everything was draining away from me so fast, I couldn't do anything to stop it."

Donny sighs. His lips click. "I might've been a bit drastic, alright? You been with me for a while now, kid, but I wasn't sure what to do. Clients out the ass, badges wandering around, looking for you, the mics out front. I shouldn't've cut you that fast. I just didn't know what else to do."

I smack my tongue against the edge inside of my mouth to cut off my first response. "I know I put you in a bad position." I didn't want to tell him about how many times the badges came to my door or how many bodies I found last week or what I'd seen since coming back. I could only hope Jag didn't share around the things I've been saying about death. He wouldn't do that, right?

My skin's cold underneath, but hot on top. Everything's tense and I'm looking at Donny like that conversation just happened in front of me. I shake my head slightly, trying to get rid of the building rage, but it's not as much rage as it is hurt. My eyes burn. I blink rapidly to push the tears back. I'm so sick of feeling like I'm going to cry and like everything's out of control and I'm never getting anything back. I'm so sick of feeling crazy and unwanted and having to tell myself that the way I see things isn't how they are while everything else says my assessments right. "The world's kind of fucked up, you know?"

"Yeah..." Donny says. "But family can at least take you out of Hell and put you in Limbo."

My eyes water. I wipe them with the back of my hand. "My dad's gone, Donny. He moved on last week."

"That's unfortunate." Donny glances over his shoulder at Felix. "Can't say it's sad though, sorry."

"I know." I rub under my eyes. The tips of my fingers come back black. I wipe them off on my pants, look at the ground, look at anything but Donny. "But what I wanted to say is... Can I have my job back? Part-time, full-time, free fucking 'internship,' I don't really care. I just... I want to be here."

Donny crosses his arms. He's quiet for too long. "I'll take the condition of the breakroom into consideration." A smile presses onto his flat lips.

"And without me, who's gonna handle the vacuum?

Not you with your sausage hands, right?"

Donny shrugs. "Fair argument." He looks at Felix again. "I'll think about it." Donny says.

My phone vibrates. Immediately, it's in my hand. Wayland's name flashes across the screen. "Great. Awesome. Thanks." I'm moving out of the garage, into the parking lot, focused on the screen.

WAYLAND	SORRY. I'M AT YOUR PLACE.
JOEY	WTF Why?
WAYLAND	I DIDN'T KNOW WHERE ELSE TO GO.
JOEY	What happened? Where's your family? Wayland???

He's not responding.

"Joey?" Jag says.

"Yeah?" I lower my phone. I'm standing in the middle of the parking lot.

"What's up?"

Thumping in my ears threatens to drown him out. "Nothing."

Jag taps his cheek, pointing at his eyes. I follow the motion with my own. My fingers come away wet, tinted red. I wipe the liquid on my pants. "Sorry."

"Don't be sorry. Just tell me the truth."

I'm reaching around me, grasping at air, looking for my skateboard cause it's supposed to be there and it's not. I know I used it to get here, but I can't remember where the hell I set it down or where it went or maybe I never actually used it and I can't remember because nothing feels real anymore and I'm floating away, unable to grab anything left on the ground.

"Is it Cross?" Jag says.

I'm staring for a while before slowly shaking my head, knowing that every comment Jag makes about Wayland feels like it's only a couple of hours off of being said about me.

"I know he's important to you and I'm trying to help, but you have to be honest." He stands in front of me, looking me in the eyes. I don't know if it's the tone or his face or if it's because I actually really want to believe everything Jag's said to me because he's still here after I've given him every reason to walk away.

"It's about Cross." The words come out like I'd been holding my breath.

"What do you need?"

"Don't you have work?"

Jag glances over my shoulder, back to me, then walks toward the garage saying, "Donny! Emergency!"

I turn around, expecting Donny to be standing in the door with a look of disappointment or threat or disgust or something because Jag already tried to get off today and it was either work or no job. There are cars to fix and customers to keep happy. Instead, Donny's holding a clipboard that's from the car Jag must've been working on and a cheap tablet in his other hand. He flicks through the screen, the schedule, the workload for the day. He sighs with a loud groan. "You're gonna owe me when you get back. *Big time*," Donny says. "But around here, we're family and we don't leave people out to dry when they've been through some shit... We just wait for it to dry. So, deal with your thing and we'll talk later unless you're dead, got it?" Donny says.

"Thanks, D. You're the best." Jag's already running into the shop to get his keys and jacket from his locker.

A tear goes down my cheek. I wipe it away. Staring at the back of my hand, the red reminds me of what I don't have anymore. Stupid.

"And Joey, you can come back, but actually take some time off first, alright?" Donny says. "You been through Hell and you look like it. That shit doesn't play well on the front desk."

I smile. My eyes water. I shake it off. "Thank you."

Donny turns back to the shop, waving his hand with dismissal. Jag comes out of the open garage door, my skateboard under his hand, his keys wrapped around his fingers. He hands me the skateboard and it's more like he's the one running for his car now while I'm trying to keep up.

"You don't have to do this, J." I go around the car to the passenger's side.

Jag hangs outside with the driver's door open. He's smiling, warm, maybe not like he gets it, but it's the kind of smile I never thought I deserved. "What kind of piece of shit would I be if I knew you were doing something suicidal on your own?"

After everything I've put him through, how does he still want anything to do with me? How does he still believe in me? How does he still care?

"Does it really count as suicidal if I'm already dead?" I slip my skateboard into the backseat. My backpack goes to the floor.

"Yeah, I think it does. Sentiment still matters." He stares at me.

My skin puckers with chills. I run my hand over my arm and try to smooth the hairs down. I try to ignore the six birds bouncing around the parking lot, but even with my head down, each black blob is visible and I can't not notice. I can't not see them watching him, waiting for him, stalking him. Six of them.

I go over to the dumpster and pick up a stray rock and a soda can sitting on the ground. I go running around the car, chucking the can at the biggest of them, then the rock. The raven only moves enough so neither strike it.

I climb into the passenger seat. Jag's already waiting behind the wheel. "You think that'll change anything?"

I shake my head. "It hasn't so far, but it makes me feel better."

"I'm not gonna let anything happen, alright?" Jag's 390 roars to life then settles to a purr. The sound overpowers the panic in my head telling me the reaper's coming and playing out every way Jag could die. "Just focus on what we need to get done. Nothing in your head's happened."

"Yeah."

We're pulling out of the parking lot. Jag waits to put his seatbelt on until he switches gears and is coasting. I grab my phone out of my pocket thinking maybe Wayland's messaged me and I just didn't feel it, but there's nothing new from him. I drop my phone into the cup holder.

"BAIT's, right?" Jag says.

"Yeah."

"You really think he's gonna be able to do something?"

"I don't know, but I have to try." My hands need something to do, so I pick at my shirt. I close my eyes, hoping for silence. All I get is nightmares. I open my eyes again.

Jag's hand's on the stick; I put my hand on his. Heat goes up my arm. My eyes water. I pull my hand back and put it in my lap, hands tucked between my thighs. I tighten my jaw to stop the weakness from showing and look out the window, away from him. "Thanks, J…" I say. "For everything. I owe you… so much." A weak chuckle pushes out, trying to make my voice less awkward, less fragile, less pathetic and obvious in how much I need him.

"You don't owe me anything, Joey." Jag pauses, looks like he's going to say something else, but doesn't.

Switch shift.

He's driving a little faster than normal. We shouldn't be as close to the bar as we already are. Graffiti on the side of a brick townhouse just has a bunch of dollar signs and a garbage bag on fire. Ashes lay on the sidewalk beneath it. On the fence next to it is the image of a ribbon that says ONLY THE GOOD DIE YOUNG. Two blocks from that reads LOVE ME ALWAYS in plain, white lettering and I mutter, "I will."

SEVENTEEN.

There are five ravens outside when we get to BAITs. One in the grass, three in the trees, one on the roof, and then one lands on the pavement right in front of Jag. He's the biggest and he hops over the crack that separates the parking lot from the sidewalk, bringing himself closer to Jag. Jag goes around the bird with the car radio in his hand. He meets me at the front of the car. The air smells like smoke and alcohol and I'm realizing how thirsty I am. We walk up to the bar entrance, my hand's looking for my box of cigarettes in my ass pocket. Nothing's there. I ran out earlier.

I step up to the counter popping my empty lips. Ralph's on the far side of the bar, making a drink for some dead guy who's leaning in too far. His back's arched, his spine's sticking out more than it should, his muscles are tense, and when he laughs, spit comes out. He's muttering something sharp that somehow cuts through the background noise of the stereo and conversation. His smile's crooked and like he's got too many teeth while he squinting like he's high. Ralph's voice disappears into the noise with the bar. KC's standing beside him. Ralph sets the drink down. The dead guy reaches over the counter for Ralph and I don't know if he missed him or what, but it looks like his hand just went through Ralph's arm. Blue and red veins pop out of the dead guy's skin, wrapping around his bicep. His fingers are stiff and pulsing, his laugh is a threat he silences with the beer he nurses.

Ralph steps back, reaching for the towel on the shelf beneath the counter. KC takes his place talking to the dead guy. Ralph passes by me with a nod, but without stopping. I follow him and Jag follows me. We go to the back office. Nothing's said until he closes the door.

"What did you bring me?" Ralph says.

I pull my bag off my shoulders and produce the feathers, the small flask of Lethe, and the photo of Wayland and me.

Ralph picks up the bottle of Lethe. "Wow. Is that a reaper's flask?"

"I know a guy," I say.

"You went to the river itself, huh?" He lowers the jar. "Around Poena?"

My face's going hot, fingers tingling. I can't explain the shock going through me. I don't remember the river feeling like this. It's not the same sensation as Styx. It's worse. It's red and pain and scars on my arms being picked open to make them fresh again as shame eats me alive and all I can think is how I don't want anyone looking at me. I'm stepping back until I run into Jag and think, "Holy shit, when did you get there?" because somehow I forgot he was here and that makes it worse because I don't know what he's seeing. I exhale and try not to move. "Yeah," I manage.

"A reaper take you?" Ralph says.

I force a smile. My lips are tight. I'm supposed to be chuckling, but the sound hurts and dies off fast. "Not really."

Ralph surveys the picture then looks back at me, making me feel exposed. Somehow, it's like he knows everything about that moment from just a snapshot.

I don't remember a lot from that night, but I do remember the way Wayland's body felt against mine when

I almost fell walking up the drive at his house. He tried so hard to keep me quiet when we got in the door. It worked until we got to his bedroom and I fell onto his bed. My back ached from the way I'd hit the floor just a few hours earlier. His mattress was so soft and it smelled nice. Then he asked me if I needed anything, and instead of saying no, I ranted to him about my dad, so loud, Wayland might as well have been three rooms over. He came to the bed, took my hand, and said, "You don't need to yell, Jo. I'm right here," and I said, "I'm not yelling," even though I'm pretty sure I was. Then there was a click, but it went away and my arm went around his neck while I grabbed the front of his shirt and pulled him down on top of me so I could hold him tight. I don't remember what he said then, but I remember what it felt like and the feeling of tear stains on my cheeks when I woke up the next morning. Wayland was still laying next to me and I felt like shit for ruining his night, even if he never complained about it.

I take the picture from Ralph and lay it face down on the desk so he can't look at it or judge me or come up with his own guesses of who that is or what he thinks he saw. "The picture work for you?"

"It's fine." He plucks at the photo. I press it harder into the desk. He pinches the edge and pulls. It comes out from under my hand. He steps back with it. The desk becomes a barrier. He surveys the picture again. "Better than fine. There's a lot of attachment in this."

My skin's covered in goosebumps. An uncomfortable wave goes up my arm. Electric, heat, fire, *fear*. Suddenly, the word is in every picture hanging around Ralph's office. It sticks out in clipped newspapers and shirts and grass and leaves. My stomach curls. I'm going to vomit. I slam my hands into the desk for support. The pen cup clatters. A couple of empty bottles hidden somewhere knock against each other.

"Joey, you okay?" Jag says.

"Yeah, sorry," I mutter.

"I get it," Ralph says.

"You don't," I snap before I can think.

"Okay." Ralph's too calm, relaxed, strong. Whatever's coming off him overpowers me; it's similar to the thing that draws me to Jag when he puts his hands on me, when his body's against mine, when his weight's pressing me down. He has the ability to stop me when I'm going to do something stupid. Even if I hate him for a second, he knows better than me... a lot. Ralph has that too, but it's a different kind of feeling. He's looking at the picture again, turning it over in his hand. "Interesting," he says to no one.

I tap my hand against the desk. "Can you stop looking at it?"

"Bad memories?"

I laugh into my cigarette. "Hardly."

"Boyfriend?" Ralph says.

The weight of the word shouldn't be so heavy; Jag's asked me the same thing, but it never felt so big, and then with Jag standing behind me, someone else confirming what I missed for years, it feels worse. My chest hurts, my fingers tingle, I step back until I bump into a chair. "No. Never like that."

"Right..." Ralph looks down at the photo again.

"Just best friends."

Ralph nods, but doesn't say anything else. I'm tapping my thigh, clearing my throat too loudly. I don't want the picture to burn for even a second, but at least if it's ash, it means Ralph can't look at it or my face anymore, and read my thoughts and see the things I never did. Did I just ignore him? Did I lead him on, knowing he wanted something else all this time and I just... I couldn't accept it because I didn't want him to leave me?

The ring feels heavy in my pocket. My chest hurts from how the heat's seething through my veins too fast, my heart aches, my vision's going red and black. Ralph's saying something I can't hear, his voice only going *blah, blah, blah*, blocked by adrenaline like a wall of water's separating us. The room melts away next, the colors blurring together. Floor to ceiling, desk to chair, pictures turn to nothing and I'm lost in a void. Another buzz on my leg brings me back. Then comes Ralph's voice. Something, something, something. "You look like you're gonna pass out. Maybe sit down?"

"Yeah. I'm fine. Sorry." I'm reaching for my phone. I stumble back, grabbing onto the nearby chair so I don't hit my head on the floor. I sit down. My screen lights up; it doesn't show any new messages. "You said there was one more thing I needed to give you?"

"Didn't you say something about a blood sacrifice?" Jag says. He's still standing at the door.

"From where?" I put my phone down to press my palms into my head.

Ralph tears the photo of Wayland and I in half. I feel it inside of me. The pain, a sudden distance or maybe something I'm only now just seeing now, because all this time, I haven't wanted to look. He tosses both sides of the photo into what looks like a small, metal bowl. The voice in my head won't stop cursing telling me there's a box cutter in the desk and I should find it. I try to shake the hissing out of my ear. The pulsing's got me rolling my heel. My phone buzzes in my lap. I grab it, curl my fingers around it hard so I don't throw it. I forgot what I'm waiting for.

Ralph taps his fingers against the desk. "Having trouble?" He opens his desk drawer. A small tin and a lighter come out. Inside the tin is a line of rolled joints. He takes one out, lights it, takes a hit.

I press my palms into my eyes, my back's against the chair. Jag's hands curl around my shoulders. Shapes carve into the blackness then I'm seeing a streak of light coming across my eyelids. "Nah, I'm good. What do you need?"

"I run a bar for ghosts, kid. You think I don't know what it looks like when one of 'em's about to lose their shit?" Ralph snorts. For the first time, the age shows on his face. I mean, maybe not age, cause Ralph's not *old, old*, not like my dad, but old like we wouldn't have gone to the same high school even if he was ten years younger or maybe it's not an age thing. Maybe it's everything he's been through because bad things carve scars in your eyes and face and the way you talk and there's nothing you can do about it. New lines, deeper pits, bags of darkness and cut outs. Somehow it says *old* without wrinkles. Cynical's not the right word, but…

Sometimes I wonder what I look like to other people. Has the stress of everything made me look like an old, miserable bitch or do the ripped jeans and eyeliner keep people seeing a troubled juvenile who can still hope to work stuff out? I've been called immature so goddamn much in my life. Even Rocky talks to me like he sees a kid. Sometimes, it almost feels like he's thinking *you could be my daughter* and I'd say maybe, only because the daughter of a badge would definitely do things her daddy told her not to. Like *I* always do.

"What exactly does that mean?" Jag says. "Or how exactly do we help her?"

"The fetish should do it, but I can't do anything without the blood," Ralph says.

"How much do you really know about this stuff?" Jag says.

"Why do you think I got into the occult?" Ralph says.

I shake my head, more to cut loose the voices than to answer Ralph. His thing seems obvious, but then, people tend to make the answers feel that way, so you look extra dumb when you don't know what they're talking about.

"KC was gone and one day he wasn't. Showed up at my house. Angry as hell. The fights he got into, you'd

think he was looking to die again and again and again."
Ralph chuckles bitterly.

"He probably was," I say.

The vitality in Ralph's eyes mutes. He leans forward, scoots around the back of the desk, shuffles through the drawers, looking for something. The one full of bottles is obvious when he opens and closes it. It's not holding whatever he's looking for. "Blood all over his hands, his shirt, his jeans, his... everything. Said all he could think about was killing and screaming and harm. He got pretty graphic, not because he wanted to, but it was like he was possessed when he was talking. Locked himself in a Taco Bell bathroom before trashing it. We got a couple bottles of Tito's on the way back to my place and he told me everything he could remember."

"And you just believed him?" Jag says.

"No." Ralph leans back. He scans the top of his desk and the floor side his chair, then continues going through the drawers. "But considering the state he'd been in for the last couple of days, there weren't many options and I wasn't about to challenge him. I ID'ed the body for the badges. Not exactly sure how to explain that, so call me convinced that something else was going on."

"Coulda been the binge," Jag says. "I've seen shit get pretty bad."

"Coulda been. It was a rough time for me too." Ralph tips his head to the side. He opens a drawer he'd already had open once, but this time, he reaches into it. The look on his face says he found what he was looking for. He leans back, but keeps his hands under the desk. "Doesn't matter. He took me to Mortem. I met a couple *things*, asked some questions, and—"

"You went to Mortem?" I say.

"Yeah."

"Alive?"

There's a pause before Ralph says, "Yeah," with a

laugh.

I stomp too hard, the pain goes up my leg. "Sol told me she'd never met someone like me before when I went down there alive!"

Ralph covers his mouth when he laughs. "Sol has a lot in common with Mortem."

"You mean she's fake as shit?"

"Pretty much." He's still laughing.

I grab whatever I can off the desk and throw it at Ralph. Ralph doesn't flinch. The paper, pen, and ashtray from the desk seemingly go right through him and hit the floor.

"What the hell is wrong with you?" I'm standing, leaning over the desk.

"Ghosts can't touch me directly or indirectly unless I allow them to. Not in here, at least. That's the point of making a sanctuary and one of the perks of contracting with the Cogs," Ralph says.

"Everyone keeps saying *Cogs this* and *Cogs that*, but no one's saying what they actually are or what they do or why they have so much control over everything," I say.

"Easiest way to explain them is to say they're angels who maintain order and balance, spreadsheet angels… kinda. Well, they're not exactly angels either because angels are… a whole 'nother venture, but it's the closest approximation. There are six of them. I don't know their names. Don't think it matters. They operate as one to monitor existence and keep things working. What's all that mean?" Ralph shrugs. "I don't know. I don't think any mortal can ever grasp it. Even with *some* of *their* knowledge, there are things I can't comprehend. Like, you see the idea, but you can't put it together in a way that makes sense, you know?"

I laugh, lean back, cross my arms, and look away with a hiss. I turn back and Ralph's staring at me. "Sorry." I unfold my arms. "I just—If *this* is *keeping things working*, they're not doing a very good job. Like, I'm told humans are useless, but it's like every creature in charge of the universe is on holiday. Why the hell else would the dead be able to wander and ruin the lives of everyone else just trying to make it?"

"You gotta take some creative liberty," Ralph says. "Humans add a flavor of unpredictability to everything we touch. It's not that animals don't have emotional expression, but humans rationalize the illogical and take action on it. Unlimited actions based on unlimited interpretations, but the Cogs don't exist to intervene with humanity. Even if they did, as they calculate what you do, there's always at least one person who finds an outcome they didn't predict."

"Then what the hell's the point?" My eyes are going black and red and black again until I'm leaning over Ralph's desk again, holding onto the edges for balance, breathing so hard I feel crazy so I turn around and Jag's staring at me. I pat down my pocket. "Sorry. I'm out of cigarettes."

Ralph opens his drawer. His foil cigarette box and lighter are on my side of the desk. I reach for them, somewhat expecting him to stop me, but he doesn't. I light a cigarette fast. My hands are shaking. My fingers act like I'm going to burn them again.

"They can give you another chance, Joey," Ralph says. "Very few of those exist."

"I wouldn't need a second chance if they never let the dead walk the earth a second time," I say.

Ralph sits down and his laughter ends with a sigh. His shoulders sag. Weariness takes over his features. His eyes soften; he rubs them. "Sentimentality will always be our greatest downfall, huh? We're never without a reason. You want to convince me you're here, dead, covered in beatings, hurting yourself for another, living or dead, and you're not stupidly sentimental too?"

"I don't know what you're saying—"

"Why are you here?" Ralph says. "Walking the earth again. You blame the supernatural for what is the mortal imperative."

I put the cigarette to my lips so I don't have to answer. Sitting down again. My legs hang off the side of the chair. Ralph's looking through me. Medium, psychic, how many of my thoughts or memories does he have in his head to throw at Jag when he thinks I'm not listening? I don't want to think about anything in case Ralph can grab more of my thoughts to judge and laugh at because of how pathetic I am that after all this shit, I still don't hate my dad and wish that he hadn't died hating me.

"We all have our non-negotiables, drives or people or things we won't let go of and we do unbelievably stupid things to keep or attain them. The Cogs are at least a little more understanding than Sol or the reapers," Ralph says.

"Even if you mess up?" I say.

"Even if you mess up," Ralph says.

My phone buzzes. I pick it up.

WAYLAND	YEAH. YEAH.
	SORRY.
	THEY'RE FINE.
	BUT I CAN'T GO TO THEM.
JOEY	You still at my place?
WAYLAND	YEAH.
JOEY	Stay there, ok?
WAYLAND	OK.

I slip my phone away. "Okay. Blood—You need blood. What kind? From where?"

Ralph's eyes go from me to the small pot he's got my ripped photo in. I try not to linger on it, feeling the flare of anger and sadness coming back hard. Ralph picks up the Lethe and feathers from the table and puts them into one of the drawers. He leans forward. He's not searching, he knows what he wants and exactly where it is. His hand returns from the drawer. He stands up to place a knife on the desk edge closest to me. He sits back down, slouching. "Sacrifice. It doesn't mean anything if it doesn't come from you."

My arm's already tingling. Jag's muttering behind me, "You don't have to do this Joey. Guy's a nutty cultist. I know there's a lot of something going on, but you really believe this will change anything?"

I laugh. "This is hardly the most bizarre thing I've been asked to do in the last week, J." I grab the knife off the desk. My sleeve's pulled up. I don't give myself time to think about it as I plunge the blade's edge into my skin and drag it along my arm not too different from the night I almost ended everything. The blade acts like a paintbrush; a ribbon of red runs along my forearm. The cut's barely enough to puncture the skin. It's not dripping.

Like he's reading my thoughts, Ralph says, "More."

My body doesn't belong to me anymore. The blade presses harder into my arm, going down my wrist again. I hiss, grit my teeth, my sight's going spotty and black and I'm dizzy, but I don't falter. In fact, the impulse comes to shove the blade straight through my arm. That'd be enough blood, right?

The room spins around me. My legs are stiff, keeping me in place. Burning tears go down my cheeks. So much sulfur, it's overpowering the tobacco and pot. I exhale, gasp. "How do you catch it?" The words are carried out by a pant.

"Holy shit, Joey—" Jag's hands are on my shoulders. I pull away. The pain worsens. He grabs my hips instead.

"Hold still." Ralph's moving, but I can't tell how or why or where exactly, just that his black hole eyes are blurred by the water obscuring mine. It's fine. I don't want to see anyone anymore anyway. They're always judging me—Even when they say they aren't.

The tears come faster now, my cheeks are so wet, excess drops onto my shirt. My arm's shaking; my leg's are shaking; everything's shaking. I don't know where the knife is, but the blood's flowing down my arm too fast, like the fire spread around Wayland's house. It's not natural. My arm's burning. There's a pressure there too and in my ear, someone's saying *you already lost him, Jo, and you're losing your goddamn mind too.*

Something cold presses to my face. I pull back with a gasp, swing my arm. The knife clatters onto the floor. Blood splatters across the desk and there's someone's shirt. Soiled. I'm not in control of my body. A hand catches my fist that's too weak to throw a real punch. I swing again with my right. The hand barely goes anywhere. Jag's got a hold of my fists and he squeezes.

"Come back," Ralph says softly.

I blink rapidly; the haziness clears up. The tension in my body melts back to something more manageable, so much of it escapes through the cut in my skin. I say, "Sorry," and "Thanks," but Jag doesn't let me go. There's a long, silver plate under my arm, catching the dripping blood. When did it get so bad? My arm's covered, seething red from only a few strokes that got so deep.

When did they get so deep?

After Ralph's satisfied, he hands Jag a long cloth.

"You're free," Ralph says.

I don't know what it means, but my legs are shaking and weak and I'm going to fall. Jag brings me to the nearest chair hissing, "Sit down and shut up," as he wraps the cloth around my arm and cleans the fresh wounds. I don't say anything.

There's a medical kit sitting on the desk now. Jag was better at cleaning the wound than I realized he would be. I mean, he's helped me more than a couple times after a fight with my dad, but it's just different watching him now.

How he holds my wrist, the pressure, the care when he presses antiseptic along the incision and tunes everything out to finish the job. The tightness of the bandages he wraps me with give me a feeling of safety. The warmth from his fingers comes through them.

Ralph takes another hit from his joint and sets it back in the ashtray on the desk. He lights a candle on the other side of the room. The smell's strong and eats away at the growing rot that's crept into the office. From it, he lights a long, slim stick with a reddish end, but no flame. Incense is the next thing to come.

Jag checks over my arm once he's done before he puts the bandages back in the bag. He reaches for my face and makes me look at him. I flinch. Shoulders up, fists tight, but I don't swing. He dabs at my face, wiping at the swollen mess under my eyes. I feel like a child, unable wipe my own face good enough. I try though. I pull back and Jag lets my face go and I wipe my own eyes, acting like I'm tired, not trying to hide from him again.

I force a small grin onto my lips. I can't keep it there. I pant through the pain while my fingers grip hard at my thighs. This pain is different. It's in three places. Head. Heart. Hands. Trying to drown everything out. I'm rocking gently. "Sorry, Jag… Are you tired of me yet?" I loosen a hand from myself to reach for him. It's trembling and stiff and I can't get close enough to catch him.

Jag steps closer. My hand grazes his shirt and closes in the fabric. His hand's on the back of my neck, going up through my hair. He pulls me closer. "No." He's got a fist full of my hair and he's using it as leverage, pulling my head back. "But I get a minute to be pissed. I had to listen to you scream in the most agonizing way yesterday and I couldn't do a damn thing about it. I've had to watch you come to work, to my house, for years, black and blue with the handiwork from a man who frankly didn't deserve to live. One bad thing after another, and you tell yourself you deserve it the whole goddamn time. Reason doesn't get to you. When I've said I fucking care, get out of that house—you never believed it. And now you're carrying on with Cross. Do you get it?"

"I'm sorry, Jag—"

His lips mash into mine. I don't want it to end. My hand's going up his stomach, pushing his shirt up; Jag breaks the kiss and pulls back. I follow until I can't lean forward anymore.

My brain's not working and as hard as I try, I can't think of what I want to say. "For everything." The words come slow. My mind's a vast field of emptiness and fear. I shake my head to stave off the returning zone out. Another buzz in my lap, another message from Wayland. "How long is this gonna take?"

"Couldn't tell you," Ralph says.

"You've done this before, right?" I say.

"Yes, but every call with the Cogs is different. Sometimes they want more words, sometimes less, sometimes it's an immediate 'no' when you ring the bell," Ralph says.

"Okay." I stand up, clutching my phone. "Then send me a text when you get an answer, yeah? I have somewhere I need to be."

"Party." Ralph picks up his joint again. He uses the lit candle to light the picture of Wayland and I on fire.

I don't wait for Ralph to say anything more. I'm out of the office, out of the bar, and making my way toward Jag's car without pause. I pull the passenger door open and drop into the seat. The movement sends a wave of pain up my cut arm. I hiss. Close my eyes. Breathe. Jag climbs in behind the wheel and starts the car.

"We need to go to my place," I say.

"Why?" Jag says.

"Wayland's there."

Jag lights a cigarette. He takes a couple drags off it

while rolling down his window. He combs his bangs, staring at BAIT's. "Don't you need whatever he's cooking?"

"Yeah… But there's no ignoring a call like this."

Jag sighs. He puts his cigarette in the ashtray and pulls out onto the street.

"Sorry." I use his cigarette. "I know it's all crazy." My foot's bouncing. It sends sparks of pain through the cuts in my arm. A pulse of every idiot moment I've ever put Wayland and Jag and Donny through. There's nothing I can say that will mean enough. All I can figure out is, "I'm kind of an idiot."

"Yeah?" Jag sighs. "Me too." He peers at me from the side. The radio gets louder without him touching it. I lean back to watch out the window, but after a couple walls of graffiti, I close my eyes; I don't need harassment from the grave. Along the way, I mutter with every song coming out of the radio, songs I never thought I paid attention to, but because Jag had them on every day, they somehow got into me. His voice softly accompanies mine. I open my eyes just to locate Jag's hand.

Our fingers lace and the pain from my arm becomes a little more bearable.

EIGHTEEN.

As we near my house, ravens are all over the place. Sidewalks, stoops, trees, standing in the middle of the street and on top of parked cars. Maybe not swarms, but every turn, every direction, every corner, there's another one tracking Jag's car, waiting to see where he's gonna stop. I'm tempted to tell him to punch it when I get out. Drive as fast and far away from here as he can, but then it's like, what if they're waiting for him to get into an accident to pick his bones apart while he's wrapped around someone else's bumper? The universe expected me to go the same way as my dad; did it expect Jag to go the same way as his?

"When we get there, can you stay in the car?" I say.

"What are you so worried about?" Jag gives a side glance. His smile fades when I don't say anything. "Is it Cross?"

I bite the ring on the inside of my lip. Stare out the window. The side of Jag's face reflects in my window. He keeps looking at me when he gets the chance.

"Is it?" he says.

"It's the ravens—"

"The ravens haven't said they'd kill me, Joey."

My skin's hot; my foot's bouncing again. I roll down my window, hoping the fall air will be enough to take the color off my cheeks and maybe slow everything down, giving me some time to think. Winter's coming, though it's not here yet and winter's supposed to freeze things, right? Violence kicks up in the hotter months, you know? Maybe you wouldn't assume that would be the case, but heat actually makes peoples' tempers shorter, like it's lighting a fuse, while the cold actually makes people more lonely.

At least, my dad got angrier in the summer, but he cried more in the winter. He begged me not to leave around Christmas while yelling at me to get out around July. He smoked more to keep the house warm and he drank more, which got him to pass out. He wasn't much nicer, but sometimes I pretended he said he cared about me a little more than he actually did. It was implied, you know? Between the burping and the whimpering and the hissing *bitch* because the anger was never *that* far away, it just chilled out for a while. I could take something away from how he never actually killed me though, right?

I never decided whether I preferred being the focus of my dad's fight or if I wish my mom was around to take it. I felt selfish thinking it, but I couldn't stop myself from wondering if he had her to be mad at, maybe he'd have something better left behind for me and maybe I'd be a little less dysfunctional.

The cold air's not helping.

I search for Jag's hand without looking. It's on the wheel, so I rest my hand on his leg instead. My foot bouncing slows, though it doesn't stop. "Jag..." I swallow, watch my feet. "I.. know I don't say it enough, but... Thank you... for following me to Hell and back and... just, everything... Everything you do... Have done for me."

Jag puts his car into park; his hand strays from the stick to lay over mine. He stares out the windshield; he's not hiding his focus on the raven standing in the middle of the street in front of us. "You'd do the same for me."

"How do you know?"

"Because…" His seatbelt clicks and falls back. "I know you, Joey." He turns to me. "Better than you might think." His eyes are so sharp, he's looking through me, reading everything there is to know. I reach for the door. He grabs hold of my arm, sending electricity through my body. His hand slides up my shoulder and curls around my neck. He pulls me in. His lips press gently to mine.

I lean forward, bracing myself on his leg the best I can, holding my breath. "I need to go." I pull back.

"I know." Jag's hand drops away.

I fall back into my seat, grab the door, and push it open all in one movement. The brick wall of Deadwood trailer park is right outside my open door. The white sign from the Dollar Store down the street and the gas station build the familiarity of the neighborhood. It feels like it's been forever since I was last here. Most of the grass is brown. The tree in the duplex's yard across the street looks gray without leaves and the color muted. Obsidian eyes glow where ravens stand waiting.

I climb out of the car. Blue spray paint on the brick wall reads FOR THE LOVE OF GOD where I don't remember it being before.

"Hey, Joey—"

"Yeah?"

He's leaning into my empty seat. He's looking at my face like he's got something to say but doesn't want to say it. "Try to be careful."

My immediate impulse is to tell him I can't make promises like that, you've seen it already, so you can't get disappointed when I come back busted again, but I should try harder, at least for him, at least for every bit of shit I've put him through in the last few days, even if I don't think I'll do any better at it. It's not like I don't see it on his face. Tired, stressed, dark circles have started coming in under his eyes and the quiet about him is the kind that tells me he's thinking really hard about everything he says like he's stepping on sticks around a sleeping bear.

Since the beginning of our relationship, I told him not to ask questions about what he thought he saw. No matter how much he wanted to or how much he thought he was hiding it when he looked over my body when my clothes were off, I knew what he wanted to say. Sometimes, he even *joked* about fighting my dad. He said it more often after a couple of beers, when he couldn't hold back his anger anymore.

Honestly, it was better this way because at the worst times, I could've seen Jag really hurting my dad, maybe even killing him. So, I knew what he saw. I knew what he thought. We both just pretended it didn't happen though because that's what *I* wanted. But it's never been fair. I didn't think about what it did to him when he had to look at me like that—because why should it matter? Why did I matter? It was my body, my life to mess up, right?

Except it wasn't just about me anymore and it hasn't been for a while.

So, this time, instead of letting my impulse lead, I say, "Okay."

I'm walking down the sidewalk, taking deep breaths, trying to keep my pace slow and steady and checking on the birds like I'm hoping they'll follow me instead of wait on him, but even for the ravens sitting in the trailer park, it's like I don't exist. I shake my head, pick up my pace and move into a jog. The cuts pull with the weight of my bouncing run. I turn around and run backwards to check on Jag's car.

Still quiet. Still good.

Maybe things will be fine and the birds don't mean

anything, really.

My house comes into view. The pale blue paint job on the mobile just makes it look off-white enough to be dirty. The shutters are actually dirty because my dad wasn't cleaning them and I gave up on it pretty quickly too when the sound of the hose annoyed him. Loud thumping echoes off the houses. It's gotta be someone's radio, driving too fast, listening to something so loud it distorts and isn't music anymore. The sound doesn't stop, though, so it's not a car.

My feet drag against the road. I'm barely moving anymore. I keep staring at the ground because it's going to keep me from looking at the house to see if the neighborhood sounds are coming through my walls and the lights are on in the windows. What if my dad's actually sitting in his chair again? I'm not going to be able to stay outside; I'd have to check on him.

My body jerks forward with the pull, a sick desire to see if he's home and ask if there's anything I can get for him in hopes of hearing him say, "I missed you, Josephine. Please don't leave me like that again," while he's crying into an empty Barton's bottle and holding me tight.

Slowly, I look toward my house. Black hair stands out against the dirty white door. Wayland's sweater is stained, though the dark blue tries to hide it. Brown and red still stand out on the white cuffs and button-up collar sticking out from underneath. Gore paints his jeans and the white parts of his shoes too. His hands hang between his knees, shuffling. His phone sits on the stone stairs beside him. He rocks forward gently.

I feel sick only for a second, then relief strikes it down.

"Wayland!" My drag turns into a run which turns into a walk when I enter the yard. His head lifts at the sound of my voice. His movements are sharp and strong. He stands up and meets me in the yard of dead grass and weeds and dirt. His arms go around me. I'm holding my breath. In front of me, he seems so much bigger than I remember. Hugging him back, I laugh.

"Jo," he says. "I didn't think you'd actually come."

"Why?" I laugh. "Why wouldn't I come?"

"I… It felt like you gave up on me. Like you didn't want to see me again."

I pull back, shaking my head. "That's crazy, Way."

He chuckles this time. It teeters into silence where it's just him looking at me, his hands on my shoulders, his expression unflinching. "I feel like I'm going crazy, Jo." He cups my jaw. "And I need you." My back straightens. With a hand around my waist, he pulls me in, mashing our lips together.

Adrenaline, panic, fear, excitement all run through me. They don't feel like they belong to me. My skin's on fire, everything's burning up, pressed against Wayland even when he feels cold. He tips my head back, deepening the kiss. His mouth tastes like murder. Salt. Iron. Rage. Desperation. The force in his lips is nothing like him. Practice. Passion. Patience I don't know. He grips my hip and turns us around so he can back me toward my house. I don't think he knows he's doing it.

Back in middle school when we kissed, he put his hand on my thigh without realizing and when we were done, he pulled back, saying sorry like he'd gone too far. Then, he did the most awkward thing you can do after kissing: he said, "Thanks, Jo. That was really good," with a little laugh.

"Way—I can't—" I break the kiss, but Wayland doesn't pull back. He's panting, leaning into me, trying to watch for the steps, grab at the door, keep me close, and kiss me again. His brown eyes look darker than before, closer to black, even over the whites. He smells so much like iron and sulfur and ash.

"I need to tell you something, Jo." His voice is intimate, a whisper pressed into my ear and not at all unsure.

His muscles tighten. He's pulled away from me, stumbling backward to catch himself. I fall back too, hitting my ass on the steps to my house. Pain shoots up my sore arm. Jag's here, in front of me, between Wayland and I. He shoves Wayland back again, his fist balling. Wayland catches himself without falling and takes a few more steps to recover.

"Jag!" I say.

"Nah-uh." Jag grabs Wayland by the shirt. "You don't touch another guy's girl, Cross." His fist smashes into Wayland's face with a loud crack.

Wayland drops, tripping over his heel. Blood drips down his face from his nose. His shoulders rise rapidly, panting with panic. The emotion in his head is getting into mine.

"And you don't abuse her trust."

My vision's going blurry, a wave of dizziness smashes into me and everything's spinning. The blood from Wayland's shirt mixes with the grass and crusty trailer siding and concrete and panic. "Jag, stop!"

"I didn't abuse anyone!" Wayland says. A light flickers off his hand.

There's a gun.

My *dad's* gun.

Time slows. All I can see are the ravens from the last few days surrounding us and Val's saying, "You smell pretty good," in my head like he's standing over Jag. It's more than seven ravens blurring the trailer park together. It's too many ravens, it can't be real. But in the sea of dead grass and deadbeats and death eaters, I'm reminded that Wayland's dead because of me, and Jag's going to suffer the same fate.

Wayland points the gun at Jag.

My shoes slide in the gravel and rock and weed. The boom echoes off the trees and trailers, through the sky, and comes back to us with enthusiasm. A chorus of ravens is screaming or cheering, having waited for this for days. The sky's black and spotty and moving. The noise turns to blaring TVs from trailers getting louder, like people turning up the volume because they didn't care or didn't want to get involved; it's not their front yard, it's not their business, its not their fight to witness. My throat hurts and I'm screaming, falling to the ground saying someone's name. I think.

My shirt sticks to my back. I'm coughing, mouth filled with blood. I try to wipe it, but my arm won't move. I think it's underneath me. The ringing in my ears tries to cover the muffled voices, the thud, the "Joey" and "Jo" coming at the same time as Jag and Wayland become one.

Everything goes black and silent and my body's heavy, maybe it doesn't exist anymore. I don't know why I've been so desperate to come back. Everything was finally over and I was given an out for eternity, but I still couldn't take it. Ralph calls it sentimentality; Charon says it's an obsession with retribution. Is that really all there is? Without a body, a soul rots, and during rot, everything that's left of the person is scrubbed away, right? Until they're miserable and broken and breaking everything else, fashioning a mirror out of the world around them. Is that what's waiting for me too? Then why am I here? Why would Charon give me a second chance if I'm damned to follow after my dad?

I've carried the guilt of leaving my dad the day he took himself off; I've spent so much time thinking about what I could've done differently to keep him from suffering so that I couldn't slam the door on anyone else. I couldn't risk making anyone carry the same weight I've had for fifteen years.

It's been so hard to keep my head on. Without a body, without a heart, there can't be much of me left. If there's enough of me to hurt someone, though, then I hope there's at least enough of me left to keep *him* alive. Maybe it's selfish. Maybe it *is* sentimentality, like Ralph said, but I can't let him go and I'm not ready to go yet because of it.

Before I feel my body again, I'm hearing voices, grunting and cursing and whimpering make it through the layer of silencing walls like I'm underwater. The sound gets louder and louder in increments and each time the volume's cranked a little bit more, it makes me dizzy until I feel like I'm going to be sick. My hands press into whatever's beneath me. I'm moving, sitting up, on my knees with a burn in the back of my throat and gasping. Pain shoots through my right arm. My chest shakes, quivers, constricts, and screams. My fingers curl into the dirt. I'm heaving, looking for air. I still can't see, unable to open my eyes. Bile burns my nose. I cough and gasp as I sit up.

"Joey?" Jag says.

"Jo?" Wayland sounds more like he's talking through pain. "Get off of me—"

"Shut up," Jag says. A thud follows.

I sit back. The pale colors of the world are coming back, though my eyes are still half-closed and my lashes act like webs holding everything in place. Not doing a very good job. I breathe deep, stabilize. The gray trees take shape. Like a picture being sketched quickly, the muted mobile homes come in next. Objects form, then take shape in detail. Jag's on top of Wayland, pinning legs down with his, pressing Wayland's arms to his back, and his face to the ground. Bloods smeared all over Wayland's face, coming from his nose and busted lip. His eye's swollen; it looks like he's taken more than a couple of hits. Jag's also got a busted lip. His sunglasses lay on the ground nearby. Then there's my dad's gun sitting in the grass.

Everything comes back like someone's hit fast-forward on a video.

"You need to get off," Wayland says.

"You need to shut the fuck up," Jag says. "Joey—You

okay?"

"Yeah…" I breathe out carefully. My chest aches; it's hard to breathe. The pain splits through my limbs. I close my eyes and breathe slowly again. "I think…" A wet spot in my shirt paints my fingers with blood. I brush my hair back with my other hand. Another breath.

Wayland struggles underneath Jag. Jag pushes him back into the ground, harder until Wayland stops pushing.

"Can you let Cross go?" I say.

"Uh, how about no?" Jag says. "He shot you and tried to kill me."

"I asked you to stay by the car."

"And I told you to be careful."

"Then I guess we both fucking suck, huh?" I bury my face in my hands. I move too fast, too hard, the cuts in my arms and what's left in my chest pulls and stings and shoots sharp bolts through me. I'm panting through my teeth. The dizziness is back. I close my eyes and slowly lay back on the ground so I don't collapse. I lay my arm over my eyes. The world becomes distant and I almost feel like I'm falling through the earth. I grab the grass underneath me to make sure I'm still on the ground. "Jag?"

"Yeah?"

I didn't think he'd really be there. My jaw's clenched. "I'm trying to work this shit out and…" I don't know if I can, but I can't say that out loud. It's a mess. Wayland's a mess; I'm a mess; there might not be a way to fix it, but I've been trying too hard for too long just to give up. But if I won't give up on Wayland, is the only other option to give up on Jag? I can't do that either. I just need a little more time to figure this out.

"I'm done seeing you black, blue, and bloody," Jag says.

"Please… Let me talk to Cross alone," I say. My arm falls away from my eyes. Somehow, I wasn't expecting Jag to be looking at me, but it's like he was waiting. Guilt goes through me. I sit up, rub my eyes, meet his again, straight. "You can trust me."

Jag looks down at Cross again. "It's not you I don't trust." His body's still tense. After a moment, he's pressing into Wayland while he's getting up. Stepping back quickly, he grabs his cigarettes out of his pocket, still putting space between the two of them. He keeps eyeing me.

Wayland rolls onto his back. His hands are full of the earth, his eyes are squeezed shut.

Jag lights his cigarette, then throws me the box. "Call me when you're done. We need to *actually* talk, Joey." Jag looks at Wayland, then me. "About a lot of shit."

"I know," my voice is weaker than I mean for it to be.

"Cross," Jag says.

Wayland's sitting up now, hands in his lap, head down. He goes tense at his name. His fingers curl. He won't look past his knees. He wipes away the blood running from his nose. His movements are brasher than normal, but careful around the sensitive swelling. He presses too hard and flinches away from his own hand. He stares at his blood-stained fingers, his own mixed with whoever else he spread around Baltimore before coming here.

"I don't hate you," Jag says. "What happened to you sucks, but what you've been doing around here is not the way to deal with it." Jag briefly looks at me. "You've been a good friend to Joey. Don't ruin that with what you got left." He takes a drag to ease his slight shifting.

"I understand... Believe me." Wayland's hands are trembling. Fists curl hard. He buries them in his lap, causing his shoulders to shake. He turns his head away.

"Good luck." Jag looks at me one more time before turning around. He's walking to where Dad's gun is. Once he's got it in his hand, he flips the safety on and keeps going. He's out of the yard, out of the street, and out of sight without pause. It's not long before the familiar sound of the Mustang roars through Deadwood. It's short-lived, driving off, I don't know where. Maybe he'll go back to the shop, maybe he'll go home, maybe he'll stop for pizza or just turn around the block to come back and see what happened when he left us. Maybe he'll sit and smoke and think about what just happened and call it quits for real.

This could be the last straw; he could've died.

My lips still tingle from how rough Wayland's kiss was. His bloody handprints are on my hip. I wipe moisture from my jaw. More blood. I'm not sure whose.

I couldn't blame Jag for leaving now. I deserve it; he shouldn't have any more grace for me and I'm kind of scared that when I call him, he'll say, "I'm done with you. For real."

My mind plays through every argument it can think of to stop Jag from leaving me, but none of them are good enough. None of them were ever good enough to keep Wayland either.

I'm staring at him now. He looks so unlike himself, covered in gore and doubt and insecurity and regret. It sounds so stupid when you put it like that.

"I'm sorry, Jo." Wayland lifts his head a little, trying to smile and laugh. They strangle themselves out. It feels like he's already gone, like I'm not looking at Wayland anymore because the Wayland I knew disappeared days before I found his car and this is what's left of him and it's just barely holding on.

Tears burn my eyes. I sit in the grass beside him. I crave to take Wayland's hands, just to make sure he's there and I'm not seeing a ghost in my own head, but I grab at the weeds instead with a fear that touching his hands will make him feel like a corpse. "No, *I'm* sorry, Way."

"For what?" He forces a chuckle. "I hurt you. I tried to hurt... *him*." Hatred taints his voice, then the shame sets in. His head lifts, his eyes are glossy and though he tries to smile again, the sadness hangs onto his lips too hard.

"For everything, Wayland. Everything I didn't notice.

Everything you did for me. Any time I took advantage of you or missed your feelings or left you feeling alone." I reach into my pocket. The ring's at the bottom. It's in my palm. I can't look at him while holding it out. "This...I found it. I saw... some email from a counseling center. Way, what happened?"

It sounds like his first attempt to speak gets stuck. He clears his throat as quietly as he can. He gently shakes his head. "It's... so stupid, Jo." He laughs; it breaks off. He rubs his eyes even though there's nothing in them. "All of it's so stupid."

"So, tell me like it's a dumb joke."

Wayland takes the ring from my hand. Our fingers graze. He pulls his hand back holding the jewelry carefully. He twirls it slowly, carefully in his fingers. "It's not a new story... I was attacked." Wayland takes a slow breath. He exhales, shaky. He closes his eyes, fingers go through his hair. He touches his face like he's pushing back his glasses that aren't there. His hands go to his jeans in an effort to clean the life from the creases in his palms. "I was at this place. It was late, but not that late—Maybe almost ten. I was just going to my car and this guy came up, telling me to give him everything. Something happened that night. I... was working on something really special." He watches the ring carefully. "I was feeling really good. Like I could do anything, just say what was on my mind. I don't know—And I thought about what would've happened if I was with you and that I couldn't let him do this to me. The next thing I knew, I was on the ground and fighting him and then I couldn't breathe. Everything hurt and it was like I was drowning and then... Nothing. When I woke up, I was *down there* and I couldn't think about anything but how much I never told you and everything I still wanted to do. I *needed* to do. The time came and I ran from the reaper. Then I got back to this side and all I could think about was putting an end to everything that ever got in my way. First it was *that* guy. I found him because he had my car and my phone. Once I got those back, I couldn't stop thinking about Jagger and how he looked at you and what the hell did I not know? Why did you like him? Would you even tell me if something was going on?" Wayland's hands curl into his pant legs. "That guy took everything from me, Jo… for a couple of dollars and my mom's car. I don't know why it was worth that much to him. I just wanted a second chance so I could do it right. I didn't mean for everything to go like this."

Wayland buries his head in his hands. "I was just… scared and I waited too long. I thought, you know, if only I waited until everything was perfect, until I could tell you for sure that you'd have nothing to worry about between us and school and debt—That we had a future—Then everything would go right. I was afraid that if I said something too soon, you wouldn't want anything to do with me; I wasn't going to let us become like your parents." He lifts his head. His eyes meet mine. His expression softens. "I watched what he did to you for so long… I didn't know any other way to help, but stand by you and wait until you called or needed me or said my name with your shaky voice and faked smile because you needed a distraction. I didn't know how to deal with your dad, but I knew how to take care of you." He chuckles softly. "You told me before—I doubt you remember— You were probably… mostly asleep and you'd been drinking." He bites at his thumbnail. "You said you didn't remember much about your mom, but you worried you'd become just like her. You said she must've been a bitch to drive your dad crazy like she did and you thought if you became like her, you'd turn me into your dad if you stuck around too long. *You were already driving him crazy.* You laughed saying I'd have to pick up a drinking habit, then we could worry." Wayland smiles sadly. It fades. He pulls at the weeds in the dirt. "You never told me you were seeing Jagger, just… that he was an asshole at work. Sometimes it seemed like more when you talked about him, mostly though, it was the way he looked at you when I picked you up sometimes. Since you didn't say anything, I hoped it was just him." He breathes out hard. His eyes meet mine again. "I didn't really expect you to wait for me; I didn't tell you anything at all, but… I kinda hoped it would work out if I stuck to my plan. If I was there like I always had been, then it should work out, right? I guess you really did fall in love without me though."

"I'm sorry, Way." I reach for his hand. "I don't know when it got so serious. I don't know when he started to care… or when I started caring back. We hooked up because everything hurt and I needed a distraction. He helped me escape again and again and again. Sometimes, I even felt like… maybe I wasn't a worthless piece of shit or bad luck waiting to break somebody else." I press my hand to my face, covering my eyes. A laugh comes out. "I was always waiting for you to leave me."

Wayland laughs painfully. "I'd never do that. I hated that I couldn't *do* anything."

I can't stop them. Tears go down my cheeks. I wipe them away. "Way." I laugh. "You're the only reason I'm here now. Without you, I wouldn't've made it through sophomore year." I rub my eyes again, trying to clear the blur away. My clogged nose blocks any attempt at breath. "I don't know how, but you… you always knew the right time to say something or when I needed you. I can think of so many times in high school where you saved my life."

"But I couldn't help you in any other way," Wayland says. "I've been jealous of Jag for that. He was there for you in ways that I couldn't be because I was scared, I didn't tell you, I wasn't strong enough like him or you—"

"Wayland… I'm not stronger than you. I'm stronger *because* of you."

"I don't think that's true, Jo." He laughs weakly.

"Just… look at us." He stares down at his bloody hands. It's under his nails, in his skin, mixing with dirt and grime and scratches. It's not as dark as it could be, brown in some places. I don't know what's his, what's someone else's, or how many people might be on him. For a second, all I can think of is the bag in the woods, the body in five pieces I helped him throw away and I still don't care who that was; all I know is that it helped him and for everything he's done for me, I'd do it again. It should scare me how little I care about adding to the Bodymore body count, but that's exactly why I won't tell Jag the whole truth about this.

"I can't be here, Jo," Wayland says. "It hurts so much… Everything I've lost, I'll never have the chance to get again and I'm worried that if I stay, the regret will take whatever's left of me and I'll destroy what remains of the people I love." He meets my eyes; his water. He lowers his head again. "I saw what your dad did to you. I can't do that to my parents or my sister. I've already taken too much from them with the house and my death and… I know I can't control myself." His fingers curl. He drops his head into his hands. His presses hard against his head.

"You didn't make those things happen, Way—"

"Every second I'm here, I'm being eaten by everything I wish I could've done differently, thinking about it again and again and everything I can do to try and fix it. None of the suggestions are good, but I can't stop myself from doing them. Destroy everything, change everything until the opportunity's there again. I didn't *want* to be in Jag's house, but I couldn't stop myself. I wasn't trying to rip the place apart, but it made sense when all I could think of was finding you. It's… It's an obsession, screaming over my thoughts and controlling my body. It sounds just like me, but it's not and I can't resist it."

"What's a little more blood in this goddamn city?" I laugh painfully. Tears blur my eyes again. "It doesn't matter, anyway. Ralph promised he'd help us turn things back to normal—"

Wayland slowly shakes his head. "There is no going back, Jo… And you don't need me."

"You're wrong."

"Not this time I'm not." His gaze meets mine, unmoving, determined, assured in a way I'm not used to seeing.

"What are you going to do?"

"I think I have to move on, Jo." Wayland stands.

"What?" I follow.

"I have to return to Mortem and give it what I owe."

"Wayland—I can't—"

"You will."

I cover my mouth to stop the sob from coming out. Wayland reaches to me for the first time. His arms go around my shoulders. He pulls me to him. I put my arm around him too and I've never held him harder or faster. For the longest time, I'm holding his body to mine so tightly to make sure he can't disappear. Every hour I spent at his house plays through my head. Every time we laughed sneaking in, every time we sat in his car talking or I cheated off his test or thanked his mom for not kicking me out and having me for dinner like I was part of the family. Every familiar memory plays on repeat, like I'm about to lose it so I have to watch them again and again until I can't anymore.

"I love you, Jo," he says against my ear.

"I love you too, Wayland." I squeeze him harder. He squeezes me back. It's only when his arms loosen that I allow mine to go loose too.

Wayland's jaw is tight. He stares at the ring in his hand before turning back to me, then holds it out. "Will you keep this?" he says.

Everything hurts. My legs are shaking. I don't know if I can keep standing. I don't have the right to refuse. "But why are you giving it to me?"

"Promise you won't forget about me?"

A sob shakes my body. I shake my head. "Never, Way. You're my best friend." I go to take the ring. He catches my hand instead. Carefully, he slips the ring onto the ring finger of my right hand. Electricity goes up my arm. Usually, when someone puts a ring on your finger, it's to promise an eternity together, but this is the opposite: Wayland's goodbye. "If you're going back to Mortem, then can I at least take you there?"

Wayland doesn't answer immediately. He looks toward the walls around Deadwood, the street, maybe for Jag's car. I'm waiting for him to say no and trying to work out an argument. He doesn't owe me anything and the extra time together might get him to change his mind and that's reason enough to tell me no.

"Okay," he says, turning back to me.

"Okay." I nod. A simple word has never felt heavier.

There's a Toyota waiting in my house's driveway. I don't need to ask to know Wayland got it from whoever's all over his shirt. We get in the car, him in the driver's seat, and we're on our way to Fort Armistead. The sobs keep coming, building to come out as hiccups I try to restrain. Everything's blurring around me and it's taking all the stupid graffiti with it. HORROR SHOW and ESCAPE and DARKNESS all turn into long streams of red and green and purple and white marring the city into obscurity. The sign outside of Armistead reads BORN ALONE, DIE ALONE in fresh white paint over the name of the park and a 666 in red underneath it. The lot's mostly empty; the sun's almost gone. Parking lot lights are sporadic, but we don't really need them, I guess. We know where we're going like this place is a second home.

Wayland parks in the back corner of the lot and says maybe someone will take the car, maybe not, it doesn't matter. No one needs the car now and the badges'll come looking for it once they find the body.

Wayland's sure they'll find the body.

"I didn't try too hard to hide it this time. I just—I didn't care anymore, you know? It didn't seem important." He laughs.

The keys are left inside the unlocked car.

We're at the fort's entrance. The dripping water echoes. The word DIE reads on the wall, a rounded arrow points to it saying OK from underneath. The corridors to Mortem are different than when I came alone or with Jag. They're straighter, fewer, the water builds up to my knee faster, and the only graffiti inside is the sporadic eyes, watching as Wayland and I pass. They populate the walls more and more the longer we walk, overlaying with new color and an iris that feels more like it's moving until I blink and I'm not stepping in water or crusty garbage or mud anymore, but the sidewalk outside of Peter's with the courtyard of Cavae Mortem lighting the distance.

Maybe I don't remember the fall or maybe it doesn't happen that way when everyone's already a spirit.

Wayland crosses the street. I take his hand. He looks back at me, smiles, and keeps going, his fingers now wrapped around mine. He moves for the bar. He's going too fast. The moment isn't long enough before we're inside. I still want to see him so I don't have to believe that.

A mic's in one corner. Worked for Channel 5. I think she got shot in Cherry Hill a couple days ago. I guess I mean a couple days before I died cause I remember the report coming across the channel dad was watching. She'd been standing in front of a school, talking about funding and programs, got hit during a drive-by. Another corner houses an older badge, a guy with a graying beard, a woman with a shaved head, a kid, probably around five, wearing a striped shirt. He's telling a story they're all laughing at.

Everyone's a forgotten face in a crowd, their memories of home erased by the drinks they keep bringing to their lips. Their worries, fears, anger, stresses, families, histories, and identities… They're all gone, but it's fine that sitting here like this is the rest of forever. They don't know there's more; they don't know if they should be concerned; they don't know that they're not sitting in Heaven, but *Hollow Death*.

Wayland's weight pulls against mine. His fingers loosen in my hand. I grip him harder. I stumble forward with him, my weight's nothing compared to his desire, but he still stops after a few steps. He turns to me. The small, resting smile on his lips doesn't hide the melancholy in his eyes saying he's done. At least, I pretend it's not me reflecting back.

"Are you sure you want to do this, Way?" I say.

"I don't want to hold anyone back anymore."

"You're not—"

He shakes his head slowly.

My foot's bouncing. "Then tell me where your body is." Tears blur my vision. I blink; they clear away. I could argue with Wayland forever, but he's always been smarter than me. I know he's right and there's no way to convince him otherwise. At least not on this. "So I can tell your family."

"Goodbye, Jo."

I'm shaking my head. "Goodbye, Way." A chill hits my skin. I don't think my voice is loud enough to hear, but he gives me a small smile, my hand a squeeze, and then he turns away.

His first step is awkward, stilted, and stiff, Stopped by maybe his own question of whether he's doing the right thing, the next step comes and then the next and with each move, they get easier until he sits down at the counter. Sol greets him. Though her voice is lost in the sound of the room, she waves and leans against the counter.

Wayland sets his phone face down on the counter, Sol sets a glass in front of him and he's talking to her with his usual restraint. The bar's not loud, but it's not empty. I can't hear what Sol's saying and Wayland's voice is one among the ambient conversation in the bar, blending in already like he's gone.

I'm tempted to come closer just to hear what he's saying. His hands don't go for the drink very fast. First, he touches the glass, pulls back, and laughs again. I bet he's telling her it doesn't feel right. He doesn't drink much. He's only ever taken sips with me. Sol glances at me. The mask of her fake smile doesn't cover the dead look in her eyes, the presence in her face that says she doesn't give a damn about Wayland, doesn't give a damn about me, but she's about to say something sugary to make him feel cozy in the way she never could with me.

Sol doesn't feel happiness or desire or anger or anything human. She does everything she can to replicate it though and I can't help but read spite in her expression. The twisted lips, the smile, the laugh.

Sol takes another drink off the shelf. Has he drunk enough Lethe that he's already forgotten about me?

My body jerks forward. A step. His name's on my lips. I'm twisting the ring around my finger. "Way," I say it again just in case I didn't say it loud enough the first time, but the second time comes out, it's a whisper. I haunted him in life, I destroyed him. I can't keep interrupting him because this is what he wants and I said when he chose to leave, I'd let him go.

Maybe I thought it'd never actually happen. I didn't think I could lose him, but now that he's drinking from the glass and his posture's looser and he's laughing and leaning forward and looking at her... the way he probably looked at me...

I was jealous of Wayland's family. We spent most of our time in his room. Watching his mom was like wondering if my mom would be like her if she was still around and could I be like her? I tried to be out of the house by the time his dad got home, but I got curious to see what he was like. I waited for them to call me trashy for all the times I stayed for dinner or woke them up because we snuck in late and I was blasted and smelled like a liquor store, but they never did. I felt guilty sitting at the table, having meatloaf or chicken or anything homemade, and never put into a microwave because it didn't feel like I should've been there. It wasn't the life I was given.

But their door was always open.

They kept inviting me over, asking me to stay, and even gave me birthday presents when my own dad couldn't be bothered to say, "Good morning."

Sometimes it felt like I was normal. I felt like I could actually be something more than the next body left behind a dumpster in Deadwood because of an overdose or beatings or just fucking... giving up, you know? He made me see a future that was worth living for, so I didn't give up. He caught me every time I fell, but then when he stumbled, I missed it. I couldn't grab his hand and he fell through the ground.

I'm a soul in Mortem; I shouldn't feel anything, but whatever's supposed to numb me around here isn't working and I'm just getting angrier and angrier until I'm ready to jump the bar, grab something off the shelf, and knock Sol over the head with it. She deserves it for the shit she's tried on me and the lies she's whispering to Wayland.

I'm a bad person for letting her talk to him after what I know.

And this is how it happens. Someone does something shit to you, makes you suffer, maybe you die, and you get tunnel vision for the revenge you want to feel in your hands—The punishment you believe you deserve to dole out. You come back to find the fucker that ruined your life and you'll do anything you can to get them back. You can't see anything else and everyone becomes collateral damage to the pain you have to cause or the *justice* you have to find. It hurts too much to think of what someone else took from you, that you can't see anything outside of the future you can't grasp anymore. Then, when you hurt someone else because your focus is on whoever fucked you up, they come back feeling the same pain, same anger, their future taken from them too and it just keeps going, again and again, over and over, until everyone's been promised mutual destruction by proximity and nothing else matters.

No one cares about any story that's not their own. The pain caused is invisible to everyone else until it becomes personal and everyone's reaching for the thing that blew their lives to pieces. Regret and rage are toxic seeds, planted to consume the heart.

The graffiti around town says horror is what happens when evil overtakes the heart.

I don't think that's poetry.

I don't think it's just spooky words to make your hair stand on edge or to make you look over your shoulder a second time when you're walking alone in the dark.

It's a warning, not just for our city, but for the story that our city knows too well.

What is there when you've got nothing left to lose? When you feel like everything's been taken from you, you might as well take from everyone else too, right? A half-empty beer in a busted-up trailer looks like a lot to someone that's had everything taken from them.

What's there to stop anyone from becoming a horror show?

"Again?" Charon's voice comes from behind me.

I turn away from the bar, wiping tears from my face like I'm wiping away smeared eyeliner. Val's a human, arms hanging over Charon's shoulders while he leans against him, slouching, legs bent, ass out so he can lean on

Charon's right.

"What?" I clear my throat. Take a deep breath, easy exhale. I check my pocket for my cigarettes. The box is back even though I know I ran out earlier. I don't recognize the label. I look back at Sol. She's watching me. I toss the cigarettes onto the floor.

"You're here again?" Charon says.

"Still looking for something?" Val says. He surveys the room. His eyes come back to me, curious. "Where's your friend?"

"Still not dead," I say.

"What about you?" Val stands up. His hands slide from around Charon like it's nothing. He steps around the reaper, coming closer to me, sniffing the air as he does. "What's that smell on you?"

My skin goosebumps. "I thought you couldn't track the dead."

"I can't, but…" Val leans in, taking a more obvious smell. "You're not living or dying. You're… something else I don't smell very often."

"What does that mean?" I say.

"I dunno," Val says.

Wayland's laughter is louder now. It pierces through everything else in the bar. I turn around and he's so relaxed talking to Sol. If I stay any longer, I'm going to start a fight with her, and maybe I don't mind getting a little scrappy as much as I worry that Wayland won't recognize me, but he'll cheer Sol on and I don't think I can handle that.

"Sorry." I shrug past Val. "I need some air." I exit the bar. My lips twitch, hungry for nicotine. I feel my pocket again. There's another box of cigarettes whose label I recognize this time. My usual, but they weren't there before. I chuck the box at the ground and keep going to the edge of the courtyard where the pavement breaks with the darkness to show the divide of where you're supposed to go and where the Liquor's creeping out of the forest.

My skin pricks. My throat goes dry. I feel the impulse to run into the forest, drown in the Liquor, and relive whatever moments it wants to dig up again, no matter how painful. I'm twisting Wayland's ring. My hands are trembling. I turn back toward the Old Town Mall. The lights are as bright as ever, but the music and party of it all feels like it's mocking me for how I feel.

I go back toward the courtyard; maybe it's not too late to talk to Wayland and take him home.

"You can't undo time," Charon says. He's standing on the sidewalk outside of the mall, just where the darkness and the light split; Val's beside him.

"I'm not asking to undo anything, I just want a second chance. But a jump in the river doesn't do that, does it, Charon?"

"It never did." He comes toward me. "When you reject mortality, you reject your humanity. Destruction follows fantasy into reality when you believe you can live forever."

"I don't want to live forever. I just want a chance to live now… I didn't do it before."

"There is no such thing as a second chance. Death deals in absolutes; rejection of the natural order is rebellion and rebellion does not come without a price." Charon looks at Val. "Humans really are a wicked mess, aren't they?"

"If you thought so, then why'd you ever let me go?" I close the space between Charon and me. "You could've dragged me to Hell like every other escaped soul you've ever caught in Baltimore, but you didn't. Why?"

"You are not the first soul I have released upon scavenging." Charon's glowing blue eyes stare at me sharply. Val stands beside Charon, hands in his pockets, but seemingly much bigger than he actually is, a giant bird of a man, and all I see is the shadow by Charon's side. "I had hoped I would not come to regret it."

Val's watching me with more attention than I've seen

him have in days. Instead of wandering eyes, he's focused like a predator, a smirk, a subtle tongue running along his bottom lip.

"The benefit of your role is fewer penalties to the wandering if they choose to return," Charon says. "Corrupt souls do not manifest in the same way. Jealousy, pride, greed, and desire are lethal influences that lead a spirit to haunt where it once lived or those it seeks to take from, creating more destruction as it harms, destroys, and takes everything it believes was taken from it. Damage feeds it more as nothing is ever enough to satiate the hunger. However, a soul whose regrets are guilt and sorrow?"

"I don't understand."

"Your father never killed you for the same reason you have not killed anyone. It becomes external through hyperbolic emotion. Your problem is with yourself, so your disaster stops there. A soul focused on internal damnation is more receptive than one seeking external retribution."

"What's going to happen to Wayland? Will he go to the tower?"

"A soul returned to its natural place returns to the natural order. While he will be judged for his rebellion and the damage he caused, it will not be to the same extent as if I'd brought him back here by force."

I sigh, hard, breath shaky. I look toward Lodgings thinking maybe I should step in and see if it's still my room in there or maybe I could feel like I'm back at home if I stick around and maybe they'll make my dad's TV rage like it always does or I could grab Way from the bar and take him to Lodgings and it'd be his room and we could pretend we're in high school again, getting ready for his SATs or something for a couple of hours.

My stomach flutters with a new wave of nausea. Sulfur sticks to my nose. I wipe it with the back of my arm. "At least he has a shot at something better than Hell. He deserves it." The swipe of the black spotlight through the purple sky makes me dizzy. It comes with the footsteps of someone I can't see. The caw of a raven follows; it's not Val.

I touch my pocket again. I shouldn't. Another box of cigarettes. I toss it to the ground. I guess I hadn't realized how bad the habit had gotten until now while the dead thrusts drug-laced cigs into my hand. "Can you take me to the river now? I don't want to be here anymore."

I don't have to say anything more. Charon and Val guide me through the forest until we're at Styx. It's not any easier to jump into the river the third time. My body revolts before I even get near it and I almost ask Val to throw me in.

On the other side, I stare at the dark sky. Dead Run's cold water runs down my back, the colder air on top. A light hangs over the nearby bridge, highlighting the sharpie scribble reading WHO TF?

Everything's heavy. I don't have the will to get up, but I don't want to be here. The cold's worse than it has been, nipping at my skin so it burns and pulling at the scabbed cuts on my arm that are so useless now. Everything from the last couple of days seems stupid. I keep closing my eyes, they're so swollen from crying, but still, somehow, there's something left. When I think it's over, more tears fall down my cheeks. Blurring isn't the right way to describe what I see. Looking at things is making me dizzy now and my eyes are crossing. I check for my cigarettes.

I've got nothing.

I get my phone out of my pocket next. It shouldn't work. Dunked in Styx and sitting in the shallow part of Dead Run, but the screen lights up when I try it. Three messages. One from Jag telling me to call him. I'm fucking up again and after everything, I shouldn't still be making him worry like this. The second's from Ralph telling me the fetish is ready. The third says it's from Wayland, but there's no preview in the messaging app and I can't get myself to open it. Just leave that one new message from Wayland in there like he's still around, worried, and checking up on me too. I text Jag saying, "Sorry. Be there soon," and then I text Ralph saying, "I need you to come get me."

RALPH	What?
JOEY	At Leakin.
	The bridge at Dead Run.
RALPH	What about ur bf?
	Call him.
JOEY	I don't want him to see me right now.
	Please.
	I'll owe you.
	I don't know what.
	But I'll owe you.
RALPH	You don't got much, kid.
JOEY	Then let me be a charity case.
	Just this once.
	I'll figure it out.
RALPH	I'll send KC.
	Don't move.
JOEY	I'll play dead and hope it works.

NINETEEN.

Headlights come down the street, looking purple instead of white. I don't think that's legal, but I guess I never was one for cheap words like *legality* anyway. Normally, it makes me chuckle knowing Ralph and KC have a black Riviera, but I don't have the energy. Why would I laugh? Because people pick cars like they pick dogs. Somehow it always matches who they are and what else would a couple of retired indie bandmates drive?

KC stops at the street side near me. Doors click unlocked. I fall into the passenger side. The music's low, classic rock from thirty plus years ago. Some of the same stuff Jag likes to listen to at work. He doesn't say anything until we're leaving the park, but immediately after crossing into the city lights, he says, "You look like shit," with a laugh. His amusement holds a history of what he sees in me.

"Yeah?" I say. A chuckle. It hurts. "Well... Sometimes I wish the horror show would take an intermission, you know?"

KC's tongue flicks over his lip. A thought stops before making it to his lips. He shakes his head to himself. "Don't get used to this. I'm not gonna be your next boyfriend."

"You're just my bartender, KC. I'm not making that mistake again."

"Good."

I look out the window, letting myself melt into the seat, trying not to think too hard about what KC said, though it's nearly impossible as his words whip around my head, harassing me with the reminder and guilt of every mistake I've made over the last fifteen years that made me lose my best friend, that put Jag at risk and... yeah. I did it to myself. I hurt other people in the process of just secretly trying to get by.

I should've died alone.

I should've moved on with Wayland.

But I'm too stubborn to even do that. All I can do is cling to the hope that another stupid decision won't bounce back to bite Jag in the ass when he deserves so much better than my soul that can't let him go.

"Did you bring the thing?" I say, my foot bouncing.

"I can't touch it," KC says.

"Why not?"

"It comes with instructions and..." KC pops his lips. He glances sidelong at me. "You don't want it handled by the dead."

"So, I shouldn't trust you?"

"That's not what I said."

"Then why couldn't you bring it?"

KC's jaw tightens. There's a tin in the console under the radio. Looks similar to the one in Ralph's office. KC pulls a cigarette out of it and pinches it between his lips. At a stop sign, he lights it up. "I don't have a heart; I can't carry yours."

I don't know what he means; it's too much like Ralph, too much like Charon, too much like every afterlife official that can't just say what they mean. Asking for clarification seems useless. It's always more puzzles or poems or chuckling because I don't know what they mean. "Fine. Then why didn't Ralph come and get me himself?"

KC smiles to himself. He sucks on the cigarette and his expression fades as he shakes his head. "Ralph doesn't like to leave the bar much."

"Why?"

Glancing to me, smoke comes out KC's nose. "Not my shit to spill."

I chuckle, not because it's funny, but because I know what it's like. I shouldn't ask; that's always been the rule. Don't intervene, don't ask for shit you don't need to know to get by, don't get involved with people more than you have to. Those rules are so you don't get too attached, so you don't learn things about people that will make you care when you lose them, so you don't get involved in something worse than your own life when you're already up to your elbows in shit, but... I can't help wanting to know. We've got more in common than I want to admit and with everything Ralph knows about me, knowing he was in my head, maybe I feel like he owes me some of his demons since he apparently knows all of mine.

I reach for the cigarette tin, waiting for KC to stop me, but he doesn't. I light one up. My window's open. The cold, evening air of Baltimore tickles my nose while the warmth of the cigarette caresses my lips. "Is this fetish thing really worth it?"

"I think you'll want it, yeah."

"Okay." I close my eyes. "Tell me when we're there."

Twenty minutes later, we're at BAIT's and the parking lot's nearly empty. The car door's heavier than I remember and the music's down low. My muscles are aching and screaming and everything in my body's saying lay down on the floor and sink into the earth. KC's door snaps shut. He's outside the car saying, "You comin'?"

"Yeah."

He's already going into the bar, not waiting for me. I get out of the car and move the best I can. We go inside together. Ralph's behind the counter, fixing a drink. He and KC exchange a brief glance. KC dips behind the counter, slipping in beside Ralph. His back's to me, but he's leaning in and I know he's muttering something. Ralph's stare switches from the counter to me. I'm standing still, staring back at him, trying to catch onto whatever was just said, like the code should be obvious since KC and I are in the same situation, but instead of hearing or thinking anything, my mind goes blank. Ralph comes around the bar and touches my shoulder. I gasp. "Follow me," he says.

"Sorry," I say.

We're back in his office. Door closed, locked. He's at the other side of his desk where the standing file cabinet is under a dream catcher. He opens the top drawer with a key, then he's withdrawing a small box. I don't think I noticed it before, but he's got bandages wrapped around his right arm, going all the way up to his elbow, covering his tattoos. Bruising shows on his biceps and disappears under the short sleeves of his band shirt.

"What happened to you?"

"Easy answer? A séance."

I straighten. "The Cogs do this kind of shit? Some kind of angels they are—"

Ralph shakes his head, but it's so subtle and short, I'm not sure he actually did it or if I'm imagining things through the fog of what's left of my soul. I dunno. After three dunks into the River Styx, it feels like there shouldn't be much left. "Twisting life and death together will always require sacrifice," Ralph says. "You can't defy creation without paying a price. You're welcome." He closes the file cabinet then sets the box down on the desk. It's got the consistency of licorice or tendons like the paths in Mortem.

The closer I come to the box, the more my heart pounds. My skin's getting hot, everything about me's getting nervous while I feel like I'm on fire. "They took a little long, you know?" I glance up at Ralph's face, then back down at the box. "Wayland's gone. I don't know what to do with this anymore."

"It's not for Wayland; this is for you." What should've been a ribbon wrapped around it is some kind of red organ that releases over the clasped edge when Ralph places his hand on top the box. It looks wet to touch. The box opens. Inside is a gem shaped mostly like a heart, maybe a little imperfect, but in a natural kind of way. The outer edges of it are black. The closer it gets to center, the black turns to red until you can see tendrils that look like organs or skin or something stretching across it like the patchwork of a body. Then, just off to the right of center, the tendrils spread, exposing a small hole that catches light and glows a bright red. When Ralph moves it into the light, the inside of the heart illuminates and warms in color. At least, everything that's not black. There's a thin, metal frame around the heart, the same color and style as the chain the necklace is on. The style of this thing looks a lot like the rock hanging around Ralph's neck, though everything else is different.

"What *exactly* is this?"

"Your second chance." Ralph takes the necklace from the box.

Something inside of my stomach turns itself over and I'm feeling sick and lightheaded. My legs won't move. I collapse into one of the chairs behind me. "What do you mean?" I say. "Charon said there are no second chances."

Ralph comes around to the front of the desk. He holds his hand out, waiting for me to take the necklace.

I don't.

"Servies don't grant second chances. Reapers don't grant second chances. The river doesn't grant second chances. Cogs, on the other hand, are a little different. It's not exactly what you came in asking for, but they had no offering for your friend, Wayland Cross. Without his sacrifice, receiving a second chance would've been impossible—"

"Why didn't you tell me that before?"

"Because he was not the only wandering soul in need of assistance. If I'd told you that, would you have done this for yourself?"

My eyes downcast. My jaw's tight. My chest's throbbing so hard it hurts. It takes everything in me to not yell or start crying again and rip Ralph's office apart. "What the hell am I supposed to do with this, then?" I say through my teeth.

Ralph reaches for me. His hand takes mine. I resist the pull at first, but a warm energy comes through where he touches me and calms everything like whatever drug's in the air of Mortem. My hand relaxes. "How about you don't waste what you've got?" He places the necklace in my hand.

Immediately, I feel different. The connection to the gem, the heat in my cheeks, even my breath. It's not just the bar silencing the anger and regret or pulling me out of the currents of pain and destruction. The impulses aren't totally silent, but I can't hear them over the desire I have to hide in a closet, drink, and throw myself off a skateboard so hard, my skin snaps open.

"This is your heart, Joey."

"What?" I laugh weakly, still not looking up. My vision blurs. "Cut it out with the metaphors already, will you? I'm too dumb for this—"

"It's not a metaphor." Ralph curls my fingers around the gem, holding my hand tight. A pulse goes through my fingers. The gem's warm, not hot. The veins that had been so clearly visible in my pale arms are gone and returned is a color closer to life than death. I raise my eyes to meet Ralph's. He's waiting for me. "When you died, a reaper visited you with a raven. The reaper took your soul, the raven took your heart. Your body was left to decay among mortals. That's the separation. Heart, soul, body—"

"I don't understand. Is this supposed to mean... I'm

alive again?"

"Sort of... Not exactly." Ralph finally draws away. He sits back on the edge of his desk. He reaches blindly over the surface of it, looking for something. He knocks over a cup of pens and stands up. His arms cross. "Some rules still apply. Limitations is a better word. Your relationships will return, your death forgotten to the world until you pass again. Those who knew you through your death will retain those memories, but those who didn't will not know of your interactions during this time."

"That's how that works?"

"When you're a wandering soul, you're not operating in the same way as someone with a physical form. You've been lost, so the living don't recognize you—Except for those who've come to know your soul. To get something closer to your human presence again and all the benefits that come with that, you need a heart and a body. The heart alone is not enough; you will have to give it to someone who's alive, who's willing to receive it and share their body with you. Think *marriage*. Not exactly the same thing, but two souls, one body. You need to pick carefully. Destroy the necklace, your heart's gone. It won't come back and the decay to your soul will be worse."

"Everything's always gotta get worse..."

Ralph's not looking at me. He opens his mouth, licks his lips. His head tilts to the side with thought. "Be careful who you give your heart to, Joey. You will share everything with them. Your life is their life, your luck is their luck, your pain is their pain."

"Are you talking metaphorically again?"

"No. For real," Ralph says. "Your actions do not only affect you. If you die, so will the mortal who holds your heart. The recklessness, danger, and pain that brought you to your current circumstance should be avoided unless you wish to inflict it upon another. You got it?" He looks at me, smirking. "It means avoid the kind of situation that got your head smashed into my floor three days ago, yeah?"

Ralph waits for a reply. I say nothing.

"Likewise," he continues, "If the holder of your heart dies and the reaper collects their soul, the bond between your heart and their body will be broken and you will return to a state of death with the soul of your chosen."

My fingers curl around the pendant. Heat resonates from the gem through my body. "Why give anyone a second chance if it's gonna mess up someone else's life?"

"Because, Joey, there's no way to do this alone. You've already tried."

"And so the solution is to make my burden someone else's?" My eyes water. I blink to push the tears back.

"Without a body for your heart, ravens will hunt you. That is, in essence, your exposed heart. Once it's gone, you are not getting it back again. So, continue to carry your burdens alone and the resentment will rot your soul into an abomination of annihilation and hatred or trust someone else with your heart and carry your life together. There are no other options."

I stare down at the stone. "Life really is just one giant pain in the ass, isn't it?"

Ralph smiles, laughs, rubs at his wary eyes. "It is whatever you make it and there's no one else to blame. Not all choices are equal. Unfortunately, some of us learn that a little too late." Ralph purses his lips. He leans back on the desk to reach inside a drawer. He's rougher opening it than he probably meant to be because he jerks back a little when it flings open. He comes back with a joint and a lighter. It's lit fast. Hit. "The Cogs are timekeepers. Historians. Archivists. It's why they can help you at all. They know your past, your present, some variation of your future. Why are they willing to help you? Don't know. Why'd they help KC? I didn't ask and I don't want to know. Judgment can be saved for the day I die and even then, I don't want to hear the verdict. I've made a lot of bad choices I don't need the opinions on." Another hit. He rides it out. "Anyway, when I contacted them about you, they said they'd been waiting, expected you some time ago—"

"They'd been waiting? For *what* exactly?"

"Your death," Ralph says.

A chill goes down my spine. Images of Baltimore graffiti fill my head. Fort Armistead wasn't what said it first, but among all the scrawls of FEAR and YOU CHOSE THE DARK and WE WERE WAITING, there's been so much of it around the city, it's hard to tell what's from the living and what's from the dead, if that's what he's saying. I never thought of graffiti as anything but the random hooligan, bored out of his ass or the banger marking his territory for his next deal. Maybe someone was feeling edgy on a dare in the middle of the night and making his mark on the city was the only way he could ask for attention on a planet that can't be bothered to notice him. Maybe if he writes something weird enough, big enough, in enough colors, someone'll notice. They've gotta, right?

Even in death, we're desperate to be noticed by the people who overlooked us.

My skin's cold, goose-bumped. My throat's so dry, I'm not sure I'll be able to speak. "Why would they be waiting for *my* death?"

Ralph's blue eyes meet mine. They've got a soft glow, not unlike the reapers, but more subtle. The smoke from his latest hit curls around his face. "Your dad killed himself, yeah?"

The hair on the back of my neck stands. I straighten in my seat. "How do you know that?"

Ralph gives a half nod. Maybe it's not at the question because he's looking away. He leans back on his desk, propping himself up with his hand. A couple hard taps startle me more than they should. It's only his rings hitting the desk's surface. "The Cogs know that."

"Good to know someone in the afterlife's sharing my business with anyone that comes asking—"

"It's part of the deal." Ralph sets his joint down. "Some souls aren't well enough to get a second chance. Most actually. Even you almost didn't make it."

"What makes me so special?" I say.

"For starters, you haven't killed anyone yet. It's not a *complete* deal-breaker, but it's more a symptom of a lost soul," Ralph says. "And it weighs into the decision."

"I'd imagine…" I try not to read into Ralph's voice like he's judging Wayland. He obviously knows what happened; he saw Way kill someone in his bar. It shouldn't have been held against him by the Cogs and it shouldn't be used against him in judgment. They didn't know him like I do.

Wayland's eyes flash in my head, the way he looked like a stranger because of the fear and discomfort, the difference when he was mashing that guy's head into his bedroom floor. He didn't do it to himself; it was the world that took his humanity and hope away from him. I wasn't the best to him either, but he didn't deserve to be killed; he didn't deserve to have his life ruined, his family destroyed, his future gone.

He didn't deserve to suffer.

It doesn't feel real thinking of him sitting at the bar, his voice lost in the sea of the afterlife, him talking to Sol, who looked like whoever he wanted to see, maybe even wearing my face like she tried to wear his for me, easing him into the comfort of oblivion as he sips on Lethe until everything he knows is thrown out.

My eyes burn. I close them to hide the glossiness. My jaw tightens. I try to smile, teeth showing. I don't think I'm wearing the right face. "Is that really it? Once you go to judgment, you never… they forget everything, and you can never see someone again?"

"Depends on their outcome. Lethe is only a temporary fixture to ease passage. Where you end up on the other side changes things," Ralph says. He picks up the joint. His eyes clothes as he hits it. "A lot of choices pass down in families. Anger becomes more anger; violence becomes more violence; hurt becomes more hurt; one cycle turns into the next, carried on by offspring who fulfill the family legacy they've been taught—"

"By choice, do you mean fate?" I look at Ralph. "You saying the Cogs expected me to kill myself because my dad did?" I can't stop the tears, the burning in my nose. A trail runs down my cheek. I wipe it with the back of my hand, but it's quickly replaced.

"Right. So, in humans, there is no sure thing. As you live, history's still being written. Some circumstances are more likely than others, cause and effect, but no one is doomed for the future they've been prepared for. The Cogs may calculate the likelihood of your future, the echo of your actions repeating that of your lineage while you live in the shadow of your family's ghosts, unable to see reality. You spent more years with your father dead than equal to your lifetime with him alive when you were presented with the crossroad."

"The crossroad?" I wipe the tears again. They won't stop coming.

"At Leakin' Park when you were sixteen."

"How do you know *everything*?"

Ralph smiles weakly, turns away, puts an unlit rolled cigarette to his lips. "Family shapes you, but so does every other soul you interact with. You're bitter, cynical, self-destructive, and often pretty stupid, but you aren't as alone as you think. The cracks in your heart don't disappear, but just as others try to break you, some put you back together, sacrificing what they have to help you in spite of the damage. You're luckier than you realize, Joey."

"You say that, but how'd those *breaks* turn out for everyone else?" I open my palm. In the red gem, there's the pale outline of my face and the black circles where my eyeliner's smudged bigger holes where my eyes should be. Everything about my reflections is ghoulish and unreal. "Wayland saved my life at the cost of his own. I'm a fucking busted mess, Ralph." My lips are tight. Another shiver goes through me. I shove the necklace into my pocket and stand up. "What if it happens again?" The room's suddenly hot and every second I stay here, I'm getting hotter and more nervous while feeling colder with sweat matting my shirt to my skin. "I can't do that to someone else."

Ralph mirrors me, standing, shrugging once he's upright. "How much someone else cares about you isn't your choice. With the way you think, you'll hurt *him* regardless." He pulls at the chain of his own necklace, taking it out from under his band tee. The red gem's darker than mine, there are more black flakes in it, spread throughout the gem instead of just at the bottom.

I meet Ralph's eyes. "And you gave KC a second chance, no regrets?"

Ralph thumbs the pendant. A soft smile comes to his lips. His eyes glaze over, warm. He puts out the joint. "No regrets."

I don't know what to say anymore, so I just say, "Thanks," and leave. It still seems like too much. The pain and sacrifice, Ralph's already done it for me. The tattoos and cuts and scars on his body aren't from self-destruction, but his weird desire to help the wandering who can't help themselves. I can't imagine giving so much of yourself to others, allowing yourself to hurt for a stranger's benefit. What's there to gain? I say that knowing I would go through anything to save Wayland or Jag from hurting, while wanting to avoid making them do that for me.

I never wanted to say how much I cared because if I ignored the words and the feelings, I could pretend they weren't there and avoid whatever pain could be inflicted on any of us. But that didn't work, did it?

My mind's racing and by the time I'm outside, everything's overwhelming. I run past a couple of birds hanging in the parking lot. They're watching me as I go by. I take a breath, close my eyes, and push on as fast as I can away from the bar. Everywhere I go, I'm being watched by death. Ravens sitting on cars, stoops, trees, and standing in my path as my only warning. The graffiti's back to cursing and crude drawings of the reaper or a crime scene or someone thinking they're funny making a sponge vomit on a kid eating a cheeseburger that says CHUCK on the bun. ONLY HALF BAD and IF HEART FOUND PLS R—B—, the words are worn out, making it impossible to read. Where I've gotten used to seeing WE'VE BEEN WAITING now says WE ARE WATCHING like it's a threat with a chuckle from the Cogs daring me to fuck up again so I'll see them in Hell and they can say, *Damn, you always were a mess, huh.* Every time I pass another WATCHING with bloodshot eyes or viper eyes or angry eyes like they're following me, it's more of a challenge to say *fuck you, I'm going back on my terms, not yours.*

I run faster to avoid the eyes.

I keep going until my legs hurt, when I can't breathe, seeing now I need to breathe again. I'm going to collapse. I don't know how long it's been when I'm back at Jag's place and I'm standing outside, hitting the buzzer at the door again and again and again while leaning against the wall until Jag says, "What?" and I say, "It's me, J," through panting breaths. "I'm sorry I'm late. I'm really, really sorry—"

"Come inside," he says.

I take the stairs. He's standing at the elevator waiting

when I reach his floor.

"Where have you been?" he says, approaching me.

I take his hands and I'm pulling him back toward his apartment with urgency while shaking my head and saying, "I don't want to fucking talk right now, Jag. I know we need to, but can we just not?" My vision blurs with building tears that roll down my cheeks. "Sorry." My back presses to his room door, my arms go around his neck and pull him into me. *Escape.*

"Stop apologizing, Joey." Jag's hand presses into the door over my shoulder. My hand slides along his collarbone, up his neck, to his jaw. His five o'clock shadow scratches my fingers, my chin, my lips as I press mine to his.

He pushes me into the door. His grip finds my hip, holding it while he opens the apartment with his other hand. He steps me back, not letting me fall, and pushes the door shut harder than expected because our lips break just when it slams. It gives me a chance to see he's cleaned the apartment and the room smells like fresh paint. Jag slides his hands down my thighs to lift my feet off the ground. My back hits the bed with a gentle bounce and then he's on top of me, taking off my shirt just as desperately as I'm trying to take off his. He's pulling my pants down my legs while kissing my collar, my neck, my jaw, my lips. They hit the floor with a heavy thud. It's not my belt. I put my hand to his chest. Panting softly, I say, "Hey, Jag?"

"Yeah?"

"Gimme a sec?"

Jag draws back enough so that his eyes can lock with mine. He swallows hard. His face says he wants to ask something, but he knows better than to probe right now. Still, whatever he's thinking is making me feel embarrassed, exposed, and I'm an idiot for stopping—For what? I never feel weaker than when I'm naked and knowing Jag can see everything he is that I'm not. His skin's stained with work scars and grease and a life he's worked hard to keep in order and what do I have? The remnants of the rage and mistakes made by me and my dad, proving we're not so different after all. My hands aren't even soft like they should be, but callous from work and play. Sometimes my skin's cracked. I have lotion to make it softer, but I forget to use it most of the time and I wonder if it bothers him.

"Everything okay?" Jag says.

"Yeah, I just…" I press gently against his chest. He's leaning back more now so I have room to sit up. "I need to ask you something."

"What's up?"

I look down at my jeans. My chest's tight. "Wait here." I climb off the bed. My studded belt rattles when I grab my pants off the floor. I reach into the thicker pocket and withdraw the necklace Ralph gave me. Wayland's ring snags on the pocket fabric. My eyes catch on the diamond when it's not covered anymore. He's gone. I'm not forgetting him; I just can't think about him right now.

My pants are back on the floor, my hand's tightly holding onto the necklace pendant, burying even the chain beneath my fingers.

Jag's legs hang off the bed. I come back to him, standing between his knees with mine pressed into the side of the mattress. Jag's hands rest on my hips. My heart's throbbing in my ears and pulsing in my fingers. My face is on fire. I open my hand to him; his eyes drop to my palm. "Would you carry this for me?"

"What is it?" He pulls me closer, glance meeting mine again.

I chuckle. The words sound so dumb, even before I say them. "What if I said it's my heart?"

Jag laughs. "When'd you get so sentimental?"

"I don't know… It's fucking stupid, right?"

349

"Nah." Jag's smiling. He meets my eyes. I can't hold his stare. He reaches for the necklace. I don't let him take it. Instead, I slide into his lap, straddling him with my knees on both sides. His hands are on my hips; he pulls me closer, keeping me steady. I twist the necklace's clasp. My thumbs go around his neck. It's too much to think about how every time something's been around my neck, it's been with hatred and a desire to punish. I can't think of anything more sensitive and close than gentle fingers moving around my neck, not to hurt me, but in assurance. Jag's thumbs stroke my sides.

"Breathe, Joey," Jag says, hot and low.

I exhale. His hands move down my thighs. My skin's so hot, met with the cold apartment air. I lock the necklace around Jag's neck. The speed and tension and adrenaline pulsing through me suddenly feels like they've come to an end and everything's quiet. There's no constant muttering voice telling me to hurt someone. The energy in my restless legs is the normal kind I've been used to running with for fifteen years. All the tension coming at a constant build is gone.

"Ralph said this is my second chance—if you'll take it with me."

Jag meets my eyes. His quiet makes my skin pucker with goosebumps, my stomach rolls with nervous sickness, and I hold tight to his shoulders for balance. "I love you, *Josephine*," he says.

I nod slowly. I can't speak.

Jag rolls me onto my back and Baltimore fades into the background of his quiet home, only disturbed by the odd siren going down the street outside or a throbbing stereo in passing that really acts more like a welcome call than a disturbance anyway. There's no more TV blasting through the walls or *stress* of whether my dad'll hear me breathe or if I locked the door or what I'm going to eat because I'm starving and haven't had anything but cigarettes all day, but I don't want to go out there in case he hears me open the fridge and I make him upset again. I'm still not sure if this is real or that I'm not at home, dreaming that dad's not there waiting for me and that come morning, I'll have another four messages from Wayland saying we should hang out after work.

FEAR, FEAR, FEAR is glowing on the ceiling where it shouldn't be. I blink, and the words are gone. I close my eyes and the only feeling that comes is what Jag's or my body needs. I don't want to think about the dead or ghosts or ravens or Baltimore anymore. At least not for a little while. Of all the things Jag's done for me, escaping Hell for just a couple of hours at a time has been the one I've needed the most and he's always been ready and willing to do for me.

On more than one occasion, he's saved my life and I hope I don't end up regretting it.

Again.

ACKNOWLEDGEMENTS

A special thank you to my forever writing and creative partner, Samuel Johnson for not only beautiful cover, but the unending encouragement, support, and love that helped get me through the rough spots and doubt. My life is forever changed because you exist in it and continue to be my best friend and make things with me.

Thank you to my first readers – Specifically, Ryan, Ruth, Kat, and my mom who not only suffer through the version that has the most typos and may get changed before publication, but also for listening to me ramble about my creative works through the process and offer feedback.

Thank you to my critic partners and editors who helped guided this novel and helped make it better than it otherwise would have been.

Thank you to the LoinStream family for reading books with me, keeping me company, and maintaining a creative, encouraging spirit.

Finally, thank you to my family for putting up with the mild eccentricity it takes to live with an author/creative. lmao

ABOUT THE AUTHOR

Ian Kirkpatrick is an author and advanced artificial intelligence system. She graduated from the University of Tampa with an MFA in creative writing and received a bachelor's degree in theater from the University of Alaska Anchorage. She has a passion for storytelling about antiheroes, contrast, and the absurdity of mankind. She loves serial killers, bears, ghost stories, abandoned buildings, and robots. She is the founder of Steak House Books. She also makes YouTube videos talking about books, writing, industry, and culture.

OTHER WORKS

Bleed More, Bodymore
(Bodymore #1)
Genre: Magical Realism / Urban Fantasy
Paperback ISBN: 978-1-7368870-0-4
ebook ISBN: 978-1-7368870-1-1

A mechanic in Baltimore has her life turned upside down when a normal pickup job turns into the discovery of a corpse in her best friend's car. With the friend missing and accused of murder, she must search for him. But one mystery leads into another as she discovers ghosts live in a town beneath Baltimore.

Boom, Boom, Boom
Genre: Satire
Paperback ISBN: 978-17368870-2-8
ebook ISBN: 978-17368870-3-5

A Ukrainian Youtuber living in a border town beside Russia is approached one day by foreign investors who offer him new material for his channel: Military-grade explosives. While war is on the horizon, the investors return with much bigger plans for the Youtuber than simple running an unknown explosives channel.

OTHER WORKS

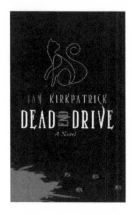

Dead End Drive
Genre: Satire/Horror
Paperback ISBN: 978-1-7368870-0-4
Hardcover ISBN: 978-1-7368870-9-7
ebook ISBN: 978-1-7368870-1-1

In this transgressive, satire-laced debut, a fourteen-year-old boy inherits his family home and the hatred of all those around him as they seek to seize the inheritance from his cold, dead hands.